ALSO BY ALICE HOFFMAN

The Marriage of Opposites

a novel

ALICE HOFFMAN

SIMON & SCHUSTER

New York   London   Toronto   Sydney   New Delhi

Simon & Schuster
1230 Avenue of the Americas
New York, NY 10020

First Simon & Schuster hardcover edition August 2015

SIMON & SCHUSTER and colophon are registered trademarks of Simon & Schuster, Inc.

For information about special discounts for bulk purchases, please contact Simon & Schuster Special Sales at 1-866-506-1949 or business@simonandschuster.com.

The Simon & Schuster Speakers Bureau can bring authors to your live event. For more information or to book an event, contact the Simon & Schuster Speakers Bureau at 1-866-248-3049 or visit our website at www.simonspeakers.com.

Interior design by Joy O'Meara

Manufactured in the United States of America

10 9 8 7 6 5 4 3 2 1

Library of Congress Cataloging-in-Publication Data
Hoffman, Alice.
    The marriage of opposites: a novel based on the life of Rachel Pizzarro / Alice Hoffman.
—First Simon & Schuster hardcover edition.
        pages ; cm
    Summary: "From the New York Times bestselling author of The Dovekeepers and The Museum of Extraordinary Things: a forbidden love story set on the tropical island of St. Thomas about the extraordinary woman who gave birth to painter Camille Pissarro, the father of Impressionism"—Provided by publisher.
    I. Title.
    PS3558.O3447M37   2015
    813'.54—dc23   2014047743

ISBN 978-1-4516-9359-1
ISBN 978-1-4516-9361-4 (ebook)

The Marriage of Opposites

CHAPTER ONE

We Followed the Turtles

CHARLOTTE AMALIE, ST. THOMAS

1807

RACHEL POMIÉ

I always left my window open at night, despite the warnings I'd been given. I rarely did as I was told. According to my mother, this had been my response to life ever since my birth, for it took three days for me to arrive in the world. As a child I did not sleep through the night, and I certainly didn't follow any rules. But I was a girl who knew what I wanted.

Other people shivered when the rains came and were chilled to the bone, but I longed for cold weather. Nights on our island were pitch dark, the air fragrant and heavy, perfect for dreaming. As soon as the light began to fade it was possible to hear the swift footsteps of lizards rattling through the leaves and the hum of the gnats as they came through the windows. Inside our stucco houses, we slept within tents made of thick white netting, meant to keep mosquitoes away. In rain barrels of drinking water we kept small fish that would eat the eggs these pests laid atop the water's surface so there would be fewer of them to plague us. All the same, huge clouds of insects drifted through the heat, especially at dusk, bringing a fever that could burn a man alive. Scores of bats descended upon our garden, flitting through the still air to drink the nectar of our flowers, until even they disappeared, settling into the branches of the trees. When they were gone there was only the quiet and the heat and the night. Heat was at the core of our lives, a shape-shifter that never was too far from the door. It made me want to step out of my clothes and dive into another life, one where there were linden trees and green lawns, where women wore black silk dresses and crinolines that rustled when they walked, a country where the moon rose like a silver disc into a cold, clear sky.

I knew where such a place could be found. Once, it had been the country of my grandparents. They had come to the New World from France, carrying with them an apple tree to remind them of the orchards they'd once owned. Our very name, Pomié, came from the fruit that they tended. My father told me that our ancestors had searched for freedom, first in Spain, then in Portugal, then in Bordeaux, the only region in France that accepted people of our faith at that time. Yet freedom was fleeting in France; our people were jailed, then murdered and burned. Those who escaped journeyed across the ocean to Mexico and Brazil, many aided by the Marrano Fernão de Loronha, who financed expeditions and hid his faith from those in power. Even Columbus, who called our island Heaven-on-earth upon spying it, was said to be one of us, searching for new land and liberty.

In 1492 Queen Isabella expelled our people from Spain on the Ninth of Av, the worst day in the history of our people. It was on this date when the first Temple in Jerusalem was destroyed by Babylonia and the second Temple was destroyed by Rome. It was on this very day, in the year 1290, that all Jews had been expelled from England. Thousands of our children were baptized and shipped to the island of São Tomé off the coast of Africa, then sold as slaves. In the year 1506 four thousand were massacred in Spain during Passover. Many converted, continuing to practice their religion underground. I pitied those who had stayed behind, forced to take on Christianity. My father had told me that in time even that sacrifice wasn't good enough; such persons were called Conversos, and were looked down upon and degraded, their property and rights taken from them. Those who survived were the ones who knew when to flee.

The Inquisition followed our people across the ocean, where they were once again murdered and cast out in Mexico and Brazil. My grandfather was among those who found themselves on the island of Saint-Domingue, and it was there both my parents were raised. But there was no peace in societies where sugarcane was king and people were enslaved. In 1754 the King of Denmark had passed an edict proclaiming that all men could practice their religions freely on St. Thomas; he outlawed new slavery and gave Jews the civil rights of other men, even granting them admission to associations such as the brotherhood of Masons, which allowed our people to do business with non-Jews. My parents came, then, to the island of the turtles, for more free people could be found here than anywhere in the new world, and people of our faith were soon accepted as Danish citizens, in 1814. Nearly everyone spoke English or French, but all were grateful for the Danish rule. In 1789 there were fewer than ten Jewish households listed in the tax registers, but in 1795, the year I was born, there were seventy-five people, with more settling on our shores each year.

Once he arrived my father swore that he would never again travel. He brought along the apple tree, and my mother, and the one man who was loyal to him.

OUR ISLAND WAS A small speck of land, little more than thirty square miles set in the blue-green sea. The original population had all vanished, destroyed by disease and murder. The native people, called the Caribs, believed their ancestors journeyed to this island from the moon; having seen the dull earth, they'd come to give it light, traveling through the clouds, drenching our island with color, so that shades of orange and blue and red were scattered everywhere. But the Caribs' ancestors were trapped here by storms and had no choice but to stay in a place where they never belonged. They wound their long, black hair into plaits of mourning both for themselves and for our world. They were right to mourn, for until the Danes brought freedom here, the island's history was one of injustice and sorrow, a society built by convicts and slaves.

AS IT TURNED OUT, the fruit of our name did not grow well in tropical weather. It was far better suited for cooler climates. My grandparents' apple tree, planted in a large ceramic pot in the courtyard, never grew any bigger. When I watered it during the dry season, it was so thirsty, it could never drink enough. Its brown leaves crinkled and sounded like fluttering moths as they fell to the ground. The fruit it bore was hard, the skin more green than red. Still this was our heritage, the fruit of France. I ate every apple I could find, no matter how bitter, until my mother found me out and slapped my face. My mother's full name was Madame Sara Monsanto Pomié, and she was a force few people would dare to go up against. Her anger was a quiet, terrifying thing.

"These apples were meant for your father," she told me when she found me gathering fruit that had fallen onto the patio. I walked away from my mother and from the tree without a word. Unlike other people, I had no fear of her. I knew she wasn't as strong as she seemed for I'd heard her weeping late into the night. I told myself I would be in Paris when I next ate the fruit of our name. Though I'd been born here, I'd always believed it was not my true home. I was trapped on this island much like the people who had come across the sky and could do nothing more than stare at the moon through the vast distance. But unlike them, I would reach my destination.

From the time I could read, I found solace in my father's library, where he collected maps of Paris, some made by the great cartographer Nicolas de Fer. I traced my hand along la rivière de Seine and memo-rized the parks and the tiny twisted streets and the paths of the Tuileries Garden, created by Catherine de' Medici in 1564, covered with ice in the winter, a cold fairyland. It was my father who first told me about Paris, as his father had told him, and to us, it was the place where everything beautiful began and ended. Although my father had never been there, I came to believe I would someday see that city for him.

At the ages of ten and eleven and twelve I would have preferred to remain in the library but was often forced to accompany my mother when she visited her friends who were members of Blessings and Peace and Loving Deeds, the association of women who did good deeds among people of our faith. I discovered that even these pious women of the Sisterhood liked to keep up with the chic styles, and several of them had come to our island directly from France. I asked the maids in these households where I might find the *Journals des dames et des modes* and *La Belle Assemblée*, the best fashion journals from Paris. Disappearing into dark dressing rooms where I didn't belong, I lay on the cool tile floor and sifted through page after thrilling page. There were cloaks with fox collars, boots in maroon leather, kidskin gloves that reached the elbow and closed with two perfectly placed pearl buttons. Occasionally, I tore out a page to keep for myself. If anyone noticed, they didn't reprimand me, for in those dressing rooms I also stumbled upon secrets best left untouched. Love notes, bottles of rum, piles of hidden coins. It seemed that some of the most prominent women in our community strayed, for Jewish women were bound by rules on every side: the rules of God, but also the rules of the Danes, and of our own leaders. We were meant to be mice, to go unnoticed so that we would not bring hatred upon our people, who had been so ill-treated in every nation. But I was not a mouse. In the fields where I walked, I was much more interested in the actions of the hawks.

NEARLY ALL OF MY father's books were printed in French, many bound in leather with gold letters embellishing the spines. Every time a ship came from France my father was waiting on the dock, there to collect a parcel so he might add another volume to his library. I disappeared into that cool, shuttered room whenever I could. Girls did not attend school, but here in the library I found my education. My father taught me to read English, and Spanish and Hebrew, along with bits of Danish and Dutch, and of course we spoke French. He educated both me and my dearest friend, Jestine, although when we read aloud he laughed at our Creole accents and he did his best to teach us the more proper pronunciations. When my mother complained that I would learn more in the kitchen, and flatly stated that Jestine shouldn't be in our house at all, my father was furious. Jestine and I slipped under his desk, our hands over our ears so we couldn't hear the bitter words between my parents. I knew my mother thought I would be better served spending time with girls of my own faith, rather than befriending someone whose mother was an African and our cook. But of course, little of what my mother wanted meant anything to me.

JESTINE WAS AFRAID OF my mother, and shy around my father, and she never came back to the library. Instead, I brought books to her house and we read on the porch, where you could see between the slats straight into the ocean. Sometimes we read aloud in dreamy voices, with accents as elegant as we could manage, but mostly, I spent my hours alone in the library. I read while my mother was out with the society of good deeds, visiting women who had no husbands and children who were orphans, the sick and infirm and needy. I knew I was safe in the library, for my mother believed it to be the domain of my father, and after their argument about girls learning to read she never again came uninvited into that room.

As a reader, I first became engrossed in *Histoires ou contes du temps passé, avec des moralités: Les Contes de ma mère l'Oye,* what the English called *Mother Goose.* In every marvelous tale collected by Charles Perrault, there was the sting of truth. As I turned the pages, I felt as if there were bees on my fingertips, for I had never felt so alive as when reading. Monsieur Perrault's stories explained my own world to me. I might not understand all that I felt, but I knew a single one of his chapters was more enlightening than a hundred conversations with my mother.

*Il était une fois une veuve qui avait deux filles: l'aînée lui ressem-
blait si fort d'humeur et de visage, que, qui la voyait, voyait la mère.
Elles étaient toutes deux si désagréables et si orgueilleuses qu'on ne
pouvait vivre avec elles.*

*Once upon a time there was a widow who had two daughters. The
elder was so much like her, both in looks and in character, that whoever saw the daughter saw the mother. They were both so disagreeable
and so proud that there was no living with them.*

Perhaps that was what my mother disliked most. I resembled her. I
could not help but wonder if for some women, that was the worst sin of all.

MY MOTHER AND I never discussed my education again, until one day
she brought a hired man into the library to clean the window glass, and
found me there. By then I was a serious girl of thirteen, nearly a woman,
but I was sprawled upon the floor, my head in a book, my hair uncombed,
my chores left to the maid. Madame Pomié threatened to throw the fairy
tales away. "Take my advice and concentrate on your duties in this
house," she told me. "Stay out of the library."

I had the nerve to respond, for I knew she wouldn't dare to deface
my father's library. "This room doesn't belong to you."

My mother sent the hired man away and shut the door. "What did
you say to me?"

"You know my father's wishes," I said. "He wants me to be educated."

I no longer cared if my mother disliked me. I didn't understand that
when I closed myself to her, I took a part of her bitterness inside me. It
was green and unforgiving, and as it grew it made me more like her. It
gave me my strength, but it gave me my weakness as well.

My mother tossed me a knowing look on the day I spoke back to her.
"I hope you have a child that causes you the misery you have caused
me," she told me with all the power of a curse.

From then on she acted as if I were invisible, unless she had a task for me or a complaint about my appearance or my deeds. Perhaps she was so cold to me because she'd lost the child that had come only nine months after my birth. He had been a boy. She had wanted to give my father a son; perhaps she thought he would love her more if she had been able to do so. I often wondered if she wished that of her two children, I'd been the one who had been taken.

Il était une fois un Roi et une Reine, qui étaient si fâchés de n'avoir point d'enfants, si fâchés qu'on ne saurait dire.

Once upon a time there was a king and queen, who were so sorry that they had no children—so sorry that it cannot be told.

My father had recovered from the loss and loved me, but my mother was inconsolable, refusing to open her door, to him or to me. By the time she was improved enough to oversee the household once more, my father no longer came home for supper. He was out until all hours. That was when I began to hear my mother weeping late into the night. There was a part of me that knew my father had left us in some deep way I didn't quite understand. I only had access to him when we were together in the library, and I loved them both—the library and my father—equally and without question.

JUST AS PERRAULT HAD interviewed the women in the salons about the stories their grandmothers had told them, I spoke to the old ladies in the market and began to write down the small miracles common only in our country. For as long as I was trapped here, I would write down these stories, along with a list of the wondrous things I myself had seen. When I went to France, I would have dozens of tales to tell, each one so fantastic people would have difficulty believing it. In our world there had been pirates with more than a dozen wives, parrots who could speak four languages, shells which opened to reveal pearls, birds as tall as men who danced for each other in the marshes, turtles that came to lay their eggs on the beach in a single mysterious night. On these occasions I would wait in the twilight with Jestine, watching as the shoreline filled with these lumbering creatures, all so intent on their mission on the worn path they always took that they didn't notice us among them. We were turtle-girls. If we had been inside of a story we would surely have grown shells and claws. In silence, we studied the beach through the falling dark. We could not light lanterns, for turtles follow the moon, and in the eyes of such creatures the moon is any globe of light, even one you hold in your hand.

I had pinched a blue notebook with fine paper made in Paris from my father's store. If anyone noticed they didn't say so, although my father's clerk, Mr. Enrique, a stern, handsome man, looked at me differently after that. The first story I wrote down was one the old ladies told about a woman who'd given birth to a turtle. They liked to take turns when they told it, so that each storyteller added a detail or two. The woman who was the turtle-girl's mother was so stunned by the green shell surrounding her baby that she ran down to the beach and left the newborn by the shore. She meant to desert the child and let it be taken out to sea with the tide, but luckily, a mother turtle with a nest of hatchlings was nearby and she raised the turtle-girl as her own. Jestine and I always searched for a turtle that was half human, with a human face and soul. She was said to have grown to be a woman who looked like any other, with long arms and legs and moss-tinted hair. You couldn't see her shell unless she was in the sea. She could have easily disguised herself and joined our world, eating in cafés, dancing with men who found her beautiful, but instead she'd chosen to live in the world of the turtles. If you happened upon her you would see that her skin was a pale green and her eyes were yellow. She had swum to every gleaming sea in the world, but always came back to our shore.

We are here, Jestine and I whispered as we stood on the beach. *O Sister,* we called. We would not forsake her or judge her if only she would show herself to us. But she never did, no matter how late we stayed, even when we waited until the last of the turtles had returned to the bay. It was clear that Jestine and I were as uncomfortable as the mysterious turtle-woman when in the company of humans. Jestine was especially shy, perhaps because she was so beautiful her mother had warned her not to be too friendly to the boys and men who might approach her. As for me, I was distrustful by nature. The two of us roamed the island as if there was no one else in the world. We would collect buckets of hermit crabs and ghost crabs and race them against one another in the sand before setting them free and watching them scramble away from us as if we were monsters.

Sometimes I was forced to bring along my younger cousin Aaron Rodrigues, who lived with us. There were three years between us and he was nothing but an annoyance to me. I was told his parents had been lost in a storm when he was little more than a baby and afterward our family had taken him in. My mother preferred him, even though he wasn't related to us by blood, perhaps because of the baby boy she lost. Girls were not worth very much in her eyes, especially a disobedient girl such as myself. Aaron was handsome, dark, with startlingly pale blue eyes. Even as he grew older, my mother still enjoyed showing him off to her friends, especially the formidable Madame Halevy, whose stern presence intimidated us all but who melted whenever she saw Aaron. *Mon chouchou*, she called him, even when he was a rowdy boy of nine. *Mon petit canard*. In return I pinched Aaron and called him a duck in English, not such a pretty word. He always gave me a wounded look, though he didn't complain. I should have been guilt-ridden, but I suppose I was a brutal girl. I knew what happened in fairy tales. The strong survived while the weak were eaten alive.

On nights when I was forced to look after Aaron, I gave him over to Jestine, who was more kindhearted than I. Perhaps because he was an orphan and Jestine had no father, she could feel compassion for him, even though he was a wild boy, who delighted in leaping from cliffs. I took to scaring him to get him to behave. He was terrified of were-wolves, half-human beasts that were said to reside on the old planta-tions. My father had assured me these were made-up stories, used by the plantation owners to frighten slaves from running away. *There is the out-side of a story, and there is the inside of a story,* he told me as we sat in his library one afternoon. *One is the fruit and may be delicious, but the other is the seed.*

By now my father had decided I'd had enough of fairy tales and was too old for such notions. Perhaps my mother had complained to him or perhaps he thought I should be more serious or maybe he simply longed for the son he'd lost and wished to educate me in the way he would have had I been a boy. Monsieur Pomié was a respected member of the Bur-ghers' Association, the businessmen's society that one must join to be a merchant, in my father's case, a shop owner who exported rum and sugar and molasses. Aaron was fated to take over his business, since girls and women could not inherit property, but perhaps my father hoped those laws would change. He began to teach me figures, so I would understand the ledgers in the store, and I was honored to be educated in a way few girls were.

All the same, I wrote down the werewolf tale the way I'd heard it from our cook, Adelle. She had told us that the werewolves were mem-bers of the old Danish families who owned slaves. Their transformation was God's punishment for their wrongdoings. You could spy their teeth and claws at night, even when they were in their human guise, so they often wore gloves and scarves, even in the hottest times of the year. *If you see such a thing,* Adelle told us, *run.*

I read this story to Aaron on a nightly basis. Though it terrified him, he always wanted to hear it again and again. It came as no surprise that he began to imagine such beasts in every dark lane and alleyway. He stayed close to Jestine, trusting her as much as he mistrusted me. Some-times I made a howling noise when I walked behind him and he'd jump as if he'd been bitten.

"Must you frighten him?" Jestine would ask me.

"Must you pity him?" I would say.

Still, I admit that on certain nights I had my own fears, not of roaming half wolves, but of our own homeland. It seemed there was an inescapable loneliness here. The bats above us, the wind from Africa, the roar of the waves. It was as if we were on the edge of the known world and could drop off into the darkness at any time. When the three of us were out together, no one knew where we were. If anything happened, we would have to save each other.

PEOPLE WHO CAME HERE from Europe often claimed they couldn't tell the difference between winter and summer on an island as mild as ours. They clearly didn't know this island. We had times of rain and wind, blue nights when a cold thread coiled through all the houses, pinching the babies and making them cry. On such nights the fish in the ponds turned black and floated to the surface. The leaves of the jasmine curled up like little frogs. But in summer, everything turned white-hot and bright in an instant, with sparks in the air that were as hot as flames. The heat stunned people who weren't used to it. Women who accompanied their husbands here from France on business often fainted moments after disembarking from their ships. They were given a drink made of palm bark and sugar water, yet many could never abide the bright light, not if they stayed here for years, not if they spent their whole lives here. They shrank into darkened rooms, keeping their window shades closed against the fierce light, not venturing out until dusk. We would see them sometimes, crying in courtyards.

"Werewolves," my cousin Aaron would declare when we passed by these houses, for their weeping sounded like howling. "No, they're not beasts," Jestine assured him. "Just lonely women from France, longing for home." But whenever we came near the old Danish estates, where there were still slaves living in shacks, we ran as fast as we could, with Aaron trailing behind us, until he grew so tall he could outrun us. Then we had to use all our strength just to keep up with him. By the age of twelve he was six feet tall, so handsome that grown women stopped on the street to call to him. Jestine made certain he didn't go to investigate when the women made clucking noises aimed at him, as if they were hens and he was a fox. I knew then, she wanted him for herself.

～❦～

EACH YEAR I HAD more stories to write down. The women at the market waited for me whenever they had a new one to tell. There was the story in which a hundred butterflies arose from a single tree all at once to form a second yellow moon, and one about a fish with the face of a horse who came galloping into the city one night, and another about a bird that flew halfway around the world for love, and was flying above us still.

I tied my notebook with ribbon and kept it beneath my pillow, far from the grasp of my mother. "Don't tell," I warned the laundry women who came to change the sheets. They understood why I would keep a secret from my mother. She had little tolerance for what she considered to be nonsense, and that included most things in this world, even the history of our people, and how we had come to be so far away from our rightful home. I knew if she found my notebook she would toss it onto the trash heap at the back of the yard. Everything I knew of our island I had learned in my father's library. It was a complicated history, for St. Thomas had traded hands many times, belonging to the Spanish, the Dutch, the English, and finally, the Danes, who sent the Danish West India Company to begin a society that was mostly concerned with trade. In 1688, of the 739 people who lived here, 317 were Europeans from eleven nations and 422 were African people, who were brought here against their will. The wretched slavers' ships docked across from schooners belonging to the relations of royalty, many of whom had been cast out from their own kingdoms and had no inheritance other than tracts of land in the mountains beside the dormant volcano known as the Quill. Pirates from all nations camped in the coves, hidden from the authorities.

Captain Kidd had roamed the shore, along with a fierce and pitiless man known as Blackbeard, who attacked ships in the harbor, kidnapping wealthy residents, taking dozens of local women as wives, and forcing women en route to America to wed him as well. He was voracious, hungry for more despite all he had. There were people who claimed he'd had twenty wives; others insisted it was more than thirty. Some he kept, some he passed on to marry his sailors.

The grass grew tall in the fields, and wild donkeys roamed freely, left behind by the pirate wives who had begun farms in an attempt to civilize their husbands. Trees from Madagascar had been brought here on their lawless ships, and after the pirate wives had been abandoned by their men, they'd sown the seeds from their homeland as if they were blood-red tears. Even now as the graves of these women went untended, and their passings unmourned, the seeds they had scattered turned the hillsides red and orange from May to September. Some called the pirates' bounty flame trees, but to us they were known as flamboyant trees, for no one could ignore their glorious blooms, with flowers that were larger than a man's open hand.

Every time I saw them I thought of these lost women.

That was what happened if you waited for love.

ON NIGHTS WHEN I couldn't sleep, I took a candle and sneaked into my father's library so that I might look at his maps of Paris. I was especially entranced by the garden of the Tuileries, for my father had recently told me the King had wanted the park for himself until Monsieur Perrault roused the crowd, insisting that each common person had a right to Paris and to that garden. From my father's books about ornithology and botanicals, I turned to François-Nicolas Martinet's illustrations for *Histoire naturelle des oiseaux* to learn about kingfishers and swans and nightingales. My father loved books of landscapes and architecture with huge hand-colored plates illustrating the gardens, and he particularly valued roses, which were not natural to our shores. White Alba roses, tea-scented roses in shades of apricot and yellow, China roses with blooms as big as plates, and Bourbon roses, which had been developed in a prince's greenhouse. In these books I discovered winter fruits most people on our island had never seen, apples and pears and blackberries and then, in the spring, raspberries and strawberries the color of gems.

I stood before the bookcases in my bare feet while outside the wind from Africa came across the sea. I was somewhere else completely, inside a story where I shivered in the snow and drew my fox cloak around me. I stepped over the ice in my fine leather boots. Once there had been a girl who slept for over a hundred years. There was a daughter who protected herself by wearing the skin of a donkey. A cat that was wiser than the men around him and earned such a huge treasure it never had to chase mice again. I kept the book of fairy tales close to my heart, the cover flaming blue. That would keep me warm, until at last I reached the place where I belonged.

⤜❦⤛

AT FIRST THERE WERE six families of our faith here who said prayers around a dining room table and formed a burial society in 1750 so they might begin a cemetery in an area that was then a wasteland called the Savan. The year after I was born the synagogue was founded, with the right to do so granted by the Danish King, Christian VII. It was called *Kahal Kadosh Beracha VeShalom*, the Holy Congregation Blessing and Peace, and our burial society was named Deeds of Lovingkindness, named for those who cared for the dead. There was a doctor employed by the congregation, and the poor were cared for. The council safeguarded our civil rights as best they could in a world where people of our faith must always be cautious, ready to swim away when need be. In return for all the synagogue did for us, decency and decorum must be observed and unity preserved at all costs. Fines were levied upon anyone who disagreed with the Reverend. Troublesome congregants would be dealt with by the committee chosen to do so. The Danish government tolerated our congregation, but any incident or infighting could bring attention to us now, and the government's acceptance of us could always change, with people executed and jailed, vanishing as if they had been enchanted and turned into stalks of grass.

By the time I was a young woman there were eighty families in our congregation. At Friday night services my mother and I sat behind a sheet of white muslin that separated the women and children from the men. My mother always sat beside Madame Halevy. Together they were a powerful force. The Sisterhood of Blessings and Peace and Loving Deeds monitored themselves and us; they were judge and jury in all social matters and on occasion were far harsher than the Danes might have been. It was their world, after all.

THE SYNAGOGUE WAS A small wooden building, lit by candles that flickered in heavy silver candlesticks brought from Spain a century ago. Someday our prayers would be recited in an elegant building made of stone, but even then, we would keep the floor as it was, made of sand, as it had been in Europe for the duration of the terrible years when we had to hide who we were, when footsteps on marble or stone might give away our place of worship to those who wished to cause us harm. The inside story of our people's lives had been kept secret for hundreds of years, a stone inside a fruit, the truth of who we were.

To outsiders, people of our faith were considered mysterious beings. There were Christians who whispered that we were like shadows, able to slip through a net like fish. If we were shadows, then our history had made us so. We went through life underwater, unseen by those in power who might turn on us. My people accounted for nearly half the European population of the island. We were called Creoles, Europeans who had never been in Europe, Jews who hadn't stopped running from persecution until we came here. Yet we still cooked our food in the French way; we added olives and chives and caperberries, in the old Spanish style. We carried our pasts with us. Perhaps that was what made us appear to be shadows, the burden we carried with us, the other lives we might have led.

My father had told me that no matter how comfortable we might feel, we must live like fish, unattached to any land. Wherever there was water, we would survive. Some fish could stay in the mud for months, even years, and when at last there was a high flooding tide, they would swim away, a dark flash, remembered only by their own kind. So perhaps the stories they told of our people were true: no net could hold us.

I KNEW I MUST do all as I was told, yet something burned inside me, a seed of defiance that must have derived from a long-ago ancestor. Perhaps my mind was inflamed from the books I had read and the worlds I had imagined. I gazed at myself in the silvered mirror in our parlor and I knew I would do as I pleased, no matter the consequences.

I rarely helped to make the Sabbath meal, as such duties did not suit my nature. I was not a cook but a huntress. Because of this, I was often sent to find a chicken in the yard behind the kitchen house, a small building made of white stucco, separate from the main house to ensure that the heat of our cookery wouldn't enter the rooms where we lived. I wore a black apron so that any blood I spilled wouldn't show. With the heat of the day rich and hot on my skin, I looked forward to Friday afternoons, when I became a killer of chickens. I listened to the thrum of the bird's heart and the beat of mine quicken together. I always said a prayer and called upon God's grace, and then I was not afraid. I was practical, and I thought it important to teach myself to face whatever other girls feared most. I stared at the clucking birds until they quieted, for they were easily calmed. Then I chose one, wrapped it in a cloth, and took its life before bringing it into the kitchen so that Adelle could pluck its feathers. In return I was given a plate of ripe sapodilla fruits, which tasted like caramel. These small egg-shaped fruits were my favorite treats; as I ate I imagined they were sweets from a shop in Paris rather than hard-shelled fruits fallen from a tree.

I couldn't remember a time when Adelle didn't work for us and I did not spend my days with her daughter. Jestine had her mother's brown skin but gray, nearly silver eyes, as if she were related to those incandescent first people who had come here to bring light from the moon. She and I did everything together. We often helped Adelle, who was the best cook on the island. Other than the library, the outdoor kitchen where Adelle worked was my favorite place. Our dinners contained my family's recipes for stews and soups from the old world, but Adelle added lime juice, papaya, banana, rosemary, all ingredients from our garden. When my mother was not at home Adelle often made us a supper of rice and beans and fried conch meat that we first had to pound tender with a hammer. At lunch we had the local cornmeal porridge called fongee, which my family thought of as food for the poor. Best were the snacks Adelle made, a most delicious mixture of mango, tamarind, gooseberries, and sugar. Jestine and I ate this with our fingers, in heaven to have something my mother would never have allowed to be served at our table, eating in a way that would have made her call us pigs.

Some people suggested that Jestine's father was a man in our congregation. No one would say who he might be, but I thought he must be rich. Adelle was a servant, but she had money enough to live in her own house near the harbor. Jestine's father had not made himself present. Jestine had never met him and didn't know his name. "It's better that way," Adelle had told her. "You can't betray what you don't know."

Jestine accepted her mother's advice, but I was too curious to be satisfied. I peered into the faces of men in our congregation, looking for features that resembled Jestine's. I was certain that she belonged to my people, and was therefore my sister, as I was hers.

The cottage where Jestine and Adelle lived was set on stilts; even if the floodwater was high enough to surround it, the house and its contents and those who lived inside would be safe. You had to jump puddles on the path if you wanted to pay a visit, and sometimes there were starfish in those puddles, stranded until the next high tide. The wide porch was constructed from wooden slats, and it was possible to look right through into the blue sea. Some of Adelle's furniture was fashioned of local mahogany, upholstered with leather and mohair seats; other pieces, a carved bureau for instance, had been imported from France. There was a lace runner on the tabletop, and kerosene lamps lit the sitting room; at night her whole house was like a lantern, a beacon on the shore.

As far as I knew, no one thought worse of Jestine because she had only a mother. Many people didn't have fathers, or at least not ones they knew. Those of mixed blood who had white fathers were given their freedom, even when a man was not cited by name, and people of mixed race accounted for more than half the population of color. Still, I was glad that I did have a father and proud that he was Moses Monsanto Pomié, a man well thought of by his neighbors, a businessman favored in all his endeavors. I was happy that I didn't have to look into men's faces, searching for a part of me, some feature that connected us by bond and blood.

Jestine never looked, no matter how I urged her to do so. She shrugged and said a mother was enough and she didn't need more. She was cautious when I was curious, kind when I was arrogant. She was far too gentle to kill a chicken, so whenever Adelle sent her to do this, I always took her place. We laughed and spoke of exchanging lives. I would have liked to live in a house where I could hear the sea in my dreams. Jestine wanted to be within the garden walls where the light had a gold tint in the evenings and bees gathered in the blooms. We would dress in each other's clothes, say good night to each other's mothers, dream each other's dreams.

But such a thing could never happen. And for this I blamed my mother. No one would trade for Sara Pomié.

"You would beg for your life back before morning," I said sadly.

Jestine knew how stern my mother was, how sharp her tongue was, how bitterly she complained. When we heard Madame Pomié's voice we always had a jolt of fear, unwilling to face her unflattering comments. In Madame's eyes, nothing we did was right.

There were days when I wished I were a boy, for if I had been I might have set off to France as soon as I turned seventeen, sailing on one of the schooners that left from the docks near Adelle's house. We had cousins who lived near Paris, and the businesses on both sides of the Atlantic helped each other: the French Pomiés shipped us fabric of all varieties, along with glassware and china, while we sent back molasses and rum and sugarcane. I ambled along the harbor, passing Fish Wharf and Cow Wharf, skipping over puddles. With every step I wished myself away to another life, one lived far from here. Adelle said that I had been on earth before. My mother didn't like this sort of talk; people of our faith didn't believe in past lives or spirits. But Adelle whispered that it was an honor to be able to reach over to the other side, the place where the lost and the found comingle. We had experimented with my powers. We went into the woods one night, just the two of us. Jestine was too afraid and went to bed early.

"It's just as well," Adelle said. "Let her stay home. Spirits can sense fear. That's one thing you don't possess."

I took pride in Adelle's estimation of me, and I tried to live up to her high opinion, even though the night was so dark and we were so deep in the hills, up near the caves where the pirates had lived.

"I want to call the pirates' wives," I said.

Adelle shook her head. "It doesn't work that way. You don't call them, they come if they wish to do so."

When I held out my hands in the pitch dark they filled with orbs of light. That meant the souls of the dead were around me. They came like moths drawn to a lantern. I felt the sting of their spirits. They whispered things I was too innocent to know about, what they had done for love, and for hate, what had happened to them at night in the arms of the men they belonged to, those they mourned and those they had wished dead.

I felt their sorrows and my heart quickened.

"Don't be afraid," Adelle said. "You're the one with the power."

I wished I were the person Adelle thought I was, but I was afraid of my own power. I suppose I was too young, and raw emotion frightened me. The idea that a woman might be willing to ruin her life for love was

far beyond my understanding. I shook my hands to disperse the spirits
into the air. I was afraid I had gone against my religion on this night, but
Adelle told me that women of every faith have power. They just have to
find it within themselves.

I painted my room a shade called haint blue. Blue kept unwanted
spirits away; ghosts and demons could not cross over water, nor could
they enter a room that was the color of the sea. I did not tell my mother
the reason I had chosen this vivid blue, knowing she would have disapproved. She said superstition was for fools. The truth was, I sometimes
regretted painting my chamber, for I often wished a spirit might travel to
me from across the water and take me with him past the hedges of jasmine, over the garden wall, back to Paris. I peered out through the vines
of oleander and bougainvillea, silver and purple in the dark. I could hear
moths fluttering, many as big as birds, as they struck against the shutters
of my room, called to the yellow light of the candle on my table. They
could not get in. Whether they were spirits, I did not know. I wondered
if all creatures were drawn to what was dangerous or if we merely
wanted light at any cost and were willing to burn for our desires.

～❧～

TIME PASSED INSIDE A dream, and soon my childhood was gone. I
thought of the fairy tales I'd read and how change came so suddenly. In
one story, a boy too ugly to be seen is transformed by his own wits and
by love. In another, a girl is given a gift that allows her to sing like a
nightingale. Perhaps I was drawn to stories in which people found their
true desires because I was a stranger to myself. Emotions stirred inside
me, but I wasn't certain what these feelings were. I understood that I
wasn't beautiful, and I knew that in our world, for a young woman, that
mattered and often changed one's destiny. I did the best with what I had.
I brushed my long, black hair a thousand strokes a day. I begged Jestine
to take a needle and pierce my ears so I could adorn myself with something prettier than my own reflection. My mother slapped my face for

disobeying her command not to scar myself in this way, but she also gave me a pair of gold earrings that had belonged to her mother. "Your grandmother made me promise I would give these to a daughter," she told me. "You may think ill of me, but I do not break my vows."

When I looked at myself in the gilt-framed mirror in the hallway, studying my black hair and dark eyes, seeing the glint of gold, I wondered if indeed I might be the sparrow who became a swan.

The women from Blessings and Peace and Loving Deeds complimented my mother when they came for tea, and for good reason. My mother had a lovely house, one of the tall stucco mansions in town, painted pink, with patios and gardens hidden behind high walls. Much of the furniture had been ordered from France by my father, who delighted in beautiful things. Madame Pomié always presented exceptional food, the latest recipes from Paris—cooked birds in pastry, a soup made of sorrel. Adelle knew not to speak when she served the ladies ginger tea for good digestion, along with butter cookies and slices of mangoes. Most often Madame Halevy led the discussions concerning anyone whose children were ill-behaved or whose husbands had an eye for other women. Such transgressions were common knowledge, and there was little tolerance for weakness or wrongdoing.

⚬⚬

THE WOMEN FROM THE congregation might appear delicate and ladylike, but on this island strength was a necessity. Most of these women could climb onto a roof before a storm to make certain that the shutters at every window were bolted shut, they could cook over an outdoor fire, kill chickens and wild waterfowl, do what they must should the tolerance of our people fade in yet another country. It was said that Madame Halevy gave birth to her first child alone while her husband was off to sea and was rumored to have cut the cord of life with a carving knife. She had lost two sons to yellow fever, but her daughter in America was said to be a great success and a great beauty. My mother was not as lucky. By the time I was of marriageable age everyone knew I was moody and disagreeable. I thought too highly of myself and was too choosy. I was already considered an old maid. Though I had masses of glossy hair that shone after I washed it with prickly pear juice, and almond-shaped eyes, I possessed a sharp face and a sharper tongue.

I had barely glanced at any of the boys who might have been interested in me, all of whom had gone on to marry other people's daughters. My father had tried to arrange a marriage for me several times with little success. People said I was difficult and would bring only trouble to my husband. Truly, I was happier on my own. I enjoyed the privacy of my room, which overlooked the courtyard, especially in the season when the frangipani flowered and the garden turned pink. I had observed the lives of other young women, and marriage seemed a difficult and hazardous path. Many children were lost, often in infancy, to malaria and yellow fever and smallpox, and young mothers died giving birth or soon after. Even with the help of maids, marriage was hard labor, not a fate I looked forward to.

I chanted the prayers of my own faith, but I remained interested in the spirit world. I knew from my readings in my father's library that our people had once believed in seers and signs. When I was alone, I studied the Book of Ezekiel and the Song of Solomon, mystical chapters filled with wonders. I knew I would be reprimanded if I were discovered reading these texts, which sang the praises of both spirit and flesh. From these readings, however, I knew our people were drawn to mysteries before we were forced to hide who we were and be most concerned with survival. Still such things were a part of us, and we remained in awe of God's miracles. When a storm came up my father asked the archangel Gabriel to protect us from woe. I often went outside and thought I saw this angel in the sky above us. He was made of golden light and of the breath of the earth. Sometimes he heard my father's prayers, and sometimes he turned away from us.

Adelle was known for having the gift of sight, and local women who were with child often came to ask her if they would have a son or a daughter. She held a ring on a chain over them and told them to be silent. If the ring moved in a circle, that meant a daughter; back and forth meant a son. She once predicted I would have many children. I laughed at the notion. She was usually correct, but in my case was most certainly wrong.

"Maybe you're confusing my fate with Jestine's," I suggested, for I didn't like children, whereas Jestine's manner with them was easy and assured.

"Everyone has her own fate," Adelle told me. "This is yours. Trust me. Even you will fall in love."

I refused to accept this prediction. I saw the constrained lives of the women in our community. I knew what had happened to the pirates' wives. "Then I'll close my door and lock it, and my fate will pass over me as the angel of death does at Passover."

"You think love is like the angel of death?" Adelle laughed at me. "You can't lock it out. It doesn't even know what a door is." She touched my head with her fingertips, as if testing for fever. "My advice for you is to accept what you don't understand."

1817

One night my father came to talk to me in the privacy of my room. It was summer and the sky was still light, streaked with a gold tint in the east, pink in the west. There was a vase of frangipani on the bureau. As my father drew up a chair, a hummingbird darted through the window to drink the nectar of the flowers. The tiny creature was there and gone so quickly I wondered if I had imagined him. Perhaps he was another spirit. Then I noticed a feather on the floor. I picked it up and slipped it under my pillow. Such things were said to bring luck.

Perhaps my distaste for the fate of most young women was my father's fault. He had educated me and schooled me in the ways of the business world, and because of this I understood, long before my mother ever knew, that the family business was faltering. It had been a season of storms, never good for the island. Merchandise loaded onto ships, headed for Charleston and New York, had been lost at sea. My father had large debts, ones he couldn't repay.

He was a busy man even in the best of times; he didn't have time for idle conversation, and so I was honored that he'd come to speak to me in the quiet of the evening. I wore a white cotton nightdress, and my hair was plaited, then pinned up. My face was scrubbed clean. My father sat in a hard-backed wooden chair with a cane seat. He wore a charcoal gray suit, formal, with pearl buttons. He was a dignified, well-mannered man. Clearly the reason for this visit was serious, for this was the same suit of clothes he wore to his shipping office.

"We must change our business and our lives, or we'll become one of the families the women from the congregation of Blessings and Peace take pity on, bringing us supper on Friday nights. I do not intend to have us living in a hut in the Savan," he told me.

I leaned forward, straining to hear his every word. Until this year my father had been so successful that people came to him for advice, and he made his suggestions in a quiet, forceful voice. He had fled from an island where there was such cruelty against Africans that the enslaved people finally rose up in a riot of blood. Like his forefathers, he knew when to depart even though it meant leaving his worldly goods behind. He'd had one slave, and that had been Mr. Enrique. Mr. Enrique was the one who told my father that the time had come, the flower of the revolution was blooming, fed by rage and despair. On Saint-Domingue, all French families were advised to leave their homes, with the men to stay and band together in safe areas where they would stand ready to fight. That was not my father's intention. Because my father was so well known and could not be seen in public without being held back to fight against the slaves, Mr. Enrique readied a boat. My mother went to the harbor with diamonds and pearls sewn into the hem of her dress, wearing a black cloak, for she was pregnant with me. Perhaps that was when I first became a burden to her. She covered her head with an embroidered shawl so she might not be noticed. There was only one way my father could have reached the ship-yard. Enrique helped him to escape by hiding him in a wicker clothes hamper he carried on his shoulders as he navigated through the mobs in the street. Like the original Moses, himself a slave whose freedom was brought about when he floated through the waters of the Nile in a basket of reeds, my father was thus brought to safety. He was so grateful that he immediately turned over the keys to his house to Mr. Enrique. He knew Enrique had saved his life, and that every day forward would be a gift not only from his maker but also from this man who had risked his own life and safety for him. In turn, Mr. Enrique gave the house to his sister and accompanied my father to St. Thomas as a free man. He said that when the mobs finally heard how my parents had escaped, he would be killed for helping them, and that when people forgot he would go back home.

But they never forgot and Mr. Enrique never returned. He lived in a house beyond our garden on the other side of the tall stucco wall. He had great affection for our island and the freedom he'd been granted. Out-side his doorway he'd planted a St. Thomas tree, whose yellow flowers were marked with red drops, said to be caused by drops of the saint's blood falling on such a plant when he was martyred. The deed to the cottage was in Mr. Enrique's name, signed by my father. Once the busi-ness was set up, Mr. Enrique worked in my father's office as a clerk. He wore a black suit every day, which only served to show off how hand-some he was. There were many women who wished to marry him, but he was a solitary person. The revolution on his island had scarred not only those who had fought in it but also those who had abandoned their homeland.

In the tax records Mr. Enrique was said to belong to Moses Pomié, but he'd been granted his freedom on the dock in Saint-Domingue, where they traded a life for a life. My father told us that our people had been slaves in the desert and because God had seen fit to set us free, none among us should ever own another man. It had been written that every man belonged to God and no one else. But did women belong to God or to the men of their family? They could not own property or businesses; only their husbands could have that honor. They must lower their eyes, behave, follow their appointed destinies. My father now told me I must trust in him and do as I was told.

"Marriage is not unlike business, and business is something you're good at, my dear."

He had finally arranged a marriage, as was the custom among our people. But I had never believed he would find a match for me. As soon as I heard that he had, a chill ran through me, even though he assured me he had chosen a good man, one who would treat me kindly. I must have paled, but before I could begin to mount my argument against the marriage, my father shook his head and took my hand in his.

"Understand," he said, gently, sadly. "It has already been agreed upon."

I knew once he gave his promise there was no breaking his word. I could feel my pulse at the base of my throat. I heard the hummingbird outside the window, the whir and beat of its wings. The man my father had chosen was wise in the ways of business but had recently had some bad turns of fortune with his ships. He had several decent ships left, and so he had come to my father, who had goods to sell but no ships on which he could transport rum and molasses to Charleston and New York. Together, they would join forces, and in this way they would both prosper. It was a partnership that would include the entire family, on this island and in Europe, as both businesses were co-owned by European relatives who had lent us money. A marriage would be a bridge between the two families, our wedding vows more binding than a legal contract.

"It's a combining of strengths," my father told me.

I said nothing, but I knew it was more. It was a combining of destinies.

Our congregation was so small there were only a few young men left unmarried. I assumed I would know the groom-to-be. But he was not one of the boys I had grown up with. When my father told me the name of my betrothed, I felt the way prisoners must when the cage that holds them is slammed shut and the key in the lock is turned. My husband-to-be was Isaac Petit, a man nearly thirty years my senior, the father of three children, the last a girl not yet a year old. It was the birth of this baby that had caused his wife to pass from our world. We had all gone to her funeral. I could not see Monsieur Petit from where I sat, but I had heard his children crying.

The losses to the Petit family seemed beyond what humankind could bear. Several children had died: a daughter, one son and then another, two twin girls who passed from this world before they could be named, and finally a beloved son named Joseph. Only two sons had survived, David and Samuel, and then, twelve days after the last baby girl was born, Madame Esther Petit, who had been suffering from childbed fever, passed away. I had seen her many times in the market square, a slim, pretty woman who had prized the red flower of the flamboyant tree. For days after her passing people left vases of them outside her husband's house.

They were all faded now, swept away.

There was a lump in my throat when I heard my fate. I thought of the map of Paris that I had memorized and my childish book of stories hidden beneath my mattress. I imagined a man I didn't even know coming into my bed. I would rather be at the bottom of the sea, but I knew I must go forward. Perhaps someone else would have begged to be released from her father's promise. But I had seen the ledgers, and I knew that there would be no house, no garden, no comfortable life as we knew it if the business stayed the same. This was why Adelle had seen an unexpected fate for me. I would be a mother before I ever was with a man or had given birth. My future was already waiting for me: the house of the red flowers, the motherless children who wept, the sorrowful man who had paid so little attention to his business after his wife died that he'd nearly been ruined.

On the night when moths twice as large as any in Paris struck against the wooden shutters, I knew this was not a dream that would be broken by morning light. I wanted nothing more than to leave St. Thomas and be sent off to Europe, even if it meant I must care for some aging relative or clean other people's homes. All the same, my father looked like an old man, beaten by fate. He was concerned for the future, but it was my future as well.

"First I will have a discussion with Monsieur Petit," I told my father. He sighed. He knew I was stubborn and had my reasons. "Must you?"

"Must you breathe to live?" Wishing to save the business didn't make me a fool. "I won't deny you what you ask, but in return, don't deny me. Send him to me."

MONSIEUR PETIT CAME A few evenings later, after his children were asleep under the watchful eye of a maid. It was late enough for the mosquitoes that swarm at dusk to have disappeared into the damp night. The bats had settled in the trees, their shadows like leaves. I could hear them breathing as they hung upside-down in the branches. I'd asked for the meeting to be informal, outside. All the same, my father introduced us formally, though surely we'd met before, although on what occasion neither of us could remember, for Monsieur Petit had been a grown man and I nothing more than a girl.

"Enchanté," Monsieur Petit said to me.

I'd been told that he'd come directly to St. Thomas from Paris, which interested me. I wished I might question him about his past there, but my father threw me a look, so I merely greeted our guest politely. The men had glasses of sherry. I had a tea of vervain, though I would have preferred rum. My mother insisted I wear one of her dresses so that I would look sophisticated, a bit older than my age. It was a gray silk frock from France, with an underskirt of crinoline that pricked at my legs, as if ants were climbing past my ankles. My hair was pulled back with combs fashioned of tortoiseshell and abalone. I knew I wasn't beautiful, but I was young, and perhaps that was enough.

My father spoke about the weather, always a topic on an island prey to storms, and then they discussed business matters, nothing too urgent. What was central to the arrangement had already been addressed before the proposal of marriage was made, in private. I asked Adelle to find out as much as she could about Monsieur Petit from the maid who cared for his children. Because of this I knew he was forty-four years of age.

Older than my father.

More than double my own age.

Earlier in the day, Jestine had come into my room. She knew what was to be, and didn't approve of arranged marriages. She gazed at the silk dress my mother had given me, then rubbed the heavy gray fabric between her fingers.

"You shouldn't wear this," she advised. The weather was sweltering, and drops of water fell into the garden even though there was no rain. "This is why French women faint."

"He's proposing tonight." I was gazing at myself in the mirror, and I didn't like what I saw. I thought I resembled my mother.

"You don't even know him. How can you marry him?" Jestine asked.

"Marriage is no different from business," I told her. I was parroting my father, but I also believed I had a duty to him.

"It should be a business of the heart and soul." Jestine lowered her voice. "We can run away and be gone before anyone notices we are missing. Let them find him another wife. We'll go to Paris."

We had always planned to journey there together, but now I shook my head. I couldn't allow my family to be financially ruined. It was the night when the turtles came to shore, but Jestine went alone to the beach while I sat in the courtyard with the man I was to marry.

"SHALL WE SPEAK TO one another plainly?" I asked Monsieur Petit when there was a lull in his conversation with my father. Adelle had always told me that a woman who acts as if she knows what she's doing gets what she wants. "And perhaps alone?"

Monsieur Petit glanced up, startled by my request. He was tall, with distinctive features. His hair was marked with gray. I'm sure a woman of his age would have found him attractive. I smiled at him with whatever small charm I might have. "Surely my father can trust you to be alone with me."

Monsieur Petit nodded. "If you wouldn't mind," he said to my father. He still had not addressed me directly.

"You're the one who might mind. She doesn't hold back her remarks." My father glanced at me with an implicit warning.

Once Monsieur Petit and I were left alone in the garden, the seriousness of the situation settled between us, a heavy weight. We were to marry, yet knew nothing of one another. We both gazed into the hedge of jasmine, embarrassed and ill at ease. The heat enveloped us. Jestine had been right. The gray silk dress was much too heavy for the season. I wished I could tear it off and toss it into the shrubbery, then sit across from my fiancé in my white cotton chemise and petticoat so I might be more at ease. My mother had forced me to wear black stockings and calf-skin boots with pearl buttons when I would have much preferred to be barefoot. I laughed to think of what Monsieur Petit's reaction might be were he faced by an unruly girl who'd slipped out of her dress. When I laughed at my imagined state, he glanced at me, confused, then studied the dark garden, as if there was something to see in the hedges.

The scent of jasmine and frangipani was dizzying, but I was used to it and kept my head. I grew braver and turned my attention to Monsieur Petit, searching his face for clues to his disposition, pleased when he looked up, then quickly looked away. My direct gaze had made him nervous. I took that to mean he would not bully me or tell me what to think. He turned to his glass of sherry as if it was the most compelling thing on earth. That was when I thought I might have the upper hand in the situation.

Monsieur Petit politely asked about my interests. Another man wouldn't have cared.

"I believe you're my interest now," I told him.

"Do you wish to know me more thoroughly before you make your decision?" he asked. "I wouldn't wish for you to be unhappy with the arrangement."

It was then I realized this was as much a business affair for Monsieur Petit as it was for me. In that instant I understood he still loved his wife.

"My father speaks well of you. I don't need to know more. But if I'm to be a mother, I wish to meet the children."

"The children are very well behaved," Monsieur Petit assured me.

I was cordial, but I made my point. "That's not the issue. If we are to be married, you need to trust my opinion, and that is, I must meet the children."

His expression was puzzled, but he nodded. He had dark eyes and tanned skin. He'd spent a good deal of time on ships before he married and had children. "Of course."

"There," I said. I could tell what happened between us would be up to me. "We've had our first fight, and are none the worse for it."

He seemed amused, and perhaps would have enjoyed further conversation, but I stood and shook his hand and told him good night. I did not wish for him to consider our meeting anything more than it was. He had a nice handshake. He did not try to overpower me, as some men might have, nor did he shrink from me. Most important, he didn't press me to account for my reasoning.

In truth, I wasn't worried that something was wrong with the children. Rather I feared that I might not be able to experience the emotion a mother should possess, due to my own fraught relationship with my mother. I knew from fairy tales about the evil deeds stepmothers might do, how black their hearts might turn. I had no idea what reaction I might have to another woman's children, especially the daughter who had caused her death. When the Petits' maid spoke with Adelle, she had divulged that even on her mistress's deathbed the ailing woman could think only of her newborn daughter. Madame was desperate to live long enough for the naming ceremony, eight days after the birth. If a baby died without a name, the spirit of Lilith, she who preceded Eve, could come for that child's spirit and claim it as her own. Madame Petit chose the name Hannah, which meant grace.

On the day after the naming, Madame was too weak to take a sip of water. She lasted four more days, but on the twelfth day she began to succumb to childbed illness. "If you don't watch over her, I'll haunt you," she had whispered to her maid, frightening the woman so deeply she rarely let go of the child even now, all these months later. She held the baby close all night, watching over her until morning, afraid not of Lilith but of Madame Petit's ghost.

The one thing that could make me walk away from this marriage bargain was if I felt nothing upon seeing the boys and the baby girl. To take care of a ghost's children, one could not feign love.

ON THE DAY I went to the Petit house, I wore what I would have to wander through the hills with Jestine. We favored plain cotton skirts that made it easy to run, in case we came upon some of the wild donkeys with nasty dispositions that might give chase, braying as they nipped at our legs. Jestine came in while I was dressing.

"If you join that family you will know only tragedy," she told me.

She had seen the boys in the market, and they looked ragged, like little criminals, even though their housemaid treated them with special kindness.

"All boys look like criminals until you wash their faces," I said. "No one could have looked more like a little thief than Aaron, and you certainly opened your heart to him."

My cousin could be selfish and stubborn, but with Jestine he was tender, a different person completely. I believe he had fallen in love with her on those nights when we were the only people in the world. She returned his love, even though she knew no one of our faith could marry a woman of African heritage. Jestine, although free, would never be recognized as one of our people. Still, Aaron was sullen if she went out with anyone else, whether it be with her mother or her cousins or, lately, even me. When men looked at her, as they always did, he was outraged. He'd gained a reputation as a hothead, someone to avoid. But while Jestine had sleepless nights, Aaron slept quite well. I knew this because when I knocked on his door to tell him his breakfast was waiting, he didn't even bother to reply. I went in anyway and sat on the edge of the bed.

"Do you love Jestine?" I had asked one day. He was a handsome man, yet still a child in many ways.

"Of course I do," he said. "But Madame can never hear of it."

"You're going to let Madame Pomié ruin your life?"

Aaron had pushed me off the bed. "There are rules," he told me. I was shocked to hear him say so. I thought of us as rebels, wandering the island, going where we pleased, even if it was something my mother had forbidden.

"You're the one who will ruin your life if you don't understand there are differences among us," he told me.

After that I didn't trust Aaron. I told Jestine a thousand times, *Don't choose him,* but she said in love there were no choices and swore one day I'd find that to be true. I could not concentrate on my books or on the stories I wrote anymore. I listened to the moth that always tried to get into my room, and I wished I could fly with it across the ocean. Perhaps in the cold my heart would freeze and I would care nothing for those I was forced to abandon.

◦∿◦

MY FATHER ESCORTED ME to the Petit house on a Sunday afternoon when the church bells were ringing. There were mountains all around town, and many of the streets were steep. One had to climb up staircases made of ballast stones from ships that had docked at the island, for thousands of such stones were unloaded when the shipmasters picked up their cargo. The Petit home was up a winding twist of a road. The house was pretty, painted yellow with a large veranda. There were green shutters at every window that could be fastened shut when there was the threat of a hurricane. Egrets were fishing in a small pond nearby, a sign of good luck despite Jestine's warnings. Egrets meant joy and happiness. I knew that much. I asked my father to fetch Monsieur Petit while I waited at the gate. I needed a moment to collect my thoughts. "Go on," I said to my father. "It's fine for me to wait on my own."

"If you're this bossy with him, he'll likely cancel the wedding," my father warned.

"If he doesn't try to please me now, what will he do when he's my husband?"

My father laughed, but he did as I asked. Standing there, I noticed egrets worked into the design of the iron fence. I wondered if Madame Petit had asked the ironworker for this pattern after watching the very birds I now spied in the pond.

I didn't go forward until my father and Monsieur Petit came out. They were so much older I felt silly being young and inexperienced, but then I saw how tentative Monsieur Petit was and I felt my strength. I nodded a greeting, then asked if they would leave.

In the bright light Monsieur Petit looked worried and even older than he had on the evening we met. "But you don't know the house."

"You plan on marrying me, yet you have discomfort about me being in your house? Do you think I'm a thief?"

He laughed. "Not at all. It's only that I wished to introduce you. For your comfort."

I assured him that women spoke to children in ways men did not understand, or so Adelle had always told me. I said I was comfortable on my own and he could return in one hour. That was time enough. In one hour I would discover all I needed to know.

"And you don't have to watch over me," I teased my father. "If anyone was to do that, it would be Monsieur Petit."

Isaac Petit looked startled. I think he was still in a dream, imagining that his wife might return to him. I saw that his posture was somewhat stooped, as if he carried sorrow on his back. All of this might have made another girl turn and run, but I had always been the sort of person to do my best no matter the situation. I went to the porch, where there was wicker furniture set out facing a long view of the harbor. The water was pale green in the shallows, turquoise in the deep. The sea changed color depending on the tides and the wind. I pried open the heavy mahogany door and slipped inside the house, where it was cooler, darkened against the summer heat with closed shutters and drawn curtains. Being inside was like drinking a glass of chilled water. I stood in the hallway and shivered, thankful to be cold.

The boys were clearly expecting a guest, for they found me in the hall fast enough. They had dressed formally for the occasion in white shirts and black trousers, their hair combed back with lavender water. They raced in and looked disappointed when they spied me lingering there.

"We thought our new mother was coming," they burst out.

I could tell they thought I was a day woman, hired to help with the laundry. My clothes were plain and I was young. Not what they had expected.

"You can have but one mother in this world and no one can take her place," I assured them.

When I asked for a tour, they showed me all the rooms they planned to show their new stepmother.

"Let's run," they said. "We're usually not allowed."

I laughed and chased them down the hall. I let them think I was the laundress; it was the best way to observe their true natures. The older boy, David, was outgoing and talkative. Samuel was the quieter one, who had green eyes, the color of the sea. There was a sadness sifting through him. He seemed older than his age, which was less than four, but I was soon reminded of how young he was. Sometime during the tour of the house, he took my hand, quite naturally. The truth was I liked the feel of his hand in mine, the heat and weight of it.

. . .

THE BOYS SHARED A room. The window opened to a stand of banana trees. From here it was possible to watch the bats at night, for those creatures love this kind of fruit, opening the peels with their hands as if they were small people. I sat with the children on the bed and heard David's stories of the bats he had seen—one that had red eyes, one that had pointed teeth, one as large as a cat that darted through the shadows to sit on the window ledge so it might peer inside the room, licking its lips. Samuel crept into my lap during this story. He shivered and kicked his feet. I leaned down and said, "Your brother is making up these stories. If he saw a bat as big as a cat it was indeed a cat. He was probably too sleepy to tell the difference."

After that Samuel seemed calmer. I thanked the boys for showing off the house.

"It's one of the prettiest on the island," I said.

"Our mother made it that way," Samuel told me.

When he let go of my hand, I felt empty. They went off to play, and I continued along the corridor so I might glance into Monsieur Petit's room. It was very neat and clean, with a huge mahogany bed. There was white mosquito netting hanging down, held in place through a hook in the wooden rafters. The duvet was a pale mint green of very soft cotton. It seemed Monsieur Petit and his wife had slept together, for she hadn't her own bedroom, as many married women did, only the nursery next door. I peered inside. The room was dark, and I wondered if I would see Madame Petit's ghost if I reached out to her, for I knew I could call spirits to me so that they flickered over my palms.

Because of this, I kept my hands closed.

I suppose I was nervous about what she might say to me. What if she warned me away? What if she uttered a jealous curse?

I found my way downstairs easily enough. I wanted to see what else I would discover in this house that had held so much sorrow, perhaps a sign that would tell me whether I should stay or go. In the parlor there was a small piano, painted white. I ran my hands over the keys without making a sound. Then I listened to a bee, tapping against the window, struggling to get inside. I could spy the sea from this room, as green as Samuel's eyes. Perhaps that was all the sign I needed.

The maid was in the kitchen, the baby in her arms as she cooked a soup for lunch. I could smell curry and chicken gravy. The maid had set out johnnycakes on a platter and was drinking a cup of steaming balsam bush tea. Hot food in hot weather, local people say. Such meals heat you up inside and then when you finish and put them aside, you feel cooler. I recognized the maid from the market—an African woman named Rosalie, who had always lived with the Petit family. Her accent was the same as ours, a rich Creole French. When she turned from the stove to see me standing there, she took a step away. The baby in her arms had golden hair and dark blue eyes, nearly violet in color. She waved her small hands at me. Perhaps this was another sign.

"May I hold her?" I asked.

The maid grasped onto her. "Maybe you're a spirit," she said, uneasy.

"I'm not. You know Adelle, who works for us. I'm Moses Pomié's daughter."

She wasn't convinced it was safe to have me in the house. "You might have come to steal her."

"I didn't. I was invited to this house by Monsieur Petit."

"He didn't invite you to hold this child. As you can see, he's not here. I am. So it's my decision."

I understood that if a person made a pledge to a ghost, she would fear being haunted if she failed to keep her word. I would have to win them both over, the maid and the spirit of the mistress of this house. I gazed at the stove. There was a heavy cast-iron pot, and the fragrance of the food was unmistakable.

"Curried lime chicken soup. That's my favorite, I must say. I'd like your recipe."

"I don't give my recipes to strangers."

By then we were speaking informally, as if we knew each other. "I'm not really a stranger." I picked up a wooden spoon from the table. "May I?"

Rosalie shrugged, so I took a taste.

"I could never make a soup as good as this one." Indeed, it was very good. But my compliment got me only so far. Rosalie was still wary, so I told her the truth about my visit. "Monsieur Petit has asked to marry me."

She nodded. "I've heard so. Not that he mentioned it to me."

"I'll likely say yes."

"You're here due to love?"

We gazed at each other. I saw that very few lies could get past this woman. "Due to circumstance."

"Because he won't love you," Rosalie informed me. She was a straightforward woman, not yet thirty. "Just so you have that clear in your mind. That won't happen. He already loved someone."

"Fine," I said. At that time I didn't care about love. I didn't even believe in it, since it had never affected me.

Rosalie saw that I was studying Hannah. She was darling, so pretty she looked like a bluebell in a garden.

"She's a very good baby." Rosalie shifted the child in her arms. "Maybe you'll spoil her."

"I won't. You won't let me."

Rosalie threw me a look. She knew what I meant. If I came to live here, I would keep her on. I would share the baby with her. She decided to let me hold Hannah. As soon as the child was in my arms, she gazed into my eyes as if we somehow knew each other.

"She doesn't like strangers," Rosalie said, "but she's taken to you."

I smoothed the baby's hair. I felt something close to my heart. "Do you think you can love someone who doesn't belong to you?"

Rosalie nodded. "I know that you can."

. . .

MY HOUR IN THE Petit house passed quickly. The sea had turned a
darker green, and pelicans wheeled across the sky. When I left, only
Monsieur Petit was waiting at the gate. He looked appealing from a distance, and I noticed that his suit was more elegant than most, presumably
tailored in France. There I was in my cotton skirt and blouse, my hair
unbraided. I felt like a child beside him as we met and shook hands. Parrots in the treetops called when we went up the hill. It was another good
sign to see parrots nearby. The Danish government had sent over mongooses to kill the many rats that made their home around the wharves,
but since rats were nocturnal, the mongooses had turned on other prey,
attacking our parrots. Now there were fewer than a hundred left in the
wild, mostly in the mountains, where the foliage was deep enough for
them to hide from these predators.

As we walked on, I realized that I no longer considered this to be
purely a business arrangement. I felt dizzy, and there was a lump in my
throat. I had fallen in love, not with Monsieur Petit but with the
children.

We were silent as we strolled through town, unpracticed in the art of
conversation with one another. When we reached my parents' house,
Isaac Petit gently placed his hand on my arm. I didn't shrink from his
touch as I'd imagined I would.

"You didn't give your opinion of the children. Were they well behaved?"

"Very much so. The maid has done well with them."

"You will, too. Children need a mother."

"I've already told them that children can have only one mother in
this world. I would not dream to think I could take your wife's place."

Monsieur Petit nodded. I saw his grief pass over his face. "You will
do well all the same," he told me.

"I want Rosalie to continue on."

"Of course. She's always been with us, and you'll need help."

He was an agreeable man, more attractive than I had first thought.

No wonder my predecessor had fallen in love with him, and slept in his bed rather than have a room of her own.

Throughout my life my mother hushed me whenever I tried to speak my mind, but if I kept silent now, I would never be able to be honest with this man, so I decided to say what another woman might keep to herself.

"When you think of the woman who is your wife, I will not expect you to think of me first," I told Monsieur Petit.

He kissed me on both cheeks, as a father might have. Jestine would have been disappointed. She would have wanted him to kiss me on the mouth, and place his hands on my waist and draw me near. But I was pleased and relieved. I was so young I believed that, when it came to a marriage, there could be matters more essential than love.

"So we have an agreement?" I said.

He laughed and looked at me. "You would have been a good businesswoman."

But such a thing did not exist in our world, not unless it came to making a marriage that would benefit all concerned.

"I'll make a good wife," I assured him. "One you won't have to love."

CHAPTER TWO

The Elixir of Life

CHARLOTTE AMALIE, ST. THOMAS

1818

RACHEL POMIÉ PETIT

Adelle and Jestine and I worked feverishly on my dress, sewing until our fingers bled. We used cornstarch to stanch the bleeding. "You may need this on your wedding night," Adelle told me. She explained how a woman bled the first time she was with her husband; she said this was natural, for a marriage was a blood pact. The wedding was in a matter of weeks. Adelle had given me some information concerning what went on between men and women; the rest I discovered from watching donkeys in the fields and listening to the whispers of the pirates' wives.

"You think he'll be like a donkey?" Jestine laughed at me. "Why marry a man at all?"

Both Jestine and Adelle thought I was making a mistake to do my father's bidding, but I didn't care to hear their opinions or warnings.

"She doesn't want to talk about love," Jestine told her mother with a grin. "She wants to marry a donkey."

"Just a man," I said. "One who understands my father's business."

"Maybe she's right." Adelle shrugged. "Since she's not bound to know love in this marriage."

What was a husband, after all, if not a partner? Why should I ask for more than that? Why should I ever want it?

~☙☙~

EVEN IF JESTINE WOULD have agreed to attend my wedding service, my mother made it clear the ceremony was only for people of our faith. The marriage prayers were recited at the same altar where Monsieur Petit's wife's funeral had been held. The synagogue was a dark building, but when light came through the windows it became a radiant place. My mother was pleased that I was to marry Monsieur Petit, and because she approved she gave me her wedding veil, smuggled from Saint-Domingue, the only thing she'd taken other than her jewels. "You're not as foolish as I thought you were," she told me.

I supposed it was a compliment.

"Marry from here." She touched her head. "Not here." She hit her chest. "Love will do nothing for you."

As soon as she offered her approval I began to doubt myself. If she thought something was right, it was usually wrong. But it was too late for me to have second thoughts. I'd given my father my word.

On the day of the ceremony I asked that branches from the flamboyant tree be placed in a vase on the altar to honor the first Madame Petit. Her husband would now be mine. He looked very somber and handsome and much too old for me. During the ceremony the boys were solemn and quiet, and Hannah did not call out once. Everyone said she was an exceptional baby, calm and sweet-natured. The wedding contract, a lavishly illustrated document bordered by gold leaf, had been signed the evening before. Time moved quickly during the service; the synagogue was so close and crowded and hot. My mother beamed with pride, which gave me a case of nerves. I felt myself grow wobbly. I refused to faint, but my heart was so loud it was all I could hear. I concentrated on a vase of pink flowers at the altar beside the branches of the flamboyant tree, placed there by Jestine, who knew bougainvillea to be my favorite flower. And then it was done. I was a married woman.

The marriage dinner was in the garden of my parents' house. Tables had been set out, and silvery lanterns were strung from the trees. Everyone was there, all of the old families from St. Croix and Saint-Domingue, and some of the newer families from Amsterdam and Morocco. My father's good friend, Monsieur DeLeon, gave a speech in which he declared that every bride should have a father as wise and kind as mine. Though I agreed, I couldn't wait to get out of my heavy wedding dress, which Jestine had already decided we would dye blue so I might get some use of it in the future.

Jestine now worked beside Adelle as a maid in our house, and had helped cook the food for the dinner, but on this night she came as a guest, invited by my father. She wore a pale pink taffeta dress. She and I had both had our hair braided by Adelle's deft hands. There were little white pearls scattered through my hair, and pink pearls threaded through Jestine's hair. People said we looked so alike we might have been sisters. I introduced her to Monsieur Petit, who took her hand and said it was a pleasure to meet such a dear friend of his wife's. Without thinking I laughed when he called me his wife. It seemed like a joke, some wild mistake. Monsieur Petit crinkled his eyes when he smiled; he wasn't the least bit insulted. I carried Hannah in the crook of my arm during the party. The boys ate cake and my father let them take sips of wine. When it grew late, I had to send the children home with Rosalie, even though Samuel held on to my skirt and said he was afraid of the bats his brother said perched on the window ledge. I whispered for him not to worry. "When I get to the house I'll take a broom and chase them away."

The night was hot and long. I drank rum punch until I was dizzy. As the evening was ending my mother took me aside. After all these years of disapproval and silence, she suddenly wanted to begin an intimate conversation concerning what went on between a husband and wife. I suppose she thought it was her obligation to do so.

"You may not like your husband's desires, but it is your duty to fulfill them, and in the end you'll become used to him. Do not fight him, and do not think he means to murder you when he takes you in his arms."

I nearly laughed out loud. "Thank you," I said, "but you don't need to say any more. My husband will instruct me."

My mother gazed at me, eyes narrowed. "You're very sure of yourself."

Perhaps she thought I was experienced in matters of a physical nature. In fact, I wasn't, which was why I'd had so much rum. A carriage took us away. Usually a bride's carriage would be decorated with ribbons and flowers, but in deference to the first Madame Petit, ours was plain. The black carriage horse was the same one that had brought her coffin to the cemetery. I went upstairs, relieved to take off my wedding clothes. Most people avoided a summer wedding, and now I understood why. It was too hot for the heavy clothes one had to wear for such an occasion. I was happy to be in my muslin undergarments, barefoot, my hair freed from the tight plaits that Adelle had decorated with pearls. The little beads scattered onto the floor, and they sounded like falling rain. Though I had never spent the night here before, I had the sense of being at home. I peered into the nursery to watch Hannah sleep, then went to look in on the boys. True enough, bats were perched on the window ledge. In the morning I would instruct Rosalie on how to place sharp shells and bits of broken glass along the casements to keep these creatures away. For now, I merely opened the window and shook a handkerchief until the night creatures flew to the treetops.

When I turned, Monsieur Petit was there.

I cared nothing for love, yet I was terrified of all I was yet to learn about my husband's desires. My mother had frightened me with her instructions.

"We are married," my husband reminded me.

I said I knew.

"What else do you know?" He was gazing at me in a way he hadn't before.

"Nothing," I admitted.

I thought of Jestine and Aaron and the way they were drawn to one another, even when they didn't wish to be. When I'd asked Jestine to teach me all she knew about love, she'd declined. "If I told you, it would all sound silly or ugly, but when it's you it will be different. You have to learn for yourself."

Monsieur Petit brought me to bed and taught me what people did in the dark. He undressed me and I let him, though I had it in my head that I could escape into the baby's room at any time, turn the key, and sleep on the floor. Monsieur put his hands on me and I let him do so. He told me he wouldn't hurt me, but everywhere he touched me I began to burn. He moved away from me to ask if I was all right. I nodded and waited for what came next. I found myself to be a bit disappointed. I'd had certain expectations, and Monsieur Petit didn't act in the manner I'd expected. I'd heard women in the market say that a man would become a beast of sorts, a slave to his desires. Certainly my mother had prepared me for some sort of violence, which in a way interested me. I thought of Perrault's story of Bluebeard, who'd had so many wives, each one mad for him despite the ill treatment they received.

Monsieur Petit, however, was quiet, possessing a tenderness I hadn't anticipated. He didn't rush anything between us, merely held me to him. I could feel the way he wanted me, and that was curious to me. It wasn't love, but he seemed to possess a sort of passion for me, perhaps a hunger he'd had since his wife had been gone. He had one hand on the small of my back. The other hand slipped between my legs. Who was I that I wanted this? I felt the heat spread out inside of me in a way I didn't understand. I could not think clearly. I believed I saw a shadow in the velvet chair against the wall. I could have sworn I heard a sigh from that area as well. A single breath. I moved away from Monsieur Petit and gazed in that direction. I had the sense that we were being watched, although aside from the two of us, the chamber appeared empty.

"Is something wrong?" my husband asked me.

I shook my head and closed my eyes. If the first Madame Petit was with us, that was her right, but it was also my right to ignore her. Before long it seemed I had drifted out of my body, as if my spirit were flitting above us. I could watch myself on the bed below. I was inside a dream, but I could feel a stab of heat inside me. Perhaps I was shivering, as if I had flown away with the moth outside the window of my bedchamber, a place where I would never sleep again.

Monsieur Petit said again that if I liked he could wait for me to become more used to him, but I said no. We were married, and because this was our wedding night I asked if on this single occasion he would think only of me rather than of his first wife. I would never ask this of him again, and when he did call me Esther on other occasions I never once complained.

~❧~

THERE WAS SO MUCH to learn about the children and the household in the first weeks I might have easily become overwhelmed, but I had Rosalie to educate me, and she was a good teacher. She told me she had been born in this country, on the grounds of one of the old Danish farms, and that she had been cooking since she was a little girl. I stood beside her in the kitchen, both of us in our aprons, our hair covered by scarves. I learned the recipes for lime chicken soup and for all her other dishes. I soon became expert in cooking the children's favorite food, the fongee porridge of cornmeal with vegetables that I myself had always enjoyed. The children's play in the muddy garden made for masses of laundry, which were hung out on two rope lines nearly every day. The clean clothes smelled like sea air, and before Rosalie pressed them with a heavy iron she sprinkled them with lavender water. David was already attending the school at the synagogue, but Samuel followed me around from room to room. I allowed the children to stay up late, for I hated to discipline them. Often Monsieur Petit read in the drawing room while I played games with the boys.

"You worried you wouldn't love them, now I'm worried that you love them too much," Rosalie warned.

"There's no such thing." I laughed.

But Rosalie said I was wrong. We sat on the porch and drank ginger tea. In a low voice she told me she'd had a baby who had died. She had loved him too much and so she took his death as a punishment from God for being too proud. The baby spit up blood and turned so hot he was on fire in her arms. The milk he drew from her breast boiled in his mouth, and perhaps that was what killed him, she whispered, his own mother's milk. She was crying as she spoke, the wound was that fresh even though the baby had been gone for several years. I slipped my arms around her and insisted that neither her God nor mine would be so cruel as to do such a thing. A baby could not drown from drinking milk. He'd clearly had yellow fever, and that was no one's fault. I was young, and I thought I understood grief, but I knew nothing. I had no idea of how deep a mother's sorrow could be.

Rosalie was polite enough not to tell me I was a fool to give her advice. I think she pitied my stupidity and saw it as innocence, so she embraced me in return and said nothing more. But after that I often heard her crying behind the stairs, and I knew it was for the baby she had loved too much.

❦

THE WOMEN FROM THE congregation invited me to join them as a member of Blessings and Peace and Loving Deeds. This was an honor and in my mind, both unexpected and unwanted. All the same, I had little choice. Monsieur Petit was an esteemed member of the community, and I was his wife. At last my mother could be proud as I sat among the women from the best families. I overheard her speaking of me. At first I thought she was referring to my predecessor, but no, when she had said Madame Petit, whose house was so lovely, whose children were so well behaved, I realized she meant me.

After tea at Madame Halevy's home, there was conversation regard-

ing orphaned children and those of our faith who did not have luck with
business or had fallen prey to illness. We planned dinners to raise funds
for those in need and wrote up reports to present to all of the committee
members. People who faltered were discussed at great length, for in a
group such as this, any hint of wickedness was worth uncovering, including those men who dared to keep two wives: a Jewish wife and another wife, and perhaps another family, living near the docks. The
scandal concerned Nathan Levy, born in Baltimore, but now a resident
of Charlotte Amalie. Levy had been granted the honor of being the
United States consul but was said to be dishonorable in his business dealings. The women seemed most concerned that he lived with an African
woman named Sandrine, flaunting the relationship in public, treating her
as though she were his wife. I'd seen them once when I was at the market
with Adelle. She had stared after them, interested.

"My mother says it's the marriage of a heron and a parrot," I said to
Adelle.

"Does she?" Adelle made a disapproving face. "Well, your mother
knows nothing. They're not birds. They're people in love."

Levy was a member of our congregation, and although there were
several letters sent to the office of the United States Secretary of State,
John Quincy Adams, in Washington, no one dared to discuss this matter
with Levy face-to-face, for he was a man of power who helped the business interests of those on the island. Rather than confront him, people
crossed the street when they saw his woman or when she and Levy
walked arm and arm near the harbor.

I went directly to Adelle's house and found Jestine on the porch,
folding laundry. "I thought you were too busy being married to come see
me," she said. "Aren't you attending a meeting today?"

"I have three children. And I left the meeting." I thought perhaps I
would find excuses not to attend any meetings to come.

Jestine threw me a dark look. "You have one true friend," she reminded me.

"Whereas you have two," I teased. "How is Aaron?"

Jestine laughed, a catch in her voice. "I haven't any idea."

She said he had been avoiding her. Twice he had not shown up at their appointed meeting place. She'd stood alone in our garden. She'd thrown stones at my cousin's window, but there had been no response.

"He's a heavy sleeper," I told her. "And you know as well as I do, he's lazy." It was, to be honest, part of his charm. He liked to take his time and have lengthy conversations with other businessmen, rather than work in our father's shop, which he clearly thought beneath him.

Jestine shook her head. "I think someone's turned him against me."

We both knew who that someone was likely to be. My mother. "We should have never let him come with us," I said to my friend. "We should have left him home when he begged to follow us. He was always a troublemaker."

"No, he wasn't." Jestine stacked the laundry neatly in a reed basket. "We inherited our troubles."

After the laundry was completed, we went into the hills, the way we used to, before I was married. Jestine was right; I'd been consumed with my new duties and hadn't been a good friend. In truth, I'd missed her. We linked arms and chattered until there was a burst of rain, and then we had to run to take cover. When the torrents ended, a pale drizzle came down around us. Everything smelled green and sweet. On this island there were a hundred varieties of rain, from blue to clear, from whirl-wind storms to a dash of dew to the driving rain of winter. We used ba-nana leaves as umbrellas and sat under the canopy of the trees. On very clear days we could see the islands that were used as pastures, Goat Is-land and Water Island, where livestock ran free, chewing the wet, salty grass. Light drifted through the raindrops and the sky broke into colors. The heat came back, and we lay down in the field. We made garlands out of tall grass and bits of twig. No one passing by would have seen us, ex-cept that the grass moved whenever we breathed.

"Have you learned to love Monsieur Petit?" Jestine asked me.

"I don't hate him."

She laughed and shook her head. "That isn't an answer! I told you not to do it. He's old enough to be your father."

"He's not my father when we're alone."

"Oh?" She smiled. "So now you know. But is it good with him in bed? Do you long for him to touch you? Yearn for him when he's not there?"

I shrugged as if I were an old married woman, though I was little more than twenty. "It's better than I thought it would be."

Jestine snorted. "Because you thought it would be hell."

I was surprised to find I was insulted on my husband's behalf. Although I didn't love him, I respected him, and surely that counted for something. Another woman would have thought him a considerate lover, but I had been inflamed by the stories I'd read and the passions of Solomon, and I wanted more. "I could not ask for a kinder man. That can't be hell."

But Jestine knew me and could see this wasn't love. "There are those who say that heaven and hell are not so far apart. They are not at opposite ends of the world beyond ours, only a step away from one another."

⁓◦⊚◦~

EVERY FRIDAY NIGHT WE had dinner with my family. I brought Rosalie along so she could watch over the children if they fell asleep, but also because I had made her a promise, which I intended to keep. I would never let Rosalie go, even though my mother had instructed me to dismiss her and get a new maid, one who hadn't been loyal to the first Madame Petit. I smiled and nodded but did the opposite. I gave Rosalie extra spending money, Saturdays and Sundays free, and warned her to stay away from my mother on Friday nights.

"I'm happy to do that," Rosalie said.

I grinned. "If only I could do the same."

All of the men in the family were now partners, members of the

Burghers' Association, for tradesmen must be accepted by the royal Danish organization in order to do business on our island. The marriage had strengthened the business, although Aaron Rodrigues wasn't happy to have Isaac Petit rise above him in a single day. My husband was a full partner, Aaron merely a distant cousin whose official title was manager, which couldn't have pleased him. I knew that he and my father had been meeting to discuss the future, and on several occasions I had heard my cousin slam out of the house, grumbling under his breath, striking the gate with a stick on his way. I heard my parents arguing in the parlor.

"There are ways around this," my mother said.

"So you can keep him here? And baby him while you treat him like a son?"

"Why not? He is a son to me."

"And what will his child be to you?" my father asked.

"What is yours to you?" my mother said coldly.

This was dangerous territory, I thought, even though I wasn't certain what my mother's meaning was.

"Am I not married to you still?" my father said, which ended the conversation.

THAT EVENING AT DINNER my father revealed that Aaron was being sent to France. My mother looked like she'd been crying, and my cousin did not look pleased by the announcement. All at once I viewed him differently. There was a hidden vulnerability inside him that was in direct opposition to the careless man he appeared to be. I suppose he'd thought he would be my father's heir, and now it was clear that honor had gone to my new husband, in the manner of the law if the oldest child was a girl, for women had no rights to property. It was a slap to Aaron, a reminder that he was not a true son, though my mother treated him as such. Yet he was not to be entirely forsaken. We had distant cousins in France, and many business connections, and Paris could not get enough of the island's rum. Aaron would be introduced to all of our relations and their friends. I felt a bitterness rise inside me. I was the one who wanted to go to Paris. Adelle always said if a person doesn't speak her mind she will carry her resentment until it burns her, as I was burning now.

"Perhaps we should be the ones sent to France," I said to my husband.

There was an immediate hush of the dinner table chatter. My father and husband both looked at me as if I was a bee with a stinger who had settled on our table without invitation.

"That wouldn't be possible," Isaac said to me. He looked over at my father, embarrassed by my outburst.

"And why not?" I had already convinced myself, now all I had to do was convince the men of my family. "The children would be in a good school and would get to know our family. It would be an adventure for them. And we could take Rosalie."

My husband shook his head. "Our life is here."

Still I didn't give up. "You came from Paris, it would be a homecoming."

My father's gaze was blistering. He didn't like to be disrespected, and this was the first time I had opposed his wishes. "You've said enough," he told me. "Your husband is an excellent partner and the business here is what matters most."

"A business you clearly don't need me for." Aaron threw his napkin onto the table and stormed out.

"Let him go," my father told my mother when she began to rise from her chair. She sank back down, near tears. "This day was bound to come," my father told her. "You have done more than enough for that boy. We will follow the law. The business will belong to Monsieur Petit. Not to Aaron."

I couldn't keep quiet. "Even if I want to leave and he doesn't? If the business is to be my husband's, do I not also have a say?"

"My apologies for her behavior," my husband said to my father, as if I were a child he had to make excuses for. He turned to me displeased.

"Say no more." He looked his age on this night, and I could see he thought me nothing more than an ill-mannered girl, too young and foolish to know enough to hold my tongue.

I thought of what Jestine had said, that we had inherited our troubles. Certainly I had inherited mine. This marriage, this man, this house, this family.

"I'll find my own way home," I told Isaac. "I'll go with Rosalie."

I left the table and followed Aaron outside. Once, he had been my baby cousin, a fondling in desperate need. Now he was a handsome man who stood alone, tossing some crumbs to the old lizard that had been his pet when he was a boy. He had only just turned twenty. He was a favorite with many of the young women in our congregation, but he'd never looked at anyone other than Jestine.

"I should be the one going to France," I told him.

"I wish it could be so. I'd be happy to stay here."

"Then let me go!" I said impulsively.

"I have no power, Rachel. Not even over my own life. At least you'll get what you want. Someday your husband will take you there."

"I plan to go with Jestine," I told him coldly.

Aaron laughed at what a fool I was. "You think you're so smart, but you don't understand anything. You're never going there with her. Just as I would never be allowed to marry her. Don't you understand she's the reason I'm being sent away?"

I felt ill. Perhaps the weather was too hot. I left my cousin and rushed along the stone path, past the fruit trees. The bananas were ripening and wasps were gathering, drawn to the sticky sugar inside the leaves. I didn't make it into the house, but instead was sick in the bushes, bringing up my dinner. Afterward, I sat back on my heels in the grass. Rosalie had come outside to search for me, and when she saw me she went to the well. She came to hand me a cup of water.

"You know what this means," she said.

All at once I did. I thought of the nights in bed with my husband, and of the first Madame Petit, who had died of childbed fever. I thought of my cousin, who had never even looked at a map of Paris and would soon be living there, staring out his window at the rain.

"They say if you're sick in the morning you'll have a daughter, and if it's in the night, you should expect a son," Rosalie announced. "It will be a boy for certain."

"I don't wish anyone to know until I'm sure."

"I'm sure."

"Well, I'm not."

I was thankful that my mother hadn't needed Jestine to serve dinner, so she was saved the dreadful news about my cousin. I went around to the patio kitchen, searching for Adelle, who I'd assumed had cooked our meal. Often she sat beside the rose tree my father had ordered from France. My mother despised and ignored the tree, she thought it too showy, but I knew that Adelle secretly watered it, perhaps to spite my mother. When I searched for her now, I found she hadn't appeared that evening. Another hired woman had helped with the dinner, one I didn't know.

"Is Adelle ill?" I asked. "Will she be back tomorrow?"

The cook threw up her hands. "I only work here!"

I went then to the bedroom where the children were sleeping and lay down beside them. I found some peace when I closed my eyes and listened to them breathing, but too soon it was time to go home. Rosalie came for us, and I carried Hannah as I followed Rosalie down the corridor. The boys clung to her as they ambled after her, sleepy and thickheaded with the heat.

When I said good night to my mother, I asked where Adelle was.

"Not here." My mother shrugged. "That's all I know."

THERE WAS A SERIES of squalls after that, with the appearance of the raging wind and rain that often comes in September. It was a terrible month, which ended with a hurricane of enormous proportions. My husband spent his nights at the office, worried over our ships at sea. Perhaps it was best for us to be apart; certainly, I had not forgiven him for taking up my father's argument against me. While he was gone, I made the best of the situation for the children. We played games, hiding under beds and in wardrobes, making birds out of paper and flying them across the rooms. We had some of the long pods from the flamboyant tree that we had set out to dry in the sun, and we used the husks the children called *shack-shacks* to make music. It was a delight to feel like a child again, but it was impossible to stay in that frame of mind for very long. The wind was screaming, and the shutters at every window needed to be nailed closed. Later I took out my notebook of stories and added a storm in which goats and sheep were lifted out of a pasture and deposited on the other side of the island, still chewing their cud. I wrote about a woman who was left behind and did her best to return to the moon, even though every storm could take her no higher than the treetops. When the center of the storm was above us, there was an odd quiet that was even more frightening than the howling of the wind. I wondered if God was above us, and if he could see our love and our fear. We all got into bed together, and Rosalie joined us. We said our prayers and she said hers as we held hands.

When the worst of the storm had passed, a stray little donkey came into the garden, drenched and bawling for its mother.

"Look who came calling!" Rosalie laughed when she looked out the back door.

The rain was still falling, and the puddles were huge, some as deep as ponds. When such things happened, fish would appear, as if brought about by magic. Samuel was terrified of the donkey at first, and hid behind my skirts. I told him it was a baby, nothing to fear.

"Let's help him," I said to Rosalie.

While I held Hannah and Samuel clung to my skirt, Rosalie and David caught the donkey with a rope, then brought it into the yard, where we offered it soft bread and milk from a tin pan. It was shy at first, but starvation got the best of it and it ate with such abandon we all laughed. Samuel soon lost his fear of the donkey. He asked if he might keep it as a pet. He had already named him Jean-François, and indeed the creature trotted over when called so. I shook my head and told Samuel no. This was a wild donkey, meant to be with its mother.

"Why does he have to be wild? Can't he be like Gus?"

Gus was a goat who lived nearby and who escaped from his pasture every once in a while to terrorize the local dogs.

"No," I told Samuel. "Some creatures are not meant to be pets."

When the sky brightened, and the donkey was well fed, we set it free. Samuel cried for so long that David teased him and called him a baby, which made him cry even harder. That night when I was putting Samuel to bed I lied and swore that I had seen the little donkey on the road with its mother, and that the day had turned out for the best. He slept easier then, his hand clutching mine. I curled up beside him rather than go into my marriage bed. But the wind arose again, hammering at the roof, and I couldn't sleep. I felt I had become a different person since moving into this house. Before I'd had no trouble killing chickens for Friday dinner, but now I wept over a wild donkey as I thought of him wandering alone. My dream for my life was slipping away from me, and perhaps that made me more tenderhearted toward this motherless creature.

I needn't have worried. In the morning the donkey was in the kitchen. He had let himself in through a door that had been blown open. Maybe it was true what they said, that donkeys and mules would not cross over a shadow, and this one had turned back when he reached the end of the property. The boys begged and begged, and even Hannah wailed and cried, reaching her hands out to the beast everyone now referred to as Jean-François. I relented. When Isaac came home at dinnertime, he found that I'd made his favorite dish, wild mushrooms and rice. I poured him a glass of rum with limewater. I said there was no reason to let our disagreement fester and interfere with our daily lives. Then I told him that the children had a pet they had named Jean-François.

"Pets are a foolish expense" was his initial comment.

"Sometimes being foolish is the right thing to do. Look at us."

"You're never foolish. I know that much."

"Not even when it comes to Paris?"

"The business cannot be run from Paris, Rachel, though I wish that it could be. Do you think I haven't thought a thousand times of leaving this place behind? I have terrible memories here. But I have to think of the children, and children expect to be fed and clothed."

"And you would be leaving Esther if you went back to Paris."

Whereas other men went to taverns in the evenings, I knew my husband went to the cemetery. Rosalie and I could both tell because there would be red mud on his shoes and red flowers in the pockets of his jacket.

"I couldn't leave," he admitted.

I went to sit on his lap. He was a kind man, and although I couldn't change his mind about Paris, when it came to the household I knew how to get what I wanted. "Be ready to be surprised."

"You always surprise me."

Because Isaac disliked dogs, he was somewhat relieved when I took him out to the barn.

"Voilà," I said. "Jean-François."

Isaac laughed, despite how tired he was. "Let me guess—he's a French donkey."

"Exactly. So we had no choice but to take him in."

Isaac stroked my hair. He was grateful that I was good to his children and humored them. "The boys talked you into this."

"Would Esther have let them keep him?"

"Esther would have been terrified of him. But she would have been glad you kept him."

I DID NOT HEAR my husband laugh again for some time. The storm was terrible for everyone, and nearly ruined us. Every workingman on our island found himself thwarted. Desolation was everywhere: roofs collapsed, houses were washed away, mudslides ruined roads and streets. The island was ravaged by destruction, and we suffered the fate of those who depended on the sea. Trading ships carrying merchandise to Charleston, including those belonging to our family, had sunk. It was a financial disaster, and Isaac spent weeks in the office, sleeping there and taking his meals at his desk, doing his best to salvage the business. Three months had passed since I'd been ill in the garden, but our bad fortune kept me from telling my husband of my condition. He didn't need more worry.

At least we still had a home. Other people were not as fortunate. Roads were impassable, and part of the shoreline had disappeared. Boats could be found on hillsides, swept there by the rising tide, broken apart so that their wooden hulls whitened and became skeletons left in among the vines. There were bodies of creatures, dogs and rats and iguanas, along the streets. Parrots in the trees drowned from turning their faces toward the sky; when they fell their feathers scattered in the mud.

I worried for Adelle's house, so close to the harbor. Neither Adelle nor Jestine now worked in my parents' home. They avoided me as well. As soon as crews had chopped up fallen trees and hauled them away, I left the children with Rosalie and made my way to their house with a satchel of food and clothes. There was a huge flood between the town and the docks, impassable. I paid a man to take me across in his canoe. Clouds reflected in the water. Everything was calm now, and the sky was an indigo color. When people in Paris thought of paradise, surely they imagined this.

The boatman dropped me off. I waded through knee-deep water until I reached Adelle's cottage. There was a starfish on the road. It was a good thing the house had been built on stilts, and that the stilts were pounded into rock, otherwise the house would have likely floated away to the other side of the world.

Adelle came onto the porch. She took the necessities I'd brought her, then hugged me close. "I'm grateful, but you shouldn't have come here," she said. The roads were dangerous, not only because of the flooding. There were looters and bands of wild dogs, all of them hungry. Adelle said that Jestine had been unwell and had taken to her bed. During the storm they had both said their last prayers as seawater rushed in through the windows. At the worst of the flooding they'd tied themselves to the cast-iron stove in the kitchen, which was the heaviest thing in the house. There was still sand on the floor, and the blue paint was pale with salt. Adelle swore that a flatfish had swum through the window, right into a cooking pot, which was God's way of seeing that they had enough to eat through the storm. They were Christians and believed in a merciful maker who would watch over them.

I told Adelle I'd come despite the floods because I missed them both. And because I had a secret. I wanted Adelle and Jestine to be the first to know.

"It's no secret, Rachel. I told you your fate before you got married. I saw that man and his children and all the other children that you'd have. Now you tell me my fate in return. Is your mother going to have me come back to her house?"

I suppose my mother had bad-mouthed Adelle and she could not get other work. I didn't mention that a hired woman was now serving dinner there. I was still confused over the matter. I asked Adelle what had happened between her and Madame Pomié, and she simply said, "We had words."

"What kind of words?"

"What kind do you think? Would your mother say anything nice to me? She didn't want me or Jestine in the house."

Just that morning my mother had ordered one of the hired men who worked in the yard to cut down the rose tree Adelle favored, but fortunately Mr. Enrique had taken it to his house before any damage was done.

"I'll speak to my mother," I promised. "You'll see. You'll be back and nothing will change."

But Adelle didn't agree. "Everything changes. Look at you. Look at Jestine."

I went into the bedroom and saw Jestine in her bed. She wore a white nightdress, and her arms were bare. It was afternoon and hot and murky, the way it is after a storm, with air that smelled like the tide. I lay down beside her, and she opened her eyes. As girls we had done everything together. At least that hadn't changed. What had happened to me had happened to her as well. I could tell from the sleepy look in her eyes, the rise in her belly. I was happy about it. Our children would be friends, although they couldn't be the cousins that they truly were. This child to come was the reason Aaron was being sent to Paris.

"We should have run away when we had the chance," Jestine said. "If you hadn't gotten married we could have gone and been there waiting for Aaron, but you had to go and fall in love with those children. I could tell after your first visit to his house that we would never get out of here."

I felt stung by her remarks. I promised that nothing would be different. I swore it on my blood. I bit my own arm and let it bleed onto the sheet. We watched as the blood formed the shape of a bird. We would still go to France, I insisted. We would leave after the children were born, despite the fact that I was a married woman. I'd lately been reading about the history of Paris, and now I told these stories to Jestine, how the streets were built over tunnels that were a thousand years old, how the Île de la Cité had been shored up by ancient ramparts to ensure that the island would never float away, no matter what floods might come. I told her Perrault's story of a girl who was in love with a beast and knew he had a true heart.

"Not that one," Jestine said.

I also recited from an old French recipe book on Esther Petit's bookshelf that I read as if it were a storybook. I'd memorized the instructions for making chestnut pastries. I recited the recipe to Jestine now, even though neither one of us had ever seen chestnuts or tasted them.

That night when I told my husband we were to have a child, he was so grateful he gave thanks to God, but in my prayers I gave thanks that there would always be ships in the harbor, there to carry us away. That night I made the pastry in the first Madame Petit's cookbook, even though I had neither chestnuts nor almond paste. I used what I had in the kitchen, molasses and papaya, and though it was not what the recipe called for, the results were delicious all the same.

MY MOTHER READIED AARON's wardrobe the following week. It was a major undertaking, and of course I agreed to assist her, but I insisted Adelle return to help us with the laundry and packing. "Does my father know you let her go?" I asked.

"She's not here. He's not blind. So he must know."

"But you told him some story. That she left because she was unhappy."

"Keep out of it," my mother said.

"I'm not afraid to tell him the truth," I told her. "He despises a liar."

It was a horrible moment between us.

"You think you are so special to have Moses Pomié's love," my mother said.

"But I do have it," I said. "Can you say the same?"

"I'll take Adelle back. But not Jestine," my mother said. Clearly she knew a romance had gone on. "Not until Aaron is gone."

Adelle came back the following day. She was quieter than usual. After a while, she and my mother took up a conversation as if nothing had happened. But it had.

The next evening, as he was preparing to go, my cousin was checking through one of the trunks he would take with him when he found a packet of lavender tucked under his freshly pressed suit. He held it up, puzzled. When he asked me what it was, I shrugged, even though I knew better. I said, "It makes your clothes smell fresh even after a long voyage." He tossed it away, saying it made him sneeze. I'm sure he had no idea what the herb was meant to do. Adelle had told me that lavender could keep a man bound to the woman who loved him. When she found the packet on the bureau later that day, she shook her head.

"I will never set eyes on that boy again."

"He might come back."

"Even if he comes back, I'll never look at him."

I WENT TO THE harbor with my parents on the day my cousin left. My mother wept as I'd never seen her do before. When Aaron came to me to say his good-byes, I threw my arm around him so I could lean close and no one would overhear. "It's your child she's having," I said.

He showed no surprise, only kissed me three times, as was the custom. I then understood that he already knew, and that he was not strong enough to give up his life and start anew. I wished this was a fairy tale and we could exchange places there on the dock, and I could be the one to leave that day. I would take nothing with me, only a map of Paris and a heavy black coat. Perhaps a cat would help me make my way and find treasure once I reached the shore of my newly claimed country. I closed my eyes and wished that when I opened them again I would find myself boarding the ship, and Aaron would stay and live in the house on stilts and we both could have the lives we were meant to have.

But when I opened my eyes he was gone and only I remained.

THAT NIGHT, I WAS even more restless than usual. I opened the windows in my bedroom. Isaac shivered as he dreamed. It was the season when the air sparked with heat in the afternoons but became damp and chill at night. I still had the same dream I'd had as a girl, and if I fell asleep the dream would come for me. There was a man in Paris who was waiting for me. He would listen to my stories, about a woman who was a turtle, and a bird that flew halfway around the world for love, and the original people that had come here from the bright side of the moon, only to be trapped, as I was. It was not fair to my husband and children, but the truth was, I still yearned for another life.

In this house the walls were not painted haint blue and spirits couldn't be kept out. That was why on certain nights when I couldn't sleep I spied the first Madame Petit in the chair in a shadowy nook that I always avoided. Rosalie said it had been my predecessor's chair. Madame Petit had often sat there before her death, rocking the baby. She had come from Paris and could never tolerate the heat. She would break out in a rash beneath the heavy fabric of the painted silk and brocade dresses she'd brought with her from France. Rosalie said she would cry when the gnats bit her, as her skin was sensitive, and she was forced to stay out of the sun, for she turned red and peeled. She had a fear of donkeys and parrots and refused to go into the countryside. She didn't like to go any farther than the front gate. Still, she had enough strength to refuse to die until her daughter had her naming day. She had loved her husband, and now I was beside him. Each night before I went to bed, I promised I would treat her children like my own. I explained that I did not love her husband, though I cared for him deeply, and that he still belonged to her. Love was out of the question for me. She needn't have any fear that I would ever take her place.

Perhaps she was watching over me during my pregnancy. As my time grew near I found I could sleep the moment I lay down in bed. Sometimes I barely had to close my eyes. I slept for hours, through the night and well into the morning, so deeply Rosalie had to shake me awake. I saw Esther Petit standing at the foot of the bed when Adelle and Jestine helped me to deliver my first child. I told her if she helped me survive this birth, I would honor her for the rest of my life. I didn't listen to people when they told me not to name my first son after a child Madame Esther Petit had lost. I went ahead and named him Joseph.

I knew who to thank for all that I had.

CHAPTER THREE

A Cold Wind

CHARLOTTE AMALIE, ST. THOMAS

1823

RACHEL POMIÉ PETIT

I n six years I added to Esther's three children with three of my own, first Joseph, then Rebecca Emma, then, a year later, Abigail Delphine. After each birth I continued the tradition of visiting the first Madame Petit to show my gratitude, leaving flowering branches on her grave. In return she gave me her blessing and allowed me to live the life that should have been hers. It was not a life in Paris, but it was one that was happily cluttered with children. Because of this, time was like a river, and I was a fish in that river, moving so quickly that the world outside my household was a blur.

Jestine often walked with me to the old Jewish cemetery when I went to pay my respects to the Petit and Pomié families. But she refused to go any farther than the gates. She was afraid of spirits, so I went on alone, and she stayed outside the gate with her daughter, Lyddie, who was four, the same age as my Joseph. I didn't tell Jestine, but sometimes I was aware of a tug when a spirit would latch on to my skirt as I turned to leave the cemetery. I felt it, a pull on my clothing, a hand around my ankle. I had great sympathy for these women snatched away by death before they'd held their children in their arms, but not so much that I intended to stay beside them. I recited the mourning prayer and they vanished, back to where they belonged.

When I left the cemetery I brushed the leaves from my hair. The fallen leaves were a sign that a ghost had been walking in the branches of the trees above me. Jestine noticed, and it proved her point. "You think those who've passed on are content to leave this world? They'll wrap themselves around you and live off your breath," she told me.

"I hold my breath when I'm in there," I assured her.

"No you don't!" She laughed at me. "I see you talking to your husband's wife, telling her news of her children."

I always left my children home with Rosalie, but I loved having Jestine's daughter along. Lyddie was an extremely beautiful child, perhaps even more beautiful than her mother, with silver-gray eyes and hair that had strands of gold running through the curls. When no one else could hear, she called me Aunt Rachel.

A new synagogue had been built with plaster covering the wooden beams and joists, for fires were common and Synagogue Hill wasn't immune to disaster. Children of our faith were taught in the new building. Lyddie went to the Moravian School, open and free for all children of color, including the children of slaves. The Moravians were some of the earliest Protestants, their faith begun by a Catholic priest named Jan Hus in the fourteenth century. Forced to leave Moravia and Bohemia by their Catholic emperor, they, like the Jews, needed to practice their beliefs underground, or flee. They arrived on the island in 1732, and soon built their church. In the new world they focused on the education of the masses, and their missionaries began the school for slaves, carrying a single mission in their teachings: *In essentials, unity; in nonessentials, liberty; and in all things love.*

I had sat in Lyddie's classroom to make certain the education was worthwhile and was astonished by the excellence of the teachers from Denmark and even more so, by the work of the teachers from America, many of them resettled Mennonites. They insisted their students sit in neat rows; each had a new pen to write with and fresh paper. Although many local people spoke Dutch Creole, the school decided most lessons would be in English. Lyddie's reading of Danish and English was far better than my own children's, her letters more beautifully shaped than my own, and her reading of French was impeccable. I occasionally dictated letters to my cousin in France for her to write down for practice. Not that he ever replied. He had disappeared from our lives, and we heard rumors about his life in Paris. Many women had fallen in love with him, and he had a wide social circle, but the family had had enough of his antics and was considering cutting him out of the business. Lyddie had no idea who Aaron Rodrigues was, which was just as well. People judge a girl's worth in many ways, but one must hope they do not include any judgment of the deeds of her father.

When Lyddie was born, the rift between my mother and Adelle became too deep to repair, and despite my threats, my mother let her go.

"That's fine," Adelle said to me. "I would not wish to work with her even if I were starving."

Because of my mother, no woman from our community would hire Adelle, and in the end she was forced to take in sailors' laundry, a job far beneath her. My mother had no idea that my father sent Adelle a monthly check or that I gave her a portion of my own household funds. Isaac never asked me why I did this, nor did he question me when I went to visit Adelle every day when she fell ill. It happened suddenly. One day she simply grew weak, as if under a spell. I went to see her, bringing my baby, Delphine, along. Adelle taught her to clap her hands and how to wave good-bye. When Adelle could no longer eat anything solid, I made her a soft fongee porridge, the same recipe she used to fix for Jestine and me when we were girls. I fed her until the day she waved me away. "Give it to the baby," she said.

Adelle's illness made breathing difficult. The day when she could no longer rise from the bed without being lifted came. Jestine sent Lyddie to fetch me because Adelle had had a dream about me. I went down to the harbor, my throat and chest aching. I was afraid of what Adelle might tell me. I hoped she didn't blame me for how cruel my mother had been, or how badly my cousin had treated Jestine. I sat on her bed. I'd left my children at home. Adelle had me lean close so no one would overhear. As it turned out she wanted to tell me more of my future. "He won't be your only husband," she said of Monsieur Petit. She sounded like a bird, distant, breathy. "If you find happiness, take it. You won't find it again. But you'll know him as soon as you see him."

There were so many questions I should have asked. I never even knew who Adelle's parents were and how she had come to be on St. Thomas or what her African name had been. I had written down so many stories, but I'd never asked Adelle for hers. I should have asked if Jestine's father was a man I knew. At the end Adelle could no longer speak and it was too late. Each evening I sat beside the bed and read to her from my old notebook, stories of the stars in the sky, how God had placed them in a path between him and us so we could always find our way to him. How a pelican had then scattered those stars above us so we could lie in our beds at night and be comforted resting beneath the path to God. How a bird had traveled halfway across the world for love.

Adelle took my hand the last time I was there. She ran a finger inside my palm. Her fingers were long and thin, and she wore a gold ring. Perhaps someone who loved her had given it to her, or perhaps she had bought the ring for herself. She would never tell. This was as close as anyone from our different worlds dared to be, for fear the past would destroy what we had. Still, the past was close, outside the door. Adelle's touch felt like the skin and bones of a bird, weightless. I shivered because I knew this was her good-bye to me.

Jestine came then, and I watched Lyddie with my own children for the next day and night. And then it happened and we lost her. I saw Jestine standing in my yard alone and I knew. I hoped Adelle's spirit would be above us in the sky to watch over us.

. . .

THE NEXT MORNING MY father called me into the library. Mr. Enrique had brought him the sad news, and my father hadn't slept. My mother was out visiting Madame Halevy, so my father and I were free to talk. I thought perhaps he had planned it that way. He asked that I place a rose from our tree at Adelle's grave. He had been sending provisions from our store to her house twice a week, and had done so ever since my mother had let her go. Now he would send the funeral dinner as well. I kissed him and thought him the most generous man in the world. We embraced each other and shed tears for Adelle, then my father stalked away. He didn't want me to know what he felt, but I heard him sobbing in the garden. If I am not mistaken, my mother, walking up from the street, heard it as well.

I went to the African churchyard for the burial. I stood outside the fence made of sticks and wire and ached for Jestine. She wore a borrowed black dress and stood with her little girl by her side, holding hands. The cemetery was different than ours. There were wooden crosses carved with angels, shells set in intricate patterns, potted vines of purple blooms. Some people were Christians; some practiced the old religions of their homelands. I knew most everyone at the service, including Mr. Enrique, who had continued on as the clerk in the office with my husband, teaching him the business I had only recently discovered that although my father had long ago granted him his freedom, Mr. Enrique was still listed in the official records as a slave. I suppose I didn't want to know these things, especially when it came to my father. I wanted to believe the world was different than it was. But there was just so much a grown woman could pretend. There was more than one world on our island, and boundaries that could not be overstepped. On the day of the funeral, I knew it was not my place to mourn with Adelle's family and friends, although when Jestine exited the churchyard, she came to kiss me.

The ground was littered with fallen leaves, so many I couldn't see the earth. That does not often happen on our island. It was as if the trees were crying. It was the coldest day anyone could remember, and butterflies froze and fell to earth. There was a shimmer of blue and white on the ground. I stood and wept, and even my tears were cold. I still have the marks from that day, though they have turned to freckles. I saw someone beyond the fence. I thought at first it was a ghost, perhaps Madame Petit, but it wasn't. I was stunned to see my mother. When she signaled to me, I went to stand beside her. She was wearing a scarf knotted over her head, perhaps so she would not be recognized as the woman who had dismissed Adelle, though surely everyone knew. My mother and I did not embrace.

The service had ended, and my mother was staring down the road at the funeral procession. Women held up straw and paper umbrellas, not against the sun or rain but to ward off the falling leaves. Jestine followed last, her daughter by her side.

"That's the child?" my mother said.

All the neighbors would now gather in Adelle's house and eat the meal my father had sent over as they remembered her life. Lyddie was holding her mother's hand. She had on a blue dress with smocking Jestine had sewn by hand. It was Adelle's favorite color, the color of protection and of faith, haint blue. I'd paid for the fabric and pearl buttons, and why shouldn't I?

I saw that my mother had taken note of the rose on Adelle's grave.

"Why do you ask about the child now?" I said to my mother. "She's nearly five years old."

My mother nodded grimly. "Maybe you'll understand when you have to protect your own family."

"What do you think I do every day?" I had six of them after all and was not yet thirty. I dreamed of storms and boats at sea and of my children drowning. I often sat in the nursery until daybreak, and Rosalie would laugh when she found me there. "You think you can protect them with your presence?" she'd said often enough. I did not answer, but if I had, I would have said, "Perhaps."

"I hope you don't visit her. If you do it will encourage her to think that life is different than it is," my mother told me.

"Jestine is well aware of what life is like," I responded coldly.

"Not Jestine." My mother was still gazing down the road. She seemed older to me on this day, her features sharper, her eyes hooded. "I'm talking about the girl."

I didn't have to listen to my mother anymore. I had done enough to please both her and my father. I'd given them my marriage and my fate. I presumed my father was at work on this day, even though Adelle had been a part of our household for so many years. At that moment I felt detached from both of my parents.

"Did you ever care about anyone but yourself?" I blurted to my mother. "No wonder my father locks himself away."

My mother gasped as if I'd struck her. "You're my daughter! I don't expect you to speak to me that way!"

I lowered my eyes and apologized. "Please forgive me." I should have honored her, and I knew that in some way I would pay for this sin of disrespect.

When I walked home a pelican followed above me. Maybe it was the bird Adelle had become, a spirit now freed. I closed my eyes and wished that she would appear in her earthly form and instruct me as she had throughout my life. I was the one who did not love my husband. I was embarrassed, because he was a good man. I had whispered a single question to Adelle before she passed on. *What is life without love?* That was when she took my hand in her own, though she was as frail and weightless as a bird. She made a circle within my palm. I knew what she was telling me. A life like that was worth nothing at all.

She had told me that Isaac would not be the only man in my life. I had begun to look for that other man. I felt like a witch, like a demon. I didn't want the spirit of my predecessor to know I was willing to betray her husband. But I couldn't resist. I gazed into the face of every man who passed by, searching for the one I was meant for.

I lived every day for my children and remained a dutiful wife. But every night I thought about my other life, the one that had yet to begin.

I WAS SO BUSY with my children I did not see my father aging. Mr. Enrique was the one who came to tell me he had died, suddenly and peacefully, in his own bed. It seemed impossible that two people I loved would die one after the other. Adelle had always told me that bad luck comes in threes. I felt a chill to imagine there was one more death in store for us.

When my mother sent for me, I put on my wedding dress, which Jestine and I had dyed blue, and went to her. It was traditional for the burial society to sit with the deceased overnight, to bathe him one last time and cover him with white linen. In the past they would have protected him from evil spirits as well, though no one believed in such things nowadays. Now it was so that the family could have some rest and peace. My mother insisted that my father be brought to the library. She became so overwrought that she had to be given smelling salts when his body was carried into the room he had so loved. I had never seen my mother quite like this, so vulnerable, her sorrow stamped on her face, her clothes wrinkled, hair uncombed. I went alone to sit beside my father. He seemed smaller in death than he had in life. The air in the room was different, still and quiet the way it was before a storm arrived. My father was wearing his nightshirt. That alone brought me to tears. The man who had commanded our family and demanded respect would never have allowed anyone to see him this way. His eyes were closed, but I half expected them to fly open so that he could order me to leave. They did not. He was gone from us. I could spy his knees, knobs of bone. His thin legs veined blue. There was a knock at the door. My mother had collected herself and had returned with a washbasin of soap and water. I had never seen her look as distraught. She had wanted his love, and had failed to have it for her own.

"Are you sure you can do this?" I asked.

"How can I be sure of anything now?" She nodded. "You see to his feet." She would take care of the rest.

I took a damp cloth and washed my father's feet. The water was cold. I looked up to see that my mother was crying as she bathed my father. We covered him with a sheet of fine white linen, then sat together without bothering to light a candle.

"I can't believe he's no longer in the world," my mother said. Her hands were in her lap and she stared straight ahead. "Now everything will change."

It was true. Some people hold a family together, and for us that person was Moses Pomié.

There were lengthening shadows in the room. The air had grown heavy and damp. I saw a trickle of water on the stucco wall, as if the house were crying. I held out my hands, as I'd done as a child. I prayed for the flicker of my father's spirit to appear, but it didn't happen. A spirit has to want to come to you. It is his choice. My father was gone, and my mother and I were in the dark, with nothing more to say to one another.

OUR TRADITION INSISTED THE dead must be buried before two days had passed. My cousin Aaron was called back to St. Thomas, though it wouldn't be possible for him to attend the funeral; it would be months before he arrived to go over business dealings and honor the dead. My father's oldest colleagues and their sons carried the coffin to the cemetery. My husband assisted as well, for he was the head of our household now. Monsieur DeLeon, my father's dearest friend, helped my mother walk to the grave site. Her cold wailing went through the streets, sharp and hard, from the center of a heart I hadn't known she had. She threw herself upon the grave and had to be lifted off before the men of the congregation could offer the mourning prayer. There were parrots in the trees, bits of red and green. Mr. Enrique stood at the rear of the gathering, wearing a black suit and a black hat. There was no one Moses Pomié had trusted more, for he would not have been alive if not for this man who had carried him to the harbor in a basket made of reeds.

The men of the congregation lowered the casket into the ground, and then took turns covering my father with shovelfuls of fresh earth. I waited until everyone was gone. Once they were through the cemetery gates, I called to Mr. Enrique and handed him the shovel so that he might have his turn. He spaded earth onto the casket for some time and then, sweating through his coat, returned the shovel to me. Women were not supposed to help in this burial ritual, but I did so anyway. In so many ways I was my father's son, therefore I acted as one now as he left our world behind.

I IMAGINED AARON RODRIGUES would be a stranger when he returned. He no longer worked for the family in France, and we rarely heard from him, although my mother addressed monthly letters to him. I assumed there were checks inside those envelopes. But as it turned out I knew him as soon as I saw him among the disembarking passengers. He was much the same, handsome and carefree. The difference was, he'd brought home a wife, a French girl named Elise, a young woman with lovely features who seemed timid, a pretty little mouse. She hesitated on the dock before being guided toward my mother to be introduced. Aaron hadn't bothered to let anyone know he'd been married. He'd clearly cut himself off from home, if that's what he still considered this island. I dreaded having to tell Jestine, who had been overjoyed to hear of his homecoming.

"My dear aunt," Aaron said, greeting my mother tenderly before bringing Elise to meet her. "I could not have had a better woman to care for me and raise me," he told his wife. "I have always considered Madame Pomié to be my mother."

Elise had red-gold hair, and her pale complexion was flushed with the heat. The crossing had clearly been difficult for her, for she seemed unsteady on land. She wore a dress that reminded me of those I'd found in a cabinet in my own house, frocks brought from Paris by the first Madame Petit, too heavy for the climate, but beautiful all the same. Elise's dress was a rose-hued silk, and there were silver threads in the smocking. She wore a cameo necklace on a plaited gold chain. After she greeted my mother, we were introduced. I didn't know what to think of her, especially when instead of greeting me with a proper hello she leaned close to whisper, asking if she might bathe immediately. Clearly unused to the rough conditions aboard the ship, she had been thinking of nothing else for days. She seemed to view me as a housemaid.

"I'm filthy," she announced, clearly embarrassed by her condition. She had a lovely voice, huskier than I'd expected. She smelled of cologne.

"You look perfect," Aaron told her.

"Looks are one thing." Elise grimaced. "I'm far from perfect." She turned to me, perhaps thinking she had found a sister of sorts, as we were nearly the same age. "Please. I would sell my soul for some soap and water."

Elise and I walked together as Aaron and my mother trailed behind. My mother was tender toward him in a way that I found frustrating. I heard her ask why he hadn't written more regularly, and then she laughed as he teased, insisting that his handwriting had always been dreadful. Besides, he said in a low voice, he had turned his attentions to finding a wife who would please her, and it was Elise's wealthy family he worked for now. Just then a lizard ran across our path. It was a small green iguana, but Elise panicked at the sight of it, stumbling and grabbing on to my arm.

"It's only a baby," I told her. "It couldn't hurt you, but you could step on it easily."

I gave Aaron's wife a day, perhaps two, before she was demanding to go home to Paris. I had seen such women from Europe, dressed in their exquisite clothes, their manners polished, organza ribbons in their hair. Soon enough they would be happy to give up their gorgeous clothes for lighter muslin shifts; their perfect upswept hair would be in tangles. They'd stand on the wharves looking out over the cruel ocean that had brought them here, wishing themselves home once more.

"Whatever that creature is, it's vile." Elise was young, and had no experience other than her life in France. She freely admitted she was spoiled, from a wealthy family that gave in to her every desire. I gazed over at Aaron, wondering if that had been the attraction. Elise was already put off by our island; she wondered aloud if there might be lions in the forests here.

I laughed. "No. This isn't Africa. The most you will see is a dog. Or a donkey. Perhaps a mongoose."

"What's that?" she wanted to know.

"A creature with a taste for parrots and bats. They don't bother people."

Elise eyed the hills with suspicion, the tumbling vines, the purple flowers, the clusters of tamarind with their seedpods hanging down like bats wrapped inside their leathery wings. "There must be snakes," she declared of the wild land beyond town. "I dread them," she confided.

There were snakes, it was true, as well as bats and rats, but I glossed over that. I certainly said nothing of the local tales of werewolves. "We have nothing that will harm you."

The heat was weighing down on us as we continued toward home. Soon enough Elise began to falter. She squinted in the harsh light and announced that she had a headache. Before I could offer my assistance, she collapsed on the road.

Aaron ran to her, motioning to me crudely. "Couldn't you help her?" he snapped, as though blaming me for his wife's delicate nature.

"Help her what? Walk? I assumed she could do that by herself."

He glared at me for mocking his wife while he lifted her, then clasped her in his arms. He had to carry her the rest of the way. "I'm so sorry, dear husband," I heard her whisper to him. She hid her face against his coat, and he did his best to cheer her. He called her his darling and his delight and vowed she was as light as a feather. But I could tell from his expression, he wasn't pleased. I could not believe he had chosen this woman, so very different from Jestine.

I walked beside my mother now, our pace evenly matched. I realized that as delighted as she was with Aaron's homecoming, his wife brought her no joy. "He brought home a feather," my mother said contemptuously. "He would have done better with a woman."

"Well, she's a feather weighted down with money. He might have had someone with more strength, but you didn't care for her," I ventured to say.

"That was impossible and you know it. I don't decide such things."

"Don't you?"

"If you think I make the rules or that I have any choice but to abide by them, you're more of a fool than I'd ever imagined. Maybe when your own children disobey you and break your heart, we can discuss such matters. Until then, I don't care for your opinions or advice. I did what I did to save him."

Once home, Aaron carried his Elise into the washroom, then left her to Rosalie and me. "This time make sure she doesn't fall," he said.

"Does she have someone to bathe her at home?" I asked.

"What is that your business?" Aaron said. "What she wants, she gets. That's the way it is when you can afford to do as you please, Rachel."

All at once, I pitied him. "Do you at least love her a little?"

"Do you think you're the one to ask such questions? You of all people, who married a business rather than a man."

"And what shall I say to the woman you do love?" I asked.

"That's my affair," my cousin told me. "Not yours."

THOUGH WE WERE PLEASANT enough to Aaron's new wife, Elise was wary of our ways from the start. She gazed at Rosalie's skin color rudely as Rosalie poured buckets of water into the bath. Before she entered the claw-foot tub, Elise cried, "The water's green. I hope there aren't frogs in there."

"Is there anything that makes you say thank you?" Rosalie said primly.

I wanted to laugh but elbowed Rosalie to hush her.

Elise threw us a look; then she slipped off all of her clothes, including her petticoat and her chemise, and tossed them on the floor. As she stepped into the bath, water sloshed over the silk. We noticed she didn't wear pantalets, which was something of a shock. She clearly liked to show herself off, and I wondered if this was how she had caught Aaron. Soft, naked skin and money.

"What kind of woman is she?" Rosalie asked me.

"One from Paris." I grinned.

"She won't last here." Rosalie shook her head. "Not for an hour."

Elise dipped her head under, and when she arose she blew out a stream of water like a dolphin. To our surprise she laughed with pleasure. "Now I feel better. And the water is wonderful, so yes, thank you! But I want more. And colder. And be sure to get me my own soap. It's in my bag."

Perhaps she was more resilient than she seemed.

I AGREED TO TAKE Elise on a tour of Charlotte Amalie while Aaron met with my husband to discuss business. The synagogue was being rebuilt after several fires; we would soon have a beautiful stone edifice and a larger congregation than ever. Wooden buildings were no longer allowed on main streets, and the new synagogue would be both fireproof and hurricane proof, with four stone pillars, each representing one of the matriarchs of our people, Sarah, Rachel, Rebecca, and Leah. There were mahogany pews made by the best furniture makers. The walls were fashioned from sand and limestone, bound with sticky near-tar-like molasses, the island's biggest export, along with rum. Despite the space for six Torahs to be housed in the mahogany ark, and the Baccarat crystal chandeliers that would be lit with oil, the floor was made of sand, there to remind the congregation of the sand floors that had muffled their footsteps when they met for prayer during times of trouble in their home countries so their presence would go unnoticed by the authorities. I explained the reason for the sand floor, so that Elise would not think our congregation barbaric. When I told her molasses had been mixed in with the mortar to bind it, and that the children said when they ran their tongues across the walls the building was sweet to the taste, she didn't believe me.

"There's quite a lot you won't believe about our island," I said. Molasses and rum were at the heart of all we were and did, since the rest of the world wanted this from us. "We have to spray salt water on the synagogue to keep the ants away."

Elise grinned and said she wanted proof, so we went around behind the building and put our tongues on the mortar as the children often did. The taste was gritty and sweet.

Elise was delighted. "It's like candy! Perhaps I've judged too quickly. Now I want to see everything it's impossible to believe." She had grown accustomed to the heat quicker than I'd imagined, perhaps because she wore lighter clothing borrowed from my mother's cabinet, a white cotton skirt and blouse.

I should have reconsidered, but I welcomed a day without the children when I could play at being a guide. I found Elise fascinating, and couldn't yet imagine how conniving she could be. I loved her chatter about Paris. She told me about the new fashions, the teashops and lounges she and her friends went to, the parks with carousels. She spoke of the leaves turning color in October, a soft gold that made the entire city glimmer, and of the snow in the winter, when she and her brothers had built forts out of ice. I felt a sort of enchantment come over me, and I wondered if this was what had happened to Aaron. A door had opened into another life.

In return for these tales, I would show her our marvels, small as they were. We went to the harbor to a café, where we drank limewater laced with a dash of rum; then we went to the fish market so Elise could gape at the piles of fish, which were so fresh they were pink and gasping. There was a fish we called ballyhoo that was a big favorite, and there were dozens lined up to be sold. All along the beach men had built fish pots in the surf out of straw and sticks and wire; fish could swim in but they couldn't get out, and we waded in to see the coils of fish within these contraptions.

I took Elise to the Petit house, and we had lunch with the children, who were all on their best behavior. She was especially charmed by the girls, Hannah, who was so lovely and polite, and the younger ones, Delphine and Emma. They were charmed in return, arguing over who would sit next to her, delighted by the way she approached a banana with a knife and fork.

"You're so fortunate," Elise said to me when Rosalie took the children inside for their naps. "Those children are treasures."

I introduced Elise to Jean-François, our pet, and after her initial fear, she calmed down and fed him oats from her hand. She told me more of her life with Aaron, the house they had in Passy, on the right side of the Seine, which her father had bought for her, the garden with linden trees, the little park she went to on sunny afternoons. I had an edge of guilt when I thought of Jestine, and how she would ache when she saw Elise. I knew my cousin had forsaken her, but I was inside a story of Paris, and I simply couldn't hear enough. In the afternoon I took Elise into the hills to search for wild donkeys. She was telling me about the goats that ate grass in the Tuileries when we spied some of the local beasts of burden. She grabbed on to me as one approached, then laughed when the donkey ran away, more frightened of us than we were of it.

"See," I told her. "No lions."

"I feel so free here." Elise had taken off her boots and was barefoot, arching her beautiful, pale feet in the tall grass. "My family always babies me, and so does my husband. I want to do something Aaron would never imagine I would do." The end of the day was nearing, and the sky was turning violet above us. "Something daring."

I asked if she'd ever been swimming in the ocean, and she laughed and said, "That's it! I'll be a mermaid! That will shock him." We went to the beach in the fading light. It was a secluded cove, surrounded by greenery, the one where the turtles came. The path went through the tamarind trees. The air was silken and the water pale blue. We wasted no time in undressing. I felt happy to be a wild girl for an afternoon. As we laughed and hid our shoes in a log, I forgot who I was with, the woman who had come to possess all that my dearest friend wanted. Or perhaps I thought I could not blame Elise for the ways in which my cousin had hurt Jestine.

We hung our dresses on a branch and walked into the water in our petticoats.

"This is madness!" Elise grinned as she went deeper into the water. A blue crab scuttled across the seafloor, and Elise shouted out, then recovered and laughed, diving in where the water was deeper and bluer. "Actually it's heaven," she called to me.

The water was so calm here. Sandfish floated below us, and we tried and failed to catch them in our hands. Even though the evening was perfect, I had a nagging feeling of dread. I thought I saw a woman, out at sea, so far in the distance it did not seem possible a human could survive.

"What do we do if someone comes onto the beach?" Elise said, when we ran out, soaking wet, our undergarments clinging to our skin. We were as good as naked if anyone spied us.

"No one ever comes here," I assured her. "It's a secret beach."

But I heard something. When I looked up I spied a figure beyond the trees, where the shadows were dark green. I recognized her shadow as she fled, for I knew her better than anyone.

AS SOON AS WE returned to my mother's house, we could hear my cousin's raised voice. He was speaking with such fury that Elise and I didn't dare go any farther. We stopped inside the corridor. My husband was in the parlor with Aaron. His expression was grim as he tried to calm him. "I'm not the one who wrote the provisions of the will. That was your uncle."

"How do I know you didn't write it and force him to sign? He was an old man."

"You are a ward, though you were called cousin. There is no relation by blood."

My father had left a gift to the synagogue and one to the Lutheran church, which was the custom. It was expected that he would leave my husband in charge of the business. To divide the company would be to weaken it, and my father wanted to keep the family's holdings together. Aaron would have a monthly check, but he was to have no say over how things were managed. After all, he had proved himself a poor business-man in France, and had lost money for our company. Our French rela-tives had relieved him of his duties, and he now worked for his wife's father, who had a prestigious store in Paris. Still, he'd clearly come back with expectations. I wondered if he thought he might inherit everything and stay on and reclaim his life, perhaps have two families, as so many men did. The one he brought to the synagogue and the one he visited on Sundays as dusk spread across the sky and he would not be spied as he made his way along the alleys beside the wharves.

We let the men speak and went to have tea with my mother.

"Don't worry, they'll come to terms," my mother assured Elise. "Men like to argue."

Elise's skin had burned during our excursion to the beach; she was flushed and overheated and soon excused herself, saying she had never been as tired in her life. As soon as Elise went to lie down, my mother grabbed my arm and whispered, "She's been here. Uninvited."

It took a while before I understood who she was talking about. Jestine.

I WENT THROUGH THE courtyard to Mr. Enrique's house. He was sit-ting outside, still dressed in the black suit he wore at the store.

"Is she here?"

"I don't get involved in these things." He looked away; therefore I knew the answer was yes.

I went inside, and there were Jestine and Lyddie sitting in the dark. The shutters were closed and only the last of the day's yellow light came through in bands. Jestine was in her best dress. She wore laced boots, and her hair was braided and pinned up. Lyddie was beside her, quiet, her hands folded on her lap. When she looked at me, I could tell she was alarmed. Jestine, on the other hand, was furious.

"You didn't think you should take it upon yourself to tell me that he had a wife?"

"I was going to," I said. But I hadn't wanted to face her.

"I suppose you were too busy. Well, don't worry, I found out. Don't you think Lyddie should meet him? A daughter should see her father at least once in her lifetime."

I asked Lyddie to wait outside with Mr. Enrique while we spoke.

"You came to see his wife," I said when the little girl had gone. "It won't lead to your happiness."

"What do I care about her?" Jestine made a face. "Lyddie is his daughter. He should know her."

"You cared enough to spy on us."

"Because you didn't even tell me he was back. You seem to care more for her than you do for me!" Jestine's voice broke. "Is she your sister now?"

"She's nothing to me," I said. It was the truth. Elise had been an amusement, nothing more. I suspected the same was true for Aaron. "And she should be nothing to you."

"I saw her fall on the road when she got off the ship, and you assisted her."

"She needed a cold bath, with her own soap from Paris."

"It didn't help her from being ugly."

We laughed at that. Elise wasn't ugly, but she certainly wasn't beautiful, like Jestine.

"I came to show him his daughter, and that is what I still intend to do. He says he wants to see her."

"You've spoken to Aaron?"

Jestine glared at me. "What do you think?"

I begged her to reconsider, but she wouldn't listen. Perhaps I should have warned her that Elise was not as weak as she might appear to be.

Jestine led Lyddie into our courtyard. All of the yellow birds that loved the sweet fruit in our garden so much some people called them sugarbirds hushed when she appeared. There was a shadow at the upstairs window.

I followed Jestine so I might stand beside her. I'd been wrong and thoughtless to befriend Elise. My cousin had been gone for more than five years. "He won't come," I warned.

"He will." Jestine held tightly to her daughter's hand. Lyddie looked over at her mother, confused.

The last of the sunlight was in our eyes, but Jestine refused to move into the shade.

"How long do you intend to stand here?" I asked. "Don't you see him for who he is by now?"

"Do you want Lyddie to have to look into every man's face, searching for herself? I have to see to this now, before he's an ocean away and she never has the chance."

My mother was the one at the window. She gazed down when she heard Jestine, then promptly closed the shutters.

"You're locking me out?" Jestine shouted.

I put a hand on her arm to hush her. "This won't work out the way you want it to."

"He'll see me." Jestine turned back to shout at the house, to my mother, I assumed, and to Aaron as well. "I'm waiting for you to show yourself. You know she's your daughter."

Surely Aaron heard her raised voice, but instead of coming to face her, my cousin played the coward and sent his wife. I suspect he feared meeting up with Jestine, and perhaps was most afraid of his own emotions. Elise came out in her rose silk dress. Jestine was too dazed to say anything as she approached.

"He asked if you would leave," Elise said.

"If I don't?" Jestine said. "What will you do then?"

"That won't happen, so we won't discuss it." Elise's eyes flitted down to Lyddie, who still held her mother's hand. Jestine glared back, fiercely protective of her daughter. Lyddie wore her blue dress, beautifully smocked. She gazed wide-eyed at the woman from France, who clearly had the upper hand.

"Is this the girl?" Elise focused her attention on Lyddie entirely. "What a pretty dress you have."

"You know who she is." Jestine's chin jutted out. "And so does he."

Jestine sounded strong, but I noticed her hands were shaking. For once I was glad I had never been in love.

"This is Lydia," I told Elise

"May I?" Elise was clearly entranced by the child. Jestine was so taken by surprise, she didn't stop Elise from questioning Lyddie about her education at the Moravian School.

"I'm going to learn four languages," Lyddie said. "I already speak Danish, and soon I'll study German and English and Spanish."

"What about French?" Elise smiled with a warmth I hadn't seen before. "Do you study that as well?"

"I'm speaking to you in French, Madame."

Elise laughed, delighted. That was when I felt a chill go through me.

Elise turned to Jestine, cool but not unfriendly now. "Let me see what I can do. I'll speak to my husband."

When Elise went inside, Jestine seemed shaken. "Who does she think she is to say 'my husband' to me?"

"That's who he is to her." I don't think Jestine had truly realized Aaron now possessed a life beyond what they'd once had together.

We left the garden and went to my house. Since Aaron and Elise had arrived, I'd been so caught up with them I'd hardly been home. My children greeted me and hugged me, then ran off to play with Lyddie. Rosalie came out to the porch and threw me a look. "Do you still live here? Or did you move back in with your mother?"

"I was trying to be polite to our guests," I said.

"Don't be. Stay at home."

Jestine was quiet during this interchange, but when Rosalie went to keep watch over the children, Jestine turned to me. "You were right. I was a fool to go there." She took my hand. She feared Elise's pleasantries had been a deception. "Don't let them do anything to me."

"They wouldn't," I assured her. "There's nothing they *can* do to you."

I truly believed that at the time.

There were green frogs in the garden, and the children were set on catching them with a net. We could hear them whooping, then gathering together to examine their catch. It was a near-perfect night, but beside me my dearest friend was crying.

WHEN I SAW MY husband later in the evening, he told me that Aaron was so angry to learn that my father hadn't left him any part of his estate that he'd already made arrangements to return to Paris. There had been threats and arguments at the store that were humiliating. My cousin's insolence drove him forward. He insisted he would take legal action. I worried for my husband's safety. "There's no need to worry," Isaac assured me. "He realized it would be worth his while to leave." My husband was clearly relieved that Aaron was preparing to go. "Your father made a wise choice. We'll all do well to be rid of him."

But we weren't rid of him so quickly that I didn't see him walking down the road toward the harbor. It was dusk, the hour when it was possible to do as one wished as darkness fell. Yet the sky was still bright in the east, and I knew where he was going. He went there every night and waited outside the house on stilts, and nothing could be done to send him away. He had come halfway around the world, after all, and found what he wanted here on our island.

THE MAIDS IN MY mother's house told me that my cousin was leaving in a matter of days. This time there would be no packet of lavender, no cause to call him back. I had gone to the store and looked through the ledgers my father had taught me to read. I found what I had suspected: Aaron was being paid off handsomely so that he would let go of the business without further argument. I'd kept away from my mother's house after the scene in the garden, not wishing to see Aaron or his wife. But on the afternoon before they were to leave, Elise arrived at my house. I was on the porch, mending my children's clothes. Their trousers and shifts always seemed torn after a day of play. I liked to sew, for my own relaxation, to clear the thoughts in my head. The last thing I expected was company.

Elise was wearing one of her beautiful dresses. Her hair was braided carefully.

"You don't like us anymore?" she said archly. "You've disappeared."

I gazed at her and saw someone different from the girl who'd walked off the boat. She held a parasol to ward off the sun, but she seemed quite steely. She spoke to me as if I were a servant rather than a relative, however distant. When some chickens came pecking around, Elise kicked up dirt to drive them away. I suppose in Paris she did as she pleased, and had everything she ever wanted.

"He said we can take her," she told me.

I was confused. Was it Aaron's intention not only to live with his wife in Paris but to have Jestine as well? Many men did so here, surely it must be the same in Paris. But such things were not spoken about, and certainly a wife would never announce that she was aware of that sort of arrangement, even if she tacitly agreed. Why on earth would Aaron inform Elise of his plan, and why would she be the one to tell me?

"And you're fine with this? You don't mind taking Jestine to Paris?"

"Jestine!" Elise laughed. "It's the girl I want. She looks enough like me for people to think I'm her mother. It's the gold in her hair."

I was speechless, though she didn't seem to notice. She went on to announce that they had decided to take Lyddie and raise her as their own. The girl was young enough so that in time she would forget Jestine and this island and the house that was so close to the sea she could hear the tides as she slept.

I listened as Elise went on at great length discussing her plans, the lycée for girls Lyddie would enter, the dozens of dresses she would buy for her, the bedchamber that was larger than the house where she lived now. There would be horses, for Elise's parents had a home in the country, and hunting dogs, and dinners on Friday nights with Elise's family.

I listened openmouthed, unbelieving and silent, until she announced that Lyddie's name would be changed to Lydia Cassin Rodrigues. Cassin was Elise's family name, and her father would be so delighted for his name to be carried on. Hearing that, I at last found my voice.

"Pardon me, but you do know who the father is?"

"A man who made a mistake, but one who has legal rights." Now I understood. Elise intended to rewrite Lyddie's history as she pleased. "He is the father and I will be the mother."

"Have your own daughter," I said harshly.

"I can't." Elise knew what she wanted, and she wasn't about to let a few words from me hurt her or change her tactics. "Put our proposal before your friend. Tell her of my plans. She will come to understand it is far better for her daughter to live with us in Paris."

I WENT TO SEE Aaron, but he shouted that he didn't want to see me. When I wouldn't give up, he came into the hall in a rage. He'd been drinking and was unstable.

"Do you know what your wife is trying to do?" I asked.

"Give my daughter a better life?"

"Better than what? Being with her own mother?"

"Rachel, you've never understood what the world is like," he told me. "You've always thought I could do as I pleased, but that's never been true."

"Because you have no courage," I said.

My cousin slapped me then. I was shocked and so was he.

"I didn't mean that," he said. "You know I didn't."

I turned and ran. There was no talking to him. We'd put a spell on him to bring him back, but we'd done so without thinking of all that enchantment might do. He was a ruined person, he was crying in the hall, and the saddest thing to me was that I could see he loved Jestine, and he wasn't going to do anything about it.

I went down to the house on stilts, my heart beating fast. I thought of what Rosalie had told me, how loving someone too much could be dangerous and how she'd been punished for her pride. When I reached the harbor I noticed there were shingles missing on the cottage, which hadn't been painted in several years. Since Adelle had passed on, things had fallen into disrepair. The same was true for my childhood house, which hadn't been the same since the death of my father.

Jestine was waiting for me on the steps. I could tell from her expression that she hadn't slept. She had been waiting for a message from my cousin, but a different one entirely. She wanted to hear him admit that he'd chosen the wrong woman and say he was coming back to her. I was reminded of the lavender Adelle had placed into my cousin's luggage to bring him back to Jestine. I wished I hadn't found it and hidden it there again after he'd discarded it. I wished he'd never returned.

I told her what Elise had proposed. Jestine said nothing, but she grew cold.

"They're going to steal her," she said.

Jestine was a free woman, but her rights were limited. She had publicly declared that Aaron was the father of the child. Everyone in our household had heard her say so, including my mother, who would certainly act against her if given half the chance.

Lyddie was inside, studying her lessons. Jestine sat there weeping. "There's no way for me to fight them. You people always get what you want."

I was stung, even though I knew what she said was true. People of my faith had fewer rights than Europeans, but compared to Jestine and Adelle we were part of the established order.

"He's found me every night he's been here," Jestine said. "I was good enough for that but not good enough to be my own daughter's mother."

Perhaps Elise had guessed and this was part of her revenge.

Jestine went inside without saying another word. I peered through the window to watch as she gathered a few belongings into a basket, then grabbed Lyddie by the hand. When they came back they took the stairs two at a time. "He'll never find us now."

Lyddie tossed a frightened look back at me as her mother hurried her along. I began to trail them, but Jestine turned around and snapped, "Don't you dare follow us! You treated that witch as if she were a sister. Now look what's happened! You're one of them."

I stood alone in the road and watched Jestine take her daughter into the mountains, where the mahogany trees were hundreds of years old, their bark made into the strongest medicine on the island. Adelle had once brought me a tea made of this bark when I fell ill as a little girl. I remembered only a haze from that time. My skin was so hot I felt that fire had been laid across my bed. I felt a wave of that heat now, and my heart sank. I feared there was no way to protect Jestine from my cousin's wife.

In the morning, our visitors were standing in our courtyard while their trunks were brought down. They waited, exchanging glances.

"Jestine won't bring Lyddie to you, if that's what you're thinking," I said.

"I don't suppose we'll see each other again." Elise kissed me goodbye. I recoiled and wished her away. My cousin looked sad and somehow resolved. He leaned close so he could whisper to me. "We made a mistake to think we could have what we wanted."

"Her mistake was you." She should never have trusted him or thought he would marry her. She should have stayed away from our courtyard.

I watched them leave our garden. My mother was so distraught she had gone to her room. Despite my cousin's failures, she still had a deep attachment to him. I think she would have been pleased if he had chosen to stay. She might even have supported him. But of course, Elise had more to offer.

Once they were on the street, I heard Elise's bright voice echo, and I was puzzled. I couldn't understand why she was so cheerful when she hadn't gotten what she wanted. I heard a burst of her laughter, and she said the name Lydia in a loving way and then went on to discuss how she had written the maids at home so the girl's room would be ready for her. All at once I knew she hadn't lost. I ran after them to the docks. I stood on the wharf, sunlight and tears clouding my eyes. I could see the rowboat of passengers that Elise and Aaron were joining, a little girl among those waiting. My cousin had hired some local men to search for Jestine. They'd found her and restrained her until they could get Lyddie away from her. The child was told that her journey was a brief trip to France, one her mother had approved. So why had her mother been sobbing when they came for them in the mountains, and why had she refused to let go of her daughter until she was held back by men who had left bruises on her arms? Lyddie asked, but these questions went unanswered. The men who'd been hired to bring the child to the wharf were sailors who cared nothing for the people of our island.

Jestine might never have been discovered, but I knew the secret places in the hills. I ran until I heard a woman crying. It was up by the caves, where ruined women often went to end their lives when they had nothing left, near the gardens of the pirate wives. The sailors who'd stolen Lyddie had left Jestine tied to a jacaranda tree. There were a dozen pelicans above her, each one perched on a higher branch. Some people believe that when a pelican cries the tears shed are as red as blood; they say the pelican will pluck the bloody feathers from its own breast to make a nest for its young despite the damage to itself.

Jestine screamed at me as I untied her. "You let them take her!"

"No," I said, but she wasn't listening to me. I broke all of my fingernails, frantic, because she was crying.

"Hurry! I have to follow them."

I knew the rowboat had left, the ship had boarded, but I stepped away once she was free and watched her run down the hill. I never knew a person to run so fast, to disappear the way ghosts do, out of our line of vision. I heard that everyone fled the dock when she got there. That people could hear her crying for miles.

No one saw Jestine for several weeks afterward. She refused to answer her door, not to me and not to anyone else. I left baskets of food, but they went untouched. I sat on the stairs until evening, but she refused to come out. My husband did everything he could. He wrote to his family in France and explained the situation. A solicitor was hired, but in the end there was little anyone could do. The laws gave Aaron Rodrigues the right to his own daughter, especially once she was on French soil. My husband went on to find a second solicitor, one who was not above paying people off to get around the law; he took the high fee Isaac sent, but though he was well connected, he could not undo what had been done. I dreamed sometimes of Lyddie on that ship, en route to Paris. In my dreams she looked toward our island. A pelican followed her until she was halfway across the Atlantic, a place that was too cold and too far to reach, even for those who loved her best.

Elise wrote me a single letter months after she'd returned to Paris. It was now summer. We hadn't heard anything of my cousin or Lyddie, therefore I was shocked to find the envelope on my table. Elise had beautiful handwriting, and the ink she used was a shade of blue so dark it was almost purple. I thought about reading the letter. I held the brass letter opener and debated. But in the end I didn't feel the message was meant for me. I brought the letter to Jestine. She had avoided me all this time, and my loneliness was like a stone in my shoe. When I knocked on the door Jestine didn't look pleased to see me, but she let me in. I knew she put blame onto me, for I had befriended the witch from Paris. That much was true, and I regretted it every day. The house felt empty when I came inside. The windows were shuttered even though it was a beautiful day. The sea was green.

"What is this supposed to be?" she said when I held out the letter.

"Something from Paris." The envelope felt hot in my hands, as if it had breath and life. "Would you rather I burned it?"

She gestured for me to hand over the letter. Then she went into her bedroom.

Whether or not she read what Elise wrote I will never know. Perhaps she cursed its author, perhaps she gave thanks for what little news she had of her daughter. When she came back the letter was folded in half. Together, we burned it in a bowl Adelle had once used to make elixirs, including the one that had saved my life. The sparks flew up. As they did I made a wish, and this one came true. From then on Jestine answered the door when I came to call. One day she was sitting in my garden, and I knew that she had forgiven me for having Aaron as my cousin and the witch from France as his wife, even though nothing was ever the same after that.

CHAPTER FOUR

If You Leave

CHARLOTTE AMALIE, ST. THOMAS

1824

RACHEL POMIÉ PETIT

When I thought of the last moments of my husband's life, the sudden stab of pain he must have felt in his heart, the speed with which he slumped over his desk on a hot afternoon, the lemon-colored sunlight falling across his shoulders, I wondered if he cried out for me, or if he had called to Esther, his beloved first wife. I hope she was standing there waiting for him, her arms outstretched to hold him, and that his spirit lifted itself out of his body with joy. On the night my husband died I came home from the office alone with his spectacles and his watch. I got into our bed and waited for the spirit of the first Madame Petit to lie down beside me and mourn with me, but she was gone. She had been there for only one reason, to watch over her husband. Now he belonged to her in the world beyond ours.

His was the third death, and the one that changed my life more than any other. Isaac was only fifty, and his death came as a complete surprise. I was just twenty-nine, too young to be a widow. I went to Jestine and asked her to make me a black dress, for I would have to wear black for the next year. She knew I didn't love Isaac, but he was my husband all the same, the father of my children. She understood my fear. I was still young and I was responsible for six children, all of whom had experienced loss.

The day of my husband's funeral was hot, the kind of weather that made people faint. It was a blur to me, and I was glad when it was over. At last dusk had fallen and the children were asleep. David, Samuel, Hannah, Joseph, Emma, and the youngest, always called by her French name, Delphine. Rosalie dozed in a chair in the nursery. I still hadn't told her that tomorrow we would be forced to leave. We could no longer afford this big house, and it would eventually be sold. In the past months the business had been failing, and it was possible that we might have to close the store, our last real asset. I dreaded Rosalie's reaction. She had lived at this address longer than I had, and was already here working for Isaac when the first Madame Petit arrived from France, limp from the heat, her freckled face flushed with exhaustion, her luggage so heavy four men had to carry her trunks from the dock. Madame's dresses from France were still in the cabinet. I intended to sell them with the household goods, though it caused me pain to do so.

On the last evening I would ever spend in my husband's house, I felt a struggle within me. I was free, unmarried, but I was also trapped. This was the moment when I'd always imagined I could begin a new life; now I wasn't so sure. The green shutters at the windows were open, and the breeze came spilling through the house. The cool stone corridors were empty, for the mahogany furniture Rosalie oiled every other week would soon be sold at auction and had already been collected in a horse-drawn cart. Adelle had cautioned me before I married that the Petit family would know only tragedy, but she'd never warned me how much I would love my children, both those I gave birth to and those I had inherited, or how that love would imprison me. In the fading light it was still so stifling that sparks of heat rose into the pockets of darkness. As I walked across the courtyard I noticed that parrots came to the stone fountain to drink. Though it was good luck to see them, especially in your own garden, this would not be my garden anymore. At the funeral, people had held wet handkerchiefs to their overheated foreheads. I'd had the sense that I was in a dream as it was happening, and that in my true life I was in my bed in Paris, under cold linen sheets pressed with lavender water, and that the rain was pouring down on the slate roof as I slept. Surely, it was only in my dreams that I was a widow with too many children and that I did not shed a tear as others wept around me.

I returned to the cemetery after the children had been comforted and had their supper, this time alone, so that I might leave branches of the flamboyant tree on Esther's grave. Her grave and Isaac's were next to each other. HUSBAND and WIFE had been written on her headstone in Hebrew, and there had always been a space for him. The branches I'd brought were only sticks, but the fragrance of the wood was sweet. I wandered through the paths, looking for spirits and finding only still, heavy air. On my way out of the cemetery I heard the gravedigger say the flowers had bloomed all at once, as if they were growing on the hillside in the season when everything turns red. I turned and saw it was true. That was how I knew my gift had been received.

IT IS FOOLISH TO cry over things you cannot change, yet on my last night in the Petit house I did exactly that as I looped a rope around the donkey's neck to lead him from the barn my husband and sons had built for him. The donkeys on the island may have been nasty things, but not this one. This one trusted me, and that is why I wept. I was not trustworthy. Later I would tell the children that Jean-François ran away and vow I could not hold him back. I had told them this once before, on the first day he came to us, but the donkey had returned of his own accord. This time I intended to bring him far into the mountains. He wouldn't find his way back now. We could no longer afford to feed him, and there wouldn't be a stable once we moved into town.

There were clouds of mosquitoes at this hour, so I slipped a white shawl over my head. The fevers here were deadly: yellow fever, malaria, illnesses few survived. I had reason to live, six of them. On nights like these I always made sure there was netting over the children's beds. They would cry tomorrow when they went out to the stable, even the oldest, David, who was nearly a man. He was as tall as his father had been, and he would turn his back to me so I wouldn't see his tears, but he would miss Jean-François as much as anyone.

After Isaac's death, I'd gathered the frightened children and assured them that it was God's will to release men from pain. Their father was gone from this world, but he would always be with them. That was what love did, it kept a person close. We covered the mirrors and tacked black fabric over the windows.

I had thought I would have to get rid of the donkey by myself, but when I stepped into the yard, Jestine was waiting for me. She had forgiven me, but there was a distance we hadn't known before, caused by Lyddie's absence. As girls we had imagined we were one spirit divided into two forms. Now, we kept things from each other, especially when it came to sorrow. We never spoke Jestine's daughter's name aloud. The word brought too much grief. The air was spicy with the scent of the bay trees as we walked together, leading poor Jean-François along. Bats hung from the branches like black leaves. As girls we had always come to this mountainside to make plans for what we would do when we were women. We used to think women our age were growing old, yet on nights such as this I felt the same as I had when we were sixteen.

"You should have gotten rid of him the first night," Jestine said of Jean-François, who balked as he was led away from home. "Now you're crying like he's your baby."

"You take him," I suggested. We still liked to argue like sisters. "He'll follow you as well as me. You could put up a barn beside your house."

"And feed him what? Oh, no. I can't have a pet. He should have stayed wild. You should never have spoiled him."

Before long, Jestine and I had walked so far the moon was hidden.

We were both deep in thought. We thought of the men we loved and the men we didn't. Though we didn't speak, our breathing was in the same rhythm. We let the donkey go on the dark road. He stood where he was, confused. Then he came up to me and nudged me. I did not shed a tear at my husband's funeral, though he was a good and decent man, but now I wept openly, sobbing, and I could not stop. Jestine slapped the donkey on his rear to force him to trot away. Still he looked back. He did not want to leave me. Who would give him bread soaked with milk as a treat? Who would brush the dust from his coat? I didn't believe I could love anyone, and yet I was in tears. I was as alone as that poor motherless creature.

Then and there I thought of all the things a woman could do to escape her life: She could walk into the water and see nothing but blue, hear nothing but the rising tide. She could leap into a ravine where the parrots were hidden in the leaves. She could climb onto a boat in the harbor, cover herself with a muslin tarp, eat limes until her journey was over. Jestine and I could make our way to France. I could leave my children until I was able to send for them; surely they would receive the blessings of our congregation, even though I had little to do with the Sisterhood. I could buy the tickets, pack a suitcase, wait for Jestine outside her house. But there on the dark road, I felt a kick inside of me, the spark of life. I had kept to myself what I knew to be true. There was a baby to come. I had known for some time, but I'd told no one, not even my husband. I had already decided to name him Isaac in honor of his father, the man I could not bring myself to love. The baby had been inside me for six months, but I wore bigger clothes and ate less.

Waiting for the third loss, I hadn't known who would live and who would die. Sorrow always comes in that number, and I had feared the child I carried might be taken. But instead it was Isaac. Tonight I told Jestine about the baby. She hugged me and said all children were gifts from God, therefore God must believe I could carry this burden, even though I was alone. I remembered what Adelle had told me, that I would love someone one day. But that day was not yesterday and it wasn't today. It was the red season, when the twisting roads were covered with petals, as if a woman had cried blood suddenly, without warning, after her heart had been broken.

WE MOVED IN WITH my mother. I wore black on that day and kept my eyes lowered. This was the last place I wanted to be, but I was a widow with six children and one still to come. I needed to practice logic and thrift. Most of our belongings had already been sold to pay off Isaac's debts. Women were entitled to no earthly goods in this world, and when the will was finally read in the parlor of my mother's house, I was passed over for a male relation in France. No one had heard of him before, no one had met him, but Isaac's family in France now owned most of the estate, including my father's store and house. We would be allowed to live off our smaller portion. A stranger would decide all of our fates. Our situation did not surprise me. I was more shocked when the will was read to discover that Rosalie was not a maid but a slave, something my husband had kept from me. Perhaps he was embarrassed, as he should have been. He was a kind man, but he believed in the social order, and his views were not mine. My father had freed Mr. Enrique before they reached this island. I begged Rosalie's forgiveness when I discovered the situation, yet again there was nothing I could do. Because I was a woman, I had no legal right. I could not change what had been written into the law.

Once I'd moved into my mother's house, I attended services on Saturday mornings and sat among the women with my mother and her good friend Madame Halevy. "You haven't been here for quite some time," Madame Halevy remarked. Nothing went unnoticed by her sharp eye.

"I was mourning my husband," I said.

"As I once mourned mine. But I didn't forsake my God."

We stared at each other, then I said, "I'm sure he will take that into consideration when you die."

"Which will be a very long time from now," Madame Halevy assured me.

I turned from both of them. Their lives had been built around our faith and our congregation, but I went to the synagogue only because I was expected to do so. When prayers were spoken, I didn't ask God for anything, nor did I beg for mercy. My life had returned to the one I'd had as a girl, only now I had six children depending on me. I was more trapped than ever. During the months that we waited for Isaac's relative to arrive and claim his property, I worked beside Rosalie at mealtime and in the laundry. There was a space between us now that I was aware of her situation, and we did not speak as freely as we had when we lived in my husband's house. There was endless work to be done, and I often was too tired to eat. Sometimes in the evening I sat in the garden and thought of my dreams and how they were further away now than they'd been when I wrote my stories in a notebook. I'd packed away my notebook. I was a disbeliever now. All the books in my father's library had been sold. I had managed to save a single volume. Perrault. But of late I hadn't the heart to read those stories and imagine cold, black nights in Paris and paths that might lead through the woods outside the city where the old châteaus could be found. My oldest daughter, Hannah, often came to sit with me, as if she could sense my despair. She was nine years old but wise beyond her years. She had always helped me take care of the younger children, who were a little troupe, always together. Although she was not my daughter by blood, she understood me and she slipped her hand into mine when she took note of my despair. I stroked her hair and was glad she had an open heart and was nothing like me. She asked me for a story, for I had often read to her from my notebook, but I said I didn't believe in such things anymore.

"You do," Hannah insisted.

I went searching for my notebook. It was in the kitchen, stored with Madame Petit's cookbooks. From then on I kept it in my bedchamber. I never lost sight of it again. I wrote in the evenings, and whenever I could I went to speak to the women in the market. *Tell me a story*, I would say to them, as if I were a child again, and they would sit beside me, near the crates of chicken or the piles of fish, and describe the wonders of our world.

LATE IN THE AFTERNOONS I visited the cemetery. On most days it was so hot steam rose from the puddles after the rain. A simple walk and I was soaking wet. At the gate, I slipped off my dress and wore my white muslin petticoat. I wanted to be the girl I used to be, to go backward in time so I might sit in the mountains and watch for parrots and believe my whole life was ahead of me. I brought branches of flamboyant flowers to place on the graves of Isaac and Esther, and the bees drifted above me, rumbling through the air. Esther's ghost had never again visited me; she must have been satisfied to have her husband back in her arms. Beside their graves there were ground doves nesting in the weave of oleander, calling to each other. Perhaps they were in love, as Esther and Isaac had been. Although I'd never loved my husband, I missed him. My milk was still in from the baby before the one I now carried. Perhaps I should have been more modest, but I didn't care, I was too hot to wear anything more than my petticoat. Sometimes I wondered what I did care about. Rosalie was the one who went to my children when they cried at night. Their cries were so distant when I was asleep that I barely recognized them. I thought perhaps I was becoming more like my mother than I'd ever imagined I could be. Cold and far away. I missed the three people who had died, and I thought perhaps I myself would be better off dead. I lay down on the soft earth of the cemetery and imagined what it might be like, even though I knew such thoughts weren't good for the baby I carried. Perhaps inside me he was crying, too.

People began to notice me in the place of the dead, there in my white undergarments, lying on my back and studying the leaves and the treetops where ghosts walked. The old men who came to pray in their black hats and prayer shawls ran away when they spied me. They covered their eyes and asked God to protect them.

My mother soon heard the rumors about me. She called me to her.

"People are starting to talk about you." She had developed a cough. Ever since the death of my father she had seemed weaker, but only in her physical aspect. Her tongue was still just as sharp. "They think you're going mad, or that you're possessed. You think you're the only one to know grief? You think I didn't lose more than my share? Cry all you want at night when you're alone in bed," my mother advised, "but compose yourself when you go out."

Other than my undergarments, the only clothing I'd worn since the funeral was the black dress Jestine had sewn for me. It was filthy. When I finally gave my mourning dress to the day woman who came to help us with the wash, the water in the tub turned black; burrs and sticks rose to the surface, for they'd stuck to the hem of my garment.

Rosalie cried when we left our house. She had good reason to do so. My mother was horrible to live with and ordered her around so that she had double the work, as well as the children to look after. Rosalie had begun to spend time out behind our house, where Mr. Enrique lived. She was younger than he by twenty years, nearly the same difference as that between me and my husband. Still he seemed like a young man whenever Rosalie came around. As for her, she sang to herself even when we did the laundry together. I knew love when I saw it, from the flattering white dress she wore, to the cakes she baked for him, to the sound of their laughter as they sat together outside his cottage. One night I waited for her, to see if I was correct. I was there when she came into the courtyard. She was aglow, singing a song I didn't recognize in a language I didn't know.

I admired Mr. Enrique, the man who had saved my father's life. I'd given him all of my father's clothes and personal belongings before my mother could stop me. He was a solitary man, but he didn't always spend his time alone. I warned Rosalie that she was not the first woman to want him and that he didn't seem to want a wife.

"It doesn't matter. I'm the best," Rosalie assured me. I suppose this is what love can do to a woman, bring her into a garden at night, convinced she somehow can affect fate's plan with her desire. Love like this was a mystery to me. I didn't understand how people allowed sheer emotion to get the better of them. You couldn't see love, or touch it, or taste it, yet it could destroy you and leave you in the dark, chasing after your own destiny.

MY SON CAME WHEN the weather changed, during the storms. The day began with blue light but ended with rain and wind. I shivered in my bed. When I was sure it was the baby's time, I begged Rosalie to get Jestine. My friend arrived quickly. She and my mother did not look at each other or speak. It was the first time they had contact since Aaron was sent to Paris. But there were no arguments, for it was business on this night, the work of bringing a child to life. My mother didn't dare to keep Jestine from our house. As she herself had never helped in a birth, I suppose she was grateful to have a more experienced woman there. When the hard pains came, my mother left my chamber. She said a verse from Isaiah as she departed, to keep Lilith away, granting the screech owl demon peace if she would stay away. At least she'd said a prayer for me, which was more than I had expected from her.

It took four hours to bring the last of Isaac's sons into the world. I swallowed my screams and my agony, but my bitterness grew. I felt it taking root in me, right beside my child. A seed that was growing greener. I bit my lips until they bled and tried to fly out of my body to escape the agony of birth. When I thought I might die, I screamed out for Isaac's first wife to take me with her. Just when I was ready to go to her, the baby arrived. He was small, but he howled like a wolf as soon as he was born, the sign of a strong constitution. Jestine wrapped him in a clean blanket and murmured a prayer under her breath, the one her mother used to say when we were ill or in need, in a language spoken in a world so far away Jestine didn't understand the meaning of the words. All the same, we both knew it was a plea for long life in this cruel and beautiful world.

It was a relief to give birth to this child, and I was grateful for the sleep I could now have. I thought perhaps my mother would now drop her antagonism toward Jestine, and show her the gratitude she deserved for bringing her new grandchild into the world. But I heard them talking out in the garden while I was dozing one afternoon, and my mother was not offering words of thanks. Their voices were rising and falling, and some of the words carried the sting of bees. Beside me, the last child I would have with Isaac was sleeping deeply, his breath even. I left him curled up and went to the open window.

"I don't want you here again," my mother said to Jestine. "I could have you arrested if I wished."

Jestine laughed. "For what?"

"Thievery."

"I was the one who was robbed! My daughter was taken by that witch, your daughter-in-law."

"You were the first to steal from me," Madame Pomié cried.

"What did I steal?" Jestine said. And then she was silent. She knew. There were tears streaking my mother's face. Aaron.

My mother shoved a strand of pearls into Jestine's hands. They were the ones she had sewn into the hem of her dress when she'd fled Saint-Domingue. "Take them. They're yours as long as I never see you again."

"Of course." Jestine looped the pearls around her throat. "I'll take the payment for your sins. But that doesn't change anything, Madame. We both lost our children because of you."

⟜❀⟞

ONCE THE BABY WAS settled I began to go to the office. I had already discussed the situation with Mr. Enrique. I thought we could see to it that the business remained in our hands, and keep the family from France at a distance. My father had taught me most of what I needed to know, and Mr. Enrique would see to the rest. We worked well together, and I quickly understood that the business was on shaky ground. Once more we were victims of the weather. In the seasons of storms we had lost both ships and merchandise. Mr. Enrique's suggestion was that we sell what was left of the shipping business, the province of my husband, and return to sales, my father's original endeavor and his best asset, the store. "Let other people run the bigger risk and earn the bigger profit. The store will provide steady income. It's safer for a woman alone with a family to care for."

I thought he was wise, and let him draw up the figures. Then I presented the plan to my mother. The very idea of sitting down with her made the rash that had disappeared once my baby was born rise again across my skin. Still, like it or not, it had to be done. My mother and I were the family now, the two of us, and perhaps we could agree upon a plan that would help us maintain some say over all the property that had once belonged to my father.

We met in my father's study. Surrounded by his empty shelves, I felt my grief over his loss all over again. I thought of the night he came to tell me I would be married, and the satisfaction I'd felt in rescuing our family from disaster. But my husband was clearly drawn to bad fortune, as Adelle had warned. Tragedy had followed him. When he combined his business with ours, instead of strengthening both, he'd brought it all down, unwise in ways of commerce and of the dangers of the weather. The pride I'd once felt for saving my father's business by agreeing to wed Isaac was a false pride. The marriage had been for nothing. But perhaps now I could truly rescue us when I presented my mother with a plan that would make the business smaller but more reliable. She glanced at the ledgers and figures, then waved her hand, impatient. "You don't think the business will be entrusted to you and Enrique, do you?"

"We work well together. So yes. It makes sense."

My mother's expression was sour. "You could never accept the fact that you were a woman and nothing more. I knew that when I was carrying you. You would cause trouble."

"I'm sorry you feel that way," I said, even though I wasn't sorry at all. I was glad to have caused her trouble.

My mother stood up, away from the desk. The meeting was over. "Your husband's family is sending his nephew from Paris. What happens next will be his decision."

I stood as well. I didn't think she could tell I was shaking. I wouldn't have wanted her to know. "You prefer a man you don't know to your own daughter?"

"It is the legal system that prefers such things, not I," my mother reminded me. "I did not inherit anything, and neither will you. But you think you're above rules, and you can do as you please. Be sure that's not what you teach your children."

I could not bring myself to tell Mr. Enrique that our plan had been overruled, but he knew. Everyone knew my husband's nephew was coming. Mr. Enrique continued to see to the business, but I took to my bed. I felt a fever come over me, a jade green fever in my heart and my bones. My bitterness, inherited from my mother. I was so ill that my mother did not protest when Rosalie called Jestine to visit me. Jestine defied my mother and came to give me ginger tea, but it was not the cure I needed. I noticed she was wearing the pearls, and she laid them on my chest; they were cold as ice. I could focus once more. Jestine said the fever was inside my mind. It was true, a black curtain had come down ever since I'd moved into my mother's house. The edges of the pink flowers on the vines at the window were blocked out by wooden shutters. I could not see anything that was beautiful.

My mother came to the doorway, a shadow. She had worn black ever since my father died. I looked at her and felt I was looking into a mirror. We resembled each other too much.

"You're not to come here again," she said to Jestine. Then she turned to me. "If you don't intend to die, you'd better get out of bed."

When she left, Jestine and I looked at each other and broke into laughter. So much for compassion.

"You would have never traded places with me," I said.

Jestine agreed with a nod. "Not for a day."

Jestine took up her satchel and brought out a gift she'd made for me, a pale green dress. It looked so fresh, like grass and new leaves. "When you're ready to give up your mourning it will be here. Then you'll show your mother you're not afraid to be who you are."

I WOULD HAVE LIKED to close my eyes and go on sleeping, but I had children, seven of them. I did what I must, but I did so as a sleepwalker, still in mourning clothes. I was not ready for the green dress. All the same, something had changed inside me. I had one goal in mind: to escape my mother's house. One afternoon I went to the store to pick up some sugar and flour for Rosalie, and Mr. Enrique signaled me to follow him. There was a staircase that led upstairs. I had remembered the area as a storeroom when we had an overabundance of goods, but now our merchandise had dwindled to a bare minimum, and the rooms revealed themselves to be lodgings. There were several bedchambers and a kitchen with an old stove left behind by the previous owners.

"We could rent this out," Mr. Enrique said. He had had some of the workmen clean the place up and collect some unused furniture, too old to sell. "Or perhaps you have an idea for this place."

I grinned. Mr. Enrique had saved me, as he'd once rescued my father. "I'll take it." I opened the shutters, and light spilled in. I could see the street and some vendors outside selling fruit.

"What will she have to say about it?" Mr. Enrique asked archly.

"She can say what she likes. It's up to the stranger from France to decide our fates. My mother has no more say than I do."

When I insisted we move into the rooms above the store, my mother didn't challenge me. Perhaps she was thankful to be rid of me. We had caused each other enough grief, and she had aged enormously. She was so ill that she spent her days in my father's chair. Often, in the dusk, a neighbor would pass by and she would call out my father's name, as if she had seen him.

Our new lodgings were crowded, and we didn't have enough furniture, but I preferred it. The younger children all shared a single room, with mattresses on the floor. The older boys, David and Samuel, slept in what had once been a parlor, and we used the kitchen as our common room. I heard Mr. Enrique in the morning, working in the office, setting out orders and keeping the ledgers. Rosalie often made him his tea. She stayed in his office for an hour or more, but I didn't complain.

WHEN MY MOTHER PASSED on, fully dressed, lying upon the bed she had shared with my father, no one was surprised. I sometimes think she willed her death. She was done with her life here and wanted nothing more than to join her husband. She left me her jewelry, the diamond earrings and brooch she'd slipped into the hem of her skirt, but everything else would belong to my husband's nephew when he came, including her house and all of her belongings. I sneaked in one night and took some of my father's maps of Paris, along with a silver pen he used. When I walked through my family's darkened house I saw sparks in the palms of my hands, but when I tried to catch them, they vanished. If I'd ever been able to call spirits to me, that gift was lost to me now.

In the garden I thought I saw the lizard that had been Aaron's pet years earlier, there beneath the bushes where the leaves were so dry they sounded like paper rustling. As I was leaving, something held me back. I turned and went to uproot the apple tree from its large ceramic pot, then dragged it along with me. I left a trail of dirt behind, and my arms were aching when I reached the little garden behind the store. I deposited the tree there for the boys to plant in the morning.

In the days that followed I accepted visitors who wished to pay their respects when they called on me with trays of food and sweets. I cannot say I felt true sorrow, and although I kept this to myself, my mother's closest friend, Madame Halevy, threw me a look when she and her maid brought us dinner, chicken curry and sweet molasses bread and several mango and coconut pastries. "Try to pretend you understand grief," Madame Halevy said in a pinched voice.

"You seem convinced you know so much more than I do," I responded ungraciously.

"Think back to this moment when you're my age," Madame Halevy told me. "Then you'll know the answer."

I wrote to Aaron, and although I didn't expect the courtesy of a letter, a few weeks after my mother's death, one arrived. He sent his regrets regarding her passing in a single line. *She was good to me when she didn't have to be.* The remainder of his brief letter concerned Jestine. I felt uncomfortable with the intimacy of his words. He missed her terribly, he wrote, and could not stomach his regret. In that way, my mother had ruined his life as well as mine. I stopped reading and brought the letter to Jestine. I sat outside while she took his letter into her bedchamber. After a while she came and joined me. I had glanced at enough of Aaron's missive to know he had written that their daughter was well cared for, as beautiful a child as she was intelligent. As if that message would lift Jestine's despair. *Perhaps I acted wrongly,* he had written, *but I acted out of love, so that she might have a better life.*

BY NOW IT WAS spring. It was the time when Jestine and I used to wait for the turtles to come to shore, but she had no interest. She didn't care what happened on our island. She looked toward France, where her heart and soul resided. When we met in the late afternoons, leaving the children in Rosalie's care, we often walked along the wharf. We watched the harbor, eyeing the ships as they came in, then we made our way home separately.

We spent our thirtieth birthdays together. We were nine months apart, but we took a day in the middle and used it for both of us. We cooked ourselves dinner at Jestine's house, a child's meal of fongee pudding and coconut cake, although we also drank plenty of rum in the hope that it would make the next year easier. We did not say aloud what we wished for, though we wished for the very same thing, to board one of those sailing ships and cross the ocean. Late in the evening, after we had

had too much rum, Jestine wept for her daughter. I stayed with her until she fell asleep. I hadn't realized how lonely it was in her house at night, like a ship lost at sea. When it was past midnight, I walked back to town, up the hill to the store. There was a certain freedom in being a widow. No one asked where I went or with whom I spent my time. Without my mother to keep an eye on me, I could do as I pleased. I wasn't afraid to be alone on the road. There were bats in every tree, but I waved my hands and drove them away as if I were a spirit. I had been young only a moment ago. I imagined that in the blink of an eye I would be old, and my life would be over before I could make it my own. Perhaps my story would not end as I had planned. Or perhaps it would change into something I had never expected, so that years from now, looking back, I would realize just how little I'd known as a young woman, precisely as Madame Halevy had said.

CHAPTER FIVE

Mortal Love

CHARLOTTE AMALIE, ST. THOMAS

1825

ABRAHAM GABRIEL FRÉDÉRIC PIZZARRO

H e arrived at 14 Dronningens Gade, in an area known as the Queen's Quarter, a day late, after a season of storms, when so many ships were lost between St. Thomas and Charleston that the indigo sea was a graveyard of sails and masts. He'd been sent a parcel that contained the keys to the properties his mother's brother had owned, as well as all of those this same uncle had inherited from his father-in-law. Abraham Gabriel Frédéric Pizzarro was twenty-two,* but he was the executor of his uncle Isaac's will and now the sole person to decide the fate of the business and of nearly a dozen relatives, all but three unrelated by blood. His family, some of who lived in Passy, just outside of Paris, and others situated in Bordeaux, where Jews had been recognized as citizens for seventy-five years, had met to decide the fate of the business. His grandfather Pierre Rodrigues Alvares Pizzarro was a Marrano from Portugal, a hidden Jew whose family had lived in that country for several generations after fleeing Spain. After much debate they had concluded

---

* The name was traditionally Pizzarro, until Camille Pissarro changed it to the French spelling in the 1880s.

that Frédéric's youth would serve him well in undertaking the long, arduous trip and help him make the adjustment to the tropics. Not many among them wished to go into a region known for yellow fever and losses at sea. Frédéric had read all of the accountings of his uncle's holdings: two houses, one store, and a failed shipping business. His uncle had left behind too many children and too many debts, all of which must be dealt with. It was up to Frédéric to turn the situation around, as it was now a family enterprise, owned in equal parts by Isaac's widow, who had no voice in business matters, and the family in France, who did. This was the law and the way property was divided. Frédéric was fluent in French and Spanish and English and Portuguese, which would be helpful despite his complete ignorance of Danish, the official language of what would be his new country, a tiny island he had never heard of before. Still, he was their choice. He was responsible, respectable, and learned in legal matters, the right man for the job.

There had been several women in Paris who were displeased to hear the news of his imminent departure. After all, Frédéric was tall, with dark hair and an easy gait, so handsome that women often chased after him, even on the street, much to his embarrassment, handing him cards with their addresses, inviting him to supper and tea. He always declined these offers of introduction. He didn't like the feeling of being hunted. He was something of a loner, and his dreams were filled with numbers and theorems. He believed in logic and had a mathematician's spirit, and he carried a memory of a section of Galileo's declaration with him. *The universe cannot be read until we have learned the language and become familiar with the characters in which it is written, which is a mathematical language.*

Without these, one is wandering in a dark labyrinth.

Some people said he was an angel, for certainly no ordinary man could act with such integrity, but he laughed when he heard these statements. He was flesh and blood. He lost his temper, made mistakes, knew fear, had wicked thoughts. At times, the intensity of his own desires un-

nerved him; they were under his control, but struggling to break free it
seemed, just beneath his skin, as if he might surprise himself with his
grasp of pure pleasure, something he rarely knew. He burned for all he
wanted, but ignored his yearnings, for he had a plan for his life, to prosper and be the man in his family that everyone could depend upon. He
wished to do this to honor his God, his faith, and his family. And so,
when they'd come to him and told him he would be leaving France, he
assumed this was God's plan. He was not an overtly religious man, but
he was a believer in miracles both small and large. The voyage had
amazed and changed him. He'd clung to the railings of the ship in the
midst of storms and let the rain splash down on him. During one particular bad tidal surge, when the waves were twenty feet high, he closed his
eyes and told his God to take him and do his will with him. When he
opened his eyes to find he was still alive, and had not washed away to a
watery death, as two other men on board had, vanishing before anyone
could lend a hand or a length of rope, he knew he had a future that was
his to claim.

He had left France as a young, naïve student, but three months at sea
with older, harder men had made the world seem like a different place,
dangerous, it was true, and mystifying, but open and fascinating, a book
he had just begun to read. Perhaps fate was not written by God but made
by men. The first week he had been too ill to leave his bunk, sickened by
the roiling sea and the metallic taste of the water from the barrel outside
his door. But by the second week, when storms returned, he pitched in
with the sailors and learned more in that one week than he had his entire
life. He learned that rats and lemons could be eaten by some men when
there was nothing in the storeroom but molded bread, just as he discovered that the stars in the southern world were far brighter than any he
had known, and that beneath the water there lived creatures so immense
they created waves, as if they were masters of the ocean, and of the universe, and of fate. He gave in to the world that was bigger and more
mysterious than he'd ever imagined, and he gave up some of the control

he'd kept over his nerves and his desires. People in Paris would have been shocked to hear how often he laughed, and how drunk he managed to get without falling on his face.

He came off the boat with his beard unshaven and his hair so long it fell into his eyes. His leather bag of belongings had been discolored by salt, and his clothing was as filthy as any common sailor's. He was still too handsome for his own good, but with lines on his face now, despite his youth, formed by the salt and the sea, and tanned skin that was a harder covering, one he'd realized he would need to survive. He knew no one in the town of Charlotte Amalie, or in St. Thomas, or anywhere else in this new world that was so bright he had to blink. The world was incandescent, on fire, and the gloom of his time at sea evaporated. He'd been babied by his mother, a favorite of the family, encouraged by his teachers and mentors. Hardship was a story he'd read about, nothing more, until this voyage, which had let him know some of what the world was like. He now understood that the sea was enormous and bottomless. It was overwhelming and gorgeous and far beyond his control, just like the rest of life. He felt a fool to ever have thought he could predict his future, for he never could have predicted a country in which the steep mountainsides were red, where flocks of birds shook themselves from the trees, like yellow flowers falling upward, into the sky.

He felt blinded by the tawny sunlight as he left the ship, and he quickly developed a squint that lasted the rest of his life. The heat was like a living thing that reached out in an embrace. If you fought it you couldn't win, so he gave in to it. That was what he'd learned at sea, not to fight the elements or, he was still learning this, his own nature. He didn't bother dressing in a jacket, as he would have done in France, but instead ducked into a cobbled alley and slipped on the one good white shirt he had left, packed away for this occasion. He'd been told some men collapsed with heat prostration in their first instants on this island. Others slowly went mad, driven to drink by boredom or weather, taking shelter in taverns and the old Danish taphuses, where they fell prey to rum. But as he went along, all he felt was free. He stood on the dock and gazed along the shore, where the houses were built on stilts, so tall they seemed like storks, their shutters painted bright hues of blue and yellow and green. Frédéric had been ill as a boy, with lung disease. In the winter in Paris he always wore two pairs of woolen socks and a heavy vest under his jacket. The heat here felt like heaven to him.

He went along the road into town, passing several busy wharves, stopping under a vine of bougainvillea so he could listen to the bees. The hum was overwhelming; he could feel the buzzing go through him and lodge somewhere inside his heart. Perhaps he had never heard anything before he'd known the sound of these bees. He was a businessman, sent to set things straight and reclaim a failing business, a serious endeavor, and yet it seemed he had walked into a dream. He spied a donkey feasting on green stalks of grass and laughed so loudly that the donkey startled, then brayed and ran away. In his bag he carried a folder of documents, along with a Bible. There was not a day that went by that he did not recite the morning and evening prayers, wearing the skullcap he carried with him. He was a Sephardic Jew whose grandfather had come from the little town called Braganza in Portugal, chased from his home in the middle of the night because of his faith with no belongings and no destination. It was in Frédéric's blood to travel. He took his prayer book from his bag and stopped in the road to give his gratitude to God, for this day and for every day to come. The time was right to thank the Almighty. A star was appearing in the still blue sky. Evening was early to come here and he hurried with his prayers. Two African men passed him by with a cart of fruits and vegetables, many kinds that Frédéric didn't recognize. There were brown fruits so sweet the flies buzzed around their bursting, ripening rinds, and orange ones that seemed to be tinted by a painter's brushstrokes. Each fruit seemed a miracle, plucked out of a dream.

"You look lost," the older man said. He spoke Spanish, the language that had always been spoken in Frédéric's home. "Are you in the right country?"

Frédéric laughed. He gave the street name he wanted, and the fruit men pointed out the way. He spied some reddish fruit in one of their baskets, the only thing he recognized. The fruit sellers said it was very rare in their country and that an old man from Saint-Domingue had planted a tree in his courtyard and it had grown so tall the fruit fell over the wall and a few people had planted seeds from this one fruit and now it grew in several gardens. They gave him one to eat, an apple, not crisp, but warm from the sunlight, the pulp dissolving in his mouth. It reminded him of home, and it was, by far, the most delicious thing he'd eaten since he'd begun his travels.

"Are you looking for a woman?" the other African man asked him, switching to French. "Or just a place to stay?"

"A place to stay," Frédéric was quick to respond. "I'm not ready to be involved with a woman."

"Who is?" the older man countered. They all laughed. Frédéric was young and handsome. His Parisian French was so precise it was nearly a different language than the Creole spoken on this island. The men probably thought he was experienced with women, but he was not. His cousins went to whorehouses, and had often insisted he go with them. On those occasions he sat on a divan in the hallway and talked with the madam about her life and gave her business advice. He had ideas about everything, and helped her to figure out ways to raise her profits.

"You prefer men?" she said to him once.

"I prefer love," he replied.

"You *are* young." She'd shrugged at his naïveté. "Come back in two years."

Now two years had passed and he was in St. Thomas, where he knew not a single soul but, if anything, was grateful for his aloneness. The world around him was an amazement, more than enough to satisfy him without the intrusion of anyone close to him. In a dream, it doesn't matter with whom you are acquainted; all that counts is what you do and see. Here every color was vibrant, a completely different palette than in Paris. The pale sky that had burned white with heat only hours ago,

when he'd stepped onto the wharf, was now washed with pink and gold.
A miracle, he thought, *with more to come.*

Frédéric knew the widow had been sent a message concerning his
arrival by the family, and that she had responded negatively. He had then
been asked to write a letter, which he'd done, though there had been no
reply. Perhaps she was expecting him, but he was filthy, in no condition
to have a formal introduction. The fruit men led him up to what they
called Synagogue Hill. They said his people mostly lived here and
wished him luck. They told him to be careful; some people thought the
old Danish families that kept slaves could turn themselves into werewolves. They ate Africans and Jews for supper. They could run faster
than any man. That was why some of the streets were made of ninety-
nine steps, so that the werewolf would stop to search for the hundredth
step, and while he did, his victim would get away.

The streets were indeed steep, and Frédéric's long legs were tired. He
noticed an address he'd seen in his legal papers, one of the houses the
family owned, empty now that the matriarch had died. It looked like the
ghost of a house in the falling dark. He spied a spiral of smoke circling
up behind the house and pushed open an iron gate so that he might see
what was there. There was a skittering that unnerved him, the flash of
some creature's tail. He thought of monsters and fierce animals, of scales
and teeth and claws. The air was perfumed, and there was fruit everywhere, growing wild, untended. No one had lived here for some time.
He went through the courtyard and opened another gate, painted green,
which led into a rear street. There was a cottage before him, and a well-
dressed black man was eating his dinner at a wooden table set out on a
small stone patio. Or at least he had been having his meal until Frédéric
came through the gate. The fellow looked up, ignoring his food. Frédéric
saw the other man's hand move. There was a gun on his lap.

"I didn't mean to disturb you," Frédéric said in Spanish. He refused
to believe it was his fate to be shot when he had just entered what he considered to be paradise.

"I'd prefer if you speak French," the other man said. "Then if I have to shoot you, at least I'll understand your last words."

More had happened to Frédéric in the hours since he'd landed at the dock in Charlotte Amalie than had occurred in all the years he'd spent in France.

"You don't have any reason to shoot me."

"Tell me why and we'll see if I believe you."

In elegant French, Frédéric quickly explained that he had only just arrived and was looking for a place to spend the night before he went to meet the widow whose business he'd been sent to oversee.

"So while you prepare to swindle the widow out of her business you wish to stay here?"

"I've been sent to run the business, not steal it. I would go there directly, but I can't present myself like this to a widow with six children."

"Seven," Mr. Enrique said. "You're behind the times."

"You know the family?"

"You clearly don't. And now you want to spend the night in the house of a stranger you've never met before?" He gazed at the intruder, and then shook his head. "Do you think you're clever enough to run a business?"

Frédéric considered himself a good judge of character. At that moment, he didn't fear for his life. If anything, he felt more alive than ever before. "Do you always have dinner with a gun over your knees?"

"I'm the watchman here, among other things. The big house is empty. There are always thieves. You can stay there for the night. In the morning I'll take you where you want to go. I think you'll need help on this island. This isn't France, you know. We have bugs that can kill you, let alone men."

Frédéric gratefully accepted the dinner he was now offered. It was a stew called callaloo, made with taro, spinach, okra, and forbidden salted meat, a dish so savory, with a flavor spiced with cloves and pods of cardamom, that it loosened his tongue. He balanced his plate on his lap and swore he'd never had as good a dinner in France. He drank something sweet, a dizzying concoction called guava berry rum, and soon found himself speaking of intensely personal matters, of his life in Paris and his family there, and of their expectations that he would return. He knew some men from the outside world hated this island—the weather, the informality of the people, the mixing of race and religion and station. But some men dissolved into it and became a part of it; they took the embrace they were offered. Frédéric already knew he was of the mind of the latter group, those who felt they'd finally come home.

He made his way to the empty house in the dark along the overgrown path that led through the garden. It was a stucco mansion with a stone foundation, with moss growing up along the stones. The scent of the flowers was dizzying. Pink blooms on vines snaked along the verandas and wound up the walls. In the hedges were nesting bananaquits, yellow birds that glowed in the dim shadows as if bands of sunlight had been painted across their chests. The front door had been left unlocked. The hinges groaned as Frédéric pushed open the door and went into the spacious, cool hallway. A bottle of rum and dusty glasses were perched on a high mahogany table. He drank directly from the bottle. A lizard peeked inside the door, then ran into the hall, hiding under a rug. Frédéric drank far too much. At home, he rarely had wine or alcohol and often had tea before bed. Here, he seemed unnaturally thirsty.

It was late when he found his way upstairs and let himself into the first bedchamber he came upon. He pushed open the shutters, disturbing the bats in the courtyard so that they all rose in a dark vortex, like smoke lifting from the trees. Drunk, he fell deeply asleep. The pillows smelled like lavender. They were almost too soft, filled with the feathers of local birds, a thousand colors inside the cotton pillow sham. That night he dreamed of Paris, and of the rain. His dreams were gray and green, filled with shadows. When he awoke the sun was blinding and his head was pounding from all the rum he'd consumed. There were pink petals on the stone floor, and the lizard was on the windowsill, a pale green thing with wide eyes, kingly, as if the house belonged to him. Frédéric rejoiced to think that this was his waking life. He offered his gratitude to his family for sending him here. On the ship he'd worried that he would fail them, that he would be better off at home, in the job he was used to, in the world that he knew. But now he understood. They had chosen correctly.

HE FOUND CLEAN CLOTHES that were nearly his size in a cupboard. They were made of lighter cloth, linen and cotton. Pale gray and white. He poured a pitcher of cold water over his head, and shaved as best he could. His hair was longer than acceptable in Paris, but here he'd seen men simply tie it back, and he did likewise. He looked through his bag for a silk scarf he wore on formal occasions.

"All set to rob the widow," Mr. Enrique said when they met up in the courtyard.

There were black birds with green throats that were no bigger than moths darting through the air, lighting on trembling branches.

"I'm here to help her. If I were a thief, there was plenty to rob in France and I would have avoided the pains of traveling here."

"Well, I don't think she'll see it that way."

They walked down the hill to the commercial district, boots clattering. The streets were filled with the din of working people and with trills of birdsong. A fellow in the market sold tamed birds, bits of yellow and pistachio-green fluttered, contained in bamboo cages. Frédéric wished he had the time to visit all the stalls and try everything before him, food of all sorts that he'd never seen before. The drinks offered had names that delighted him: pumpkin punch, peanut punch, coconut water, lemon tea. There was fruit on the trees, and in the distance the mountains looked red rather than green. It was May, and the first flowering of the flamboyant trees had begun. The air was thick with salt and the scent of limes. They passed a café where fishermen, already back from the sea, were bolting down their breakfasts.

"Let's stop and get ourselves a meal," Frédéric suggested. The fish soup looked especially delicious, and the scent of curry drifted toward them.

Mr. Enrique threw his companion a look. "There are some things you should know about this place." He realized now how young and naïve his companion was. "Your people were granted full rights on this island, other than the fact that they cannot marry out of their race, but mine don't have that benefit. There is no selling of human life since the first part of the century; the Danish government saw to that when they took the island. But those who came here as slaves, remain so. True, many people of color here are free, but that doesn't mean you can publicly sit down for a meal with me."

Frédéric shrugged. "We could take it with us."

"I wouldn't be served at this establishment. We'd have to go down the street, and there isn't time."

Frédéric laughed. "Because the widow is waiting. Snoring in a chair?"

He clearly had a vision of her, and Mr. Enrique gave him a hard look.

"You should know the widow isn't old. She's not what you expect. She understands the business and is bright."

"And you know this because?"

"I was her father's clerk, and then your uncle's clerk, and now it appears I'll be yours as well. That is, if she allows you into the office."

"I am the heir to my uncle's estate, which includes her father's properties. I'm afraid she has no choice," Frédéric informed his companion, his more serious side emerging.

"That may be, but she'd probably do better running the business than anyone, if it was not against the law for a woman to do so."

They had reached the store, which was already bustling at this hour. Frédéric admired the stone and stucco façade. Enrique explained that above the commercial area were the rooms where the widow and her children lived. This was just as well. The estate wished to sell the house where his uncle Isaac had lived, and the house of his uncle's mother-in-law, where Frédéric had spent the night. He thought of his dreams of rain and felt a chill. He had just turned twenty-two, and all at once he felt his youth, how little he knew about the lives of others: widows, children, dying men. He was about to enter into the daily life of people he didn't know. He hesitated at the door. There was a hedge of those same pink flowers he'd seen in the stucco house, and the bees seemed to have followed him. He closed his eyes for a moment and listened to their buzzing, then suddenly felt he was being watched. He gazed upward, squinting, but all he saw were some lace curtains, made in France.

Once they were inside the main hall, Enrique directed him to the widow's lodgings, before continuing on to the office at the rear of the store. Frédéric went through a side door and took the stairs to the modest living quarters. In France, this would have been considered the home of a person with little means. He had the key to the place and was legally the owner of everything, but felt too uncomfortable to use the key unannounced, so he knocked at the door. Frédéric heard people talking inside, the rise and fall of voices speaking French. He rapped on the wood again, and again there was no answer. He waited in the corridor for some time, long enough for him to realize no one would likely respond, and so he used one of the keys that had been sent to him.

There was a click, and then the door opened into the world he'd been sent to manage and guide. He hadn't expected the scene before him, two boys who were nearly men gathering some books, so many children at the table he could not count them all, an African woman seeing to their breakfasts, admonishing them for being greedy and late, a little boy and some even younger girls, barefoot, their hair braided and pinned up. They were Emma and Delphine, so close in age they seemed to be twins. It barely mattered how many there were; he could not see any of them clearly as his attention was riveted on the woman who came out of a bedchamber, wearing a white shift, her masses of dark hair loose, a baby at her hip. He thought of a white rose, for there were some in his parents' garden outside Paris, blooms which grew on thin, wavering branches covered by thorns. The woman appeared to have just come from her bed. Her clothes were loose and light enough for him to see her form. He found himself immobilized, there on the threshold of a home to which he hadn't been invited or, it seemed, expected.

A little girl saw him first and pointed. "Qui est cet homme?" she asked in a singsong. It would take weeks before he could tell which one was Delphine and which was Emma. The rest of the children, who had been as noisy as birds, quieted, staring with suspicion. The black woman said, "What do you think you're doing here?" in accented English. They were all speaking to him at once, except the dark-haired woman dressed in white, who merely raised her eyes to his. She gazed at him coldly, not wanting him to realize how handsome she found him. There was a soulful cast to his features, as if he revealed his innermost self. She saw that he was wearing gray leather boots and she knew he was from Paris, and at that instant Rachel Pomié Petit, who had the sharpest tongue on St. Thomas, found she could not speak.

Frédéric ignored the others and managed to walk up to the lady of the house and introduce himself. He could imagine what a fool he must have seemed to Mr. Enrique when he spoke of her as if she were an old woman. He'd been warned that she was not what he expected. He managed to introduce himself and to say surely she must have received the letter stating he would be arriving from France.

"My goal is to help you in any way I can," he assured her. "S'il vous plaît, permettez-moi de vous aider."

The widow stared at him. His accent was perfect; careless and elegant. She laughed and said, "Before I'm dressed or after?"

He realized she wore a chemise and a petticoat, not a white dress. He could not quite remember her name, but then the African woman called her Rachel—a familiarity that never would have occurred in France between mistress and servant. He recalled what he'd read in the files he carried with him. Rachel Pomié Petit, born in St. Thomas, daughter of a well-respected shop owner named Moses Pomié, married to his uncle Isaac when she was not much more than a girl.

The children had gone back to the business of getting ready for the day. The older boys continued to stare at Frédéric, uneasy, perhaps because he was not that much older than they, but the younger ones paid him no mind. He felt surrounded by mayhem, the children finishing their food, the maid, who was called Rosalie, clearing up as best she could, shouting out instructions that the children more or less ignored. Frédéric could see only the woman before him. The rest faded away, sinking out of his line of vision. He would always think of the scent of molasses from the store downstairs when he thought of this day, the morning when he fell in love with a woman who had seven children.

"I had Rosalie go down to the boat to meet you yesterday, but you weren't there," Rachel told him. His posture was so straight, not like that of the men in St. Thomas, who slouched in the heat. He stood the way she imagined all men in Paris did, with a natural grace. "I thought you'd changed your mind and stayed in Paris, which made me think all the more of you."

"You've been there?" he said to engage her in a conversation that might make them less uncomfortable with their situation, more social, if that was possible.

"Not quite yet." When she laughed she looked like a girl to him, no older than himself, though she was, technically, his aunt, and seven years older. The amount of time that Jacob had served to win his Rachel in the Bible, though each year had seemed like a day because of the love he felt for her.

"Well, I'm flattered that you thought of me at all," he said. "I didn't want to disturb you, so I imposed on your clerk and spent the night in your parents' house."

"How quickly you moved in to what was once ours. You've come from Paris to this dot in the ocean to claim what belonged to my husband and my father, and, if the laws cared anything for women, to me."

There was color rising in her face and throat as she spoke. Clearly she resented him. She had begged Isaac's family in France to trust her with the business, and in response they sent this tall young man who stood in her kitchen, surprised by everything he encountered. It was as if a heron had flown in through the window and then had frozen, shocked by the peculiar manners of humankind. Rachel studied him more carefully now, for he was equally strange to her. His Parisian accent, the way he ran his hand over his brow when he was speaking, his eyes, which appeared to change color depending on the light. Despite his youth, he seemed commanding in some way, comfortable with himself in a manner she assumed a man educated in Paris might be. She'd seen him from her window and had immediately known he was the one. The man who'd come to take over her life. She'd taken note of how good-looking he was, how French in character he seemed due to his extreme composure. Well, face-to-face, he was no longer quite so composed. He plucked at a thread on his shirt. Rachel recognized his jacket and trousers. "You're wearing my cousin's clothes, I see."

"Am I? They're only borrowed. I'll give them back, of course. Certainly I'm not a thief. I assure you, I'm here to help. Nothing more."

This wasn't entirely true. The Petit family in France was claiming what was legally theirs, half of the business, and they wished it to prosper, so he was there for reasons other than assisting her, no matter how he claimed to be at her service. He was here for the family. Now that he stood before her, he felt somewhat pained by the legal arrangements he was sent to oversee.

"Keep the clothing," the widow told him. "My cousin won't be returning. He's wise enough to stay in Paris. But please excuse me while I find my own clothes."

Frédéric waited at the table while the widow dressed and the children were sent off to school. He would have liked some tea, but did not ask for fear of overstepping his welcome. He wondered what sort of tea they drank here. Surely it was made of roses and jasmine rather than mere black tea leaves. The maid put a cup before him, as if she'd read his mind. Lemon and ginger. Sweet and sour.

"She's not going to like you," Rosalie told him. The maid had the baby on her lap, but she kept her eye on him. "So don't even try."

Rachel returned in a pale green dress, her hair knotted at the back of her head. It was the first time she had not worn her mourning clothes. Instead, she'd slipped on the dress Jestine had made. She told herself the dress was the first thing she found in her bureau, but that was not exactly the truth. The dress had pearl buttons, as French dresses often had, and a crinoline trimmed with lace.

No longer caught unawares, Rachel seemed different, more distant. Frédéric wanted that other moment back, when she'd first come out of her chamber, unguarded, her hair falling down her back. There were thousands of women in Paris wearing silk dresses, but he'd seen not a single one in a white shift.

"I presume you're here for business, so we should begin," she said to him formally.

One of the children sang a bit of a song, and Rachel laughed and once again was the woman he'd first spied, her upturned face filling with light, her mouth dark and beautiful. He felt he was seeing a secret, a vision granted to only a few. He could feel his desire when she glanced at him. As she caught his eye, her expression had darkened. Perhaps she could read his thoughts, which were embarrassing even to himself. The things he wished to do to this woman, he could not have brought himself to say aloud.

Rosalie went out with the children, and for a moment it was awkward between them, two strangers in a small room, the plates and dishes left on the table with crusts of bread and bits of fruit, flies gathering on the rims. The heat of the day was beginning. There was nothing and everything to say. Women were not supposed to be alone with men, but he was family and so young, only a few years older than David, the household's oldest boy. Surely there was nothing wrong in being in the same room.

She gave Frédéric another cup of tea and accidentally spilled some on his hand. He couldn't have cared less. He let the pain radiate through him. It seemed all of his senses were heightened. Though he assured her it was fine, and she hadn't burned him, she was unsure and placed a cool washcloth on his skin. His expression was unreadable. He didn't even seem to blink. There was a salve she could get for him.

"It will just take a minute," she said.

He told her please not to bother, he was fine. She took the cloth away and saw a blister rising. She could feel her concern but also much more. Something far too hot. She felt as if she were the one who might faint. He was right, she must let it be. She turned her back to him and wrung out the dishcloth. She was thinking too much about him already. He looked like a man who had stepped out of a cold world, in his gray boots, with his black hair tied back and his posture so straight, even though he'd been burned.

"We should go," she said.

"We should," he agreed.

They went downstairs, and Rachel introduced him to Monsieur Farvelle, who was now running the daily goings-on at the store. The air was so sweet it was difficult to breathe. Soon Frédéric would learn that everything on this island carried the aroma of molasses, but for now he equated the scent with desire. While the men spoke, Frédéric took a cursory glance at the shop books, quickly spying dozens of errors. Rachel sat in a chair, her hands folded, watching him. He felt himself grow feverish under her glance. He gently pointed out a few errors to Farvelle, who was not at all pleased to be upbraided by a stranger, and one as young as his own son.

"You're good at numbers," Rachel said, as they went to the shipping office at the rear of the store.

"I dream of them."

She laughed. "That's an odd dream to have. But who am I to talk? I dream of rain."

The corridor was small and packed with boxes. There were dust motes in the air, some as big as moths. He could not keep his eyes off her. He wondered if it had been her bed that he'd slept in, in the big house, and if the dream he'd had had been hers. He had despised rain when he was in France, but now he longed for that rainy dream, for the bed that might be hers, the pillows that were so deep, the open window and the yellow morning light and the cool, green dream they had shared.

She brought him to Mr. Enrique, who shook his hand and said, "Good morning, sir," as if they'd never met or discussed life on a personal level.

"Good morning," Frédéric replied, quite confused about the intricacies of social expectations here. He understood that he should follow Mr. Enrique's lead and act as if last night had never happened, and they had never dined together and discussed their personal histories. In Paris one's place in society was set; an individual did not have much to do with those outside his own position and faith. Jews were in a circle with other Jews, bankers with bankers, and so on. It all made perfect sense. Later Frédéric would understand that on this island there were the rules of what should be, and then the deeper truth of what actually was. People knew each other intimately, and then pretended they'd never met.

"First things first. Mr. Enrique is not to be removed from his position," Rachel told Frédéric, although she had no right to give orders.

"Of course." Frédéric did not wish his stewardship to be unpleasant, and there was no cause to disagree. It was in his best interest to keep Mr. Enrique on.

"And I need these papers signed immediately."

Rachel shoved a document in front of him, which he scanned, trying to make sense of it, though she was hurrying him along, handing over a pen, pointing out the place for his signature. When he hesitated she put her hands on her hips.

"I see you don't trust me, but I'm sure you will expect me to trust you," she said.

"Is business about trust or knowledge?" Frédéric asked. "I'm here to do what's best for you."

"This is best. These papers allow Rosalie to be a free woman. I haven't the right to do the signing."

Now he understood, Rosalie was a slave. He supposed she was, in essence, part of his uncle's estate, not that there was any reason for the family in France to be notified of this, for it was a violation of the deepest human right. Rachel was watching him carefully, and he could tell this was a moment in which she would either praise or condemn him. He already knew he didn't wish to lose her.

"Of course," he said once again.

When he glanced up, the widow and her clerk were exchanging a pleased look.

Frédéric handed her the document. She did not thank him, but rather studied him more closely than before. She was staring at his jacket. It was as if she could see beneath his clothes. "I presume you gave him my cousin's clothes," she said to Mr. Enrique in a teasing tone.

"He wasn't given them. He took what he wanted, though he swears he's not a thief." Mr. Enrique and Rachel often shared jokes, and they did so now, at Frédéric's expense. "You should be careful that he doesn't take too much from you without asking."

Rachel turned to glance at the nephew of her husband, the young man from France who was too handsome for his own good, who dreamed of numbers, who took what he wanted, and who now hung his head, embarrassed at the very idea of being judged untrustworthy, even if they were merely having fun with him.

"What do you have to say for yourself?" Rachel asked him. "Do you plan to steal from me?" She said so to taunt him, but all of her intentions took a turn when he raised his eyes. His look went through her. His eyes were some color that she couldn't define, a gray or green. They were the color of rain. She hadn't known rain could have a color; she'd thought it was clear, but she'd been mistaken.

"I would only take what you offered," he said.

Rachel was impressed by his forthrightness and not at all offended, as another woman might have been. If anything, she felt her interest deepen.

Something had come to her from Paris at last.

⟲❧⟳

FRÉDÉRIC WAS QUICKLY GRANTED his Burgher Brief by the business association, which allowed him to take over his uncle's holdings and be accepted into the community. He lived in a spare room in the store, below the apartment, beside the office where he worked. It was expected that he would move to his own lodgings when a property became available, not that he was in a hurry. He didn't even look for other accommodations, or respond to suggestions offered by the men of the congregation who knew of boardinghouses and rooms to let. He said he was too busy, and his time was taken up with his uncle's business matters, but the truth was, he did not wish to go anywhere else. In his current room there was a single window that let in more sunlight than had streamed through all of the windows in his family's home in France combined. Here, every day was a joy, bathed in light. Bananaquits nested outside his window and woke him with their song. Yet no matter how hot the weather, every night he dreamed of rain. It poured down in his dreams, and when he woke he felt much as a drowning man pulled from the sea might have as air rushed back into his being.

Inconveniences did not matter. He did not care for luxury. There was an outhouse beyond the shop and a washbasin on the dresser. He shaved only every other day, and tied his hair back with a string of leather. He sold the houses first, which paid off debts and gave the business a tidy sum to invest. Rachel came with him to walk through the empty houses. First they went to his uncle Isaac's house. There was an echo on the tile floors, a thickness to the air. She stopped on the threshold of the chamber she had shared with her husband and held out her hands as if in some sort of prayer. Frédéric stood beside her, his throat raw.

"She's gone." Rachel's expression was grave, her black eyes piercing.

"She?" Frédéric asked, thinking he must have heard incorrectly. Surely it was his uncle Isaac to whom Rachel referred.

"The ghost."

"Ah," Frédéric said, relieved that she was not still mourning her husband. "So the house was haunted."

"You don't believe me?" Rachel threw her shoulders back as if ready for a fight. "She was his first wife. The one he loved."

"He loved you," Frédéric said before he thought better of it.

"Why would you say that?"

Frédéric shrugged. "Because he'd be a fool not to."

They walked along the empty loggia that adjoined the rooms. All the furnishings had been sold and taken away. There was a poppet in a corner, a child's toy.

"You've seen the way he managed the business." Rachel's voice was soft. It was terrible to walk through an empty house, lost by mistakes of fortune. "Maybe he was a fool."

"Well, I'm not," Frédéric said simply.

They went out to the porch, then down to the gate decorated with herons. The sky was opalescent. Rachel shielded her eyes so that she might look into his. Doing so was like stepping into the rain.

MR. ENRIQUE WAS GIVEN the title of manager, and in return he worked long hours, teaching Frédéric the business. He was a good teacher and as talented at numbers as Frédéric was. Rosalie often brought them their dinner when they worked into the night. It wasn't long before Frédéric realized there was something between them, a tenderness brought by years of intimacy. "Your wife?" he asked one evening.

"Is that your business?" Enrique turned away, and Frédéric dropped the subject.

Later, as they were closing up the office for the day, Enrique said, "I had a wife once, but we argued. Now I don't know if she's alive. This was all on another island, another lifetime. So how can I marry?"

They kept their attention on the ledgers after that, for a discussion of one's personal life could lead to trouble. They both agreed that the store was the most profitable piece of the estate, and they concentrated on increasing the importance of sales, as Mr. Enrique suggested, for the shipping business was besieged by bad weather and pirates and taxes. Fate was a terrible business partner, Mr. Enrique told him. Frédéric took his manager's advice in all things: they would sell molasses and rum and let other men take their chances on shipping and ruination.

When he wasn't careful, Frédéric dreamed of Rachel. He kept his distance. He heard stories about her at the synagogue. He overheard other women say she thought too highly of herself, that she spoke her mind as if she were a man and was never polite to the other ladies. He walked away from such conversations. It was none of his business anyway. Still, when members of Blessings and Peace invited him to dinners, he had little choice but to attend. They were formal events, and he had only one black suit, which Rosalie pressed for him every time he went out in the evenings. He realized he was being introduced to all of the unwed young women and girls. At one dinner he was so overheated and nervous that he went into the courtyard, taking a glass of rum with him. It was even hotter outside, but at least he was alone. Or so he thought. At first there seemed to be a heron on the patio, one of those strange blue birds he'd spied in the marshes. Then Frédéric realized it was one of the older women from the congregation, wearing an azure-colored dress.

"Do you know what a sin is?" the old woman called to him.

"Pardon?" he said, taken aback. He waved away the moths that seemed to be attracted to the hair tonic he used.

"It's what you want and know you cannot have." It was Madame Halevy.

"Are you referring to the rum?" he asked in an amused tone.

"I'm referring to desire," Madame Halevy said.

"Well, thank you for your interest." Frédéric was doing his best to keep his wits about him. He thought perhaps he had run into a mind reader. He'd heard there were such women on this island.

"It's not interest." The old woman signaled him to help her up from the stone bench, and he had little choice but to do so. "It's a warning," she went on. "So you understand there is a covenant against incest."

"Madame, I'm sure I don't know what you're talking about."

"As a brother cannot lie with a sister, nor a father with a daughter, neither can a nephew and an aunt. You do not need to share blood to be in the same family."

He felt like thrashing her, old bones and all, but was polite, as he had been taught to be. "I don't know what would make you say such a thing," he said in a cold tone.

"Rachel makes me say such a thing," Madame Halevy said. "She has never understood she must obey the rules. For both your sakes, I'm hoping that you do."

He helped the old woman inside, then fled from the congregation. From then on, he kept to himself. The old woman's warning had made him reexamine his actions. Now when he had free time he explored the island. He swam in a waterfall that Enrique mentioned, a secret place set in a marshy area that was a nesting place for herons. Frédéric's first real bath, not one from a washbasin, was had among tiny blue fish that flashed around him. He quickly accepted the local wisdom that it was better to drink rum rather than wine. Rum kept away diseases, as did the netting that he strung around his small bed. Sometimes he went back to the place where he'd heard bees on his first day in Charlotte Amalie. He closed his eyes and listened to the thrum as bees darted among the flowers, and despite his resolve not to do so, he thought of Rachel.

When he visited his uncle's widow on Friday night after services, he was schooled in the proper way to hold a baby on his lap while he took his dinner. He tutored the boys with their schoolwork, and thought David had an especially good head for numbers. He told himself, and anyone who might bother to ask, that he went to the Friday-night dinners to be polite, and because it was his duty, and because in some way he was now the man of the house. At these times, and at all times, he did everything he could not to look at Rachel or imagine her in her white shift. Yet he seemed to have memorized that garment: the seams, the pearl buttons, the way it fit her body, the way he might undo it and tear it off her body, the way she might beg him to do so. He was furious with himself for thoughts he could not seem to control.

She was seven years older than he, and had lived a lifetime in those seven years. She had been a married woman, a widow, a mother, and he was nothing more than a young man who was good at numbers. Once, after leaving, he stopped on the street and glanced into the window. He saw her unpin her black hair. He stood there even though he knew she would remove her dress. It was as if his imagining had been willed into being and he couldn't turn away. Those next few movements when she stepped out of her clothes undid him. He could not look away. He heard bees somewhere, but he couldn't have told whether they were beside him in a hedge or halfway across the island. Afterward he walked through town, and then into the hills; he trekked for miles and miles, hoping he could walk away his thoughts. He found himself lost in a meadow. Everything was pitch. He felt alone in all the world, more so even than when he was at sea, where no one would have known if he slipped into the waves. He panicked when he saw eyes staring at him through the dark. He thought he had come upon the devil, and that the devil had been the one to give him the thoughts he had about Rachel, and now he would be punished. But when he looked more carefully he saw it was only a goat, kept behind a wooden fence, staring out at him. He laughed at himself and his fears then. He had told Rachel he wasn't a fool, but now he appeared to be one.

ONE EVENING AT FRIDAY-NIGHT dinner, Rachel touched his hand with hers while passing him his plate. It was nothing, a passing stroke, yet his flesh burned. He did not care to have his meal. He saw her later, pouring cold water on her own hands, and then, quite suddenly, he knew she felt as he did. After that he worked harder, kept later hours. He wrote to his family in France, long letters about the business, and did not mention her. At night he listened to the whir of mosquitoes and moths. He felt the blue-black darkness all around him. He wished that when he awoke he would find that he'd forgotten the first time he saw her.

There was a night she came to his room when he was asleep. He was dreaming that she was there in her white petticoat, and when he opened his eyes there she was, holding a lantern. She whispered, "Hurry up, get dressed," then went into the corridor to wait for him. He leapt from bed and pulled on his clothes, hurrying to see if she had been real or the work of a fevered brain. He carried his boots and darted into the corridor. She laughed when she saw him rush from his room, so tall and lanky and disoriented, wiping the sleep from his eyes.

"You look like you expected something else," she said, for she was fully clothed in her green dress and she wore a light cape.

Her amusement made him slightly angry, or perhaps it was the pure hurt he felt when he thought about the fact that she had belonged to his uncle, an old man who had ruined the business. "You came to me," he said coldly, then instantly regretted his tone.

"So I did." She nodded, chastised. "I don't deny it."

It was as though everyone else in the household had disappeared, magicked away in the blue night. Rosalie lived with them during the week. She slept in her own room when she cared for the children, the door open so she could hear the babies if they woke. All were asleep. No one seemed a part of this world, except for the widow and her nephew. The air was heavy, enchanted, and the frogs made a singing noise that was urgent and low. A few days earlier, Frédéric had discovered a frog under his pillow, green with a red dot on its back.

"Poisonous," Rosalie had declared when he described the creature at breakfast. "You'd better watch out for yourself. This isn't Paris."

He'd learned later on from the children that this wasn't true, the frog was harmless and Rosalie was having fun with him. Now every time Rosalie saw him, she said, "Are you watching out for frogs?" It had become something of a joke between them.

But his uncle's widow leading him out into the dark night was not a joke. He thought he could hear his own heart, and he hoped she couldn't hear the thudding, as if he were a schoolboy who couldn't control himself. They went down the steep street, empty now, and headed out of town. The air was soft and thick as they approached a beach Rachel wanted him to see. It was the time when the turtles came to shore. She explained they could not hold a lantern, for it would confuse the creatures that had come to lay their eggs, drawn from the sea by the moon's light. She blew out the flame, and then they lay down in the sand. He stretched himself out beside her, the length of their bodies against each other. She told him about the turtle that was half human, who looked enough like a woman, and made every man who saw her fall in love with her. Some of her suitors dove into the water after her, even the ones who didn't know how to swim, but she didn't look back.

This story worried Frédéric. Was it a warning or a confession? Was she telling him to stay away, or urging him to follow her?

"I used to come here with my best friend, but she doesn't want to see miracles anymore," Rachel confided. "She doesn't believe in them, but I'm surprised to say I do."

He was grateful to whoever this friend was; her lack of faith meant he was the one who was beside Rachel to see the miracle of this night. The sand was cold and damp, the air nearly wet as the sea, but he was burning up now. He couldn't believe she didn't know, and he half expected her to slap him for his thoughts, but when she looked at him he saw a sort of compassion in her eyes, as if she pitied him for being human, and perhaps she pitied herself as well.

There were hundreds of turtles coming from the sea. Some walked right past them, lumbering across the beach, intent on finding the perfect stretch of sand in which to nest. The moon was pale and full beneath banks of clouds, and there were pinpricks of stars. The brightest light came from the reflections of the whitecaps of the sea. And then the clouds shifted and the moon lit a path for the turtles; the beach turned green as more and more made their way ashore. It took all night for the turtles to lay their eggs, and to hide them under the sand, and then, at last, exhausted, to return to the sea.

As Rachel and Frédéric walked home, morning was breaking through the sky. The world was pale and beautiful, filled with a weave of birdsong, music so loud it seemed to Frédéric that his head would burst. They had not slept, and so the night seemed to have lasted far longer than any ordinary night.

"I should hate you," Rachel said.

She was wound up in a nameless longing, and she blamed him for her raw emotions. His presence was like a spell, his name an incantation. She had been avoiding him, but that tactic hadn't worked. She hadn't been to the cemetery once since his arrival. She ignored her children when they cried. She locked herself in her chamber every night and stared into the mirror, wondering if she was old, and if there was a cure for aging, some leaf or herb she might ingest or apply to make him want her. She should have had nothing to do with him, he was the enemy, the unwanted relative, but now it was too late. She knew too much about him, and everything he did took on a cast of intimacy. How he hung his jacket on the chair before he set to work, how he cut his food so carefully, how he looked at her when he thought her back was turned to him, how he gasped when the first turtles went past, how he'd moaned when she accidentally touched him the first time. Adelle had told her that her fate was waiting for her, and that she would recognize it when it arrived.

He pulled her to him when they passed the door of a neighbor's house, into the dark entryway, where he kissed her. He was so ardent that she could hardly catch her breath, but she did not consider telling him this could not be. She felt his heat as he shifted his hands inside her cloak, then inside her dress, the one Jestine had made her to remind her of spring. Now she knew, after seven children, after all these years of waiting for another life, listening for rain: This was what love was. She did not stop him, but fell into him, and then there was a noise, a bird perhaps, and he startled and quickly moved away as if he'd committed a criminal offense. In the traditions of their society, what he had done was both immoral and illegal. He apologized and left her at her door without another word.

HE TOLD HIMSELF THE relationship with his uncle's wife couldn't go any further. He spent his evenings with Enrique and no longer came to the dinner table on Friday nights. It didn't matter if he and Rachel were related by marriage rather than by blood—such things could not happen within a family, there was a covenant against it, as he had recently been reminded. His hours at the synagogue increased. He had been known as a pious man, now people wondered if perhaps he wished to be considered for the governing board, as the synagogue appeared to be his life. Was it pride or penance that made him sweep out the entranceway, gather prayer books, tend to the garden, pulling out weeds by hand? Either way, he was to be commended, and people spoke of him fondly and with pride.

When he saw Rachel in the store or on the street, he lowered his eyes. He made certain to call her Madame Petit, to remind himself that she was his uncle's widow, nothing more. He'd been enchanted. It happened to men on this island. He'd heard stories about it in the taverns and taphuses, men who lost sight of themselves and jumped off cliffs, swam out to sea, swore they saw women in the treetops or beneath the water.

He tried his best to be sociable, and accepted invitations from those who wished to know him better. All the same, he fidgeted and stammered when he spoke. He soon got the reputation of being shy, for he often excused himself, leaving before dessert was served. He was too pious, perhaps, to be looking for a wife. He went to bed early, blew out his lantern, tried his best to sleep. He knew that she was in the room above his. He often heard something outside his door. It was not a frog. Frogs made no noise. It was his uncle's widow, wandering through the store. In his imaginings she was wearing the white shift, a rose in the dark night. Once he dreamed she was in his arms, that she'd come into his room, and to his bed. She wanted him in that dream, and told him what to do and how to please her. In the morning, when he licked his lips he tasted molasses. He often thought of the old woman in the garden. Again, she must have read his mind, for she wrote a note, brought to him by an ancient maid who could barely walk down the path. *Ne détruisez pas cette famille et, en même temps, vous-même. Do not destroy yourself and this family.*

"Do you have a reply for Madame Halevy?" the maid asked him.

There were bees in the garden and a tree that was said to have come all the way from France and the sort of heat that made you want to close your eyes and dream.

"No," Frédéric told her. "I do not."

⌒∾⌒

THE SUMMER CAME AND went, the heat of it a mystery and a delight to him. He wanted something burned out of him. He went to the waterfall at dusk, the hour when the mosquitoes appeared and most people knew enough to stay away, and he submerged himself in the cool brackish water. The children adored him. He played with the young ones in the garden and taught the older boys about the business. The little girl, Delphine, was especially attached to him. She accidentally called him Papa one glimmering afternoon, and afterward he did not play with them as often, and he asked the children to call him Monsieur Frédéric. Because he no longer ate with them, Rachel left a plate in the corridor for him on Friday nights.

"You prefer to eat in your own room?" she asked.

"There's no reason for me to impose on your family," he responded.

"You've already imposed a thousand times over, what difference does another dinner make?"

"So you admit it, I've imposed," he said.

"Frédéric," his uncle's wife said in a soft voice. "I will not bite you if that's what you're afraid of."

"I'm not," he was quick to say, for in his dreams he wanted exactly that.

He continued to take his dinner at a desk in his room, and even then, he could not enjoy his meal. He lost weight. He often could not sleep. But he stayed away from his uncle's wife, though he thought he heard her, now and then, late at night. Or perhaps that was only his wish. That one day she would step over the threshold and tell him that she wanted him, and he would respond gratefully, willingly, without any attempt to stop.

HE DIDN'T KNOW HE was ill at first, for the weather was changing, and there was the sudden damp chill that comes when the air is windy and blue. Summer was over, and he thought it was the coolness of the season rather than his own constitution that made him feel so weak. He had been in Charlotte Amalie for eight months. More and more he considered going back to Paris to stop himself from acting on impulse, a challenge every day. He could have Mr. Enrique take over the day-to-day business, for they were equals when it came to such things, and he trusted the clerk's good sense, but he stayed because he could not imagine the world without the widow. Paris became more and more distant, darker, a place of overcast skies, a mottled fish-colored river running through it.

And then the darkness gathered within him and he could feel it like a cloud inside his lungs, and he became ill. There were trade winds from Africa that rattled the leaves, and flocks of birds overhead flew south. The darkness of his home had followed him here. He was freezing cold. He couldn't keep food down, and then he could not sleep. He felt something creep into his bones, as if he were under a spell. His sleep lasted too long and he couldn't force himself to wake. On days when it was chilly he sweated through his clothes, and then in the bright sunlight he shivered. Maybe such things happened on this island, and a man had to fight this kind of exhaustion any way he could. He drank rum for its healing properties. He ate only fruit. He wore his jacket when he went to bed, and kept his boots on as well, to keep him warm. He saw the frog again, and he wondered if it had poisoned him. It sat beside his bed, but he was too tired to catch it and set it into the garden.

One morning he did not arrive at the office. Mr. Enrique found him in his chamber, shivering in his small bed, his clothes strewn around his room, plates of uneaten food on his desk. It was an unseasonably warm day, and the temperature was ninety-four degrees. Frédéric called for a quilt and then another blanket. The doctor came and said it might be yellow fever, they would have to wait and see. He let some of Frédéric's blood. Frédéric didn't seem to notice, not the cut with the scalpel or the loss of blood or the fact that he was talking out loud, saying what he should not. Rachel and Rosalie took turns holding cold wet cloths to his face. Once Rachel put her hand inside his shirt, and felt for his heart. He was burning there, too.

She went to the cemetery and brought the last of the boughs of that season's red flowers. She begged her predecessor for help in keeping death away from him. She had cared for Esther's children and loved them as though they were her own, surely she should be granted this one wish. But his illness grew worse. It seemed that Esther no longer listened to her. Her ghost had dissolved as soon as her husband joined her. It was no longer possible to reach her.

Monsieur DeLeon, along with some of the elders from the synagogue, came to pay their respects. They gathered around Frédéric's bed and said the evening prayers. There were ten of them, a minyan, the number of men needed in the Jewish faith for an official gathering. "We are here for him," Monsieur DeLeon said as the men left. "For his time in this world and in the next."

All at once Rachel understood they expected Frédéric to die. She saw how veined with pallor he was, the tinge of yellow around his eyes, his listless form. Seeing him this way, she knew what must be done, just as she knew she didn't much care what the doctor or the men from the congregation predicted.

Though Jestine no longer liked to be around children, she had been keeping Rachel's with her, in case the fever was one that might spread. She hadn't hesitated to take them in. Now Rachel returned to the house on stilts. All of her children were asleep on quilts spread upon the floor, breathing softly, lulled by the sound of the sea.

"I need you to help me," she told Jestine.

Rachel's hair was in tangles and she wore an old skirt, one she used to put on when they escaped into the hills to do as they pleased for an afternoon. Again, Jestine didn't hesitate. They woke David, the eldest, and told him he was in charge. He was sixteen, old enough to be responsible. If he was shocked by his stepmother's appearance and how rail thin she was, he didn't say.

Jestine found a lantern and wrapped a shawl around her shoulders. They went into the hills, to an herb man Adelle often went to for help. Jestine had been there once as a child and believed she might be able to find his house. Rachel thought about Paris as they walked through the dark, slapping away mosquitoes. The bells in the chapels, the stones on the streets, the doves in the parks, the lawns that were a deep, velvet green. If Frédéric had stayed there he would never have become ill. Rachel's resolve to make her way to France was like a stone inside of her, rattling as she walked through the tall weeds. Frogs sang beside a stream. She wondered if Lyddie had already begun to forget everything she had known of their world: the dark woods that tumbled down the mountainside, the heavy curtain of dampness in the air, the purple flowers growing on vines, the hummingbirds that came to drink from blossoms in the gardens, her mother, her aunt Rachel, her life before she was taken.

Rachel and Jestine held hands as they made their way through the dark. Before they knew it they had found the cottage. The herb man

stood on the threshold. He was old, but he hadn't been sleeping. It was as
if he'd known someone was coming here to him. They told him Adelle
had spoken highly of him and his cures. He invited Jestine in but insisted
that Rachel wait outside. Perhaps he didn't trust her. She didn't mind.
Jestine went into his cottage alone. She told him there was a man suffering from fever and chills and the doctor could not name his disease. It
seemed like yellow fever, but he burned with such intensity the doctor
thought it was too late for him.

"This disease takes three cures," the herbalist said.

"Does it?" Jestine was skeptical. "Does that mean you will charge me
three prices?"

The herb man gave her a swift glance, but he did not answer. He
made a tea mixture from the leaves of the silk-cotton tree that would be
healing, and then he made a second packet of tea from the bark of a mahogany tree mixed with salt that would relieve fever. Finally he made a
poultice from the tamarind tree, brought to this island from Africa, to
relieve both fever and pain, especially in the liver, where yellow fever
collected.

He wanted to be paid for his work, as any man would. All Jestine had
to offer was Rachel's mother's pearls strung around her throat, which she
handed over willingly. "I never liked them," she told Rachel later. "They
felt cold on my skin."

After Jestine had paid for the cures, she came out of the herbalist's
house. She held a package tied with string. "He asked me to kiss him for
luck," she told Rachel. "I told him if this man of yours lives, I'll send you
back to kiss him, and he said that would be fine."

They walked back through the vines.

Rachel was thoughtful. "He's not my man."

Jestine looked at her, then they both laughed.

"You can't fool me," Jestine said. "Just everybody else."

They passed a ring of stones that was all that remained of a house
that had been abandoned. A fire had recently been lit, leaving a charred

odor. Cooking utensils were scattered about. Someone was moving in, trying to rebuild.

"Be careful with this," Jestine said when she handed over the remedy. They had reached the outskirts of the city. Everything was midnight blue, the way it is in dreams. "Maybe his fate is already set down. If you save him you may change everything that would have happened if his illness had taken him, the good along with the bad."

Rachel hardly listened. She already knew this time she would decide her own fate. She hurried home, running most of the way. Rosalie had been sitting up with Frédéric, and now Rachel told her she could go.

"What if you need me?" Rosalie said.

"I already needed you and you were always here, but Mr. Enrique doesn't need to be lonely tonight."

When Rosalie was gone, Rachel made the first tea and carried it to Frédéric's room. He was disappearing; she could barely see him beneath the quilt. The room was so quiet she could hear a moth at the window. The same moth she had heard as a girl when she wished to wake up on the other side of the world, in a bed in Paris.

Frédéric sat up when she asked him to, but he was so weak that swallowing the tea was difficult. When she made the second tea, he could take only a few sips, so she had to feed him with a spoon. As he drank the tea she told him a story about a bird as tall as a man who danced in a marsh and made his beloved fall in love with him. She wept as she told the story, consumed with panic and the thought that Frédéric might die. She laid the poultice over his broad chest, covering his heart and lungs, and then his liver, where the illness dwelled. His body responded to her, he moved toward her without thinking. She did not know why she was shivering. It was brutally hot and Rachel was drenched with sweat. She took off everything but her white chemise underbodice and pantalets. Still she was burning. She feared she had caught the disease, but she didn't care. She got into bed beside him and pulled the quilt over them.

Rosalie found them that way in the morning, wrapped around each

other as drowning people are said to be, so that it is often impossible to
tell who was meant to be the rescuer, and who had been drowning. She
had been expecting as much, and she hadn't been surprised when Rachel
sent her away. She knew what love could do to a person. She would wait
till the next day to collect the children, and let Rachel and this young
man go on sleeping. They held on to each other, dreaming of rain.

THE NEW SYNAGOGUE WAS finally finished in that year, with mahogany benches and an altar set in the center of the hall, in the Spanish style.
It had taken a long time, but now it was perfect, and no fire or storm
could pull it down. There was a low carved wall separating the women
from the men. The floor was kept as sand, as it had been in the past in
Spain and Portugal, though there were many Jews recently arrived from
Denmark and Amsterdam who thought it madness to have this daily reminder of a brutal history when every prayer was a secret and every Jew
was an enemy of the state. Rachel Pomié Petit was past thirty now, and
although she'd been considered plain as a girl, she had become quite
beautiful, her dark hair wound up and kept in place with tortoiseshell
combs, her eyes like black water. Getting older had given her more definition. There was a ferocity to her features now. It was difficult to fault
her, for after all her losses she'd managed better than most women in her
situation. She ran her household frugally, her business was prospering at
last, and her children were well mannered. The boys that had been her
husband's were both considered men now and worked in the store alongside the nephew from Paris.

As for that handsome man, Frédéric Pizzarro, he, too, had turned out
to be standoffish after such a promising start. He refused all overtures of
friendship, though he came to pray every morning and every evening.
He excused himself from social events and dinners, even when the most
accomplished women from the Sisterhood invited him. There were
daughters who would have liked to have gotten to know him better,
young women who were clearly interested. One, Maria Mendes, was so

intent on charming him that she took to waiting outside the store on a daily basis, dressed in her finery. She was only nineteen, quite beautiful, but Frédéric treated her as if she were a child. "I'm sorry," he said to her, after he'd realized she was pursuing him. "I am much too busy to do anything other than attend to business."

She didn't give up, for all men say they're busy until they're not, and then one day, as she stood there patiently, waiting for him to change his mind, a pitcher of water was poured down from an upstairs window, drenching her. She looked up, sputtering, and although the window was being closed and the person responsible was backing away, she told her friends she'd spied the widow's shadow. Rachel Pomié Petit was like a spider, Maria said, her web stretched out to keep other women from Monsieur Pizzarro. Frédéric was still well thought of even though he was not socially inclined; he was considered to be a man of integrity who honored God every day. It was said he retreated to his room after work. His interests were mostly those of the mind. He was known to be a great reader, and he tutored the Petit children in mathematics. He was often seen with the children, who had grown more than accustomed to him, treating him as if he were an older, wiser brother. When work and studies were completed, he took them to the wharf to go fishing. He liked to run, for the sheer joy of it, and the boys often went running with him through the streets, down toward the beaches. There was nothing suspicious about all this, and yet there were those in the congregation who felt Pizzarro's presence in the widow's home was improper. He should find his own house, his own woman, these people said. He had helped her long enough.

One of the men from the congregation passed by the Petit store on a dark, blue night, and after he did, nothing was the same. Whether his knowledge of the situation was gained by accident or by design, he never said, but when this gentleman, a young cousin of Madame Jobart, glanced at the window he spied a woman in Frédéric Pizzarro's room. The curtains were drawn, but he was able to see her, naked, on the bed. The truth was this prying man had crept quite close to the window. From his hiding place beneath a vine of bougainvillea he had heard a woman moaning with desire. He waited in the shrubbery, listening; when he reported his story he failed to mention that he had reached through the open window to lift the curtains, the better to see. It was Isaac Petit's widow he spied, and despite what people said about her cold nature, she was clearly more than friendly to her young nephew, and it seemed she was sharing not only her home, but also his bed.

News of the scandal went from house to house, like the angel of death on the eve of Passover. It appeared like a mist, red in color, sifting down chimneys and through windows. Now when Rachel Petit walked through town she did not have to bypass anyone, they avoided her. Her path was red, for she had committed a sin in the eyes of their faith. People crossed the street rather than confront her, as they had when they saw Nathan Levy with his African wife. The rumors had not yet come inside the Petit house, and the couple thought no one knew. At the dinner table, with the children around them, Rachel and Frédéric made certain not to sit too near to each other. But at night, when everyone else was asleep, they drew the curtains, then closed the shutters tightly and latched them, as people did whenever there was a storm brewing. It was possible that they had the sense they had been spied upon, for now they always found each other in the dark.

TWO WOMEN FROM THE congregation, old friends of Rachel's mother, invited her to tea. She refused. She sent a note thanking them and stating she was far too busy. She had her children, the store, endless responsibilities, and therefore sent regrets. Her lack of time was not the only reason she did not wish to see them, and the older women knew this. They wanted to discuss the red mist, the rumors that had caused a division in their community and might soon have Europeans looking too closely at the congregation's affairs. They wanted to remind Rachel of her debt to her mother's memory, so they came to her. They waited outside the shop, and when Rachel came out, carrying her youngest child, Isaac, born months after his father's death, with two other children trailing behind her, her mother's friends followed her into the street and talked to her there, as they would a common whore. The women were Madame Halevy and Madame Jobart, Sara Pomié's closest friends. They had been to the Pomié house nearly every week when Rachel's mother was alive, and had attended both Rachel's wedding and her parents' funerals. They had been among the mourners at Isaac Petit's funeral and had noticed that his widow did not cry. All the same, they'd had their maids deliver baskets of food for her children and black mourning clothing for Rachel, who insisted upon wearing a single black dress. Now they noticed she had on a pretty green frock, inappropriate for a woman who had lost her husband less than a year earlier.

"Many women are delirious after their husbands' death," Madame Halevy said to her. "They stay in a sort of madness for months, or even years. Madame Jobart and I are both widows. We understand your grief." She looked at Rachel carefully. "If grief is what it is."

"What are you suggesting?" Rachel said, curious to see just how brutally honest Madame Halevy would be.

"I'm suggesting you listen to someone older and wiser for once in your life."

It was an honor to be addressed by Madame Halevy, but Rachel did not consider her advice worth having. She knew why her mother's friends had come. It was not out of concern, but rather an issue of control. They would tell her that the situation in her house was improper and Rachel should be looking for a husband among the older, widowed men in the congregation.

"Some women turn to the wrong person for solace," Madame Halevy told Rachel.

"Do they?" Rachel said. "Do they turn to you?"

"Let us help you," Madame Jobart suggested. She was involved at the synagogue's school, and had gone so far as to question Rachel's children.

They called Monsieur Pizzarro Freddy, and they didn't seem to understand what she meant when she asked where he slept. *His room,* she had been told by one of the sons. *I don't think he sleeps,* she had been told by the other. "Once you are involved in the right activities," Madame Jobart now suggested to Rachel, "you avoid any actions that can lead to disaster."

"Perhaps we can help find you a suitable match," Madame Halevy added.

The children, quiet and well behaved, were listening in. Isaac was quiet in his mother's arms, his eyes wide.

"Thank you for your consideration." Rachel's face was burning. She was certain they had a list of old men who would just as soon have a maid as a wife. She swallowed the words she wished to say, having practiced trying to tame her arrogance in every conversation she had ever had with her mother. "At the moment I'm quite busy with my children."

"We would hate to see you make a mistake," the women who were not her friends told her.

"Everyone makes mistakes," Rachel said.

"Not like this," she was told by Madame Halevy. She pulled Rachel aside. "I spoke with Frédéric," she said. "But it is clear he is under some sort of spell."

"You spoke with him?" Rachel was furious. "Who are you to say anything?"

"I was your mother's friend, therefore I am trying to do as she would have if she were still alive. Your feelings about this man may seem earth-shattering now, but what is love if not an enchantment. Is it worth it to destroy the lives of your children? If you choose to be an outcast, so be it, but it will be their fate as well."

"What do you know about love?"

"It's ruin I know about," Madame Halevy told her. "Be as smart as you think you are. Put your heart away and listen to me."

Rachel took the children home and left them in Rosalie's care. She

needed time to think things through. She walked along the beach where
the turtles nested, where she and Frédéric had lain together in the sand
watching a miracle. She considered what Rosalie said could happen if
you loved someone too much. She remembered everything Jestine had
lost in the name of love. Her thoughts were scattered and she could not
gather them together. And then she realized she could not act on thoughts
alone.

At night she lay beside Frédéric in his small bed. She went there after
the children were asleep, moving so quietly through the corridors that
she might well have been a ghost herself. Sometimes she could hear the
rain when they fell asleep together. He would say how wrong it was,
how he was betraying his uncle and, most important, defiling her. It was
at these times she remembered how young he was. He had no idea she
didn't care about any of that. And anyway, such regret did not stop him.
He often pushed a chair against the door so none of the children could
wander in accidentally. He kept a hand over her mouth so she would not
cry out, but there was a time when neither could control themselves.
Emma came to the door, frightened, asking if there were ghosts in the
house for she had heard their moaning. Rachel slipped on her nightgown
and opened the door; she scooped her daughter up to put her back to
bed. "There are no such things," she whispered. But Emma had seen a
ghost in her mother's bed. He had taken on the form of their beloved
Freddy. In the morning Emma left a circle of salt around the chair where
her uncle usually sat, for Rosalie had said that spirits feared not only the
color blue but the sting of salt as well.

That same night Frédéric asked to marry her. He did it in the French
manner, formally. He had planned the evening, asking Rosalie to take the
children out, going to the finest jewelers, where he bought a slim gold
band that was exquisite, with hallmarks from France. He took pink flowers from the garden for their table, but was stung while doing so. When
he came inside with the bougainvillea, Rachel saw that he'd been hurt.
She paid no attention to the flowers, but instead took his fingers into her

mouth. The old women in town said a bee sting could be soothed in this manner, but Frédéric was inflamed. He took her to bed right then and wouldn't let her leave, even when Rosalie called for her that supper needed to be started. He kept one hand over her mouth so she couldn't answer, and she bit him as she had in his dream, and he laughed to think there was so little room between the everyday world and his dreams.

At last, Rachel moved away and slipped on her dress. While her back was turned, Frédéric went onto one knee, without a stitch of clothing on, and asked her to be his wife. Rachel laughed so hard she collapsed beside him on the floor.

Frédéric shook his head, hurt. "You're laughing at me."

"I'm not," she insisted. "It's simply that we can't."

"Of course we can." He stood and turned away from her as he began to dress.

Rachel went to embrace him, resting her head against his back. She felt everything inside of him, including the hurt she had just caused him. She loved him twice as much as she had only a moment ago.

"Are you certain you want to face Madame Halevy?" she asked.

Now it was his turn to laugh. "I thought you had no fear of that witch. I know that I don't. This is our business, not hers or anyone else's. In the end they'll be won over."

"You don't know these people. They have lived a hundred lives of suffering, all for their freedom. There's a reason for their rules and a reason they can't abide people like me. They will turn against us."

"No," Frédéric insisted. "They'll have no choice but to accept us."

He kissed her without stopping, and she knew what Madame Halevy had said was true, and that she would bring ruin on them if it was her fate to do so.

She said yes to his proposal, but refused to wear his ring until they were wed. She walked along the beach in the evenings, wondering if she should reconsider. She was the older, more experienced person. She should have known better and called a halt to their love affair. She could have written to his family and insisted they bring him home and send someone in his place, an old uncle, a married couple, the nastiest man in the family.

She had tried her best to keep Frédéric away. After Isaac's death she had written a letter to his nephew, suggesting he stay in France. *Thank you for your kindness, but don't feel you must come to our Island, for I am fine on my own.* He'd written back, *Of course I will come to assist you.* She had cursed him, but in the morning after she'd read his response she'd woken to rainfall though it was the dry season. Now she reread his letter and noticed a line scrawled beneath his name she'd overlooked before.

I will think of nothing but you.

Every night she walked farther, until there came an evening when she was so deep in thought she paid no attention to her whereabouts. Before she knew it she was lost, even though she'd spent her childhood in these hills. She found herself on a path that led into the mountains. She heard running water. The waterfall. It sounded like a heartbeat. She thought about love and what a mystery it was, how when it came it seemed to be inevitable.

She had stumbled upon the herbalist's house. She had no idea how she had discovered this place, which was so hidden even Jestine had had trouble remembering where it was. Perhaps everything that had happened was meant to be, for this was where her love had led her. The herb man came outside as if he'd been expecting her. She owed him something, it was true. "Thank you for giving me my life," she said. She kissed him then, and although he neither thanked her nor stopped her, he accepted her gratitude.

THEY WENT TO THE synagogue to ask to be married. They wore their best clothes when they went. Both were rattled, filled with nerves. But they needn't have dressed in their finery for the occasion, as they were not allowed into the Reverend's office. His secretary said he was too busy, and when they'd sat there for more than four hours, with people going in and out to meet with the Reverend, Frédéric rapped on the door. Now his secretary told Frédéric the good man had gone home to dinner. They went back the next day, and again they were denied. They did this for a week, wearing the same clothes. Each day they were told the Reverend could not see them and each day they waited on a carved wooden bench. At last the Reverend sent them a written message that his assistant brought into the corridor where they were waiting. Frédéric read it, then crumpled it, dropping it on the floor before he stalked away. Alone in the corridor, Rachel bent to retrieve the missive directed to Frédéric.

It is a sin and an abomination to lay with a member of your own family, as well as a criminal act. We suggest you return to Paris.

Frédéric was waiting for her on the street. Rachel had brought along her mother's wedding veil. She gave it to the first woman who passed by, a young African woman who thanked her for the gift, for it was beautiful French lace.

"I never cared for it," Rachel told Frédéric.

He laughed, which was a relief. He had seemed so hurt and confused to have been turned away and told he was a criminal.

"I never care for anyone's opinion of me either," Rachel said.

"I've heard that about you." He grinned at her. "I've heard many things about you."

"It's all true." Rachel might have felt herself to be a fool, wearing her best clothing and standing in the street, but she did not. They walked back the way they had come. Some who spied on them said they were hand in hand, though they were so close to one another it was difficult to tell.

IT WAS A SURPRISE to some and not to others when, two years after her husband died, and less than a year after his nephew had arrived on the island, Rachel Pomié Petit appeared to be expecting a child. She acted as if no one noticed, but in fact she was all anyone could talk about. In every household the scandal was discussed at breakfast and then again at the dinner table. Those who so blatantly broke rules usually had the decency to disappear; they withdrew from the congregation and went to the Carolinas or South America rather than bring shame upon their people. But not Rachel Pomié Petit. If anything, she grew more defiant with each passing day. Some people said that a pelican flew above her when she brought her children to the synagogue's school, perhaps to prevent taunts from the other children. As it was, no one said a word about her condition. Not the children or their parents or the women of Blessings and Peace and Loving Kindness. They were all waiting to see what would happen next.

That handsome man, Frédéric Pizzarro, still came to the synagogue to pray in the morning and at sundown, even though no one spoke to him and no man would sit next to him. He didn't seem to mind. He had been something of a loner since he'd first arrived. When Rachel Pomié Petit was too huge for anyone to ignore her circumstances, she stayed at home, where it was said that Frédéric Pizzarro had moved into her room without the benefit of a marriage contract.

The family in Bordeaux, business partners worried for their financial future, heard the gossip and immediately denounced the relationship. The couple didn't seem to notice their disapproval, or if they did, they didn't care. Frédéric did not answer the frantic letters from his relatives, but merely continued to send a monthly business report. When the baby's time came, on a bright February day, Rachel called for Jestine, who helped to deliver her. After only a few weeks Madame Petit could be seen carrying the baby through town as if she were a married woman, as if the father of her child was not the nephew of her husband, as if sin was the last thing on her mind.

CHAPTER SIX

The Night of the Old Year

CHARLOTTE AMALIE, ST. THOMAS

1826

RACHEL POMIÉ PETIT PIZZARRO

I f I had locked myself away to wear mourning clothes for the rest of my life the members of the congregation would have certainly approved. Many would have preferred I give my baby to a family who couldn't have a child of their own. Every door shut. When I walked through the marketplace the other women passed by, ignoring me. I was a cautionary tale, and young girls especially fled from me. I came to understand why the pirates' wives had lived alone in the caves, not wanting even one another's company. It was easier not to face judgment, especially from your own kind.

We named our son Joseph Félix, a second son named after my predecessor's child to bring good fortune. But he was a pale, quiet child who never fussed, too quiet, I believed. I wondered if he'd been cursed as I carried him, if the whispers about me had seeped inside and harmed him in some way, for he was listless and seemed to lack spirit. I kept him close, and at night I often took him into bed with us, so that our bodies might warm him and keep him safe despite the cold reception of our own people. For months after the birth, Frédéric had gone to the elders of our community, begging them to let us marry, but each time he was refused. The Reverend would not see him, and when Frédéric insisted on intruding on the council, the elders who made decisions for all, they disrespected him, suggesting that he find his own lodgings and look for a suitable wife.

Frédéric told me that Monsieur DeLeon had taken him aside. He cared for me and had known me since I was a child. "I've done all I can on your behalf," he told Frédéric, "and will continue to do so, but this has always been the rule here. No marriage inside of a family."

"I'm not her family," Frédéric insisted.

"Do you run her father's business? Are you her husband's nephew?" The men exchanged a look. "On this island, that's family," Monsieur DeLeon informed him.

The council's advice was that Frédéric return to France with haste, before the Danish authorities became interested in what was a personal matter between Jews. Frédéric came home from this meeting exhausted and sick at heart. He had always been the good son, the reliable brother and cousin, the young man who could be called upon and trusted. The judgments of others weighed upon him. Rosalie told me that in the market, people said I was a witch and had cast a spell upon him, and perhaps that was true. Indeed I wanted him to defy everyone, even God if necessary, not that I believed God would be against a love like ours. We had nothing to repent for and nothing to feel guilty about.

Because we were unmarried, my son's name wasn't written into the Book of Life, which charted every birth, marriage, and death in our community. That meant he did not exist within God's sight, and should he die, he could not be buried in our cemetery. Eight days after our son's birth, Monsieur DeLeon brought over a man whose duty it was to circumcise boys of our faith. The ceremony was performed after dusk, when no one was aware that this man was in my house. Rosalie cleaned off the kitchen table, and put down a clean white linen, and even when there was blood the child did not cry.

Since no one at the synagogue would list him in the official records, I was forced to see to it myself. The old man who was the caretaker let me in because I behaved as though I belonged. I told him I'd been sent to tidy up and brought a broom along to convince him. A woman who knows what she wants, Adelle always told me, is likely to receive it. I was sure of myself, at least on the outside. I nodded and passed through the synagogue's gates without the least bit of trouble. The caretaker bowed and called me Madame. I didn't correct him or let him know that most people in the congregation would have referred to me as a whore. I thought I spied a heron in the garden, or perhaps it was a woman sitting in the dappled shade where there was a small stone fountain.

It was exactly two o'clock, the hottest hour of the day, when most people went home to drowse in their parlors or bedchambers, and the stores and cafés were shuttered. My youngest children were being cared for by Rosalie, which allowed me the freedom to ensure that my newborn would be known to God. I found the most recent book and wrote in the date of Joseph Félix Pizzarro's birth, with myself and Frédéric listed as his parents. My script was careful and legible, so that no one would refute my son's rights to be a member of our community. When I put away the book, I discovered that the files could indeed do with tidying, though I had no intention of doing so.

Funnels of dust rose into the air. Many of the papers piled up were decades old, the ink faded on those that had been exposed to the sunlight. My father had taught me how to read documents and ledgers, but these files were completely disorganized. In the Books of Life, records had been charted one on top of the other, in spidery scrawls set down by a series of secretaries and assistants, all of whom had invented their own puzzling systems of notation. Perhaps it was fate, or perhaps it was God's will, that I should stumble upon my cousin Aaron's birth record. The date set down was three years after my own birth. I'd always been told Aaron's parents had been lost at sea, and that they were distant relatives, but this document showed otherwise. He'd had an unmarried

mother, a member of our congregation. The symbol for this was an *X*. I
scanned through the files, and this symbol occurred many times. I wondered how many women had lost their children due to a single letter.
Aaron's father had been marked down as unknown. *Inconnu.* Aaron's
mother's name had been inked out, making her unknown as well. I could
not read the original print even when I held the paper to the light. My
mother had been listed as the official guardian, and the baby's surname,
Rodrigues, was one of her family names long before they had fled Spain
and Portugal.

There was no way to know if the woman who'd given Aaron life had
surrendered him of her own accord, or if he'd been taken from her. Most
likely she'd had little choice in the matter; perhaps she'd eased her mind
by imagining that a wind had carried him away so that he might be sheltered in a treetop, watched over by parrots until my mother came for
him, delighted to claim the son she'd always wanted. What Aaron had
told me in the garden long ago had been true. Our mother would never
have allowed him to marry Jestine.

ONE AFTERNOON MADAME HALEVY was waiting for me when I left
our store. It had been months since she and Madame Jobart had tried to
persuade me to allow them to find me a suitable match, another husband
I didn't want or love. I was sure I wouldn't be interested in whatever
Madame Halevy had to say now. I did my best to disappear, hurrying
away. But she followed as if she were a much younger woman, despite
her cane.

"I haven't given up on you," she called.

"Please do." I went on, but Madame Halevy surprised me by keeping
pace. I had no choice but to stop and face her.

"Your mother loved you no matter what you think," she said. "You
don't know all the circumstances."

My mother had always said there was no finer woman in St. Thomas
than Madame Halevy, but she seemed like a snake to me, coiled and wait-

ing. She wanted to convince me to think as she did. "Thank you for that information," I said wryly. "Had you not told me I never would have known."

"Sara Pomié was a compassionate woman. She wanted the best for our people. And for you." Madame Halevy took my arm. We stood in the shadows. I felt mesmerized somehow; a sparrow to her snake. "If she saw what you were doing now, she would be horrified. Unmarried and living with that man. Searching the office of the Reverend." She threw me a look. "Did you think you'd find God in those files?"

So she had been spying on me after all. I pulled away from her. "I also knew my mother," I said. "Nothing I did was right in her eyes. If the goal of my life was to please her, I would have already failed a dozen times over."

"You were a difficult baby, now you're a difficult woman," Madame Halevy chided. "You cried all night, I remember it well. Your mother used to call me to her so she could get a few hours of sleep. Believe me, her husband wasn't there."

"Do not discuss my father," I said.

"I know you from the beginning, so let me tell you in no uncertain terms that this scandal you're creating affects us all. There are quiet sins and ones that echo for everyone. This situation is larger than your petty needs. People look at Jews with hatred and mistrust, and if we're fighting with each other it gives them all the more reason to despise us. We have to live with no stain upon us."

"Is that why the Book of Life is changed when it suits the congregation? To make certain that the facts fit our beliefs?"

Her eyes narrowed. "You saw changes?"

"Names inked out. People erased."

Madame Halevy was blunt. "We have to protect ourselves."

"Tell this to the Reverend," I suggested. "I'm sure he'll agree with you. Better still, tell it to his first wife. She died in childbirth and he was married again within a year to the girl of his choice. My first husband did the same when he married me to save his business, and I never questioned why my life was worth so much less than his."

"Rachel." Madame Halevy stopped me. "Do you think this scandal won't come back to haunt you?"

I wasn't afraid of ghosts and I told her so. I'd been haunted before, and had lived to tell the tale. I thanked her politely and excused myself. I could feel her watching me as I walked away, but I didn't care. Perhaps Madame had good intentions, but intentions were not enough. I'd thrown my fate away once, and I would never again allow other people's opinions rule my life. As a girl I'd done what was necessary, but I was a girl no longer.

Adelle had promised I would have another husband.

This time I would choose who that would be.

WHEN FRÉDÉRIC COULD GET no further with the Reverend, I insisted upon going with him to plead our case. My weapons were bitterness and a righteous attitude. Frédéric was still a young man, with a young man's certainty that right would win out, whereas I knew we must fight for what we wanted. The weather was wet, with a storm brewing out to sea. It was a bad omen, and sure enough the Reverend's wife refused to let us in the door. Women were to stay at home, especially sinners such as myself. She let us stand in the rain as it began to pour down upon us.

The Reverend's wife did not look at me but instead stared at the ground. There were red ants, the kind you don't want to come across barefoot. The Reverend's wife was shaking. "You need to leave or the authorities will be called." Her face was flushed and she stumbled over her words. Clearly she'd been told what to say to us.

I was a woman with eight children, the daughter of Moses Pomié, the proprietress of the largest store on the island, a lifelong resident of Charlotte Amalie, a full member of the congregation, yet I stood there drenched, as though I were a beggar woman. Frédéric took my arm. Unlike me, he had a kind, forgiving heart, and he did not wish to insult anyone. "There's no point in us being here. Let's not degrade ourselves any longer."

But I refused to leave. If anyone told me no, my back went up. I grew claws and teeth. I'd had so many arguments with my mother as a girl I was well trained in such things. I stepped closer to the Reverend's wife. There was barely any space between us. A heat came off me, as if I were boiling inside. She backed away.

"We have a right to speak to your husband," I told her.

Her name, I knew, was Sara, my mother's name. She was younger than I, though her husband was nearly fifty. His first wife had died in childbirth, as the first Madame Petit had, and of the same cause, childbed fever. In her case, however, the baby had died as well. There should have been a bond between us because of the similarities of our histories, but there was not. And so I called upon the ghost of the Reverend's first wife along with the ghost of the first Madame Petit to stand beside me. I would bring flowers to their graves. I would say a prayer in their names and light a candle every night if they would give me the strength to stand up for myself.

The Reverend's wife told me there was nothing she could do for me, then shut the door. But I now had the two wives from the world beyond ours standing beside me, good, obedient women who had given up their lives doing as other people saw fit. I could feel their energy, the life force that had been stolen from them. Perhaps some of my courage came from them. I began to rap on the heavy door, then to pound on it. I didn't care if my hands bled. Let them. I was ready to fight. When I began to shout and cry out, Frédéric couldn't stop me, though he tried his best, fearing I would bring the Danish authorities upon us.

At last the Reverend came to the door. We told him it was love that had drawn us together, and that such a thing was a gift from God. He shook his head and said ours was a destroying sort of love.

I felt a dark tangle of humiliation, the bitterness growing inside me.

"See what you've done," Frédéric said to the Reverend. "She'll be made ill by this."

"What I've done?" The Reverend showed little sympathy for me. "You weren't much more than a boy and she preyed upon you. I don't blame you for any of this. I blame her."

The Reverend glared at me as if I were a foul sorceress, eyeing my clothes, now drenched and clinging to me. My black hair was uncombed, my boots slick with mud. I held up the hem of my skirts to keep them dry with no success. I likely appeared to be a witch, with a witch's desires.

"Do not speak about her in that manner," Frédéric said sternly. "Our people are brothers and sisters, not enemies."

"You are indeed like brother and sister. That is the point." The Reverend's voice was raised. "Do you not understand? You are relatives and therefore cannot wed. It is against our morals and our laws. If you continue, nothing good can come of this."

"But it has already," Frédéric said.

He meant our love and our child. The door was slammed shut, and we walked away, the rain pouring down, as it did in our dreams. I had a chill. Perhaps I had made a terrible error and had dragged the person I loved most in the world into hell. I looked at Frédéric. As if he could read my innermost thoughts he said, "I regret nothing."

Nor did I.

When we arrived home I was still shivering. Rosalie heated water and I bathed in the tub. I was reminded of that horrible woman Elise who had come from France to steal Jestine's child. I slipped beneath the water, as Elise had done, and studied the ceiling until I came up sputtering. I hated rules, and law, and morals that were twisted into whatever people wished them to be. I didn't step out of the tub until the water was tepid. By then I had come up with a plan. My father always said that I thought like a man, and perhaps there was some truth in that comment. I did not relish the role of sitting idly by with my needlework and baking, seeing to the children while the world made decisions all around me.

I went to my desk to draw up my proposal to present to Frédéric.

We would go over the Reverend's head and petition the Grand Rabbi in Denmark for the legal right to wed.

Such things were not done. We would insult both the Reverend and our entire community. We would make them look powerless and small in the eyes of the Grand Rabbi in Denmark, but this island was small, that was the truth, and the people around us were nothing more than tiny figures when viewed from above. We had no other choice. Surely God would see that, and would bless our endeavors. I had a flicker of belief inside me.

Frédéric wrote the letter and read it aloud. I approved the sentiments within. The flicker grew brighter. I began to pray, silently, in the garden. Perhaps we had not been forsaken, and if we could address God more directly, he might hear us. We went over the letter several times that week, examining each word until at last it was done. Frédéric took it to the post office, and I waited outside, my cloak covering me, though the air was warm. Sending our letter was not unlike creating a bomb that could explode at any time, anywhere.

Frédéric came down the stairs of the post office. The deed was done, and could not be undone. He was so young. Just looking at him tore at my heart. That night in our bed we did not speak, but instead embraced each other as we had the first night we were together, when I thought he might die of fever. Perhaps we were both in a fever to act so rashly and insult our entire community. The letter that would change our fate was on its way to Denmark, and we were safe in our bed. I could think of little but that pale envelope traveling across an ocean, innocent, mere parchment and ink, until it was opened and read. Then our lives would never be the same. We would be considered traitors willing to betray our own people. The only one who wouldn't judge what I'd done was Jestine. She understood love. *What destroys you saves you*, she had told me. Now I knew what she meant. My love for Frédéric would ruin me, yet I wouldn't have it any other way.

❧

I BEGAN TO OBSERVE things I hadn't taken note of before. Perhaps I'd been naïve or possibly I simply hadn't wished to see the cruelty around us, but it was there, on every street of Charlotte Amalie, and out in the countryside where the manor houses stood. Danish law decreed there was to be no more slavery, but those slaves already owned were still considered property. They were given Sundays off as if they were free people and could sail to a neighboring island to visit family, but when they returned on Monday they were slaves once more. On our island more than half of the African population was free, and that included most everyone who had a European father, but the rest were enslaved, mere property.

I now had a better sense of how an individual's fate could be based on arbitrary rulings, invented by men for profit of one sort or another. If I had lived in Denmark, I could have married Frédéric. It was a larger community, and we could have disappeared into the outskirts of a city and do as we wished. Here, I was a sinner. I had been blind to the pain of others until I had my own burden to carry. Now when I saw slaves in the market I didn't know how they contained themselves. They were denied rights to their own lives, their own flesh and blood and breath. To beg for salvation and find none and still have faith was a mystery to me. I felt abandoned by God and by my people. Although I lit the candles, I did not say prayers on Friday nights anymore. I left that to my beloved, who still believed.

OUR SON WAS LESS than a year old when the Grand Rabbi allowed us to wed with a legal document from the highest authority. Our wedding contract came from Denmark. It was a plain document, but it carried weight because it was signed by the ultimate voice in our congregation. In the paper, the *Tidende*, the next day, November 22, 1826, we paid to have an announcement printed and had the same announcement published in the *St. Thomas Times: By license of His Most Gracious Majesty King Frédéric VI they had become married according to the Israelitish ritual.*

We thought we could resume our lives, and would no longer be considered outcasts, but the next day when Frédéric came home from the store he had the new issue of the *Tidende*.

"You don't want to look at this," he said.

He tried to burn it in the stove, but I took it from his hands and read the announcement page. We were denounced by the congregation, who proclaimed we had married *without the knowledge of the Rulers and Wardens of the synagogue, nor was the Ceremony performed according to the usual custom.*

OUR OWN PEOPLE WISHED to punish us for going over the Reverend's head. Once Jews started doing as they pleased, outside the confines of the law, anything could happen, the synagogue might fall, the world as they knew it might disappear. The Danish government might be incited to act against us, and then a new onslaught might begin. And so the president of the congregation had gone to the newspaper, making us a scandal for the whole island to view. Letters had gone out from the Reverend's secretary to the chief Rabbis in London, and Amsterdam, and Copenhagen. Protestants, Africans, Catholics, people in every reach of society had read about us, for in every kitchen we were the topic of discussion. *The good man and the enchantress.* Some people said I was made of molasses; one bite and you couldn't get enough. They said I turned into a bird during the day, and flew over the island looking for my enemies so I might soar down and peck at them, and if I grew angry enough I might leave sparks of fire on their roofs. Then at night I became a woman again, they said, slipping into my man's bed. Before he could call out to God to protect him, before he could escape, I had my arms around him.

The viciousness of the attack against us in such a public forum was unheard of. My children needed to be protected. The older ones had already heard grumblings about us in town and in the store, but we kept the seriousness of the situation from the younger ones. Rosalie, I knew, pitied me.

"It doesn't matter what people say," she told me. "He's already your husband."

Rosalie understood wanting what you could not have, as Mr. Enrique had a wife on another island and could not marry her. But I was not as patient or as tolerant as she was. The green bitterness growing inside me was a dangerous flower. I could taste the tang of sourness it gave off, like arsenic, the poison left out for the mongooses sent here from the other side of the world.

In a few weeks letters began to arrive from the Petit family, as they tried to gain control of the business. They were half owners, after all, having inherited what had once been my father's holdings along with my first husband's estate. The St. Thomas newspaper had been sent to them, and they were in shock, afraid their assets on our island would disappear if left in our hands. Frédéric put the letters away, but I found them. The family had written that he was too young and they'd been mistaken to send him; he was now obligated to give over control and send the ledgers and records of the business to France. But he did no such thing. He may have been young, but he was stubborn, a believer in doing what was morally right, even if it meant breaking the law.

We soon received a letter from the congregation stating they had begun a correspondence with the Rabbi in Copenhagen and had asked that the King's court undo our marriage, which they stated was granted outside of Jewish law. We were under siege. Frédéric and all the children fell ill with some mysterious sickness that made them unable to eat. I boiled herbs and made a tea from berries and ginger, and they began to heal. But the case against us went on.

Because of the pressure from the community, the King's court suddenly reversed itself, declaring our marriage illegal, stating that we had not presented ourselves as Jews when we asked for permission to marry. I was officially a sinner, damned by the Grand Rabbi. Now women spat on the street when they saw me. I began to carry an apple inside my shawl, not out of hunger but because it was the fruit of our family and I believed it might ward off any curses set against me. Soon I stopped going out. I locked myself in the house and wore black again.

Rosalie came to my bedside. "Don't let them win," she told me.

"They have."

"They think they have. But they can't if you don't allow it."

Still, I stayed in bed for nearly a week until Rosalie said I had to let her change the bed linen. When I got out of bed she dumped a pitcher of water on my head. I screamed, and stood there sputtering and water-logged while my youngest children laughed at me.

"If you can't wake up, then we'll do it for you," Rosalie said.

I was sopping and stunned, but something inside me awoke, the self I was, the woman who knew what she wanted and what she must have. I threw my arms around Rosalie in gratitude. Then I dressed and readied myself for the world, driven by anger and desire, but perhaps that is always what drives a woman to fight back. I had my sons go into the hills and cut down armfuls of flowers from the flamboyant tree. I took these with me and went to the cemetery. I wrapped the branches in wet muslin so they might bloom with a deeper scarlet shade. Dusk was near. The blue-tinted light sifted over me as I prayed at the grave of Esther Petit. I left her armfuls of the flowers she favored. Then I looked for the grave of the Reverend's first wife. I had brought her something special as well, an apple from the tree my father had been sent long ago from France, the one that had lost most of its leaves in the heat of the fire, but still bore fruit. I begged the Reverend's first wife to tell her husband, who was still on earth, to let us be. Perhaps he'd never known love himself in his marriages, but surely even he should be able to see it when it was right before his eyes.

WE WENT ON ABOUT our lives as if we were the only people in the world. I found several white strands in my hair, and Jestine pulled them out at the root. We sat on her porch and watched the sea, and waited for what would happen next, as we used to do when we were girls, when our lives seemed like a story we ourselves could tell. I still dreamed of Paris, only now when I dreamed I was walking through the Tuileries and I was searching for someone, driven by panic, running through the rain. Some nights I couldn't breathe, and Frédéric woke me, assuring me that he would be with me always and that I needn't search for him. I suppose I had been talking in my sleep. I held him close and kissed him until I couldn't think.

When we wed we did not mention our intentions to the congregation, or to the elders, or to the Reverend who'd made us stand in the rain. We had no license to wed, but we did so anyway. The small gathering was held in the parlor of Monsieur DeLeon's large house. He had given a speech at my first wedding and had not abandoned me even though he made it clear he did not approve of my choices. He had helped me out of respect for my father, inviting ten men who had been bar mitzvah to be our witnesses. All of them wore black, as if attending a funeral. DeLeon was a learned man, as my father had been, and he spoke the prayers the Reverend should have said. The ten pious men were uncomfortable with the proceedings, but they murmured *Amen*. I knew that as soon as the service was over Monsieur DeLeon would not wish to see me or speak to me lest he be cast out of the community.

That night I was a married woman. As a marriage gift Frédéric presented me with a copy of Redouté's illustrated book of roses, *Choix Des Plus Belles Fleurs*, printed in France. No other man would know I wanted that book more than anything, more than diamonds or pearls. We lay in bed and turned the pages; the heavy paper was scented with salt from the volume's journey across the sea. "Are you happy with it?" my husband said to me. I hesitated to say what I felt, for I loved him too much and was afraid I would be punished for doing so. Still, I said, "Yes," and we didn't leave our chamber for twelve hours.

Rosalie teased me about that every day afterward. "Married people don't act like you do," she said.

• • •

BY THE TIME OUR second son, Moses Alfred, was born, three years later, his name was entered into the synagogue books beneath his brother's name. This time I did not have to break in and do it myself, the Reverend's secretary made the entry. Rosalie thought it was perhaps because I named this second baby for my father, who was so beloved in St. Thomas, and for the patriarch who had brought our people to freedom. Frédéric believed it was because the congregation was tired of the scandal. We had outlasted them, he said. He laughed and kissed me and asked who among them could deny we were anything other than an old married couple with or without the Reverend's blessing. My husband and Rosalie could think what they liked. I knew the truth. If the congregation was no longer set against us it was due to the Reverend's wife, the one who was dead and buried whose ghost I honored, and the living one I'd petitioned for help.

Still, we were outcasts and we lived our lives as such. On Saturdays Frédéric said prayers in the garden with the boys, and then we went to Market Square, where people who were not of our faith spent their free day. There were over a dozen nationalities listed in St. Thomas and so many foods to choose from in the marketplace on Saturdays that it was like a carnival. I always craved Spanish food, eggs and sardines and olives, and we had *maubie*, a drink of fermented bark made from the maubie tree, not alcoholic, but laced with cinnamon, delicious when you'd acquired a taste for it. The Jewish businesses, including our own, were closed on Saturdays, and all shops were closed between twelve and two every day, so we often went swimming on Saturday afternoons, trekking down to the beach where the turtles came one day a year. I went in the water in my underclothes, since I was with my children. Hannah was always there, watching over them. Now thirteen, she was better at mothering than I was. I thought she must have learned what a kind heart was in the twelve days her mother had lived. Her pale hair was gold in the sunlight and I prayed she would have an easier time in this world than most women did. When she came to sit beside me, I felt her mother's love around us both as leaves fell from the trees even though there was no breeze and the air was still.

IN THE YEAR 1830, our third son was born on July 10. Jestine and Rosalie were with me, which was fortunate, for this was not an easy birth. This baby had a mind of his own and didn't care how much pain he caused me. I choked on my own screams, and Frédéric and the children were ushered from the house. It was not until much later that Jestine admitted that both she and Rosalie thought they might lose me, for the labor lasted three days and three nights, and every hour was an agony. I had begun talking to the spirits. When Jestine and Rosalie realized I was in deep conversation with the first Madame Petit, as if I were planning to join her, they became so frightened they took a vow that they would do all they could to save me should it come to a choice. They would let the baby go, and pull me back to life.

I knew nothing of this, of course. I was in a fevered state and didn't notice that Rosalie was crying. I was burning up as if I were overtaken by something stronger than myself, and the aching I felt was different than it had been with any other birth. Before he appeared, this child was difficult, intent on causing me pain. Yet when he was born, I loved him best, precisely because of our struggle, a secret I kept from all the others. I had named him Abraham, after his father's first name; then Jacobo, after Jacob from the Bible; then Camille, to always remind him that he was French. He was most like me and had my faults. He did not sleep but cried through the night, just as Madame Halevy said I had done. When I went to hold him he pulled away from me. He was perfect, a beautiful baby, but I wondered if his sleeplessness was due to an illness.

Even beneath Jestine's tender touch this baby seemed unsettled. When I hadn't slept for two weeks straight and Jacobo wasn't gaining any weight, I knew what we must do. I asked Jestine if she would come with me back to the herb man, though neither of us was certain he was still alive. He'd been ancient when we last saw him, and if people in town went to call on him they did not say so, for such engagements were made to combat troubles and tragedies.

It was the center of a hot, green summer; still I bundled up the baby in a cotton blanket to ensure against chills. We brought a pitcher of lime-water with us. I had gold coins with me as well, so this time I could pay the price for a cure. We were slower than we'd been when we were girls who ran through the hills chasing donkeys or being chased by them. We spotted some now, eating dried grass along the road. I wondered if Jean-François, once my children's pet, was among them. When I said so, Jestine shook her head.

"If he is, you don't want to know. You'll just break your heart all over again for a creature that should be wild anyway."

Still I whistled and called out his name. All of the donkeys glanced up at us. Jestine started laughing. "See!" she said. "If he's among them he's no different than they are now. You did yourself and him a favor when you set him free."

But I saw the eyes of one of the donkeys set on me, and I knew. It was Jean-François. The pet I'd walked into the hills late one night that had tried to follow me home.

Jestine saw the look on my face. "Now you're going to cry," she declared.

"Unlikely," I answered.

I turned away so she wouldn't see my tears. In my arms, my baby was fretting. Jestine looped an arm around my waist.

"You have a soft heart," she said. "Don't worry. I won't tell anyone."

We both laughed then. No one knew me the way she did, not even Frédéric. Whoever knows you when you are young can look inside you and see the person you once were, and maybe still are at certain times. I went ahead and let myself cry, then pulled myself together.

The light was yellow now, hotter. We went on to the herb man's house. Our route brought us past the waterfall that fell into a pool where tiny blue fish slipped through the shallows. I wished we could strip off our clothing and immerse ourselves in the cool water, but we continued on, past tangles of vines, some with thorns, some without. There was a hush here, and Jacobo was quiet, I think for the first time in his two weeks of life. We walked on, through the coils of greenery, light-footed, almost as if we were girls once more. There were ruins, a manor house from a hundred years earlier, crumbling into stone dust, and stalks of sugarcane grew wild. At last we reached the clearing where the herb man had his hut. Someone was living here, that much was certain. There were embers in a little fire pit, and some pots and pans scattered about. Jestine didn't know I had once come here myself to thank the herb man. She didn't know I had kissed him. She started to go into the house, but I said I would do it this time. I wasn't afraid. If anyone was to pay for a cure for my baby, it should be me.

"Do you want me to ask for something for you, too?" I said before I went in.

Jestine's expression shifted, and I saw her grief. "Ask him to get me back everything I lost. See if he can do that for me."

I rapped on the door and was told to come inside. The baby was fussing, but only a little. I had to get used to the dark. I spied the herb man in his chair. He looked so old, as if he was already in another world.

"Do you remember me?" I asked.

He shrugged. It didn't matter. "Is that the problem?" He nodded at my baby.

"He doesn't sleep or eat."

I brought Jacobo closer so that he could be examined. The herb man opened the blanket and studied the baby's form. My son threw his arms up and cried with a deep voice.

"He's strong," the herb man said. "He has no fever. He just has other things on his mind."

"What other things?" I couldn't imagine what a baby might be thinking of other than sleep and milk and the warmth of his mother's arms.

"He sees what you can't see." The baby had quieted and was staring into the herb man's eyes. "Maybe he sees my death. I wouldn't be surprised if he sees how I'll go out and lie in the grass and blink and be gone. I'll travel right up to the stars and look down at him. Or maybe he just sees the shadows on the wall."

The herbalist signaled for me to wrap up my baby. As I did he slowly got up and brought forth a bottle of a brown liquid made of soursop and powdered herbs. He gave me a bundle of soursop tree leaves to rub over the baby's blankets. The herb man was so old he could barely walk. I wondered how he fed himself, and I thought perhaps I should leave fruit and bread every week. He came to take the baby from my arms.

"He'll sleep with one drop of this every night. Then he'll get used to sleeping. He will look forward to it. But it won't change who he is or how he sees."

The herb man gave the baby a drop of the mixture to drink from his finger. My son made a face, but he closed his eyes.

"Whenever you do this let him hear your voice. Then he will know you will always be there for him. Speak now," he told me.

I was so taken aback, I began to tell the first story that came to me, the one that had always terrified Aaron. Surely it was wrong to speak of werewolves in the presence of an infant, but I did. I murmured of how the old Danish families had to pay a price for their cruelty, how when the moon was full they felt their bodies would become covered with hair and their claws would come in. By the time I was done, my child was asleep.

"He likes stories with teeth," the herbalist said happily. "Another sign of his strength."

It was then I noticed the pearls around the herbalist's neck, the ones my mother had sewn into the hem of her skirt when my parents fled Saint-Domingue, the ones my grandmother had brought when she escaped from Spain. Jestine had paid for Frédéric's life with them.

The herb man caught me staring. "You like these?" he said, holding up the pearls. "I'm making sure the bad luck in them wears off."

I took out a gold coin and put it on the table. It was too much for a sleep cure and we both knew it. I explained that I wanted the pearls back.

"Someone needs them," I said. "She wants to get back what she lost."

"You give them to her, you'll give her your luck, too," the old man said. "Are you sure about that?"

I said I was. I owed it to her.

He took off the strand of pearls and gave them to me. They were so hot they burned my hand. I was about to put another gold coin on the table, but the herb man stopped me.

"What good will that do me where I'm going?" he said. "I like something more than coins."

So I kissed him, as I'd done before.

We were halfway down the hill when I handed Jestine the pearls. There were already clouds of mosquitoes hovering over the waterfall when we passed by. "You should have what was meant to be yours," I told my friend. Jestine gave me a look, then she slipped the pearls around her throat and kissed me. I gave her my luck, and was happy to do so.

As we continued on the road I held my child close so he would hear the sound of my voice, as the herbalist had bade me to do. I told him the story of the turtle woman who couldn't decide whether or not to be human, and of the fish who had the face of a horse, and of a donkey who had the name of a French boy and came running home to supper whenever he was called. By the time we reached our street my baby was slumbering, as if he'd never had any difficulty.

1831

On the night before one year ended and another began there was a special celebration on our island, when the tired, old year was swept away, a time when wrongs were forgotten and hope was restored. It was a rowdy party that included the entire city, and what was done on that night was overlooked, left unjudged. You could kiss a stranger on the street, drink all night, engage in a fistfight, gamble, run wild, and still be absolved of any wrongdoing. Sometimes I thought it was the only night when some people on our island possessed the ability to forgive in our unfair world. People of color and Europeans, the poor and the rich, some descended from royalty and others from slaves, flooded the streets to dance. Already many people of color were free on our island, and soon they would be granted the rights of citizenship and be welcomed into the Burghers' Association so they could set up business, just as Jews would soon be granted the rights to marry non-Jews, though few would do so and dare face the congregation's wrath.

On this one night, however, everyone was equal on the street. Some wore masks, so they would not be recognized by their mothers or wives or by neighbors who might reveal any trespasses committed and create a scandal. The celebration began at four in the afternoon and went on all night; even the slaves were free to do as they pleased, dancing and forming into bands of musicians, with many playing the drums called Gumbe. In our community only men were allowed to attend this party, but I had never listened to rules. I hadn't even told Frédéric where I was going. I had kissed him good-bye and left him to read over the ledgers. Rosalie promised to stay with the children until midnight, then she was leaving to be with Mr. Enrique. I wore the green dress Jestine had sewn for me when I thought I would wear black for the rest of my life. I braided my hair, took off my rings, found a mask hidden in a bureau. My husband trusted me and asked no questions, which made me love him all the more. I would create still another scandal if anyone knew that I went alone through the city, doing as I pleased. I put my children to bed and went down the stairs in the dark.

There was Jestine, waiting for me. We both slipped on our masks made of feathers so we could not be recognized. Jestine was wearing my mother's pearls, the ones I'd bargained for with my good fortune. There were always men who chased after my friend, for even masked she was clearly the most beautiful woman in the crowd. She paid no attention. Perhaps we had indeed changed places and she no longer believed in love. She had one person in mind, her child, and that left no room for anyone else. People thought we were sisters and addressed us as such, and we laughed and drank rum at a stand on the street.

"I'm the pretty sister, but you're the one who gets what she wants," Jestine said.

It was true. I had ten children and a man I loved. No matter what my problems were, and how my own people shunned me, I was blessed by the many riches of my life.

"The whole world starts again in a few hours. You're supposed to have hope tonight," I told Jestine.

"I do. I hope that the red-haired woman dies a terrible death."

Such things should not be said aloud, but I understood, and I joined her in this wish. We raised our glasses and drank to the Frenchwoman's death. I had no qualms about doing so.

We wandered through the drunken crowd, past Glass Bottle Alley and Ding Alley, all places we weren't supposed to be. We went to a food stand, bought cups of guava berry rum, cheered the musicians, walked through town, hand in hand. We were out till the stars began to disappear from the sky.

HOURS LATER THE FIRE started. A fight had begun, and a kerosene lantern had been kicked over. In moments, wooden buildings went up like straw. I was in bed with my husband when we heard what we thought was one of the children screaming. But it was the wind that had picked up and the cry of fire as one building after the other caught. Frédéric was out of bed in an instant. He pulled on trousers and a shirt. I loved to see his broad shoulders and muscular arms when he was dressing. I wished he would stay beside me, and leave the fire to others, but he wasn't a person who would recoil from the possibility of harm to himself.

"Start pouring water around the house," he told me. "Don't leave the hill."

I felt panicked when he went out. I called his name but he was gone. I didn't care about anyone but him. There was a heaviness inside me, as if my life had left me. I went to the window to look for him, but he had turned the corner, and had taken the steps down the hill, already on his way to the synagogue, where a bucket brigade had begun to wet down buildings. Every effort was made, with the men working even harder when the breezes came up, soaking every wall and roof. I woke Rosalie, and we did the same with our home and store, with the help of the older children. The air was thick with sparks and smoke, but we worked away, our clothes drenched. I thought of Jestine alone at the harbor, pouring buckets of seawater on her porch and along the perimeter of her house. By then, flocks of birds were overhead in the dark sky, fleeing the smoke, taking wing on a course that led past Jestine's house, out to sea. The pelican who had always nested on our roof, who I'd believed carried Adelle's spirit, left that night when sparks fell into its nest. I felt an emptiness without that bird above me, there like one of the stars that rose above us in the sky.

The fire raged for two days, during which time we stayed close to home—wetting down the street and garden with bucket after bucket. Our rain barrel ran dry, and I had to send the boys dashing to the harbor to fill buckets with salt water. I counted the minutes until they were back home, safe from the flames. Cinders stung our clothes and eyes. Birds that had waited too long fell from the sky, bodies smashed on the road, their feathers drifting through puddles. I climbed out onto the roof and the children handed me buckets of green seawater to pour over the eaves. There was no birdsong, no chatter on the street, no ships' horns, only something that sounded like a cry. For two days we barely ate or slept. Frédéric had not returned. I felt I had lost half of myself, more than half, actually, for I was nothing without him. Many people had been killed or wounded in the fires, and over a thousand buildings had burned to the ground. I mourned for our city, but there was only one person I waited for at the gate, my heart knotted with fear. My hair was loose, thick with ash; my hands had blistered from lugging pails of water with handles so hot from the fires they had burned marks into my palms.

When my husband at last came home he was black with soot. I didn't care, but went to embrace him. I felt my heart had been returned to me.

I wept but did not let him see me do so. I had to let him be himself, a young, hopeful man. I could not burden him with the depth of my love and how afraid I was when I thought I might lose him. I stepped away so that he might wash the fire off him.

He stripped off his clothes and stood in the garden while he poured buckets of water over himself. Soon enough, the ground was black. Even after he'd washed, when he came to bed he smelled of smoke. "No one spoke to me," he told me. "They let me help, but when it was over, and everything had burned down, they turned from me. Not a single man from the congregation greeted me by name."

I heard the hurt and confusion in his voice, and I thought that whatever happened, whether our marriage was ever considered legal or whether we were forever outside the law, I would never trust anyone in our community. An outcast was an outcast, even when the tide turned. I would always be the woman who was a sinner. I could turn men into pillars of salt, enchant them to do my bidding, make them beg to come into my bed. My green-edged bitterness was running through my blood. Yet, despite my hatred for those men who had turned their backs on Frédéric, I was able to love my husband completely. He was such a beautiful man, both his physical self and the soul that he carried. That night in our bed he lay beside me with ashes still threaded through his dark hair, his long arms twisted around me.

The city was in ruins, with smoke rising from burned houses, and we were two people who had been scorned, but in truth I felt more fortunate than most, despite having handed over my measure of luck to Jestine. I thanked the women whose spirits walked in the trees above my head when I visited the cemetery. In the morning, when I looked into our garden, branches of our apple tree lay strewn upon the stones of the patio, the leaves burned off. But the bark was still green. This tree from France had survived both sea voyages and hurricanes. It had been transplanted whenever our family had to flee, the last time dug up with my own hands when I stole it from the garden of my parents' house. I did not think fire would be the end of it, although from that time onward, it gave fruit only once a year, more bitter than ever, but delicious when steeped in a mixture of equal parts molasses and rum.

WHEN MY FOURTH SON with Frédéric was born, I named him Aaron Gustave, hoping my choice would cleanse that name, but it was likely a mistake. Jestine refused to look at the baby, and later, when she relented, she called him Gus, which was the name of a goat that had belonged to one of our neighbors. Even I had to laugh at that.

I now had eleven children, for I considered my stepchildren my own, though they were now grown. I still worried for Félix, the one who was in my womb when I stood on the Reverend's doorstep. He was fragile, quick to take a chill, very quiet with shining dark eyes. And then in the following year I lost a baby who was even more fragile, a boy who arrived far too soon, when I was by myself in the garden. I had a stab of pain, then crouched down, as the pirates' wives must have done, alone and unaided. He arrived dead before he came to life, and so he could not be named or protected from Lilith. I felt robbed and told no one of my loss. It was only Frédéric and myself at the funeral, which we could not have in the synagogue. There was a single gravedigger whom we hired, a man not of our faith. We went at dusk, that blue empty time. I laid the child to rest beside my father, who I hoped would watch over him in the world to come, if such a thing existed. I did not weep, although my husband sobbed. When he knelt and cried out to God, I felt my bitterness burn inside me. We released the gravedigger and took up a shovel ourselves and buried our child together. Now our boy with no name would be among the spirits.

❧

IN THE YEAR OF 1833, the elders of our congregation agreed that our marriage was legal and wrote our union down in their book. It was there, for everyone to see. We were officially husband and wife. I am not certain what changed, but perhaps we had been more of a scandal as outsiders than we would be as members of the synagogue. Frédéric immediately began to go to services, but I declined. I waited for him in the garden on Saturdays, and we would sit together then and he would say a prayer for me, and for our children, and our household.

I did not expect God's forgiveness, for I had done as I pleased. Nor did I expect luck, for I had given mine away. I had done so in the hope that Jestine would be granted good fortune, but she was still in her house by the sea, still in mourning. I had written several letters to Aaron, but had received no reply. I tried to make him understand the grief his actions had caused, and begged him to consider allowing Lyddie to return. There was no response, until late one day Frédéric came to our rooms. It was the busy season, so I was surprised to see that he had left the store while Rosalie and I were preparing the Friday night dinner. My husband brought me into the garden, where we could have some privacy. He looked worried, and so many thoughts went through my head that I felt a wash of relief when he gave me an envelope from France. When he'd gone to the post office, the letter had been waiting.

"From your cousin, I assume," he said.

I opened the letter with a paring knife left out in the yard. The blade was rusty and left a mark the color of blood. I examined the handwriting. "From his wife."

I did not read any more, but instead decided to bring the letter to its rightful recipient. I took Jacobo with me. He was then nearly four, a quiet child who often refused to do as he was told. In truth, I still loved Jacobo more dearly than any of the others, though I hid the fact that I favored him. He was both clever and dreamy, interested in the adult world, which the other children ignored.

"You can help me carry a package," I told him. He always liked to be useful. We took some fruit and slices of the cassava bread that Rosalie had baked that morning and brought the food up into the hills before going on to Jestine's. I wanted favor, and I hoped my gifts might bring this. We left the offerings in the doorway of the herb man's house. I saw signs of life: pots, pans, and a bucket of water.

"Is this a werewolf's house?" my son asked. I had read him all my stories, and he liked to hear that one over and over again. But now his eyes were wide.

"Oh, no," I told him. "A good man lives here. We leave him some food because he's very old."

Another frightened child might hide behind his mother's skirts, but my son peered through a window. It was covered with two boards with some meshing attached to keep the mosquitoes out. The herbalist was likely in bed, or watching us, waiting for us to leave. There were some parrots in the tamarind trees, and the leaves shook down on us. "It's raining," Jacobo said, and he gathered the leaves and set them at the herb man's doorstep as yet another gift.

We went along the path that seemed to change every time I took it. We came upon donkeys and crouched down to watch them. Jacobo was entranced. When I held a finger to my lips he nodded and agreed to be silent so we wouldn't frighten the creatures away.

"One of them is Jean-François," I whispered.

My son shook his head. "Donkeys don't have names," he whispered back.

He was very sure of himself even then. I should have known there would be trouble between us, for our temperaments were too alike, but instead I laughed and the donkeys scattered and we watched them disappear into the hills.

THERE HAD BEEN A terrible hurricane some months before, and many of the buildings at the harbor were still in bad shape. My husband had paid some men to fix Jestine's roof and fashion new wooden shutters that she could close from the inside when bad weather struck. She had painted them blue and white. Many of the palm trees had been toppled, and they still lay on the side of the road. I had the letter tucked into the bodice of my dress. It felt heavy, like a stone. I held Jacobo's hand, but he broke away and ran to Jestine's house, climbing up the steps two at a time while I held my breath, frightened he might fall and be swept away to sea.

There were many skilled tailors in our country; it was a useful trade on an island where sailors often needed to be fitted for entire new wardrobes. But no one's work was as fine as Jestine's. She had learned her craft when she made my wedding dress, and then my mourning dress, and then my spring-green dress. She had made all of Lyddie's clothes. Now she had begun her own elite business. There was a list of women waiting to purchase her handiwork. She was a talented seamstress, but even more important, she could imagine a dress like no other. She called each one by name: The Storm, for an inky silk creation she'd begun during the hurricane when the wind swept inside her house. The Moth, pale gray linen from France, so luminous and lovely, she hated to sell it to the ugly old woman who had commissioned it. Now she was working on Starlight, fashioned of silvery damask, a fabric that would reflect light into the wearer's face so that no one would be able to gaze away. Once again, for the old lady who didn't deserve such beauty. There was a spool of white thread beside Jestine and handfuls of crystal beads.

Jacobo loved to visit here and made himself right at home. Jestine was like a dear auntie to him, and the truth was I was jealous. They talked about things I didn't care about, the color of the sea, and of palm leaves, and rejoiced over how many shades of red there were. My boy went inside and lay down on Jestine's bed, pulling the thin blue quilt over himself. Ever since he'd had a drink from the herbalist's potion, he'd been an excellent sleeper. Jestine and I laughed to think of the time when he was an infant and kept me up all night with his screams.

At last, I handed Jestine the letter. The sewing fell from her lap in a coil when she saw it. The needle she held pricked her skin, and a single drop of blood fell from her finger. Later she would use a limewater paste to remove it from the fabric, but every time the ugly woman wore the dress in public and I saw her, I remembered this day.

"It might be bad news," Jestine said.

I knew what she was thinking. A letter after all this time might mean Lyddie was afflicted in some way; perhaps she had died. It had been ten years since she had been stolen, time enough for anything to happen.

"You read it to me." Jestine was shivering as she thrust the letter back into my hands.

I noticed there was a pelican nesting on the new roof, perhaps the one who had flown from my house during the Night of the Old Year fire. My luck, I was certain, was now Jestine's. Such thoughts gave me the courage to open the letter and read, though at first my heart was in my throat.

> *I have often thought of writing to you in the past, but will make this brief due to the circumstances. I thought you should know that your daughter had grown into a beautiful woman. On the trip to France I feared she might die from a fever. She fell into a deep sleep and when she woke, she remembered little, not even her own name.*
>
> *Now, she is engaged to be married. She is still young and must wait two years before she is wed.*

I raised my eyes to see Jestine weeping. She had cast away the dress she had been working on so that her tears wouldn't ruin the fabric.

"Jestine," I said. I put the letter down.

She shook her head. "They almost killed her with their love. Go on. Read it."

I thought of Elise in our bathtub, her red hair streaming down her back, her pale skin scattered with freckles, cavorting in the water as if she was nothing more than a simple, mindless girl. Perhaps I learned that people were not always what they appeared to be from that time.

> *I beg you to be happy for the joy in her life, and not to despise me for giving her a better one than she might have had if she'd stayed on*

your island. I imagine you must curse me every day, but please know
I have always loved her.

I'm writing you this news in the hope that it can bring you happi-
ness as well.

We both had thought of Lyddie frozen at the age when she was taken. She was a little girl to us, not a young woman engaged to be wed.

Elise's monogram was imprinted in the letter paper. "We should burn this," I said.

On this day the sea was smooth and glassy. It seemed a person could walk all the way across it, on the backs of the turtles, until she reached the shoreline of France and the salt flats of the ancient city of La Rochelle. I wished it were so, just as I wished I could give my friend back her daughter. I would have even given her one of mine, but such things were impossible.

We went inside Jestine's house and made a fongee pudding out of cornmeal for our dinner. We saved a bowl for Jacobo to have when his nap was through, but for now we left him to his dreams. This porridge had been Lyddie's favorite meal when she was wrapped inside the life that should have been hers. We did not set a plate for her to help bring her back home, for people say such actions call to a person's spirit, and we feared we would disrupt the happiness she had found with the man she was to marry. But we burned the letter after we had eaten. We saw that the smoke was blue, a sign that the writer did not have long to live. Surely that was why my cousin's wife had written after all this time as an attempt to free herself of her sins. Yet there was no regret in her message, no apology, not even any gratitude. If it were me, I would have indeed cursed her. But Jestine simply poured water on the ashes, to make certain any flaming sparks were drowned. We threw what was left into the sea.

My son woke then, and he ran to us. But it was Jestine he threw his arms around, not me.

CHAPTER SEVEN

The Escape Artist

CHARLOTTE AMALIE, ST. THOMAS

1841

JACOBO CAMILLE PIZZARRO

I wanted my freedom from the start. I did not wish to go to school and would have preferred to walk through the streets of the city, skirting the harbor, making my way to the shore so I could study waves, sand, birds, light. This was my library, the landscape around me, luminous and white-hot or starry and black. I liked to be with everyday people, watching them work, especially at the docks, where there was a riot of color, and a rush of great excitement every time a ship arrived, for that was the way the world came to us and woke us up with news and events and people. We had small lives here. Each group stayed to themselves, and people of our faith were very close-knit. My older brothers and sisters had all attended European schools, and several had left the island due to marriage. But we younger brothers did not attend the school at the synagogue, rebuilt from stone and brick after the fire that had burned it to the ground. Nor did we go to any of the schools that non-Jewish Europeans attended. We were outcasts, and as far as I was concerned this was good luck. So much the better.

But my mother insisted that all children must be taught to read and write, and she brought us to the school run by the Moravians, missionaries from Denmark. The Moravians on St. Thomas had been funded a hundred years earlier by the Danish princess Charlotta Amalia, the beloved wife of King Christian V, born in 1650, and it was her name that graced our capital city. My brothers and I were the only Europeans to attend this school, and at first the other students gawked and joked about us, but that didn't last long. We had to work too hard for there to be time for ridicule. We were taught in English, Danish, and German. At home we spoke French, and I didn't know a word of these languages, so I sat there in a dream state. I wondered if this was how our dog, called Souris—meaning mouse—felt when my sisters would chatter to him. Souris was a descendant of one of the dogs brought here by pirates from Madagascar, common on our island, a breed that was white and fluffy as cotton, but tough when it came to chasing after rats and lizards. My sisters, especially Delphine, liked to dress him up in a baby's bonnet and have him sit on a chair for tea, and my father, who was easygoing, allowed this. My father loved peace and quiet; he was most interested in figures and ledgers. He was soft-spoken, though, and had a big heart. I think when my mother's back was turned, he gave my sisters biscuits to share with Souris and laughed along with them at the dog's antics. Delphine was his favorite; she was so pretty it was hard to say no to her. It seemed far easier to say no to me, for when I begged my father to let me escape from hours wasted at school, he told me every man should be educated. I knew he would not go against my mother. He never would.

Luckily, at the new school I sat beside a girl named Marianna King, who grinned at my confusion and whispered in French, "Pretend you know what they're saying and eventually you will." This turned out to be true, although it took months for the miracle of my understanding to occur. During that time everyone came to believe I was an idiot, and perhaps some of them thought that was why I was in this school with people of color, rather than in the school run by the synagogue like other boys of my faith.

But my idiocy in matters of scholarship was not the reason I was there. Something had happened years before I was born, and people of our own faith were not friendly to us. We had not been made to feel welcome to worship in the synagogue. I had once or twice sneaked up the marble steps so I might slip through the gated courtyard to peer inside. I saw the mahogany cabinet that was home to the Torahs, the scrolls of our law, and the huge tablets with the rules of Moses inscribed upon them. There was a domed ceiling, and at night the house of worship was lit by candlelight, so that the ceiling glowed as if it were the firmament. *Blessed be he that cometh in the name of the Lord.* But I had come out of curiosity and wonder, rather than drawn there by faith. Our family was not invited to holiday dinners, parties, funerals, or weddings. I knew that my parents had offended the Reverend and a scandal had ensued. My mother never once admitted this to me, but I'd heard gossip, and my older brothers had told me they'd been born before my parents had been officially married. I found this difficult to believe.

Perhaps my family's standing was fueled by the fact that no one liked my mother. Only her maid, Rosalie, defended her headstrong ways. Rosalie had cause to favor my mother, for it was my mother who had insisted that my father hire a solicitor to search for his manager's wife on another island. In doing so, he had discovered that this wife had died ten years earlier. Mr. Enrique was therefore free to marry Rosalie. For that reason alone, Rosalie was loyal, and though they belonged to different societies, the two were faithful to one another. Tell one a secret and it was as good as telling the other.

My mother had arranged to hold Rosalie's wedding in the garden of the house where my mother had grown up, opposite the cottage where Mr. Enrique, and now Rosalie, would live. She rented it from the new family in residence without bothering to mention it was not a Jewish wedding, but rather a marriage for African people. The new owners of the house closed their shutters and went out for the evening. Because of this they missed how ethereal their garden became on the wedding night, enchanted, lit by candlelight. The music was wonderful, flutes and the drums. We were the only Europeans invited. There was dancing until all hours, and my brothers enjoyed watching the women dressed in their finery. But I preferred to be in the back of the garden, where I could examine the pink flowers of the bougainvillea growing up the stucco walls in huge bunches. There was an ancient lizard beneath a hedge that barely moved when I studied his form. I sketched with a stick in the dirt, trying to capture the outlines of a century plant with huge gray-green leaves. Mr. Enrique worked with my father. On this night he was wearing a formal suit and vest ordered from Paris, a gift from my mother. He surprised me when he came into the garden. He was now a married man, and perhaps he needed a quiet moment to think through his new standing in life. He was at least twenty years older than his bride, respected by my family and by his community.

"Marriage is a lot of noise," he said, but he looked pleased.

My mother had told me that if Mr. Enrique hadn't saved my grandfather I wouldn't be alive, so I was a little in awe of him.

"A piece of paper doesn't mean anything," the new groom went on. "Your mother knows that."

From early on, I was aware that just because something was a rule, it wasn't necessarily fair. My mother glared at other women of our faith on the street for they never greeted her, and when they came to shop in our store, there was no conversation. However, the love between my parents was unlike what I saw between other married couples, who were dutiful toward one another, often referring to each other as Madame and Monsieur after decades of marriage. My parents could not restrain their emotions. Sometimes I heard murmuring and laughter from their chamber at night, and often I saw them holding hands when they thought no one was near. Their love was a mystery to me, and yet it was part of our lives, a door that shut out the rest of us, a place inhabited by them alone. I would not like to have witnessed anyone say a bad word about my father in my mother's presence. She was fierce, and when I was very young

I wondered if she'd been bit by one of the werewolves in the stories she told me. I had seen her gazing at the moon as such creatures are said to do, as if she recognized something up above us that was invisible to the human eye.

My mother lit the candles on Friday night, but she did not pray. My father, on the other hand, was an extremely pious man. Though he was not welcome at the synagogue, he prayed in the yard every morning and at dusk. I would watch him sometimes, bowing to God, his voice like a river, rising up in shades of gold and blue.

"Do you think God hears him?" my mother once asked me. I was only a boy, but she often asked me questions she might have posed to another adult.

"I think he hears God," I said.

My mother looked at me hard, to see if I was making a joke. I wasn't. I thought perhaps it was more important to listen than to be heard. I kept a vigil into the night listening to the moths at the window, the frogs in the puddles, the wind that came from across the ocean.

My family's disagreement with the synagogue was the reason I attended school with people of color, something so unusual most of the students couldn't help but gape when my mother and Jestine enrolled us. Jestine was like an aunt to me, especially as we had no extended family on St. Thomas. Since I had few dealings with people of our own faith, I did not understand why the other students seemed so stunned by my arrival. My brothers were standoffish, embarrassed to be so different, but I was pleased. Jestine had told me this was the best school on the island and promised me I would find my calling here. Our teachers were religious, dedicated people whose goal was to bring education to the new world, and they were tolerant of race and religion in ways that astounded and refreshed me. Even as a very young child, I did not approve of dictates, and thought even less of those who enforced them, those who were our elders and called themselves our betters. These were the same people who spat on the street after my mother passed by. If I had not been born a rebel, if the treatment of my parents hadn't turned me into a radical, then I had been made one by the injustices I saw on our island. From the very start I wondered about the meaning of freedom. My mother said I asked too many questions. *You look too deeply into things. Don't make trouble,* she said. A laughable statement considering all the trouble she'd made for our family, and how my father still had to remind her not to speak her mind in public, for she often held nothing back. Her tongue was sharp, and when she was angry I avoided her as best I could.

THE TRUTH WAS, I was happy not to be at the school at the synagogue because I could escape the extra work of learning Hebrew and studying the Torah. At the Moravian School we learned Bible stories as well, but they were about Jesus, whom I had not heard of before, and of the possibilities of salvation, despite our sins on earth. Such stories were interesting to me, and over the years I was in school I paid careful attention to them. The idea that God would have a son on earth was particularly fascinating. It made God seem closer to humanity, more involved with our daily trials. I had struggled with the concept of a God that would let his people suffer, and make the world we lived in so unequal, especially when I passed the shantytowns on my way to school, for it was a long walk and I dawdled behind my brothers so I might take it all in. Was it fair that some people on this island should live in huge houses surrounded by courtyards filled with fruit trees while others lived in shacks? In the stories we were told, Jesus was an outcast and a rebel. He was a Jew who would not bow down to the Romans or to any authority other than God. I grew to admire him, something I would not have dared mention to my mother. I was not a believer in the Christian faith, merely an interested observer. I said *amen* at the end of their prayers, then had pangs of guilt.

I asked Marianna about this one day, and she shrugged. She told me her family practiced the old religion from Africa. "At school you have to pretend you accept their faith. My family doesn't believe in such things. I just go along with these stories."

In that instant I saw that we were the same—disbelievers surrounded by believers. Outcasts on an island where we were not equals, she less equal than I because of her color and sex. I felt a tightness in my throat due to this bond, and an understanding of the world that would stay with me all the rest of my life. I was eight or nine at the time, but later, I came to feel that this was my first moment of true love: to know and be known by someone. It did not hurt that Marianna was beautiful, more so as we got older. She had high cheekbones and was very dark, with light-filled eyes flecked with green. When she smiled, the world was something new to me. This is what I wished for, even as a boy: to see what was there, but also what was underneath flesh and blood, core and pit, leaf and stem. Above all else, despite my mother's warnings, I wished to *see*.

I began to draw in class. I had no idea that I had any particular talent until people told me so. Other children gathered around and asked me to draw this or that. They flattered me and begged me for my art. Sometimes I complied, drawing their faces or the form of a donkey, but mostly I did as I pleased. I had always looked at the world as if it were a puzzle—whether it was a scene, a landscape, or a person—the pieces dissolved inside my mind so that I then could put them back together to form a whole. This made sense when I began to draw, creating the elements one image at a time until the world appeared on the paper. Instead of going directly home, as my brothers did, I went to the beach and drew Marianna, using a bit of charcoal and some heavy paper I took from the storeroom at school. I drew Marianna so many times I knew her face better than my own. I felt I had come upon the core of the meaning of life, to discover and re-create beauty. We spent hours together, but after a while this stopped. Marianna's mother caught us together. She grabbed me and told me that if I bothered her daughter again she would have me beaten. I doubted this, but Marianna was too afraid of misbehaving to see me anymore. We were only children and Marianna was respectful; in many ways she was more grown up than I. She told me she could no longer be my friend. I understood. My sisters were the same when it came to our mother's demands. They did as she said. They didn't want trouble.

When Marianna could no longer spend time with me after school, I did not give up art. I drew the island around me, beginning with a palm tree. I sketched it section by section, leaf by leaf. I became the palm tree as I did this, knowing it inside out. The undersides of the leaves, which I did not draw, I still knew inside my head. I dreamed of whatever I drew: the palm fronds, a bat hanging from a tamarind tree, a woman walking down the street with a basket of laundry under her arm. I did not have much to do with my brothers and sisters. They were busy, the older ones working in the store, the younger ones interested in their studies. Sometimes I caught my mother studying me. She had a cautious expression at these times, as if I were a specimen she was studying under glass.

When I was a young boy they called me Marmotte, sleepyhead. I could nap under the table with ease. My parents said they often found me dozing on a bench in the garden, or on the beach while the other children played and swam. Now that I was older I didn't sleep much. When I did, I dreamed of color. Of blue, mostly, in every shade, for our island is made up of the many delicate hues of that color. In the hottest months I dreamed also of green. On those occasions I awoke dizzy, as if I had slept in a field. I smelled wet grass, snarls of berries on vines, honey-scented flowers. And so it came to be that I carried these colors with me, awake or asleep. It didn't matter if I was in the classroom or in my parents' house; I was somewhere else as well. Inside blue, inside green, inside a palm tree, inside Marianna's light-flecked eyes.

Being an outcast meant I possessed a sort of freedom I wouldn't have had otherwise, and that was what I wanted from the time I could crawl. As a boy I was a loner. There were days when no one knew where I was. I pinched paper and brushes from my father's store, then went into the hills and soon learned to make my own pigments from nature: red petals, mud, clamshells, nut shells. I often used planks of wood as my canvases. I used a knife and created my images in slices. I learned much about dyes for my paints from Jestine. As close as my mother was to Rosalie, Jestine was the only person my mother truly confided in, though their relationship was a rocky one, with ups and downs I didn't understand. Sometimes when my mother came to visit, Jestine would act as if she couldn't hear her at the door. This could go on for months, and then one day Jestine would embrace my mother as if she were a sister.

Jestine was a dressmaker, the best there was. I often went to her house at the harbor, where she had vats of dye set out on the porch in a line of brilliant color. When one of the dresses she made was particularly beautiful she would say, "This still isn't worthy of my daughter." She had no daughter, so I assumed that she hoped to have one someday, or perhaps it was just a saying.

"Yes, it's beautiful enough," I would tell her, but she would always shake her head.

"You don't know," she'd say. "You're too young."

I found it much easier to talk to Jestine than to my mother. I was closer to her and could talk to her about things my mother would never have understood. It was in our conversations that I first learned about color, how tint laid upon tint created a mist of a certain shade. Jestine had told me never to rush something I was creating, but instead to let it come into being as if it had a soul of its own. It was so pleasant to be at Jestine's house. My mother watched me like a hawk, as if waiting for bad traits to surface. She kept that hawk eye on me in a manner that made me want to run away from her. But Jestine let me be.

I loved my homeland, yet I wanted to leave. I walked alleyways lined with warehouses that led down to the harbor. The desire to travel was in my blood. I watched the boats depart from the wharves and wished I were on one. I didn't care what the destination was: South America, New York, Europe. I was willing to go anywhere, greedy for all the color in the world. I watched the reflections of clouds disappearing into the water and thought that in another harbor the water might be an entirely different color, the sky a soft dove gray, the mountains forest green, the ice-cold waves a deep and endless indigo.

Jestine allowed me a glimpse of the person my mother once had been.

I made a remark about how my mother understood nothing about the beauty of our world, that she was focused only on household chores and on my father. Jestine told me I was wrong. She took me to a field where she said she and my mother used to go whenever they could run off from their chores. She said the only task my mother enjoyed was killing chickens for the Friday night dinner, a fact that made me laugh. There were blue snails climbing up the tamarind trees, and seawater cut through the field in a crisscross of salty, shallow pools. It was here, Jestine said, they would lie in the grass without moving, except for breathing out and in, which moved the grass in waves, like the sea. I couldn't imagine my mother as a girl, but I painted the grass and the red flowering trees and the gleam of the water in my next painting. I did my best to show the wind in blues and overlapping grays.

Jestine next took me to a stretch of beach where she said turtles came once a year to lay their eggs. It was the place where she and my mother would hide in the dark. They would pretend they were girls who were half turtle and imagine that they would swim away and never look back. The sky was midnight blue, one of the colors I loved to paint with, a shade I often dreamed of. I painted the beach and a palm tree that unfolded like a flower. In the shadows there were turtles, their shells a green-black from the depths of the sea.

Then we went to stand outside the shop, beneath my mother's window. Jestine said, *She fell in love looking outside onto this street.* The street was yellow, with rose-colored blooms in the hedges. We went on through our section of town, to the big house where my grandparents had lived, where the oldest lizard on the island hid in the courtyard.

I remembered Rosalie's wedding and the garden aglow that night. My mother had come looking for me. She thought I'd disappeared to sleep in a quiet place, but I was crouched beside the bushes, looking for the lizard. "My cousin used to do what you're doing. He could call the iguana to him. He was such a handsome boy."

Perhaps my mother forgot she was speaking to me. She let slip that when she had come to her first husband's house, Rosalie had been a slave. She hadn't been aware of this until Monsieur Petit died and the will was read. The first thing my mother had done as a widow was to have papers drawn up for Rosalie's emancipation. But she had to wait for my father to come from France to sign those papers, because a woman hadn't the legal right to do so. At Rosalie's wedding a hundred candles had been lit, and it seemed as if the stars had fallen from the sky. In bringing me back to that house, Jestine reminded me of the moment when my mother and I stood in the garden. When I went home, I took out my paint and brushes and did my best to create the rooms inside my grandfather's house without ever having seen them. The walls were in tints of pistachio and salmon and pale gold.

I practiced my art until I was ready to complete a real portrait. I chose to sketch Jestine as she worked dyeing clothes, and then to paint that image. When I sketched her I saw something in her face I hadn't noticed before. All at once I saw that the color of grief was blue and that it radiated from her. I painted her in that shade. Flesh tones didn't show the real substance of people, neither their physical aspects nor their souls.

Since I'd begun the painting I found I had difficulty sleeping. I thought about Jestine's mention of a dress for her daughter, and the color of sorrow, and my mother standing in the garden watching me, suspicious, as if I was her cousin from long ago. I thought of things I had overheard when my mother and Jestine had no idea I was listening. I wasn't really paying attention, yet still I heard bits of conversation. *How could a person be so selfish? How could love turn to ash? Why would God allow cruelty in the world if he truly were watching over his sons and his daughters?*

The next day I worked up enough courage to question my mother. I found her in the kitchen with Rosalie. They were discussing dinner, something they did nearly every day, and yet they seemed to find the subject endlessly fascinating. Would we have chicken or fish? Would the sauce be sweet or sour?

"Does Jestine have a daughter?" I asked.

My mother and Rosalie exchanged a look. They kept cooking the Friday night meal, slamming around cast-iron pots. They had decided we would have chicken flavored with thyme and parsley and tomatoes, along with a cornmeal porridge and loaves of hot bread. My father would say the blessing over the meal, and then my brothers and I, starving by the end of the day, would grab for what we wanted until my mother clapped her hands and told us to be civilized. Usually I would have tried to sneak a bit of the food that was being prepared, but on this day I merely studied my mother, who was clearly upset by my question.

"You're a busybody," Rosalie told me in her matter-of-fact way. She was always protecting my mother, telling me to hush, saying I should keep my thoughts to myself.

I didn't back down. "She mentioned a daughter."

My mother shrugged. "She had one once," she admitted.

I'd had my suspicions, yet was shocked to hear this news. "And? What happened to her?"

"Ask Jestine," my mother suggested.

I knew my mother. That was it. She turned her back and would say no more.

The next time I saw Jestine I asked if it was true, if she'd had a daughter.

"It is true. Maybe you're too young to know about such things."

"I'm not," I told her.

She fixed on me with her deep-set gray eyes as if searching for something. For a moment I thought she might tell me to leave, but she didn't. She gestured to the sea. "My daughter was stolen."

"Stolen? Who took her?" At that moment I envisioned myself a hero jumping up to track down her missing child. I would swoop in to thwart the abductors, and perhaps prove to my mother that I was worth more than she thought.

"Ask your mother who the thief is," Jestine said with an odd sort of calm. "She knows well enough."

I never liked to be between the two of them, and I had begun to realize whatever had happened was at the root of all their squabbles. I was afraid to say more to my mother. I feared she would clamp down on those few small freedoms I had. I secretly worked on my painting of Jestine, keeping it in the back room of the store where there were barrels of grain and rice. I thought it was the best work I had yet done, different than my other paintings, more layered and complicated, and yet simple in its emotion. One day I came for it and found it was gone. I was burning with rage. At least I knew who the thief was. There was only one person who continually told me that drawing and painting were a waste of my time. One person who shook her head as if I were doing something shameful when I leafed through illustrated books so that I might study the work of the great masters that I someday hoped to see for myself in the Louvre.

My mother was in the garden where we had fruit trees, including an old twisted apple tree. The bark was black as a snakeskin. Sometimes Rosalie made a cake from the apples, adding herbs and spices. No matter what she did, any recipe made from the fruit of this tree was bitter, though my mother seemed to enjoy it.

As I approached, my mother looked me up and down. "You should be concentrating on your studies," she said before I had time to formulate a single word. Perhaps she had seen the stain of dye on my shirt. "I know what you've been doing," she informed me.

"There's nothing wrong in what I do." I could feel some shackle being thrown off. I didn't feel the fear I usually experienced when I talked back to her.

"In fact there is," my mother said. "The way you paint doesn't look anything like this world. I worry that you have something wrong with your vision."

"You think this world is all there is?" I was both insulted and embarrassed. The colors I used might not have been of this world; instead they showed what lay below the surface of this world, the spark of color at the deepest core. "If your eyes see everything, did they see who stole Jestine's daughter?"

My mother lowered the basket of apples. I think she took in who I was for the first time, a person who would not easily bow to someone's command. Perhaps for the first time I allowed my real self to be seen. A pelican flew overhead, and cast its shadow upon us. All at once, my mother regained her composure.

"That is none of your business," she said. "It's Jestine's affair. No one else's."

AFTER THAT MY FATHER told me I would work in the store on Sundays. I was perhaps ten at the time and already knew I would rather be anywhere else. My older brothers all worked at the store, and I did the best I could, but I was easily bored by figures. When my inability to add was discovered, I was given the job of making certain the shelves were filled and dusted. Then I could easily take off into the storeroom. I pilfered a drawing pad, and though I felt guilty, I was delighted with my new possession, and used burned wood as charcoal for my sketches.

One of my duties was to carry packages home for the ladies who shopped with us, and I enjoyed this, for it gave me back a bit of my independence. Sometimes the ladies presented me with a coin, which I saved up, hoping for a box of pastel chalks. Once I carried the groceries of a Madame Halevy, a very old woman who barely looked at me. She was a bit terrifying, like the old lizard in the garden of my grandfather's house. When we got to her home, a huge stucco mansion painted firefly yellow, she told me she wanted me to bring the packages inside. Then she demanded that I put the flour and molasses and ground sugar in the pantry, where such things were kept away from beetles and stinging ants. She had both an indoor and an outdoor kitchen, and I wondered if she was so rich she had two of everything. She sat at the table and studied me as I worked, calling out where the items should be placed. When I was done she told me to sit across from her.

I saw the folds in her skin, the white film over her pale eyes. I found all of this very interesting. One of her hands had a tremor she couldn't control, and I had the notion she might grab me and shake the life out of me there in her kitchen if she disapproved of anything I did or said. Yet I was more curious than I was frightened. She took off her thick white gloves; they were an old-fashioned accessory that only the very old ladies on the island kept to anymore. It was far too hot for gloves. I would have loved a glass of limeade, but I didn't ask for anything.

"Would you like to know the truth about your family?" she asked.

I made a face. "Truth is different things to different people." Frankly I was parroting Jestine, who had told me this.

Madame Halevy laughed. "It's one thing when your mother sleeps with a nephew young enough to be her son, then marries him when the congregation denies the union, and yet another when she still thinks she's better than everyone."

"Maybe she is." I might have been ten, but I was sly. My mother and I had our problems, but that was private. All the same, I was glad to be told information I had mostly guessed at before.

Madame Halevy laughed again. I could tell she had taken a liking to me despite herself.

"Would you like to come to our school and learn Hebrew?" she asked.

I shrugged. "I'm not much of a student."

"Well then, would you like to know what happened to Jestine's daughter?" she asked.

I was stunned by this offer, and it must have showed in my face. The old lady smiled. She had my interest now. I realized that other than her maid, who sometimes came to shop at our store, Madame lived alone. Her husband and children had passed on, aside from one daughter, who I'd heard had gone to America. Perhaps she was lonely and wished to speak freely to someone. What danger was a ten-year-old child?

"Come to tea tomorrow," she said.

At dinner with my family that evening, I mentioned that I had carried Madame Halevy's groceries to her house.

"That witch," my mother said. She spat on the floor.

"She was a friend of your grandmother's," my father told me. Then when my mother shot him a look, he added, "Long ago."

I saw my mother that night, standing outside, feeding a pelican that lived on Jestine's roof but sometimes came to our garden. I recognized the bird because it had a ruff of gray feathers around its throat. My mother gave it not merely fish bones but an entire small fish, cooked and spiced. She talked to the bird as if it were human, conversing with it though its only response was to stare back at her. "You agree with me," I heard her say to the bird. My mother was crouching down near the frangipani as though she were a girl. The sky was a soft, fragile blue. The air itself was tinted an inky shade, as if there were drops of water in the veil that surrounded us. I could see my mother as Jestine had described her: a girl who ran off into the countryside to look for turtles and birds, who intended to fly away, or jump into the sea and be carried to another shore.

I could not sleep that night and dreamed of shades of aquamarine and navy and indigo. All day next day in school I thought about whether or not I should return to Madame Halevy's house when I knew my mother wouldn't approve. Marianna and I still shared a desk, but next year I would have to share my desk with a boy. By then we would be considered too old to sit together innocently. I had the sense that soon enough this would be my long ago.

At three o'clock I went to Madame Halevy's and knocked at the back door, and the maid let me in. "She had me make banana cake for you," the maid said. She was nearly as old as Madame Halevy, and I knew that when she came into the store, my brothers made fun of how stooped she was. "I haven't made it in so long I forgot the recipe," the maid told me. "Eat it anyway so she won't yell at me."

Madame was waiting for me in the dining room. It was an elegant room filled with antiques from France: silver candlesticks, expensive china, a lace runner on the table. There were emerald-green cut-velvet chairs sent from France, and the rugs were handwoven, spun of pale gold wool. The light coming in through the window was obscured by silk curtains and turned red as it filtered across the floor.

"There you are," she said to me. "I thought you might come back. I'm a good judge of character."

We had our tea, and I ate an entire slice of the nearly inedible cake to please the maid. The crumbs stuck in my throat, and I had to wash them down with cold ginger tea before I could speak.

"You were going to tell me about Jestine's daughter," I reminded Madame.

I thought she must be eighty or so. Maybe ninety. She wore two gold rings.

"I was very close to your grandmother. She was a lovely person and the best friend I could have had, like a sister. The good deeds that she did have gone unknown. But she didn't get along with your mother. No one likes a headstrong girl who won't do as she's told. Your grandmother adopted a boy out of the kindness of her heart. She treated him like a son, and I suppose your mother resented that. Maybe this caused a rift between mother and daughter that was never healed. Or maybe it was because your mother always tried to get what she wanted by any means necessary, even if it would ruin her own children's lives."

I ate another slice of the horrid banana cake and kept listening. I noticed the old Madame's eyes were so pale they were like stones on the beach. I wondered if she could see through the white film. The angles of her face were sharp, planes in the shape of a bird's wing. Loss had cut into her and left a mark. I could see that she had once been strikingly beautiful. She had an entire book of stories inside her, waiting to be told, but she didn't give anything away without a cost. I knew she wanted something from me, though I couldn't imagine what that might be.

After a while she waved her hand, dismissing me. "Come back on Thursday if you want to hear more."

I thanked her formally, and she took my hand. She was strong when she held on to me. She wasn't quick to let go.

"Tell your mother you were here. Ask her if she has anything to say to me."

I was confused. Here were two women who clearly hated each other, and yet they were interested in one another's lives. When I returned home I told my mother of my visit simply to see her reaction. She was sitting with my sister Hannah, who was a grown woman, and very close to my mother. When I told them where I'd been, Hannah and my mother exchanged a glance. My sister was of marriageable age, and I knew there was a young man she met late in the evening. I'd heard their voices in the small yard behind our store. There was some bitterness involved, and some intrigue, for he came only at night, when no one knew he was there. I soon understood my sister was not considered good enough for his family.

"You visit Madame Halevy?" My mother seemed genuinely shocked. It had been years since she'd had anything to do with people of our faith. On an island as small as ours, they had needed to try hard to avoid each other, but they had managed. The street could always be crossed, after all, when you saw someone you didn't wish to greet.

"She wants to know if you have anything to say to her." I was a calm, detached messenger, but inwardly excited to annoy my mother. I felt the drama of the situation, and believed that for once I had the upper hand.

I noticed that Hannah tugged on my mother's arm, urging her to give me an answer.

"Tell her she's a witch," my mother said.

The very next day, Hannah was waiting for me when I was let out of school in the afternoon. We walked together for a while. The sea was aquamarine, the sun so bright we squinted just to see. The world was light and white. We'd had different parents, but she was the sister I felt closest to. She was tall with blue eyes and pale red hair. Anyone could tell Hannah wasn't directly related to my mother. She had a sweet nature that was to be found nowhere else in our family.

"When you go to see Madame, tell her our mother sends her best regards, and asks for her forgiveness."

I was many things, but not a liar.

"Hannah," I said. "Our mother would have my hide if I said that. And I doubt that Madame Halevy would believe me."

My sister explained that she wished to be wed to a man from the congregation whom she'd met when he came to our store, but since my mother and father's marriage was still such a sore point, this man could not tell his family of his love for her. We were outcasts and he was an upstanding member of the community. He was a cousin of Madame Halevy, and her good wishes could change everything if she was inclined to help. Hannah was flushed as she talked to me. I realized she was beyond the age most girls were when they married. She was animated as she spoke, her pale skin flushed with heat, and with something I was too young to recognize as desire. I saw there was blue thread in the yellow dress she wore, a ribbon that was nearly invisible to the naked eye.

I worked in the store that day, beside my three brothers, who were better at any task than I was. At the end of the day I took a bottle of rum, wrapped it in burlap, and put it in my schoolbag. I had recently turned eleven, and after that birthday my father had sat down with me for a talk. He wanted me to learn Hebrew so that I might be bar mitzvah when I turned thirteen. He told me the synagogue would not be able to deny me this, but I thought they likely would and I had no interest in my lessons, other than the fact that the teacher he had found for me, a Mr. Lieber, was an affable, learned man from Amsterdam who told me stories I enjoyed hearing. He spoke of skating on the canals, but more interesting to me was the color of his childhood world, for it was incandescent and white, with snow falling everywhere, onto the frozen river, onto his eyelashes. I thought about the many shades of white there might be: white with cold blue, and white with gold, and silver-white falling from the night sky.

I'd learned some Hebrew from Mr. Lieber, but all in all, despite my father's good intentions, I was a terrible student.

I went for my lesson on the day I was to visit Madame Halevy, but as usual I wasn't prepared.

"I notice you don't study," Mr. Lieber said to me. "If you did it might change things."

"I'm a bad student."

Lieber shook his head. "You're a disinterested student."

I presented Mr. Lieber with the bottle of rum I'd taken from the store, and asked if I might skip my lessons from now on. I would instead stop by, say hello, then be on my way, ready to wander into the mountains with my sketch pad or, something I failed to mention, sit in Madame Halevy's dining room and listen to her stories.

"And what do I tell your father?" Mr. Lieber asked me.

"Tell him I'm a work in progress," I suggested.

"Is there anything you care about?" he asked me.

It was a difficult question, but I knew the answer. I cared about light, color, bone structure, the movement of the leaves on the lime trees, the luminous scales of fish in the harbor. I did not know how to explain this, so I said, "There is. But it's not in any book."

"At least you're honest," he said to me.

We shook hands, he accepted the rum, and then I went to Madame Halevy's. The more she refused to tell me the story of Jestine's daughter, the more I wanted to hear it. I think I was obsessed. I loved Jestine and could not stand to think of her in pain. It was as if the mystery of the world would be revealed to me once I understood what had happened to this girl.

The maid had prepared a mango pastry that was syrupy and brought flies to it. "Here's our little guest," she said when I walked through the door. I was as tall as she, so I laughed. I had inherited my father's height and was the tallest fellow in my classroom, as well as the laziest when it came to my studies.

I went to sit at the dining room table. The lace runner, from Burgundy, was set over the gleaming mahogany. I saw now it was frayed, thin as tissue. Upon inspection, I realized the silverware was twisted and very old, brought from France two generations ago. Some of it had turned black due to the salt air. Everything that had been new and beautiful was ancient now. The island's weather was not good for preserving delicate things.

Madame Halevy came in to greet me. "Your mother has a message for me?"

"She does indeed." I still wasn't sure of what my response would be.

Madame seemed to like the pastry her maid had concocted; she dug right in, so I pretended to eat to be polite. Mostly I pushed the crust around my plate. The pastry was pale and flakey, the color of damp sand. I decided to give Madame Halevy the message constructed by my sister. "My mother sends you her best wishes and asks that you forgive her all of her transgressions."

"Does she?" Madame Halevy said thoughtfully. Her eyes were bright beneath the white film that covered them. I could see the intelligence in her expression. I didn't think for a minute that she believed me. "How is your sister Hannah?" she asked. She was cagey at all times.

"Fine." I nodded. "Ready to get married."

I wasn't certain if I should speak of this or not, so I concentrated on my tea. The china was from Paris, gold and green, bone thin. I added sugar, and then, as people on our island did, a dash of molasses. It made a very sweet and delicious mixture.

"Married properly in the synagogue?" Madame Halevy asked.

"That is her wish," I said.

"What your parents did tore apart the community. We are too few, and we as a people have suffered at the hands of too many to fight among ourselves like chickens."

I remembered something Jestine had told me. "My mother used to kill chickens on Fridays when she was a girl. She said she enjoyed it."

Madame Halevy laughed grimly. "I'm not surprised. Enough for today. I will take your sister's wish into consideration."

"What about Jestine's daughter?" She seemed to have forgotten her promise to tell me the story.

"Tell your mother I accept her apology. I invite her and your father for dinner next Friday night. Hannah can come with them. We'll all go to services first. Come back after that happens and I'll tell you the story."

In order to hear the end of the story I had to accomplish a task I thought might be impossible. I had to convince people who hadn't spoken to each other in over ten years to take up polite conversation across the dinner table. It felt like a Herculean undertaking. I thought about my father praying in the garden, alone. He was a good man, and sometimes he went past the synagogue at night and prayed at the doorstep. I wondered if my mother had placed some sort of spell on him that bound him to her. If I ever pledged myself to a woman she would need to have a kind and open heart and understand there was another way of seeing the world beyond the rules we had been taught.

I stopped in the kitchen on my way out of Madame's house. The maid was still there, preparing dinner. She had made loaves of cassava bread that smelled heavenly. Her name was Helena James, she told me, and now that I seemed to be a fixture in the house, we should know one another. We shook hands solemnly. We were the only two people Madame had in her home. She went to services, and to meetings of the Sisterhood, but she liked to be alone in her house. However, Mrs. James told me that her employer looked forward to my visits. Madame had lost two children to fevers, and a third had left for Charleston and was rarely heard from. Her daughter had an entire family in America whom Madame Halevy had never met. I stayed for a while and sketched Mrs. James as she diced vegetables and fruit with a sharp paring knife. Mrs. James favored mangoes because they brought good health. She informed me that a person could live on mangoes alone and that the pirates used to do exactly that for months on end. Mrs. James was not a great cook, far from it, but her cassava bread was a miracle. I would be happy to have her bread for every meal. I enjoyed her unruffled manner, and the fact that she liked to talk. When I idly brought up Jestine, not imagining I would have any more information from the maid than I'd had from Madame Halevy, Mrs. James shook her head sadly. "I don't talk about bad luck. Best forgotten about."

"I don't believe in luck," I said.

Mrs. James laughed and said, "You're too young to know what you believe." She looked to make sure that we were indeed alone in the kitchen and wouldn't be overheard. "Abduction," Mrs. James whispered to me then. It sounded like a religious act. I thought it was perhaps a practice at the church or one of the African meetinghouses. I rolled that word around inside my head all that day. When I next went to Mr. Lieber's to drop by so it would appear I was studying, he was napping. I took the opportunity to look through his library. I found the word in a small leather-bound dictionary. *Capture. Abducción. Enlèvement.* It was as Jestine had told me. Her daughter had been stolen.

Hannah had to direct me on how best to renew relations between our mother and her old enemy. I went to speak to my parents after dinner. They were sitting in the parlor on a settee, close to each other, deep in conversation. My mother had her hand inside my father's sleeve. It was as if she was a vine encircling his arm beneath the white linen. It was an oddly intimate gesture, one that made me uncomfortable for reasons I didn't understand. From the doorway they looked like the lovers I sometimes spied by the harbor who were so intent on each other they seemed to have forgotten there was a world outside themselves. I saw a smile on my mother's face that surprised me. As soon as I stumbled near, she looked up. The smile quickly disappeared.

"Don't you announce yourself?" she said to me. "You move the way thieves do."

"I have an invitation," I declared. "Friday night dinner at Madame Halevy's."

My voice sounded unsure, perhaps because of my mother's darkening expression.

"Did I hear you correctly?" she asked.

"After services," I said. "The two of you, and Hannah."

"We're not welcome at services," my mother said. "And who asked you to interfere?"

"You'll be welcome," I said, enjoying the power of knowing more than my mother.

"Fine." My father seemed pleased. "We accept. We'll come to dinner. After services."

ON THE FOLLOWING FRIDAY my sister took an hour to dress. I could hear conversation blooming down the hall as Rosalie helped her get ready. They laughed and talked about hats and shoes. My parents seemed nervous. In fact, they'd been quiet all that day, exchanging glances. I heard my father say, "What more can they do to us? Perhaps the time has come to move forward."

"That time came and went," my mother responded.

I wondered if whatever had happened in the synagogue was the seed of her bitterness. The shadows around her appeared green, lengthening along the mosaic floor as the hour grew later and the time for her to return to the congregation approached. For an instant I saw her as she must have been when she was young and unsure of herself. Her familiar features shifted and seemed vulnerable and unformed. I had the sense I was looking straight through time. Later I studied myself in a dim, silvered mirror. I didn't like to think I resembled her, but our eyes were the same. Dark and filled with defiance.

I went to the synagogue for the first time that night. I had never walked inside before, only peeked in, and now I was stunned by how beautiful it was. A sort of hush stirred within me, and I thought about God abiding in a place, listening to the prayers that were sent to him. I wore a black suit and white shirt borrowed from one of my brothers. Everything was too big, so my father nodded for me to tuck in the tails of the shirt. "I hope you learned your Hebrew," he joked.

I hadn't, and I was forced to mumble along when prayers were said. My father and I stood with the men, while Hannah and my mother remained with the women. I caught a glimpse of Madame Halevy. She wore a lace shawl and a plum-colored dress. She raised her eyes to me, and a message flickered across her face. I had done well to bring my parents here, and she was pleased. My mother narrowed her eyes and gazed at me, and I quickly looked away from the women. I stared straight ahead to the altar in the center of the room. Despite my mother's questioning look, I felt oddly pleased to have assisted Madame Halevy.

When we left, people stared at us. A few men came to my father and shook his hand. With their greeting, my family was accepted back into the congregation. My mother held her tongue and merely nodded to the women who had ignored her for so long.

I hadn't been invited to join the adults for dinner; instead I sat in the kitchen with Helena James. Mrs. James had made a chicken dumpling stew, the wonderful cassava bread, and the terrible mango pastry. "Madame's favorite," she said. She told me she had been working for Madame Halevy for almost fifty years. She had helped her raise her children and they'd all loved mango pastry. "Just like you," she said.

I ate everything on my plate, of course.

I could hear voices rise and fall in the dining room. I waited for an argument, and my mother's sharp tone of anger, but heard nothing. I must have fallen asleep with my head on the kitchen table. All at once it was late; my parents were leaving and Hannah was embraced by Madame Halevy, who called her a most charming guest.

That evening was the end of our shunning as the cloud cast over my family evaporated into mist. After that time no one mentioned the scandal and the years when no one would speak to us. I believe that after that night, letters were sent to the King's court and to the Rabbi in Denmark, withdrawing any complaint against my parents. Customers now spoke with us as if we were part of their family. Every once in a while my mother looked at me, as if trying to figure me out. How had I accomplished this fragile peace after so many years of war between her and everyone else of our faith? She pursed her lips, and seemed to wonder who I was. But that was nothing new, and I went my own way. I had several friends at school now, boys who had to work in the fields after classes or fished alongside their brothers. I went out on skiffs with them sometimes, but they called me lazy because I wanted to sketch them as they worked rather than join in the fishing. My closest friends were Peter and Elijah, two brothers, one older than I was and one a year younger. In order to join in I learned how to fish, and how to clean the catch. I got to know the water and saw its many layers, the sea creatures floating below us, pale gold and red fish, moss-green seaweed, shells that glowed like opals, fire, stars dropped into the sea. I began to look at working people in a different way, and took to sketching them as they labored.

In a matter of weeks Hannah had her proposal and my father began to attend services at the synagogue regularly in the mornings and on Friday nights. The family went to services every Friday night as well. I often skipped out and took the opportunity I was afforded of having these nights to myself. I went to the harbor to sketch and even made some money when sailors wanted their portraits made. In the evenings my father still said his prayers in our garden, privately and alone. I could hear his blessings rise up through my window. He was still in his thirties then, still a young man, serious, interested in the world around us. He liked to talk to working people and appreciated them, as I did. When we walked together he would ask questions about the simplest things, for he hadn't grown up on this island and every bird and flower interested him, as they interested me. I felt closer to him as I grew older, and I think he felt close to me. He often spoke to me as if I were a friend as well as a son. He said that when he came to this island he had been bewitched. He laughed when he said this, but he still seemed mystified by the turns his life had taken. I told him then of my interest in sketching and painting. When I said color was everything, he nodded, agreeing. He remembered his first glimpse of the turquoise sea, the red hillsides, the flocks of brilliant birds. Once we took a vine of bougainvillea and removed every bloom, twisting them carefully and laying them out upon the ground to study the varying shades of scarlet and pink. On another night, as we walked along the wharves to check on a shipment to the store, he told me that he and my mother often had the same dream. I could see that this was part of the enchantment he'd spoken of.

I CONTINUED TO BRING Madame Halevy her groceries, still waiting for the story she'd promised to tell, but somehow always managed to avoid. Sometimes I would run into Marianna on the street. She would laugh when she saw me carrying the sacks of flour and bags of vegetables. "You're going to the mean old lady's house? Why do you do this? You're not her servant."

I couldn't explain. Perhaps I'd simply gotten used to going to Madame's huge stucco house. It was in disrepair, as she had no sons to shore up the walls and roof, and no money for servants other than Mrs. James. Still, I went. I appreciated the way the shadows drifted across her garden, falling through illuminated bands of yellow light, and admired her home, the old dishes on her table, the peonies she raised in her garden, apricot and pink, some as big as plates. I found the tilt of Mrs. James's head pleasing as she chopped up onions and mint, and perhaps more than anything I liked the way Madame Halevy and Mrs. James admired my abilities; both old ladies applauded when I could fix even the simplest thing. Many times I took up a hammer and nails and did the best I could to repair the shutters or the porch.

During one of my visits I found a small portrait of a girl on a shelf. A blue-eyed child I assumed was the daughter who lived in Charleston. For some reason, I knew not to ask about her. I'd come to understand that Madame Halevy would tell me her stories in her own time.

One day she surprised me. Instead of waiting for my visit, Madame came to me. When I left work, she was waiting outside the store. In the full sunlight I saw how ancient she was. Surely more than ninety years on earth. I saw, too, how frail she was. I could nearly spy her heart beating with the strain of having walked uphill to the store. Mr. Enrique carted out a metal chair for her, since she was clearly exhausted.

"I would have brought you your groceries," I told her. It was noon, and the heat of the day was upon us.

Madame Halevy gave me some money and asked me to purchase molasses and sugar. A few other things: some mint, some nuts. Not much. She wanted Helena James to make a special cake for the next time I visited.

"Walk me home," she said when I had finished her shopping and returned with her purchases. We went slowly and in silence, but soon she began to talk. "The worst that can happen is that you lose a child. My younger son was about your age when I lost him from yellow fever. He was twelve."

I was happy that she thought I was older than I was.

"My other boy was fourteen. I lost him the next season. I covered every window. I wouldn't let him go outside, but somehow the fever followed him into his room." She lowered her voice. "It was fate," she said. "I couldn't fight it."

"And your daughter?" I said.

"She's alive," Madame said. "That's all one can ask for."

And yet all the while I'd known her she had not received a single letter from Charleston. Though I posted the ones she wrote to her daughter, there had been no reply. Several times I'd had the urge to tear open one of the letters Madame Halevy wrote and see what she had to say to her daughter in America, but I didn't have the heart to do so.

"Your grandmother lost a baby boy," she told me now. "You can't know what that does to a person. He was born and died in the same day. I know because I was there. I was her friend and I watched her cry. It brought her some solace to take in a baby who had been abandoned. She raised him and loved him as her own. Your grandmother did everything for him. She could not have done more. Unfortunately, the ending was not as anyone would have wished. You want to think the best of your child, so you look the other way when you see failures. Maybe it was because she spoiled him. He squandered vast sums from the business. Part of it was bad judgment. I believe he gambled. Do you ever go to see the cockfights?"

The fights occurred every night and every weekend, and I had been to several. I'd stood in the background with my friends from school as their fathers and brothers bet on which rooster would live and which would die. Once blood splashed over my shoes, and I could feel how hot it was, and how hot the men's tempers were. I knew Madame would disapprove.

"I've heard of them," I said.

She laughed. "Yes, I'm sure." She really could see right through me. "Well, the son of my dear friend was a darling boy, but he had been cast away as an infant and perhaps that abandonment left its mark. I told her to be stricter, but she had a tender heart when it came to this boy. I'm telling you this because he was the father of Jestine's daughter. He was in love with Jestine, but he couldn't go against his mother, and she said they couldn't marry. Jestine was not a member of the faith he'd been raised in. But that didn't stop him from making a child with her. You understand me?"

I nodded. I knew as much about sex as any eleven-year-old boy, perhaps a bit more because my friend Elijah had given me some of the details.

"The affair was a mistake," Madame continued, "but when you make a mistake you take care of it, you take responsibility, don't you agree?" I mumbled that I did, so she went on. "He left, and that would have been the end of it, but he came back. He and his wife were childless. They're the ones who took Jestine's daughter."

"You can't just take someone," I said. "That's theft."

"You are twelve," Madame replied. Again, I didn't correct her. "Do you know that women have few rights? And African people even fewer?

People are stolen every day, dear boy. And there are those of us who feel she was taken to a better life."

The heat was strong and my companion faltered as we went on, though she had her cane. She had to lean against a building we passed. After that we stopped every once in a while so that Madame Halevy could rest. When she was quite tired, she sat on a stone wall beside an orchard. There were some parrots that she pointed out to me, slashes of bright green and scarlet among the leaves. "When I was a girl there were hundreds of them," she said. "You probably guess that I'm a hundred years old myself and that I can't even remember being young. Do you think you'll get old?" she asked me.

"I'll probably die before I do, in a fight or a fall." I saw myself as a hero not as an old man with a long beard. "Maybe on a boat. Or in the mountains."

"Unlikely. No. You'll be an old man who has to sit on a stone wall, and when you do, you'll think of me."

When we reached the old mansion, I asked Madame where Jestine's daughter had been taken.

"Paris. If she's still alive. It's been years. You lose people sometimes, you know. You don't expect to, but then it happens and you can't get them back."

We went into the kitchen, where Mrs. James took the groceries from us and asked Madame Halevy what on earth she was thinking to be walking through town on such a hot day. People fainted in weather like this. She should stay behind the shutters, which would block out the too bright sunlight.

"I had to tell this boy the end of the story."

"It's not the end," I said. "You don't know if she's still in Paris."

"The end of that story," Madame Halevy corrected me. "Jestine's not the only one with a story, you know. There are people who die all of a sudden, as if their hearts exploded. But for others it takes a long time. They walk around, as if they're still alive, and it's years before you realize nothing's there."

"Enough of this," Mrs. James told us. We were told to remove ourselves from the kitchen and she would bring us limewater to refresh us. She would add a splash of rum for Madame. After she brought our drinks, Madame and I sat together in the parlor. It was much cooler there, with a breeze. The paint on the walls was faded, I saw, with patches of plaster showing through. There were dark veins of soot in the window glass.

I realized that my companion's eyes were closed and that she had fallen asleep. The stray bands of sunlight in the room were lemony, with a dusky brilliance. There was the scent of verbena. I closed my eyes and dreamed of walking along a path of pale red earth under a soft cloudy sky. There were birds I didn't recognize. I woke with a jolt of fear. My companion was already awake, watching over me. I realized then she hadn't said one word about her own daughter, and I asked after her. Why had she gone to Charleston? Why didn't she answer Madame's letters?

"I've decided I don't want to burden you with my story. I think I'll fold it up and take it with me when I go. You're too nice a boy to carry something that doesn't belong to you for the sake of an old lady who won't be in this world much longer."

She patted my arm, and I realized then that I was not just a delivery boy to her. She had become attached to me, and I to her.

Afterward, I kept thinking about her story, folded into a desk drawer or in her night table or perhaps in a pocket she had sewn, close to her heart. I intended to go back to see her, but a shipment came in from Portugal of all manner of fabrics, embroideries and lace and flowered muslins. My father insisted I help my brothers unload the shipment and store everything neatly folded in tissue paper. I did put something aside, perhaps you can say I stole it, though I didn't think of it that way. It was a lace table runner to replace the frayed one on Madame's table. I never got to give it to her. Madame Halevy died the next week. I attended the funeral at the synagogue. People prayed and I saw my father there among the men. I followed the mourners and the Reverend to the Jewish cemetery.

I was wearing my brother's black suit, the one I'd worn to her dinner, though I'd gotten no farther than her kitchen. I didn't understand the way I felt, my heart knotted, as if I had suffered a great loss. I barely knew Madame Halevy, and she had never finished her story. Then I understood that when someone begins to tell you her story, you are entwined together. Perhaps even more so if the ending hasn't been divulged. It was exactly like dreaming the same dream, then waking too soon and never finding out what had happened. I watched leaves fall as the mourning prayers were recited. People here say that means a spirit is walking above you, in the trees, and that once a soul is free to join with them she can walk all the way to the world to come. That was a story I decided to believe.

I OFTEN THOUGHT OF Madame Halevy's son, lost when he was only a year older than I was, and the second son that she tried to protect from fever by keeping him inside for a year. Time seemed different to me, less spread out in front of me. I saw it now as a box. I was inching my way across that box, and before long I would reach the other side. I often imagined myself as that old man sitting on a stone wall, the one Madame Halevy had predicted I'd be.

I stepped back into my own life. I concentrated on my painting. My mother glared and asked how I thought I would make my living as a man.

"There's only one thing I want to do," I said. "I intend to do it."

"Whoever says that is a fool."

"Were you a fool to live as you pleased?"

"That's none of your business," my mother told me. I laughed at that. After all, the decisions she'd made had formed my life.

I stomped out of the house. If I had only a limited amount of time, I planned to do as I pleased. I painted for hours, finding shelter on rainy days deep in the woods in a shack that had been deserted. I stumbled upon it by accident and immediately decided it should be mine. The woods were green and shadowy, and there were gumbo-limbo trees, whose red bark fell off in strips like skin off a sunburned man. I knocked on the door, and when there was no answer, I pushed it open. No one had lived in this place for a long time. It was as if it had been waiting for me.

I liked the way the light came in through the windows, falling through the trees in slashes of brightness. I painted like a madman, covering the walls of the shack with portraits and then with landscapes, one on top of another. Outside the grass was high and birds swooped down to catch mosquitoes at dusk. I stayed so late I brought candles with me, so that I might paint far into the evening. Colors changed in these conditions. The light flickered as if stars were trapped inside with me. I saw differently; objects became cloudy, then bright. There were all sorts of ancient herbs hanging from the ceiling on lengths of old rope. The scent in the shack was of anise, wood, and mint. Every time I went home I felt as though I were leaving my true self behind, that I was leaving the real person crouched down near a wall flecked with color, whereas the boy who walked through his family's home was nothing more than a ghost.

One day as I was painting, trying to perfect the definition of a human hand and using my own as a model, I saw a shadow. Marianna was outside. I went out and stood in the grass beside her. She no longer went to school. Her mother needed her in their laundry business. They took in laundry from sailors and often found trinkets in the pockets of their clothes, shells from across the world, keys to hotel rooms in Europe and South America, addresses of women these sailors had once loved. Marianna showed me how she could carry a basket of laundry on her head. She did so perfectly. I tried, and when it fell she laughed at me. I invited her into the shack, but she shook her head, and took a step back. Something crossed her face, an expression I didn't recognize.

"There was an old man who lived here. He used to put spells on people and save dying men. He could heal people whom no one else could, but you had to pay him with something that was dear to you. I wouldn't go in there," she said. "And I wouldn't go with you."

Our differences were there between us and I hated that. I turned and went inside. She followed me and stood on the threshold. I could tell, our friendship was over. She was too grown up, she told me. Not a schoolgirl anymore. She proved that to me by kissing me. Then she vanished so quickly it seemed she had never been there. I had dreamed it surely. There were footsteps in the grass, but soon they disappeared too. I am embarrassed to admit, I cried, for she had been my truest friend, and she wasn't that anymore. I'd had the first stirrings of love, but it didn't matter.

I hoped that the old man who had lived here could heal me. I painted and painted, desperate, hoping for a vision the healer might send me. I sat on the floor and looked around me, and all at once I realized I had my answer. I had sketched my hand as if it was made out of palm fronds and meadows. This island was inside of me. I had captured light, heat, grass, sky. I had it all in my hands.

1842

Just before my twelfth birthday my father called me to him. He gave me an envelope. The paper was a fair sky blue. When I opened the envelope I found a ticket for passage on a schooner. I thought I was dreaming. I pinched my own leg and it smarted. My mother was standing in the doorway. There was her green-tinged shadow. It was likely she knew I wasn't going to my lessons. Certainly, she knew I was not interested in the family business. Now I was being sent to relatives in Paris, and to a school there to study with a Monsieur Savary. My parents were not pleased with my schoolwork, and they thought my world should be broadened. Clearly, they feared for my future or they would not have taken such a radical step. I would miss Hannah's wedding, I would miss my own birthday and celebrate it not at home with my family but in a land I'd only seen in drawings, living with people I'd never met before.

I didn't know how to feel. St. Thomas was all I knew, and I wondered if going away might change me in ways that made me into someone else; if I might become more like the boys my age from the congregation who abided by their parents' laws and rules. I was defiant, and I supposed I was being punished for that. In the days that followed I went wandering and didn't come home till morning. Sometimes I saw the slim deer that were brought here for the sole purpose of being hunted more than a hundred years earlier, creatures that had become so shy of human contact they were rarely seen. I stood outside a ring in the countryside where there was cockfighting. Men were drinking hard and betting on their roosters, and there was the scent of blood. My blood raced as well, and I drank a fair amount when I could manage to get hold of a bottle. My friends, the two brothers, were wary of me now. Perhaps our differences were too much for our friendship in this time and place. My mother would have disapproved of my being there at the ring, she would think the men barbaric. And yet Jestine had told me my own mother seemed to enjoy dispatching chickens when she was a girl. So there it was: my mother was a hypocrite and a stranger. She did one thing, but insisted I do the other. I realized that I hated her. This was not what I was supposed to feel and so I hated myself as well.

I found myself at the harbor one day when the sky was still dark. I walked around taking in the scents and sounds, then I went to sit on Jestine's steps. I wished that she had been my mother, for she understood me in a way my own never would. There were still the last few stars in the sky, their dim light reflecting in the water. Jestine emerged from the cottage with mugs of coffee mixed with sugar. Her hands were dyed indigo blue from the dresses she had tinted that day.

"You can't sleep," she said. "Neither can I."

"I know what happened," I said. "I'm going to Paris. When I get there I'll look for your daughter."

"Looking never did anyone any good."

I amended my words. "I'll find her."

Jestine nodded and patted my back. I felt that she had faith in me, even though I was a boy. She went inside, and I drank my coffee. She came back with a letter in a sealed envelope. "I wrote this the day they took her."

I folded the letter into my jacket. The paper felt soft, like silk, as if it had been touched ten thousand times. I folded it the way Madame Halevy had folded up her own story.

I arrived home when dawn was breaking, walking through clouds of mosquitoes. The light was a pale pink. I thought I would sneak into the house, but as it turned out my mother couldn't sleep either. She was waiting for me outside, sitting on the metal chair that had been left there ever since Madame Halevy had come for me in one of the last weeks of her life.

"Let me guess. You were at Jestine's." My mother sounded hurt.

"To say good-bye," I told her, for there was nothing wrong in that.

My mother led me upstairs without a word. She didn't berate me or punish me for being out all night. We were quiet on the staircase so we wouldn't wake my brothers and sisters. Outside the birds were stirring, and there was a haze of mist as the heat of the day settled onto the streets. My father had already been to the garden to say his prayers and left for the synagogue to offer his help to those in need. My mother hadn't told him I was missing. She didn't like to worry my father; she was tender with him in a way she wasn't with anyone else. Now she opened the door to the chamber she shared with him, a room we children were never invited into. To my great surprise there was my painting of Jestine, the one that had been taken from the storeroom. It had been hung upon the wall. My mother had tears in her eyes, something I had never seen before. I was confused. She had told me my paintings were nothing like the real world, and yet she'd kept this one. Because my mother was a stranger to me, I had always thought I was a stranger to her as well. Now I wasn't so certain.

"You think I don't see what Jestine sees, but I do," my mother said. "I know you have talent. But you must put it aside. I want you to study hard. When you come back the business will be waiting for you. You were always the one I wanted to take over. Before you do, I'm sending you to Paris so you can have what I didn't."

I couldn't have been more surprised if she had told me she wasn't my mother. Her black hair was loose and her eyes were wet and dark. I saw something new in her, the person Jestine had told me about.

"My father was like you," she said. "He saw no differences among people. He believed that every man had rights in this world. I know he believed that women had rights as well, for he treated me as he would have a son, until the rules we lived by made it impossible. Some things are impossible, it's true." My mother was weeping then. "But some things are not," she said.

I realized what I would miss most about my home were the colors, the light, the flowers, the fields, the women at their work, carrying baskets of laundry. I would miss Jestine, and my sister Hannah, and if the nights were cold enough, and the snow was silver-white, I would likely miss my mother as well.

I COULD NOT SLEEP on the night before I left. I went walking in the dark and met Marianna on the beach. We sat there, hands intertwined. She cried when I told her I was leaving. "Yes, go," she said to me, but she still held my hand. By the time I came back she would probably be married. She would sit on this beach with somebody else. But I would carry every detail about her with me.

When I packed in the morning I found a sachet of some herb in my luggage. I sniffed it. There was the scent of lavender. Pleasant enough. I meant to keep it with my belongings, but in my haste I left it on the bureau. I was late and had to race to catch the boat, and so I did not have time for proper good-byes. My mother ran after me and insisted on embracing me.

"Come back to me," she said, as if it was a hex of some sort.

Her eyes were bright, and if she were anyone else I would have thought she shed tears. I kissed her three times, and then embraced my father and my brothers and sisters. I should have been afraid to leave my home and everything I had known. I was a boy and France was a long way off, but the journey didn't unnerve me. I was ready for the seas and skies and storms.

The boat was a dream and the world at sea was a haze of life. Everyone spoke another language, and men twice my age offered me rum. I sketched whenever I could. The seabirds hovering, the lamps that burned at night, the men who worked so hard their arms were huge with muscles. The voyage seemed to take forever, and then, quite suddenly, we could see the shore. When I arrived in France, the twilight was gray, a shade I'd never seen before, and the silvery sky seemed within reach. I took note of chimneys and cobblestones as a pale green rain began to fall down. It was autumn, a season I had never known but fell in love with immediately. The air smelled like smoke. The leaves on the trees were yellow and copper. The clouds went on forever, banks of gray and blue and a shade of pink so fragile it was fading as I watched. All around me, for as far as the eye could see, were colors I had never observed before: the emerald lawns, the deep brown-green chestnut trees, the lime-colored vines, the rooftops smudged black and midnight blue. There were a thousand different blues all around me in the falling dusk. They shifted like waves in the sea. I took one breath of Paris and I knew. At last, at the age of twelve, four thousand miles away from home, I was free.

CHAPTER EIGHT

A Distant Planet

PARIS

1847

LYDIA CASSIN RODRIGUES COHEN

I t was raining and she was home alone. From the window she could see a chestnut tree, raindrops splattering against the black bark. In that tree was a nightingale, which was silent at this hour. Usually such birds began to migrate to West Africa at this time of year, but this one had stayed on in their garden. The air was luminous and damp. The children, ages four, two, and one, were out with the maid, dressed in boots and cloaks so they might collect leaves in the park. Her husband, Henri Cohen, was a partner in a small family banking company and often came home late for dinner. Sometimes she worried, for France was politically unstable, with demonstrations against the King where violence often erupted. Henri was the love of her life and always catered to her, but he was a logical person and would likely think she was mad if she told him she thought that her mother, who had died nearly five years earlier, had come back to her in the form of a nightingale, and that whenever she saw the bird in their garden, she felt a shiver go through her. When this happened, she would go to close the mauve silk curtains, because she'd have a breathless feeling, as if she were running through a field with the sun beating down on her, as if she were a million miles away, about to explode with light.

There was a certain sadness around her lately. Her father was ill. He had a lung disease and everyone hoped he would last the year, but as the days passed, that seemed unlikely. He didn't wish to see anyone, only the nurse who cared for him. Lydia found herself thinking that this woman, Marie, had been his mistress even when her mother was alive, for Madame Cassin Rodrigues had disliked her and at the end had begged for another caretaker. Now this Marie had moved into his house in Passy, where she took care of Lydia's father with extreme tenderness. She spoke with familiarity. Once, when Monsieur Rodrigues had balked at taking his medicine, Lydia had overheard Marie say, *But, Aaron, you must*, with an authority more suited to a wife than a nurse.

Lydia's father had said something the last time she'd visited with the children that had unsettled her. He was in a chair by the window overlooking the garden. He'd been a tall man, but now he was stooped. He had a long face that had once been so handsome few women had been able to look away. He was concentrating on the outside world. In his view, there were still a few stray poppies in bloom despite the season. Shades of orange and red. Plumes of tall grass grew untended. She'd brought him tea and was crouched beside his chair so she might add sugar to his cup with a pair of tongs.

He gazed at her so deeply she was flustered. "I wish you hadn't had your mother's silver eyes," he said. "They remind me of her every day."

Startled, she acted as if he hadn't said something so odd. She asked him if he wanted cream as well as sugar, and he shook his head. Her mother's eyes were blue, as were her father's and her own, though hers were, indeed, paler, and on cloudy days, they turned a fragile gray. She had a strange flicker in the pit of her stomach. There was a light inside she sometimes felt, a sharp, stinging brightness.

Her father was becoming more and more distraught, revealing a depth of feeling she hadn't thought him capable of.

"I betrayed her," he said mournfully. "What sort of man acts like that?"

"I'll get you a blanket," Lydia said, for he was shivering.

"I should have left you where you belonged," he said to her then. "I shouldn't have been your father."

She went to get the blanket and realized there were tears running down her face. Her father had always been somewhat distant, but now his words felt like an attack. Was he saying he had never loved her? What she had done to deserve this, she had no idea. Perhaps it was his illness speaking, nothing more.

She passed a gilded mirror in the hall and stared at her reflection. In this mirror her eyes did indeed look as silver as the glass.

She'd been disturbed ever since. And there was something else: a boy had been following her. It had been going on for some time. A tall boy who was almost a man. At first she thought she was imagining it. She was at the park with her three daughters and they were playing in the leaves when she noticed a shadow falling over them. She had dreams of shadows, of people who came to her to tell her secrets, but this was daylight in the park. She wore a silky woolen cape that was the color of wine along with a pretty gray dress and high-laced boots. She gazed up and the shadow darted away. She hurried the children from the park, past the green wooden benches, along the gravel paths, home to safety. She locked the doors, drew the curtains, put the children to bed. Later, when she glanced out at the street, she thought she saw him again, a tall, thin boy in an overcoat, boots, a black cap, who rubbed his hands together, as if he were freezing even though it was only October, that smoky, beautiful month when the leaves on the plane trees turned brown before slowly curling up into brittle ash.

In bed with her husband she whispered that her father was dying and that she'd felt he'd never loved her.

"It doesn't matter," Henri said. "I do."

She didn't tell him about the boy on the street or the comment about the silver eyes.

They went to Friday night services with the children, and often had dinner with Henri's parents, who treated Lydia as if she were a daughter. The Cohens had only sons, Henri and his two younger brothers, and they were delighted with Lydia's charm. She had a slight accent, which they teased her about, and a longing for spice in her tea, which they thought unusual and amusing. They were a jolly family, different from her own. Her mother had been moody and, although loving, not socially inclined. She didn't care to go out, and the few friends she had came to visit her for tea or drinks as if she were an invalid, which she was not. Her father, rarely at home, was distant, more so since he'd been unwell. She wondered where he'd been all those nights when he failed to appear for dinner. Perhaps he'd been a ladies' man all along.

Henri's mother's sister, his aunt Sophie, had been a girlhood friend of Lydia's mother who she'd often visited, and so it seemed they were meant to be family. Everyone agreed, they were fated. Henri was tall and had sharply defined features, a large, beautiful head, and luminous eyes. He was quite handsome, but there was more to him. He was capable, adept at business, but he was a man of deep emotion, something his brothers teased him about. He was an ardent stargazer and had a telescope set up in the garden, and a smaller scope that he carried with him, as another man might carry a cane. He was not a banker at heart but a scientist and an observer of nature. He was elated by the discovery of a new planet the previous year and, only recently, the detection of its moon.

"There's always more to discover in this world," he told Lydia cheerfully.

She loved how easy it was for Henri to be made happy. He was the opposite of her father in this way, for her father had always been a man who had to have more and more. The new planet was invisible to the naked eye, though it had been spied occasionally, by Galileo for instance, who mistook it for a fixed star. On the night of the family dinner when Aunt Sophie came from Lyon, Henri was in the garden with his father and brothers, discussing the mysterious nature of the heavens. There had recently been a lunar eclipse, and ever since, the men in the family had held regular meetings to watch the sky. They called themselves *Société des Astronomes Amateurs*.

The women remained in the parlor. Madame Sophie had been to their wedding, but Lydia had never spent time with her, and she found the older woman to be captivating. She was a great storyteller, and though she was widowed and had none of her own, she adored children. She told fairy tales wherein men were turned into swans and girls had to find their way through the woods. Because of this Lydia's oldest daughter liked to keep bread crumbs beside her bed, even though they brought mice into the room. The girls were already drowsing in their mother's arms by the time tonight's story had ended. It was a tale about sisters who had fallen in love, one with a hunter, the second with a bear, the third with a prince who was penniless. Madame Cohen, the doting grandmother, had gone upstairs to put the girls to bed after the story of the sisters had been told.

"I can see why my mother so enjoyed your friendship when you were girls," Lydia said as the men were looking at the stars. She was wearing blue, her favorite color, a dress fashioned of silk damask. She often dressed her girls in three different shades of blue. Tonight she'd chosen teal for Amelia, indigo for Mirabelle, and soft sky blue for Leah, who was little more than a baby but did her best to keep up with her sisters, toddling after them. They were darling children, adored by Henri's parents. Lydia wished her mother had lived to see them. Surely she would have delighted in them. Her father had taken little notice of his granddaughters, although he insisted on visiting each one on the day after her birth. Now, Lydia wondered if he was looking for those silver eyes he'd spoken of. He had not a worry. The three girls' eyes were blue.

"Elise was a complicated woman," Sophie said as they had their coffee. "I suppose that's what interested me. You expected one thing of her and she turned and did something completely out of character. People who thought she was nothing more than a pretty doll had a surprise coming to them. She could be quite vicious if the need arose. But if she was your friend, she was that for all eternity."

"Between us things were quite simple," Lydia said. "I always knew I could depend on her. I suppose that's why I miss her so. She was the person I could count on no matter what. Now it's Henri. So I'm fortunate in my choice." She noticed Sophie staring. "Do my eyes look silver to you?" she blurted.

Sophie laughed. "Not at all."

The men had returned from their stargazing, clapping the frost from their coats. It had been a lovely evening. The guests were getting ready to leave when Sophie suggested she and Lydia have tea together, just the two of them. Lydia agreed, imagining this was an invitation that would occur sometime in the future, but the very next day Sophie arrived at three o'clock. It was inconvenient, really, and unexpected, such things were usually scheduled, but there was nothing Lydia could do but ask the maid to take the children to the park. While the maid readied the girls, Lydia would have to brew the tea herself. She chose jasmine, the scent of which always made her sad, yet she favored it. Sophie sat across from her and apologized for coming unannounced. "If I've overstepped, I didn't mean to. I had no intention to upset you."

"It's fine," Lydia replied, confused, meaning it was quite all right for her to come without first sending a note. "You don't upset me in the least."

"But perhaps I will in what I say." Sophie treaded carefully.

"Oh, say what you will," Lydia responded, still puzzled by the intensity of this surprise visit. "I can't imagine I'd be offended."

"I'm glad you feel that way. I can't imagine it would matter now, with Elise gone. And when you asked about the color of your eyes, I felt I might be free to speak to you. Before that, I wasn't certain you knew."

"As I said, between my mother and myself, things were simple. She called me her great and wonderful gift."

"So you were aware that she couldn't have children." Sophie appeared relieved. "But of course she would have told you."

Lydia did not move, for fear she would betray herself. She knew nothing of this. Her heart was twisted inside her chest. The maid, already wearing her cape, brought almond cakes with sugar frosting. She had bundled up the children, who followed at her heels. It was unseasonably cold, but the park awaited. The girls were ushered from the house. The tea was poured. Jasmine tea was from Japan, deliciously fragrant with a woodsy, floral scent and a pale green color in the bone china cups. Lydia felt as though something was stuck in her throat; she found she couldn't even swallow a sip of tea.

"She wanted you desperately," Lydia's visitor went on, "and was so delighted when you entered her life. You were indeed a treasure and a gift. As long as you know that."

"How did that entrance occur?" When Aunt Sophie looked puzzled by the question, posed by one who supposedly knew her own history, Lydia added, "I can never remember the details."

She was cold as she poured more tea for her guest, despite the fire in the grate. She heard the nightingale in the yard. It was a large garden, but the bird always perched in the same tree. The one outside her window.

"Who can remember details?" Sophie shrugged. "Some days I can barely remember my own name!"

"Was I a foundling?"

"No. Of course not. You are your father's child—I believe from a marriage before he wed your mother. It seems your mother kept some details to herself."

"She did." Lydia nodded.

"I know she wanted to tell you more about the situation. I remember discussing it with her. But when do you tell a daughter that another woman gave birth to her? I suppose you were grown up when she informed you."

Lydia tried to straighten out her thoughts, but the fact that her mother, who had been her biggest champion and the person closest to her in the world, was not a blood relation or her birth mother was staggering. "No. It was only recently," she lied. The lie was like a block of ice, and yet Sophie seemed to believe her.

"Well, she worried over what to say for years. She never told me the details, or I would tell you now myself. Only that she had given you a far better life than the one you would have had. I assume there was some scandal involved. But scandal is everywhere, isn't it?"

The news about her parentage changed things in a way Lydia didn't understand. She felt angry at herself, for taking everything at face value, and angry with her mother for dying without telling her the truth.

That night she held her daughters close, and swore she would never betray them. She wanted to ask her father to reveal who her true mother had been, but when she went to visit him, Marie, the nurse, said he was too ill for company and turned her away. She stood outside the house of white stone where she'd grown up, where the vines wound up the walls to the chamber in which she'd slept as a child, and she felt a stranger.

"Would you ever lie to me?" she asked Henri later on.

"What would I lie about?" he responded.

The weather was chill, but they were in the garden, looking at stars. The nightingale fluttered from branch to branch, but didn't sing a note. Henri was kindhearted, a truly good man, and her mother had been his champion. "I think he's the one for you," Lydia recalled her saying. "He won't break your heart."

Henri dreamed of constellations, he'd told her, and of her.

Her own dreams were unreachable, dissolving into mist before she could reach them in her waking state. *I don't dream*, she insisted when he questioned her, yet the statement felt like a lie. There were birds she couldn't quite see. Voices she couldn't quite hear. The sound of the sea.

Henri tried to show her Neptune, but she couldn't spy it through the telescope. Just a blue whirl beside some hot white specks. She thought about her mother not being her mother, and everything that had happened between them. Now when she looked back, the tiniest nod or glance took on new meaning. *I love you anyway. I love you more. You're mine. I'm yours.*

As she'd aged, her mother's pale red hair had turned white. She remained stylish, and to some, especially her maids, her cold eye was fearsome. She liked things done with style, her style. She had her own chamber, with red lacquered walls and dove-gray bedcoverings. Lydia's father's room was down the hall, and smelled of cigar smoke. Her mother said she could not stand the smoke, or his sputtering snore, but there was more, a distance between them. As for her father, he gave her mother gifts on a regular basis, but managed to stay clear of her and lead his own life. He had an apartment somewhere; it was said to be used for business meetings. Sometimes when her father looked at her mother, Lydia saw a sort of surprise behind his eyes, as if he'd wandered into the wrong house and had come home to the wrong wife.

Before she died her mother had said, "Always pay heed to the woman who comes before you. If he's treated her badly, he will treat you much the same."

They'd been alone in her room, with a fire going to take the chill off, though it was May. Lydia, already married and in love, had laughed. "In Henri's case," she'd said, "that would be his mother." But when she'd begun to see Marie in the house so soon after her mother's death, she believed she understood her mother's message. Her father had not been faithful. The extravagant gifts he'd given to his wife—a ruby pendant from India, silk dresses, strands of pearls, creamy cameos—he had likely given to other women as well. Looking back, Lydia remembered walking into shops with her mother and having the salesgirl say Monsieur Rodrigues had just been in to buy a present and being confused about why such a statement should bring her mother to tears.

LYDIA WENT AGAIN TO see her father on a cold November day. The leaves were red and brown. A mist sifted down from the damp sky. Later it would rain, but not now. She wore a heavy black cape— her funeral

cape, she realized—bought for her mother's funeral in the Jewish cemetery in Passy. She knocked formally on the door, her own door, where
she'd grown up. Marie answered, surprised to see her. Her father was
resting.

"He's my father, and I want to see him," Lydia told the nurse.

She walked inside and didn't listen to any protestations. She'd been
up the stairs a thousand times before. She passed her mother's room and
continued on. Her father was in bed. The bed had been pulled to the
window so he might look outside. He turned to her, thinking she was
Marie. The nurse had followed and was right behind her. Lydia thought
her father's eyes brightened when he saw her. Perhaps there was some
affection there, after all.

"He's very tired," Marie said.

There was no refuting this; all the same Lydia told Marie she was the
one who must leave. Lydia made certain to close the door after the nurse
edged into the hallway, then returned to the bedside, where she sat in a
hard-backed chair. Her father's eyes flitted over to her, then away.

"I hear a bird," he said.

The rain had begun. There were no birds.

"She wasn't my mother?"

There was a white film over his eyes, which were still very blue.

"You were born in St. Thomas," he said.

Her mother had told her this. Lydia had been born there during their
travels. Though her mother said they left that far-off island when she
was a baby, Lydia had some memory of a long trip, and of her mother
singing to her as the waves hit against them, of miles and miles of blue
sea. Now she wondered if it was possible for an infant to have such memories, for her girls remembered nothing from their babyhood. She'd
gone so far as to question them, and they could not recall the songs she'd
sung to them or the days she'd paced the floor with them. Those first
memories were fainter than shadows on the wall.

"To your first wife?" Lydia put forth.

"Well, I couldn't marry her," her father said. "Wasn't that obvious? We weren't allowed."

"Why not?" Lydia asked, more confused than ever.

"Do you think I ever loved anyone else?" her father said. His eyes were so pale it seemed possible to look through them into a part of him she'd never seen before. He seemed completely unfamiliar to Lydia, a lost man. He reached for her. In that instant, Lydia felt like pulling away, but she forced herself to grasp his hand. She hadn't expected his hand to feel so light, as if beneath the skin there were nothing more than the bones of a bird. "Don't do what they tell you to," he said.

Marie came in, with a maid in tow, interrupting, insisting it was time for her father to sleep. Lydia was rushed from the room. She stood in the hall, mortified, while Marie sang to him as she settled him in his bed. When he was dozing, Marie came out to the hallway to escort her from the house.

"Your father has very little time left," she said. "I won't have him bothered."

"I wasn't bothering him."

"I think I know when he's tired."

Lydia felt like saying, *Heed the woman before you. He'll treat you as badly as he treated her.* In fact her father had disappeared for over a week after her mother's funeral. People said it was sorrow that had caused his absence, but now Lydia wasn't so sure. Surely there was another woman, most likely one of his friends' wives. That was the way such things were done. Affairs were kept quiet, and maintained within a single circle, people of the same standing and faith. The nurse was not of their faith; any relationship with her would not be serious, so it was absurd for her to act as if she were the woman of the house. It was unlikely her father would leave anything to his nurse in his will if that was what this was all about. And then she saw it as she was leaving the room. A flash of red at Marie's throat. The ruby from India that had belonged to her mother.

Lydia turned and left, grief-stricken. After a while she saw the boy following her through the streets. She hadn't thought of him for days. Perhaps she should have been frightened, but it was otherwise. She felt grateful not to be alone. She liked the idea of having a companion. Once she dropped a glove purposely, and when she retrieved it she turned her head in order to see him more clearly. He was no ghost, and was clearly flesh, perhaps sixteen or so, as tall as Henri, quite serious in his demeanor. He looked like a man, but there was something boyish about his posture. He ran a hand through his long, dark hair. He stopped when she did and turned to study a garden, overgrown with lime trees and weeds, then he gazed at her again. She gestured to him, but he looked panicked and backed away.

Soon after, her father died. His death was a hollow thud. Lydia went to the service and to the burial but remembered little. Only the ice-cold air as the men took turns shoveling dirt over the coffin. The sobs of the nurse. A nightingale in a tree bringing forth a ribbon of song, even though it was daylight, the wrong hour for such a creature to sing. The house was sold quickly. Although the money from the sale came to Lydia and Henri, when they went to close up the house most of the belongings were gone, the walls stripped of their paintings, and all of Lydia's mother's jewelry, the cameos and gold necklaces and, of course, the ruby, had disappeared. The rooms echoed.

"We can go to a solicitor," Henri said. "Track down this Marie."

"No," Lydia told him. "Let her be."

She stood at the glass doors to the garden while Henri went through her father's desk. Later that evening, when they had gone home, Lydia was awakened by the scent of something burning. She crept down the stairs, on which there was soft red Oriental carpeting. Her husband was burning documents in a large copper pan in the kitchen, the window open to ensure that the smoke would escape. A wind blew through the house. Unless Lydia was mistaken the smoke was tinted blue.

"What are you doing?" she asked.

"He wrote poetry," Henri said. "To some woman. I didn't think you'd want to see. They're not particularly good."

Some of it was burned, but she told him to stop and took up the sheaves of paper. She went to the pantry, a small wooden corridor where they stored flour and spices, and sat on a stool. She read them all and afterward felt as if she had swallowed stones. He loved someone, that much was clear. He called her a red flower, a star in the sky, a woman who could swim with turtles, who would never let him go, not that he wanted his freedom, not that he had ever wanted anything but her.

IN THE FOLLOWING DAYS Lydia searched through her memories, but they were hazy, bursts of events she'd experienced as a child and then as a young woman—lessons, parties, dinners, and finally meeting Henri, the moment when everything became brighter. At night, however, stranger images came into her dreams. She managed to catch bits and pieces, and she arose from her bed with peculiar tableaus in her mind: fields of tall yellow grass, a pool of tiny fish, the sound of the sea, red flowers tumbling down a hillside, her little girls with their eyes turned silver, a boy who tracked her in his black coat. She asked the maid if she'd ever been aware of someone following when she took the children to the park.

"It began two years ago," the maid confided. "I didn't wish to upset you. I shooed him away, but twice he had the nerve to come to the door. I told him never to return, but then he came again, to the back door, like a servant. He apologized for using the front door, and for trailing after us."

"But for what reason?" Lydia asked. She had grown cold with something that was not quite fear. Perhaps it was an odd excitement.

The maid shrugged. "I never gave him time to speak his mind. I didn't think it was proper. He was nervous and shy, yet he continued coming round until one night I greeted him with a hammer in my hands, and he hasn't come back since."

Lydia did not know what to do about her pursuer or even what to think. Evidently he had been searching them out for some time, years in fact. And then as she had dinner with her daughters one night, just the four of them, as Henri would be home late from work what she should do came to her as a dream might, suddenly and fully formed. She would turn the tables and follow the boy. She would become a shadow as he dodged away from spying on her. She felt a thrill inside her, as if she were waking up, taking control of her life. She played for hours with her girls, games of hide-and-seek, which perfectly suited her intention for finding her follower. By the end of the evening there was not a single place in the house—not the cellar, not the kitchen, not the tiniest bureau—where she could not find her daughters if she put her mind to it. She would do the same to catch the boy in the black coat.

As it turned out, she noticed him in the synagogue on Friday night. This was luck, indeed. Perhaps he had often been there and she'd never noticed, as the men and women were separated. But now that she'd spied him she felt her pulse quicken. She told her mother-in-law she had a headache and needed some air, leaving her children in Madame Cohen's care. She went outside and headed for home, knowing what would happen, sensing the shadow behind her. She felt her pursuer, his tentative gait, his nervous posture, his youth. There was a comforting familiarity in his presence; it was as if her own past were following her. She entered her house, then watched him from the window. When he turned to leave, thinking she had retired for the evening, she sneaked back out through the garden, ready to turn the tables. She was light on her feet, wearing her woolen cape. The air was cold and smelled sweet, as if the dark was made of molasses. The cobblestones were slippery from an earlier shower. She trudged after him through the dark streets for nearly half an hour. Just when she thought she must turn back, and felt irretrievably lost, he arrived at a tall brick house. They were still in the Jewish quarter. Luckily a neighbor passed by and Lydia asked who lived at this address. The name was Pizzarro.

She thought about that name as she found her way home. That night she dreamed of a place where there were huge teal-colored birds trailing through a marsh. They walked as people did, regally, as if they were kings and queens. When she awoke she was steaming with sweat. She was in her chilly bedchamber, her sleeping husband beside her, the stars outside their window, but her skin was flushed with heat. She remembered looking down through the slats of a porch to gaze at the movement of the waves.

SHE WROTE A NOTE introducing herself to the lady of the house, which her maid delivered, and in return she received an invitation to tea. She went alone without mentioning her outing to Henri. She was treated warmly by Madame Pizzarro. Hers was a large family, originally from Spain, with many children in and out of the house. Lydia revealed her reason for coming, which sounded quite logical—now that her children were growing older she wished to expand her circle and become more involved with the synagogue. She said she'd been told Madame Pizzarro might help her meet other women in the congregation. Madame laughed and said her own children were growing older as well, but she had little time to visit with the Sisterhood, for she'd been helping out with a nephew for the past few years, a boy who was a boarding student at a nearby academy but who spent most of his time with his extended family. He sometimes spent weekends with his grandparents, Joseph and Ann-Felicité Pizzarro, whose son, the boy's father, managed a family business in St. Thomas.

Lydia felt a jolt upon hearing a mention of St. Thomas. It was her birthplace, yet she knew nothing of it.

"How odd," she said. "I was born there during a visit my parents made."

As it turned out the nephew had arrived at the age of twelve and would be returning home at the end of the year, having studied at the Savary Academy for several years under the tutelage of Monsieur Savary, an expert in drawing and painting. The boy, whose father was a Pizzarro who lived halfway across the world, had become a good student and an excellent painter. At first his hosts did their best not to encourage

their ward in this thankless arena; business was a more appropriate calling, and the one his parents wished him to pursue. But his teacher had
applauded his artistry, calling him extraordinary. In fact Madame and her
husband were rather proud of a small oil painting on the wall the boy had
given them.

"Everyone believes we purchased it from a great artist, and we never
say it's only by our nephew. He takes delight in people's confusion, and
so do we. For all we know he'll be a great artist someday."

Lydia went for a closer look. The painting, in a gold-leaf frame, was
luminous in tone. She was drawn to the image and could see why people
assumed an expert had crafted it. A woman carried a basket of laundry to a
house set upon stilts, the turquoise sea behind her, her expression serene.

Lydia sat down, overheated again and agitated in a way she couldn't
understand. She had a flash of something, perhaps a memory, perhaps a
fear. She explained that she had headaches. But that was a lie. It was the
painting that had affected her. She had the odd sense that she herself had
been in that very same place. If you ventured along the road you would
see red flowers in the hills, tumbling down like a staircase. They were the
ones she dreamed of, and when she woke she still imagined them, as if
petals had been set in her path as she walked her girls around the neighborhood.

At last the boy she was waiting for came home from school with Madame's two sons, their maleness filling up the house with their deep
voices and the clatter of their books and belongings and the scent of cold
air and sweat. Madame Pizzarro's sons ambled past, already in boisterous
conversation, on their way to have a late tea. Then the nephew came in,
reading as he walked.

"Does no one greet a guest?" Madame Pizzarro called. Lydia recognized the tall boy who was so intent on his book. "How about my dear
nephew?"

The boy looked up. He seemed a confident fellow, but when he saw
Lydia he immediately grew pale. She thought perhaps he stumbled. He

was so angular and thin that his trousers seemed too big for him, and his jacket too small for his long arms.

"This is Madame Cohen," the hostess continued.

Lydia walked to him and offered her hand. "I think we've met."

His hand in hers was rougher than she'd expected, stained with faint blotches of paint.

"We may have," the boy said cautiously.

"You're an artist?"

"Yes." He was a bit defiant in his answer, his hackles raised. "Perhaps you'd like to tell me it's a waste of my time."

"Not at all," she responded.

He almost smiled then. He was no longer a ghost. He looked at her, concerned, more vulnerable than she would have imagined.

"Lyddie," he said.

"Madame Cohen!" his aunt corrected him. "Where have everyone's manners gone?"

"Out the window," the boy said. "Where they belong."

Lydia thought of what her father had said during their last visit. *Don't do what they tell you to.*

"He came to us as Jacobo, a cousin several times removed. But once he arrived in Paris he took his middle name. Camille."

The boy shrugged. "People change."

"He's become French through and through," his aunt said, pleased.

Because dark was already falling, and Lydia was a woman alone, it made sense when she asked if the boy could accompany her on her way home. His aunt was only too happy for him to be useful. Jacobo Camille Pizzarro held open the double glass doors, and they stepped into the smoky air of November. The streets glittered wet with rain and the air was a mist.

"How long has this been going on?" Lydia asked.

"This?" He was wary; perhaps he thought she meant to catch him in a trap of his own admission and call the authorities.

"Your pursuit."

"I'll be going back soon, home, but I've been following you ever since I arrived in France."

"Since you were twelve!" She laughed, then saw his expression. It was true.

"Well, not precisely. It took me the best of a year to locate your father's address, and then months more before I realized you no longer lived there. And then, of course, I didn't know you had taken your husband's name, so I was lost again. It was nearly three years before I found you."

"Three years!" She was quite amazed.

"Your maid turned me away every time I came to call. I thought if I approached you in a public place you might have me arrested."

"Arrest a boy?" Lydia laughed.

"I was afraid I would offend you. I suppose, after a while, I lost my courage."

"But not your resolve! I presume you follow me because you have something to say to me," Lydia said gently. He was only a boy, and he had an artist's soul, so perhaps he simply wished to paint her portrait and admired her for the character of her face.

All in all, she only wanted to know the cause of his attraction. Her husband would be getting home soon. He was at this very moment at the family office with his brothers, shrugging on his soft woolen overcoat, thinking about the dinner that awaited, the wife at the door, the stars that would appear in the pale twilight.

"If you had ever stopped and spoken to me, I would have been relieved," he told her. "For a very long time you failed to notice me. And every time I meant to talk to you, I was uncertain all over again. You seem so happy."

She smiled. He was so serious and earnest. He did seem older than his age. "And what do you have to tell me that would make me less so?"

"We're somewhat related," he told her.

"Are we?"

"We're both from St. Thomas."

"Yes. I've discovered I was born there."

"It's a very small place." He scowled at the memory. "Too small."

They walked along as if the rest of Paris did not exist. Perhaps because he admired all things French and would be leaving at the end of the school term, Camille was glum. He said there was little freedom where he came from; his mother watched over him too closely, and he was expected to live a life like that of his father and brothers, a life that he already knew he would reject. "Shopkeepers," he said of them. "Concerned with ledgers and sales. At least here in Paris the workingman is rising up to claim what he deserves."

"People must shop," Lydia reminded him.

"Must they? Perhaps all shops should throw open their doors and let those in need take what they must." He looked at her for a reaction.

"Perhaps. I don't know the answer to the world's woes. I barely know the answer to my own." The loss of her father had affected her more strongly than she imagined. She sometimes worried about her own children becoming orphaned, her most dire fear.

They passed the park where he had often watched her. Sometimes he'd sat here and sketched. His teacher, Monsieur Savary, had suggested that he carry his artist's materials with him, for a subject often appeared when one least expected it to do so. A leaf, a woman, a shaded path.

Artists were those with supporters, wealthy families or patrons. They went to the Académie and studied with masters, and few were allowed into such society. He was a Jew, from St. Thomas, seventeen years old, with no financial backing. His lanky form was stooped with regret as they walked on. And he was nervous now that he was in Lyddie's presence. Time and again he might have spoken to her, but on each of these occasions he didn't feel up to the task of telling her the truth. She seemed far too content for the message he'd brought. But now she spoke of woes, and he wondered if perhaps he should have told her long ago.

She suggested they sit on a bench in the park, though it was damp. She had a shiver inside of her. When she thought back, there was only so far she could reach. Her father had told her she was very ill as a child. That they'd been traveling and she'd had such a high fever she'd had a loss of memory. He said she had spoken four languages, but when she recovered she'd forgotten all but French. Something haunted her about that time. Occasionally she used a word from some unknown language when speaking to her daughters. Once when they looked at the night sky she said *stjerne,* and the girls had asked what she meant and she simply had no idea.

"I made a promise to find you; otherwise I would have given up." Camille took an envelope from the inner lining of his coat. "Your mother wrote this to you on the day you were abducted."

Lydia laughed, then held a hand over her mouth. A soft sob escaped. It was a ridiculous remark, yet it rang with a certain truth, particularly after her conversation with Madame Sophie.

"My father was my father, was he not?" she said.

The boy nodded. "He was raised by my family. He was orphaned somehow."

"*Abducted* is not the right word if I was raised by my own father."

"But it is. You were stolen." This was what he'd come to say and couldn't before. "From your mother."

Lydia let those words settle inside her.

"They tied her to a tree and had hired men standing guard. She's been waiting for you all this time. I need to know what I should say to her when I return."

It was now fully dark. Men in overcoats and hats were walking past, on their way home. The sky was ink, the boy noticed this, ebony at the edges, midnight blue in the center. Only bits of pale light still remained. The city was a miracle, and the idea that he would be leaving it depressed him immensely.

"What was my mother to you?" Lydia asked.

"A friend of our family. And with her mother, for a time, our maid."

"A maid?" She was puzzled.

"And I must tell you, I suppose, because of the world we live in, she was of African heritage."

"I see," Lydia said, although she didn't quite. She was a Jewish woman and the wife of Henri Cohen and the mother of three daughters and a resident of Paris for so long she could remember nothing of a deeper past. She took the letter the boy offered and opened the envelope. The paper felt like silk, watery; it had been flattened and creased a hundred times over. The print was faded, pale, but she could read it well enough.

My darling, my daughter, my star, my life.

I would not have given you up for anything in the world. Not for any amount of money, not for any promise, not even if they said it was a better future. You were meant to be with me, and no one, not on earth and not in heaven, could have ever loved you more.

You can be whoever you want to be, but you will always be my child, and we will always belong to each other, even if we never speak or see each other again.

She folded the paper back into the envelope, and slid it and her hands inside her cape. They were ice-cold. She was stunned and yet, at the same time, not surprised to discover that someone had loved her beyond measure.

"I need time," she said when she could speak. "To think about this."

"Of course." This boy, Camille, was quite unusual. He seemed an equal. A man from St. Thomas who could understand what a man who had been born and raised in Paris never could. He rose to leave her to her thoughts.

"What will you do when you go home?" she asked.

"I'll pretend to be who they want me to be." He grinned then, and she saw his youth. "But it won't work. In the end I'll have to disappoint someone. Either them, or myself."

She herself did not think she could go home yet. She went to a restaurant instead and said she was to meet her husband there, for a woman on her own was not allowed inside. She sat in the lounge and ordered an aperitif and drank it. She shivered, realizing that she was always cold. She had been since the time she'd had that fever. She wondered what had come before and why she could remember only bits and pieces: a red flower, a woman's voice, a bird that was bright yellow. All at once she knew this was the woman her father had written about and loved. The boy could easily be a liar, the letter forged, the information untrue. But she believed it. He had been following her for so long. He'd known her when she hadn't known herself, for if this letter was indeed from the woman who had given her life, then Lydia was no longer sure who she was. Certainly not the same woman who had walked into Madame Pizzarro's house.

When the manager came and asked if she would like him to send a driver and a carriage for her husband, stating that she could not continue to drink on her own, she shook her head and asked that the aperitif be put on her husband's account. Everything looked new to her, the way things look in dreams. In dreams, the same street one walks along daily becomes a mystery, the stone gray color of the pavement turns to silver and then to gold and then the street disappears completely.

When she at last arrived home, Henri was at the door, worried.

"I couldn't imagine what had happened." He embraced her, so grateful for her well-being he didn't notice that she didn't respond. The children had been given dinner and had been sent to bed by the maid. Her name was Ava; she originally came from the Loire Valley, not Jewish, a working girl from a farm. Lydia had never asked if she had brothers and sisters. They spoke only of the details of daily life. What the menu would be, what the yardman had failed to do, how the children were growing so quickly, like sprouts. Even when the maid had confided about the boy who'd often come to the back door, Lydia hadn't thought to ask if she'd been frightened or confused by a stranger. Lydia felt flushed with guilt to think she'd never spoken to this woman about anything deeper than menus and household duties; she'd never asked a question, never had any interest.

While she was preparing for bed in her dressing room, she went to the mirror and studied her reflection. She was the same and yet brand new.

It was true. Her eyes were silver.

✐

SHE REREAD THE LETTER whenever she was alone. And then one day she took up a pen and paper and wrote back. She told her mother everything she remembered. How ill she had become on the ship. How she had refused to eat and they'd made her drink hot lemon juice to break her fever. She admitted that she could now speak only French, but that her French was flawless, so that everyone assumed she'd been born in Paris. She wrote that she dreamed of teal-colored birds that danced for each other, and that when she had such dreams she awoke crying. She wrote a letter every day for twenty days, and in each she told more of the story of her life. It was as if she was writing her diary all at once, from the time she woke from the fever on the boat to this very day. She was afraid to mail them for some reason. She had a peculiar fear that if she posted them, they would vanish or be stolen and would never reach their intended reader. Instead, she folded them into a small wooden box in which she kept lavender sachets. She didn't notice how quickly time was passing. Snow fell in early December.

"Will you be going home for Christmas?" she asked the maid, Ava.

They were in the kitchen together, making notes regarding the pantry. Ava seemed shocked to be asked her plans.

"If I can have the time," she said, wary. "I would like to."

"Is it a farm?"

"Oh, yes," Ava said, her cheeks flushed, cheerful to think about her family home. "Mostly chickens and goats."

"By all means go home. You'll be paid for your time."

Snow was falling when Lydia wrote her thirtieth letter. It was Christmas Eve, a time when they always stayed at home. It was not their holiday to celebrate, but there was a peacefulness when the city was deeply quiet, so different than it had been during the riots of the past year. Lydia was in the parlor and the children were asleep. Henri came in from the garden. It was a clear night, and he had been looking at the constellations. He clapped the stray flakes of snow from his coat. There was a fire in the fireplace, an envelope on Lydia's lap, and the small dog the children had begged for, whom they called Lapin, Bunny, was napping on a small moss-green pillow.

"If we have a son," Henri said. "We should call him Leo. For the lion of the stars."

"What if I wasn't who you thought I was?" Lydia asked. Her pretty face was furrowed with worry.

Henri sat beside her. "Is this about your father? That he didn't leave much? You know I don't care. We're fine, Lydia. There's no cause to fret."

"I believe that my father may have been a horrible person. He may have done something awful."

"Well, he's gone, so it doesn't really matter. Neither does the money. The old house brought a good amount. Our girls won't be in need."

"But what if I wasn't who you thought I was."

He got them both a drink and sat beside her again.

"You think I don't know you?" he asked.

It was the moment when she could easily have embraced him and thrown the thirtieth letter onto the fire, which was already burning so brightly. She thought about a summer trip she'd made with her parents, to the sea, when she was a girl. They were in the ancient city of La Rochelle, famous for its fields of salt and Roman ruins. She'd never been to the ocean before, but she was entranced. Perhaps she was only seven, little more. She heard her name being spoken in a soft voice, as if some-one who knew her was calling to her. She walked over the stones, there for all eternity, made of a soft-clay mineral, filled with the fossils of snails and sea creatures that had lived before there were men and women. Her mother rushed after her, frightened. *Don't you dare,* her mother cried. Lydia thought her mother feared she would drown or be taken up in the undertow. Now she realized that wasn't it at all. It was how easily she was called to the sea, how familiar it seemed to her, how right and how beautiful, as if she belonged to it and it to her.

In bed she told her husband everything. She could not look at him as she spoke.

If one is not born of a Jewish mother, it is impossible to be consid-ered a member of the faith, and if she was not, their girls were not either.

"Easily rectified. Conversion is possible if we feel the need," Henri said.

"I cannot convert from who I am, Henri. My mother's mother was an African slave."

"Who your parents were means nothing to me," Henri told her. "It's your heart I want."

Her false mother had been right about one thing: he was a man who would not harm her. As for her heart, it was already broken. That was the source of the fever that had caused her to lose her past and herself.

"And your family?" Lydia asked. "What will it mean to them?"

"There is no need to confide in them, or to invite them into the inti-mate details of our life."

Then she knew: he feared they would not be as open as he was to her true history. The business was a family business, based as much on rela-tionships as on the ebb and flow of the banking world. All of their deal-ings were held within their community with other Jewish families. The unrest around the King, Louis-Philippe, had had little to do with people of their faith in the past, but his lack of concern for working people had touched off serious uprisings. There were days when black smoke filled the city; angry crowds gathered, provoked by how little the King cared for those who felt disenfranchised. For the Cohens, the desire was to keep on in a normal working manner, and that did not include a daughter-in-law whose background would call attention to them. Still, Lydia did not wish to lie to her own children's grandparents, uncles, and aunts.

"What if I wanted them to know?" she said. "What if not being myself had made me ill?"

"Are you ill?" he said, concerned.

"I have been in the past, and would be again."

Henri held her close. "It's your choice. Whatever you decide makes no difference to me."

The snow continued to fall; still, she heard the nightingale. Lydia wept to think she had not left it any seeds or fruit, and that it might perish on this night. Yet, she did not go to it, but listened until silence overtook her. At last she slept and dreamed of the sea, and when she woke the sky was clear. The snow covered everything and was so deep it had stopped all of Paris. Before she turned to her husband, or looked in on her children, she slipped on her boots and woolen cape and went into the garden.

The bird was in the snow, frozen, feathers silvered with ice. Lydia knelt. She lifted the nearly weightless body and laid it across her knees. She had always half thought she'd imagined the bird and its song, but no, it was real. The morning was so hushed she could hear her own pulse, and then her ragged breathing, and something like a sob. She took the bird around the side of the house, where the trash barrels and coal bin were kept. She lifted the cover of one of the barrels and dropped the nightingale in. She felt a shudder go through her when she heard the soft thump. She had always thought her mother was in the garden singing to her, watching over her. But no longer. The woman who had raised her was nothing to her anymore.

The winter went on. Frozen, gray, with hard frosts that were followed by drizzles of snow. She did not see the boy on the street or in the synagogue. Perhaps he was busy with his last term of school. Perhaps he had said all he had to say to her. She found that she missed his presence. Once she walked past his aunt's house, but didn't dare to go to the door. He'd said he was leaving at the end of the school term. Paris itself was mayhem. The King had been overthrown, and the factions of his opposition now turned against each other. There was a lawlessness in the streets they hadn't seen before. Henri suggested that Lydia and the girls stay close to home. For weeks on end their parlor was their world, and Lydia put off changing that world, at least for a while. The girls wore their blue dresses and danced as the snow, in record amounts, fell down and bonfires burned black in the distance.

Lydia discovered that she was pregnant in the spring. She felt different than she had during her other pregnancies, and she guessed the baby was a boy. If it were, they would call him Leo, after the lion in the sky. Henri had said nothing she had discovered about herself mattered, and to him it didn't. But of course, there was the rest of the world. She thought about that every time she went out, had a conversation with her neighbors, discussed dinner with Ava. She thought of her children and this son-to-be and what they would have to deal with being their true selves. On some afternoons she wandered off by herself. She did this on Saturdays, letting her mother-in-law take the children to the synagogue, saying her pregnancy made her dizzy. That was not the truth. She took a streetcar to the Montmartre district, where African women worked in the market. Many of them sold baskets woven out of coils of straw, handcrafted, and so beautiful they made tears spring to her eyes. She bought one in a market stall from a woman from Senegal. There were birds in some of the hanging baskets, bright, flittering bits of orange and yellow. The basket she bought was a small oval, and the straw smelled like cardamom. She kept it on her writing table, and held it up to breathe in the scent of the straw. Her heart, though broken, still beat.

In bed she and Henri held each other without speaking and made love with urgency, as if the world was ending and the storm was outside the door.

She sent the boy Camille a note asking if he would meet her in the park. It was nearly June, the time he would be leaving, a lucky thing, for the riots would grow worse until Napoleon III was elected later that year. He would remember France as it was when he first arrived, all color and light and beauty. Lydia waited on the bench as her children played with Ava watching over them. She now knew that the maid had two brothers, and that one would like to come to Paris and go to school, but there wasn't money enough, and besides, there was the farm to care for. Lydia thought perhaps she would offer her help to Ava's brother. It was the least she could do.

Camille was even taller now; he'd become more of a man in a matter of months.

"You've been avoiding me," Lydia said as lightly as she could. "After all these years you seem to have deserted me."

"I thought you'd never want to see me again," he admitted.

"Why would that be?"

Camille shrugged. "Perhaps you liked your life as it was."

"It was a lie. How can anyone like that?"

He had a blue canvas bag. "I brought you something. A gift before I leave."

It was a painting of this very park, and of her three children, and of the chestnut tree. The park benches looked glittery, as if a rain had fallen. The painted air was a strange blue color, as if the artist had managed to catch bits of mist and add them to his paints.

She thanked him and kissed his cheek. She was so grateful, but if he wished to give her a gift this wasn't the one she wanted. She whispered what she most desired and he nodded, then jotted a note concerning the one she preferred. She then gave him the box of sixty letters. She had written in tiny print, which allowed her to tell the entire story of her life as it had been so far, the stolen years her mother knew nothing about.

Camille took the letters and said his good-byes. He had been following her for so long, it seemed odd that he would leave her in this park and not shadow her on her walk home. He knew her route, knew the way she ran a hand through her youngest daughter's hair, and that she usually stopped to look in the branches of the chestnut tree in her yard to see if there were birds nesting there. Before he left, Lydia embraced him. He had become quite dear to her.

"Tell my mother I'm about to give birth to a boy," she told him. "We're naming him Leo. I was going to write that in today's letter, but I'm telling you instead."

Camille walked away, then turned back to her and waved before loping off. He left Paris soon after, packing up nearly six years of his life into two small suitcases and a leather trunk. He hated to return home, and could barely bring himself to think of what was waiting for him. His mother's demands, a job at the store, his paints drying up in the heat of August, the girl he yearned for, Marianna, already married. He would give himself two years, and then, if it was as bad as he imagined it would be, he would find a way to leave. He had that in his blood, a history of men who knew when to stay and when to run away, men who could tell when it was time to find another life and another land.

Soon after he left, Lydia went to the Pizzarro house. Camille's aunt welcomed her when the maid ushered her into the drawing room.

"This is unexpected. But a pleasure!"

They had not seen each other since Lydia's initial visit. Tea was offered, but tea had not brought Lydia to this house, and so she said perhaps another time.

"You must miss your nephew," Lydia said.

"Oh, we do," Madame Pizzarro said warmly.

"As do I. We became very close. We both were born in St. Thomas, and so he granted me something to remind me of that place."

Lydia took out the note Camille had left with her, written hastily in the park, a grin on his face as he complied with her wishes. He wrote to ask that the painting in his aunt and uncle's parlor be given to Madame Cohen on the day she came calling. Madame Pizzarro frowned as she read it. She had grown accustomed to the painting and did not wish to part with it.

"I'd have to discuss this with my husband," she said. "We had it framed at quite some expense."

"I can pay you for that. I know you admire the painting, but it means so much to me. More than you can know." Lydia had gone to stand in front of it. A woman carrying a basket of laundry, the sea behind her. Lydia knew what was inside the house on stilts and what was down the road where the donkeys ate tall grass and dodged toward you if you dared to pull their tails. The disease and shock that had left her without a memory was returning, bit by bit. She found she understood English, and she referred to foods with unfamiliar words, calling the porridge her daughters ate in the mornings fongee and making them laugh.

She was so overcome that she began to sob.

"My dear!" Madame Pizarro said. "Please don't do that!"

"I'm so sorry," Lydia said. "I'm so terribly sorry." She could hardly get the words out in French. She thought of an odd phrase—*Jeg er ked af*—unsure of what it meant. "I truly don't think I can live without it."

"That's very clear," Madame Pizarro said, signaling to her maid to find some brown wrapping paper. "It's yours, my dear."

When she was given the painting, Lydia thanked her hostess and wished her well. She went into the corridor for her cloak and stood there for a few moments to collect herself. The heat inside her felt like the heat on this road leading down to the harbor on days when this woman held her hand. *Do not run too far from me,* she always said. At last, Lydia ventured into the street. It was nearly summer and the trees smelled sweet. The sound of birdsong echoed in the pale blue air, haint blue, the boy Camille had called this shade. He said it kept the ghosts away. It was the color of the sky in the painting she now had of her mother, whose name was Jestine, and who had been waiting for her daughter ever since she had been stolen, convinced that one day sixty letters would arrive in a box scented with lavender, the herb that always brings a person home.

CHAPTER NINE

The Ground That We Walk Upon

CHARLOTTE AMALIE, ST. THOMAS

1848

JACOBO CAMILLE PIZZARRO

He slept for eighteen hours straight after he got off the boat. When he woke it was as if he'd traveled not across the ocean but across time itself. Backward into the heat, listening to the goats' bells in the hills and the fluttering of moths bumping against the shutters of his darkened chamber. He considered himself to be a man, but here he was still thought of as a boy. Half asleep and half dressed, he made his way to the kitchen, where Rosalie had the fongee porridge of his childhood waiting for him in a yellow bowl, the same bowl he had used when he was a boy who followed at his mother's heels. He thanked Rosalie, announcing that her cookery tasted much better than anything he'd had in Paris. It was true, the porridge was more than mere sustenance; it brought back his childhood and everything it contained, like an enchantment. As he stood watching Rosalie at the stove, listening to her lilting French, it was as if he'd been charmed into remembering everything he had known on the island, the things he loved as well as the reasons he couldn't wait to get away.

The major reason he had wanted to stay in France was evident as soon as he returned to his small bedchamber. There he found his mother unpacking his luggage, rooting around in the large trunk that had been battered from his voyage, the wood damaged by salt air and the rough treatment of its delivery.

"What do you think you're doing?" he shouted, forgetting in that moment all aspects of courtesy and respect. "Do I have no privacy whatsoever?"

He went to stand in front of the trunk in which he'd stored six years of his life, protective, guarding its contents, already embattled with the woman who'd given him his life. He loomed over his mother. Perhaps his expression was more fierce than he'd meant for it to be. For an instant she appeared to be afraid of him.

"Mother," he said, backing down. "I am used to my privacy."

"Do you have something to hide?" She'd recovered from the initial shock of his aggressive stance.

"My belongings are my business." He was scowling, his anger now directed to himself for his rude behavior, which was indeed childish. In Paris his aunt had been too busy to know where he was half the time. He suspected she was involved with one of his uncle's business partners, who called at odd hours. This hadn't bothered him at all. His life had been his own, and his artistry had been appreciated by his teachers and his fellow students.

"It's your father's trunk," his mother informed him, putting him in his place. "He paid for it, not you."

"Then let him be the one to look through it."

But Rachel had already spied the box packed alongside his clothing. Her expression darkened as she reached for it. She glared at him and held it in her hands. "Light as a feather, Jacobo."

"It has nothing to do with you," he replied. "And please do not refer to me that way."

He no longer thought of himself as Jacobo, but as Camille, his French name. But perhaps it was Jacobo, the boy he used to be, who was trying his best not to be affected by his mother's disapproval. He reached for the wooden box, a bit unsure of himself. People in Charlotte Amalie used to say that Rachel Pizzarro could turn herself into a snake or a witch. They said if you crossed her you'd likely never sleep again. Even he'd heard the rumors, whispers that her blood was made of molasses, which drew men to her even when they had no reason to desire her. Camille took a step away from his mother. She looked no older than when he'd left, although there was a white streak in her hair that hadn't been there before.

"It's for Jestine," he admitted, and then was angry with himself for feeling the need to appease her.

When she heard this, Rachel's countenance changed into something unreadable.

"And it's such an important item that you are willing to disrespect your mother? Did you know it took three days for you to be born? Three days when I might have died."

Camille's face flushed with shame. She had told him this many times before. "Mother, I apologize. But you must understand I'm not a child."

She was unfazed. "You are my child."

There was no way to refute this.

"Though you have changed your name," she added.

"My father calls himself by his third name." He had a point in this, for his father was referred to as Frédéric rather than Abraham or Gabriel.

"True enough. Well, you will evidently do as you please, so by all means, go to Jestine," she said, surprising him. "If I'm not mistaken, she's been waiting all these years to hear from you."

He took the opportunity to leave immediately, before his father requested he report to the office, a fate he dreaded as surely as if he'd had a prison sentence hanging over him.

He was unused to St. Thomas after his time away and was struck by the heat as if he'd never lived here. He broke into a sweat as he made his way to the harbor, his clothes drenched as the strong sunlight went through the fabric, through his skin it seemed. He felt as though he were a stranger, surrounded by the clatter of men at work at their fish pots in the harbor, the boats being readied for service, the crowds heading to the market. And then, all of a sudden, the enchantment came over him again, and he was home. A wind from Africa rose up, palm trees swayed, and a cloud of white birds took flight, a breathing, living cloud. Like the breakfast he'd had, the landscape was a familiar part of him that surfaced in his dreams and in his art. Once his past had come back to him, he no longer had to think about where he was going. His feet knew the path, though some houses and shops had disappeared and new ones had appeared. He had come here so often with his mother, left to amuse himself while she and Jestine spoke of things he was not supposed to know about: gossip, tragedy, snippets of their daily lives.

JESTINE WAS HANGING UP herbs to dry that she would later use in her dyes, but she stopped as soon as she saw him. She felt a sort of lightness enter her body, as if she were a younger woman. She had been waiting for his return and had half expected Lyddie would be beside him on this day, even though she'd read the thief's letter and knew a return was impossible. Lyddie was a married woman now, and it was not so easy to leave one's husband behind and come across the world to a mother she didn't know.

As soon as her friend's son came up the stairs, Jestine threw her arms around him. After returning her embrace, he backed away, grinning. He asked her to call him by his French name, Camille.

"I suppose Paris changed you," Jestine said as she appraised him. "You're certainly taller."

"I'm the same in one way: I told you I would find her and I did."

Jestine wrinkled her brow, not yet knowing what to believe. "You saw her with your own eyes?"

"Many times."

"How many times?"

Camille laughed. "Too many to count. Trust me! She's real and well and very much alive."

"She has a husband?"

He nodded. "And three daughters."

"Three?" Jestine felt her head swim as he recited their names. Amelia, Mirabelle, Leah. Had there ever been such beautiful names? Girls formed of her own blood and hope. When he'd left, Camille now told her, there'd also been another baby to come, one they planned to call Leo if it was a boy. He waited while Jestine took a moment for herself. She sat on the stair, keeping one hand upon the banister to steady herself. Despite her age, she was still beautiful. As always she wore the rope of pearls Camille remembered she favored even when she was in her work clothes, as she was today, a plain cotton dress with a black apron, to ensure that the dyes she used wouldn't stain her good clothing. He could tell his news came as something of a shock. The details about her daughter were now spun into the thin thread of daily life.

Indeed, something inside Jestine made it difficult for her to breathe. It was as if there was a bubble rising up through her chest. It was clawing at her, everything she didn't want to feel but felt anyway. A desire for revenge for all she'd lost. Not only a daughter had been stolen but an entire family.

Camille went to get her some water. Jestine berated herself; she refused to ruin this moment thinking of the demon in the silk dress, a dress they thought so astoundingly beautiful, though it was nothing compared with her own designs. Camille returned, and Jestine took a few sips of water. When she had her breath again, she made him describe everything in the greatest detail: the children and the house where her daughter lived, the way she walked and spoke, the nearby park with its linden trees and green benches with wrought-iron armrests, the snow that lined the cobblestones, like white powder that stuck to your boots, the husband who looked at stars in the garden, the silver color of her eyes.

"And what of her mother?" Jestine asked. It was bright, so she shielded her eyes. Her voice was flat, and Camille couldn't tell what her emotion was.

"You're her mother," he was quick to say.

Jestine smiled. He had a kind heart. "The one who stole her."

"Dead. I never met her."

She nodded, then, satisfied. It was not everything, but it was something. The next question was more complicated. "And the father?"

"Gone as well."

She felt a pang of regret upon hearing this news.

Camille gave her the box containing her daughter's letters. Jestine opened the container and was overcome by the scent of lavender. "My darling boy," she said, thanking him. "You did what you said you would." Then she waved him away. She wanted to be alone with the letters.

"Are you sure?" Camille said, concerned for her well-being, fearing her daughter's words and life might be too much for her to take in all at once. In this light Jestine did not look as young as he remembered. There was a slight tremor in her hands. But she had been waiting more than twenty years for what she had now received.

"Very sure."

When he left she went up the stairs, inside the cool shadows of the house. She felt clearheaded now. Not dizzy in the least. She thought about the day Rachel came to see her when they were both first expecting, and how they had lain in bed together to dream about their children-to-be. Now she took the letters and lay down to read until there was no longer any light. After that she lit the lantern so that she might continue on.

I did not know if you would want to hear from me.
If you might hate me for not remembering.
They took away everything.
They took away my world.

But now that the boy has come to see me, it has come back to me. I remember the waves and the sound of water beneath the porch. I remember that you told me about the day the fish swam into your own mother's cooking pot when there was a storm. You told me about the dangerous season, from October to May, when storms flew across the ocean from Africa. If a big wave comes, your mother told you, hold on to me. Because she did not trust the world and had no reason to, she had faith in her own abilities to protect you. She tied herself to the cast-iron stove, then tied you to her. It was the same with us. I would sit out on the porch and you would tie my foot to the post so that no waves could carry me away. You were never going to let me go. I remember your voice when you told me so, when the men who took me to the ship tied you to a tree. You could not get to me to keep me safe. I remember there was a pelican above us and you told it to peck out your eyes as a payment if need be, but to keep me safe.

The bird must have known you would need your eyes to see me when we meet again, so she let you be, flew after me and watched as I went onto the ship into the arms of a woman I didn't recognize. The pelican followed us so far out to sea I wondered how she would ever get home. I wondered if I would ever see you again. I shouted into the sky, "Go back to her and tell her I'm not gone from her."

I remember it now as I write to you as if it were only hours ago, and all of the time that has come between us never happened at all.

❦

CAMILLE WORKED IN HIS father's shop as a shipping clerk, but at night, he paced his room, restless, out of place, living a life he was not meant for. In their bedchamber, Frédéric and Rachel whispered about him. They heard his footsteps and knew he couldn't sleep. He, whom they'd called Marmotte when he was a boy because he could sleep anywhere no matter what disturbances there might be, was now an insomniac, bleary-eyed in the mornings and in a foul humor. Perhaps they

should not have sent him to school in France. Despite the difficulties between them, Rachel loved him perhaps too much. It was not right to
prefer one child over the others, so she hid her emotions; he had no idea
he was a bright light to her. More so than ever now that he had returned.
She had hoped it would have done some good for him to see the world
beyond theirs, as she had failed to do.

His parents waited for him to fit in and feel more suited to the business, but that did not happen. Everything he did was a disaster. He
spilled ink, filed shipping orders incorrectly, and avoided his desk. After
dinner, and after the dressing-down he would receive from his brothers
for his many mistakes, errors he freely admitted to, he isolated himself in
his room. He waited until everyone else was asleep, then left the apartment. He did not see his mother at the window watching him wander
into the street, hands in his pockets, wearing black trousers and a white
shirt. He was tall and lanky and resembled his father in his younger days.
Although he was not as handsome, he was compelling. He was quiet but
arrogant, with a sort of fire that came from desire. Women looked at
him, curious, wondering what made him so proud. There was something
he wanted badly, anyone could see that. A yearning he didn't speak of.
He looked past the people around him. He was a shipping clerk, but he
seemed to think he was something more.

Though he was a man in form and age, he carried a boy's rebellion
on his shoulders. He dared the world to try to rein him in the way wild
boys often do. He had vowed to himself that he would not be at anyone's
mercy and he had little fear of authority, yet he was eighteen, and his
father's son. He did the work he was told to do, no matter how his resentment might build. And it did build, each day, until there was a wall between him and the rest of the family.

In the back room of the store, he thought he might explode from all
of those meaningless hours seeing to the ledgers. Math was difficult and
pointless, and he cared nothing for finance. Money was a ruination, in his
opinion, needed only to survive. Those who had it considered them-

selves blessed; those who did not were cursed for reasons that made no sense to him, mere circumstance and luck. He sketched in the margins of the ledgers, images of the workers who delivered molasses and rum to the back door, with cloths tied around their foreheads so that sweat wouldn't run into their eyes as they labored. Then for a week he sketched seabirds, seeing the creatures in parts, as he used to when he was first beginning to draw: wings, feet, talons, beak. He spent hours drawing the sawlike fronds of palm trees, the ridges in each leaf distinct and individually lined. This was his release, until his father found him out and had him painstakingly rewrite the ledger pages he had ruined with his sketches.

After that Frédéric moved Camille to the front of the store to see if he would fare any better in that position. He did not. Being polite to customers who spoke to him rudely and dealing with their petty orders and concerns maddened him. He pouted and was silent. He lost his appetite and became even lankier than before. His older brothers made sure to tease him and let him know he was inept; he needed to be broken and understand he was beneath them and must do as he was told.

Taking orders did not come naturally to Camille. He burned, but kept quiet. Monsieur Savary had told him to take the opinions of only those he respected and ignore the rest. "Do not react to all the world may throw on you," his teacher had advised. Camille had realized the truth of this advice in the many hours he had spent at the Louvre, studying the great masters. Each artist had to find his own path, regardless of the current mode and criticisms. He stood before da Vinci's great works, every painting a world unto itself, but each clearly seen through the eyes of a singular master. It was through this single vision that the work had risen to the heights of art and artistry. This was why da Vinci had understood the true artist as no other man did.

Unfortunately, Camille himself was trapped from such flight, unable to lead an artist's life, a victim of the bourgeois fate he'd been born into. He would have liked to open the storerooms and call for local people to come and take what they needed, free of charge, until at last the store was emptied and he was freed from its prison. Since this was impossible, he walked at night to ease his rage, stalking the streets he remembered, but remembered in a mist of thought, as if he'd walked them in a dream.

He longed for Paris and for the route he used to take to school through the pleasant streets of Passy, for the tall, ivy-covered house he'd found when he followed Jestine's daughter to her home. He thought of the snow under his boots, the chestnut trees in leaf in April, each leaf so pale it was nearly white, the moss-green benches in the Tuileries, the sky filled with clouds, the gray rain that glowed green with light, the fields outside Passy where mustard seed and poppies grew in a riot of color. Here in St. Thomas daylight was so bright a man had to shut his eyes against the sun until colors and objects shifted into points of light. Red, green, yellow, and a thousand shades of blue.

He again came to know the narrow streets of Charlotte Amalie, taking the curved, sheer alleys made entirely of steps, where it was said werewolves used to roam. Most often he found himself heading into the countryside, for it was there he felt most comfortable. He remembered that as a boy he'd had the ability, as most islanders did, to switch to a sort of night vision; as soon as dusk fell the horizon was engulfed in the glimmering dark, an all-consuming shadow within a shadow. He made his way on the sandy roads, avoiding ditches that swelled with puddles when there had been rain. The night world was blue and black; a hot velvet curtain dropped down from the branches of the trees. He walked through it and felt the dampness on his skin, the pinpricks of insect bites, the wind when it wound through the trees and passed him by as if it were a creature with a mind of its own. Here on the hillsides there were the old stands of mahogany, and so many birds that he could hear them nesting, fluttering above him as they rested. Leaves fell down on his head, and he remembered some old story about how the spirits of the dead walked about in the trees. He was used to dark nights, he had known such nights from the start of his existence, but when he thought of his years in Paris what he yearned for most was the light, the yellow glow of morning, the green shadows of the afternoon, the silver radiance of winter splintering like ice on a windowpane.

He became silent and grudging as days and months went on, a tall, dark figure moping through the dusk on an empty road. When he saw groups of children in their yards he raised his hand to wave hello, but he was a ragged stranger and they shrieked and scattered, racing inside their houses. He began to spend nights in the herb man's house, where he had gone to paint as a boy. It had been a secret place then, and it was now, abandoned for so long even the few people who had known of it had forgotten it was ever there. He always blundered upon it in his ramblings out of sheer luck. Or perhaps he'd been led there in the way a dreamer comes upon a dream he'd had years earlier. Everything was the same now that he'd returned, and yet it was different, as a painting with layer upon layer of paint splattered upon the canvas. There was an old cotton mattress left on the floor, which he stuffed with newly dried grass. The hut smelled of his childhood, when his mother used to take him everywhere and he'd hear bits of conversation he knew he shouldn't and he was given hard molasses candies to keep him silent and happy. He used mud and straw to caulk the holes in the walls to keep out the mongooses that found shelter from storms. He took branches to sweep out the curled, desiccated bodies of beetles littering the corners of the room. It was the season when nighthawks migrated, and he heard them crying as they lit in the trees, exhausted from their flight. In the dark, there was a world of insects hitting against the roof and walls, with moths and mosquitoes doing their best to get through the shutters when he illuminated the room. He burned a candle anyway, though it drew thousands of insects to beat their wings against the wire and there was a constant whirring sound. He needed at least some faint light so that he might paint.

He worked at an old, handcrafted table that gave off the odor of herbs that had been chopped on its soft wooden surface. His paper became scented by rosemary and lavender, stained by guava berry. His art softened in the candlelight, and he saw objects as washed with blue and gold. He had taken paints and pencils from the store and had brought pastels and chalk with him from France. He drew over the boyish designs that had covered the walls and began to remake the world as he observed it now, as a man. His teacher had told him to embrace the landscape of his youth, as it had been the cradle of who he was as an artist, but also to see it through his current experience. *Sometimes you must close your eyes in order to see*, his teacher had suggested, therefore Camille imagined what he would see when the sun arose. The deep red of the mahogany trees, the brilliant shades of scarlet flowers, the emerald of the hills, the women in their muslin dresses on their way to work in town, passing by with the laundry they had washed in huge pots set over fires.

A waterfall was nearby, and he often went to drink and bathe there. One early morning, on his way back to the store, a place he thought of as his penance for the years of freedom he'd had in Paris, he got on his knees and drank deeply. When he started off again, he stumbled over something. He stopped, stunned by what he saw, but too curious to turn away. His mouth was still dripping water. The sun was warm on his back. He had come upon bones cast into the tall grass. A man's remains, picked clean over the years by birds and mongooses and field rats. Some of the bones had been scattered by animals and weather, yet the skeleton still retained the shape of a man. From the position of the skull, it seemed he had been resting there, sleeping perhaps, out in the open country when he passed away. Camille lay down beside the bones so he might hear what the dead man heard. He listened to the drone of mosquitoes and flies, to the lulling sound of water in the nearby pool. He closed his eyes and dreamed he was the herbalist holding a baby, staring into its wide eyes, seeing his own death. Shadows from the clouds passed over him, and he remembered when he could not sleep as a babe, when he wanted to see the world so desperately he would not dare to blink.

He woke with a start in the middle of the day, alive and young. He was so grateful not to be a dead man, and to have the world to dive into.

He was late for work, and he knew, as he ran back to town, he would be in trouble, yet again. He had not been able to steer clear of it since he'd been back. They said he'd changed, his sullen moodiness, his criticism of his family and the politics of the island. But perhaps he was only more himself, a man with his own opinions now, though his parents clearly considered him too young to have the right to act upon his needs and desires.

HE THOUGHT ABOUT HIS constricted life a few evenings later when he spied Marianna at the harbor. He'd been hoping to run into her. He was at a café when he saw her in the marketplace. A married woman wearing golden earrings, talking with her friends. She was as beautiful as ever, perhaps more so, but she wasn't Marianna King anymore, the waiter told him when he asked about her current situation. Her married name was Morris. He thought back to when she knew him better than anyone. He caught her eye, but she had no expression, merely stared back as if he were a rude stranger gawking. She then avoided his glance and went on talking with her friends. A knife went through him. His brothers were right. He was no one. He kept an eye on Marianna all the same. When she left and started for home, he followed. Unlike Lydia, who had no idea she was being followed for months on end, Marianna sensed her stalker, and turned to face him.

"What do you think you're doing?" She sounded truly frightened. "Stay away from me."

"It's me," he said, plaintive, once more the confused boy who'd sat beside her at school while she explained the Bible stories they were told by their teachers. "Don't you recognize me?"

"That's exactly why I'm telling you to stay away. We're not children. We can't do as we please. I have a husband."

He felt like a fool. She must have known he was pained by her reaction, for her expression softened.

"Don't you know what this place is like? Have you been away that long? Just because we went to school together, we don't live in the same world. And we're certainly not the same people we once were."

He promised he would not seek her out, or follow her, or even greet her should their paths cross again, if that was what she wished.

"Who said anything about what I wish? I'm just telling you how things are, just like I always did. You should be grateful to me."

MARIANNA WAS RIGHT IN saying he was not the same person he'd been when he left, and his family had been right as well. The world had opened to him, and as it was doing so he had closed the door on this island, which ran on rules he found heartless and inhuman. When he'd first returned from Paris, and asked his family to call him by his third name, Camille, so that he could at least keep something of his life in Paris, his brothers had mocked him. *Be whoever you want,* his brother Alfred said, *just do your work.* The family did as he wished, except for his mother, who preferred not to say his name at all rather than to change it. She referred to him as *he,* more a stranger than a son. *He's not happy with the food. He came in late for work. He disappeared. He does not wish to join us for dinner.* And, when Camille refused to go to the synagogue—*He no longer appears to be a member of our faith.*

In Paris he didn't have to struggle with his people's history every time he spoke the name Jacobo aloud. He was just a man, not a Jew but an artist. This sense of being an outsider was not an issue for his parents, who were now accepted by people of their faith and had no wish to know any Europeans outside the community. Within the family there was no discussion of the rift his parents' marriage had once caused. The shame of having children born before they were officially wed was never spoken of, although this was still a topic discussed in other households, behind closed doors. Most people didn't even remember why the congregation had been so enraged and why the Pizzarro children had gone to the Moravian School. All the years of bad blood had evaporated, and his brothers and sisters seemed to have forgotten those times.

"That was so long ago," said his sister Hannah, now a mother herself. Her wedding was said to have been the turning point, but perhaps it was the dinner at Madame Halevy's. When that night was ending, and his parents had thanked their hostess and walked into the courtyard, Madame had come into the kitchen where Camille had been waiting with Mrs. James. "Now your grandmother and I are even," she told him, insisting he take a piece of pastry with him, though he would only toss it out for the birds when he reached the road. "Always pay back what you owe. Remember that," Madame Halevy told him, patting him on the arm.

Frédéric Pizzarro now went to synagogue every day for the morning prayers. At first Camille accompanied his father and brothers on Friday nights, but unlike them he could not forget how these same people they prayed with had disrespected his mother, treating her as if she were a ghost. He supposed he held a grudge. He stopped going. Instead, he found himself drawn to the Lutheran church run by the Moravian brothers, his teachers, who had begun the school for slaves. Those Bible stories he had been told as a child had stayed with him, and he thought of Jesus as a great teacher, a rebel who refused to see the poor and disenfranchised mistreated. He went to the church sometimes and sat with his eyes closed, listening to the hymns, songs in Danish and German.

He owed his father his loyalty; therefore he did not mention his visits to the church, nor did he outwardly complain about how miserable he was since his return from Paris. His older brothers were happy in the family business, and the problems with the Petits in France had been dealt with. A new business had been formed, with his sister's in-laws, one more profitable than the old business. The future was the family's interest. So who was he to think of the past? For him this island was a mist of all that had once been, a past that enveloped him every day. Certainly he felt this each time he visited Madame Halevy's grave and left a stone behind, for remembrance. He had done as he'd been told. He had not forgotten her. Whenever he left the cemetery the leaves shook down

into his hair and he felt Madame nearby, reminding him to see to his duties, and pay back every favor.

He often brought bags of groceries to Madame Halevy's maid, who
had gone to live with one of her daughters on the outskirts of the city.
Mrs. James was very old now, and her family took care of her. Camille
made sure to include bananas and mangoes so she could make her desserts. "I'll have my daughter bring a cake to your house," she always
told him.

"Please, no. Thank you but please, make something for your grandchildren." He still did not favor sweets.

"People think they knew Madame, but they didn't," Helena James
said one day. She'd made a guava berry custard, which she insisted he
try. "She wasn't mean the way they said."

Camille grinned. He had spooned much of the custard into the
hedges when she turned away, and now bees hovered around. "She loved
your desserts."

Mrs. James nodded as if this was a given, then went on. "I suppose
she told you the story about Jestine because she also had a daughter that
she lost."

"The one in Charleston?" Camille spooned up the last of the pudding, thanked his hostess, and returned the china bowl to her. It was one
of Madame Halevy's. Everything in her kitchen had been given to
Helena.

"When you work in someone's house you know things about them
they don't know about themselves. Whatever they try to hide, you see,
even when you don't want to find it out. You open a drawer, there it is.
Once you know, there's nothing you can do about it but pity them.
Here's the truth about Madame." Mrs. James glanced around to make
certain no one was near before going on. "The pain was not that her
daughter went to Charleston but that she had to go away."

"And why was that?" Camille asked, although he was not as interested as he might have been. He had taken up his sketch pad, and was

doing his best to record Mrs. James's hands, her beautiful, long fingers, adorned with the two gold rings Madame Halevy had always worn. She'd given them to Mrs. James, rather than to her own daughter.

"It's an old story," Helena James said. "It's the past and over and done with, as good as buried with the dead once I'm gone."

CAMILLE UNDERSTOOD THAT PEOPLE often wanted to erase the pain of what they'd been through, to reinvent the past and their part in it. He'd seen this for himself in the Market Square on July 3, when the proclamation emancipating all slaves in the Danish West Indies was read. It was a joyously received, a long-overdue declaration brought about by the King's governor, Peter von Scholten, who himself had a common-law wife who was a free woman of mixed blood. Eight thousand slaves on St. Croix living under appalling conditions had demanded and been granted emancipation from the Danish government, and von Scholten had been there to witness how this could be accomplished without bloodshed. He had set the same process to work in St. Thomas, and at last the King had granted these demands.

Camille was glad to be there for the changes that were taking place, a witness to these cruel laws abolished. He noticed those who had been in favor of slavery and who'd been forced to free their workers now behaved as if they had never used such labor. Most of the African slaves were from Ghana, for the Danes had a fort there, one identical to the fort on their own shore. It was the gate to hell, and it would now be closed. People threw paper and bark inside the doorways of the fort and watched as the windows lit up with a flickering orange light, as if the fort were a lantern that could send a message across the ocean. *No more,* was the message. *Not in our life and time.*

There was a great party in the public square that lasted most of the week. Because the date was the third, all that year babies were given names with three letters, for three was clearly a lucky number. But for many people there was a bitterness ingrained in the celebration, for they had been granted something that should have been theirs all along. For the older people, it was also a time of mourning for all the years and lives that had been stolen.

Rosalie went to the grave of the child she had lost. She wished he was alive and had grown up to become a young man who could celebrate freedom for all on their island. She took the fallen leaves from her hair and placed them under her pillow so she would dream of her baby. She no longer thought he'd been taken because she loved him too much. That was foolishness someone had told her, that she'd drowned him, poisoning him with her own milk, and she'd taken the blame upon herself. The truth of the matter was, she loved Enrique too much as well, and her love had done no damage. He was still on this earth, alive and well, the handsome man she first saw in the garden of the Pomiés' beautiful old house where strangers from Amsterdam lived now. She could hear these new people talking when she sat outside the cottage where she lived with Enrique, though she did not understand Dutch. She still worried about bad fortune even though she no longer believed love carried a curse. She feared that Enrique would be taken from her. But fate surprised her, and on the occasion of the proclamation she felt something she had felt only once before, the flicker of life.

She told Enrique that night, knowing he had always wanted a son. He said she could name the baby after the child she lost. That first baby's name had been Leland Frost, a name she had told no one, and his father had been a sailor from St. Croix who had drowned. "No," Rosalie said after carefully considering. "He'll be his own person. He'll have his own name."

That was when she knew they would be starting everything all over again. They sat outside and had their dinner and watched the fires on the hill all around the fort, with orange and red flashes leaping upward. She had been attached to the motherless Pomié children, then Rachel had surprised her when she came to the house and asked for her help. Rachel had been so young and inexperienced, Rosalie had felt pity for her. But that was a long time ago, after the first Madame Pomié had taken ill and wept and Rosalie had wept with her. But a servant, no matter how beloved, was not a friend, and a slave was a shadow, nothing more. The sparks from the celebrations were so bright they looked like stars. It was the last night of the old world. *Good riddance,* Rosalie thought. She'd name this boy a name no one else had, so he could someday be his own man, one who could stand up to the devil himself.

There were bonfires all around Skytsborg Tower, called Sky Tower, built in 1678 on the highest point overlooking the harbor. It was here that the pirate Blackbeard, born Edward Teach, had lived during his time on the island. Blackbeard was rumored to light cannon fuses dipped into limewater under his hat and in his beard so that smoke would encircle him. He would look as fierce as the devil, and some people believed that he was. His enemies so feared him they would simply turn over their boats and goods to him and even grant him their wives. His fourteen wives got the worst of the bargain, for he'd abandoned each one. Their skeletons could still be found in the hillside caves. Camille had come upon their wild gardens while he walked at night, so deep in the thickets they'd disappeared for a hundred years. Here untended avocado plants and patches of mint and juniper grew wild, rambling down hillsides, mixing with native plants. He sketched the jumbled remains, an exotic mixture of hope and despair, with vines run riot. Some gardens were bordered by seashells and rocks, others had tumbled-down fences made of bones and rocks, still another was surrounded by banks of pink and red that had all sprung from a single rosebush brought from Madagascar. He liked to search for these gardens when he went into the countryside to visit Helena James, bringing her delicacies he'd filched from the storeroom. Chocolates from France, coconut syrup, oranges sent from Florida. If he found bougainvillea, he plucked some vines and brought them along as well, then sketched them as they trembled in a vase on her table.

"There's going to be trouble," Mrs. James told him one day as they sat outside and ate oranges cut into slices with a bone-handled knife that

had once been on Madame Halevy's kitchen table. "The daughter's returning, even though she swore to her mother she'd never come back
here. My daughter heard about it from a woman she knows who works at
the hotel."

"Why would she come now? Madame Halevy has been gone for
some time."

"Exactly why. Think about it. Now with her mother buried so long
she can't walk out of her grave, the daughter finally is here to see what
she can get."

Camille asked around on the docks so he might ease Helena James's
worries. He'd found that the old lady was right. The daughter had already arrived and was staying at the Commercial Hotel. She'd had a
meeting with a local solicitor known for his aggressive manner. Camille
posted himself outside the hotel at the coffeehouse, where he ordered
one coffee, and then another. The waiter, a fellow he knew named Jack
Highfield, pointed her out when she left the hotel, a woman in her fifties,
well dressed, with a brash sort of American ease. She wore no hat, and
white leather buttoned boots showed under her green muslin dress. Since
Camille was adept at following people, he set off to see what he might
discover. Madame Halevy's daughter went directly to the St. Thomas
Savings Bank. Camille went in after she left, but he didn't know anyone
there, and the manager was too busy to meet with him. There were now
more than forty thousand people on the island, and it was no longer possible to know everyone, along with their business, although in the Jewish
community news still traveled quickly.

Camille had Hannah question the women of the Sisterhood, and of
course they knew the reasons behind Madame Halevy's daughter coming to visit. Rebecca Halevy-Stein had come for her mother's estate. The
old mansion had stood empty—there had been talk of ghosts and bad
luck—and was only now finally sold, to an Ashkenazi family recently
arrived from Germany via Amsterdam. Mrs. Halevy-Stein had returned
so that she might collect her mother's belongings, but when she went to

the house there was almost nothing there. Years had passed, and what Madame had not given away had been seen as abandoned and therefore fair game, taken home by various deliverymen and the construction people hired to repair the roof or the shutters or the falling-down stonework.

When Camille made his report to Helena James, the news of Mrs. Halevy-Stein's doings did not comfort her. Rather it made her more anxious. "She's going to come after me. Even though I helped raise her, she was always selfish and thinking about no one but herself. Her mother would say the very same thing if she was alive."

In fact, Mrs. Halevy-Stein did intend to visit Mrs. James, along with her solicitor, Edwin Holloway, who was not from the community but was instead a resettled American from South Carolina. They'd known each other in Charleston. Camille was aware of their meeting because one of Helena James's grandsons, a boy of seven or eight named Richard, came running into the store, out of breath, frantic, not even having taken the time to put on his shoes. He was a faster runner barefoot, he claimed, just as Camille had been as a boy. Camille slipped on his own shoes, however, when the boy came to tug on his shirtsleeve. He was no longer used to jogging along over sand and stones.

The boy hurried him. "My grandmother thinks you should come and speak for her."

Frédéric overheard and took Camille aside before he could leave the store. "How are you involved?"

When Camille explained that Mrs. James had worked for Madame Halevy for years, and was afraid of the daughter, Frédéric slipped on his jacket.

"Shall we?" he said, with the clear intention of accompanying his son.

Camille grinned, surprised but pleased not to have to face Mrs. Halevy-Stein and her solicitor alone. After all, he knew nothing of business matters, as his father was well aware, and Frédéric was respected for his professional acumen.

They followed Mrs. James's grandson out of town. He was indeed fast, and Camille and his father had trouble keeping pace.

"I used to be able to run like that," Camille said.

"So did I," his father informed him.

They went uphill as quickly as they could, clouds of dust rising. It was noon, and too hot for such activities. Camille and his father both wore jackets, due to the serious nature of the occasion, and were therefore sweating through their clothes.

"They're going to take away my grandmother's dishes," the boy, Richard, said. "They came with boxes and some donkeys. They're going to steal everything she has."

"They're not taking anything," Frédéric assured him.

But when they got to the little house on a hillside, they saw that several wooden crates had, indeed, been brought from town and set out in the yard. Frédéric went and immediately introduced himself to Holloway, the solicitor, who although new in Charlotte Amalie, knew of Monsieur Pizzarro and his store.

"I suspect there's been some confusion," Holloway said. "There are some items here that belonged to my client's mother. Perhaps this good woman Mrs. James has had them in safekeeping, but now my client wishes to collect them for her home in Charleston."

Madame Halevy's daughter, the one she had lost, was so cool the heat didn't seem to affect her in the least. She was tall and well formed, an attractive woman. She came to join the discussion, and Pizzarro wondered if that's what women from Charleston did, act as if they had the rights of men. "I'm thankful that our maid took care of these household items," she said in her soft, measured voice, "but they belong to me."

Camille glanced over at Helena James, who shook her head. He elbowed his father and motioned this was not true.

"I'm afraid your mother left these items to Mrs. James," Frédéric Pizzarro said.

"Really?" Rebecca Halevy-Stein turned to the maid. "What kind of china is it?"

"It's the green set. The one Madame liked to use for dinner."

Mrs. Halevy-Stein smirked as she faced Monsieur Pizzarro. "It's Limoges. Imported from France and quite treasured. They are meant to be in my home."

"Your mother didn't like for you to use them because you chipped them," Mrs. James said. "You know that to be true."

"Do you have a written statement in your mother's hand that these are her belongings and meant to go to you?" Monsieur Pizzarro asked Mrs. Halevy-Stein.

"I am my mother's daughter." Mrs. Halevy-Stein was agitated. "You heard Helena. She admits they came from my mother's house. They were used at dinner." She took note of something else, and her eyes widened. "And that's the table they set." Mrs. Halevy pointed into the house. The door was open. "It's there in the front room. Mahogany. Handmade."

Monsieur Pizzarro shrugged. This proved nothing. "Perhaps the dishes were borrowed from Mrs. James so that Madame Halevy might use them in her home."

The solicitor Holloway laughed at the preposterousness of the suggestion that a woman of wealth and standing within her community would need to borrow dishes from her maid. He then saw Monsieur Pizzarro's expression. "You're not serious?"

Monsieur Pizzarro turned to his son. "You dined with Madame Halevy. Did you ever see these dishes in her house?"

"I never saw them," Camille said. But of course he'd never looked. He usually had his dessert on an earthenware platter.

Rebecca Halevy-Stein was a pale blonde; now her skin flushed with anger, even more so when she noticed a flash of gold on Mrs. James's hands. "What do you have there?"

Mrs. James hid her hands under her skirts.

"Those are my mother's rings," Mrs. Halevy-Stein said, turning to her solicitor. "She has them on right now!"

"She gave them to me," Mrs. James told Camille. "She wanted me to have them."

"This may be an issue for the courts," Holloway said.

"Not without some paperwork." Frédéric stared the solicitor down. "Is there a will? You say there's not. Is there a document connecting your client with Madame Halevy's personal items? It doesn't seem to exist."

"I came from Charleston to take care of this," Mrs. Halevy-Stein said. "I made a long trip, and I did so in good faith."

"You didn't come even once when your mother was alive," Helena said before she could stop herself. "And you and I know why. It had nothing to do with faith."

The younger woman turned to Mrs. James. "I should have my mother's rings," she said. "As far as I'm concerned they've been stolen, along with everything else. Does this woman have a paper that states they're hers?" she asked Monsieur Pizzarro. "Did my mother sign a document stating so?"

Mrs. James gazed at Madame Halevy's daughter and shook her head. "I made your porridge when you were a baby. I know you, and I know why you didn't come back. You never wrote to ask what happened, just left everything in your mother's hands. I'm the one who helped her. I helped her and she was grateful. So if you want to go to court and charge me with something, then I suppose you will."

The air felt as it did when rain would soon begin, a prickly shock of heat with a measure of cold, dampness mixing into the atmosphere.

"Charge me, Rebecca," Mrs. James said. "Bring me to court. See if what it gets you is worth the trouble. I have the story, and I've kept it to myself."

Mrs. Halevy-Stein studied the maid, then turned to her solicitor. "This is ridiculous. Let's just deal with the house."

"But the crates?" Holloway said, confused. "All of your mother's belongings? Surely they're worth something."

"I'm not going to fight with an old woman." Rebecca Halevy-Stein reached for her purse so she could pay off the men who'd brought the crates and donkeys up the hill and were waiting to fill them with furniture and dishes. "I hope you're happy," she said to Mrs. James.

"Happiness is for fools." Helena James shrugged. "So I wish that for you."

When the unwanted guests had left, and the donkeys and the crates were gone as well, the Pizzarro father and son were given cups of maubie and thanked by the family. Mrs. James went in to get a coconut cake she had made. She signaled for Camille to help her inside. There was a hole in the roof so that the smoke and cooking smells could escape. The stove was tiny, but the oven was clearly big enough for Mrs. James's baking.

"Your father's a good man," she said.

"Yes." Today Camille had seen the righteousness inside his father that he hadn't been aware of before. His father was a quiet, solemn man, and Camille had always assumed the battle with the synagogue had been his mother's doing; now he wasn't so sure. His father, he now understood, was a fighter.

"I'm going to use the green plates you never saw in Madame's house," Mrs. James said. "The cake will look just right on them."

Because Camille was tall and could reach, she directed him to take the plates from a special place in the cabinet that had once stood in Madame Halevy's kitchen. She still called him Jacobo, and he didn't correct her.

"Madame Halevy would be glad you have the dishes," he said. "They're in the right home."

"She didn't live to tell you all of her story. She thought about it, and we talked about it, then she died. So I can say now that the end of the story was that she died and her daughter never came to see her. But it's the middle of the story that matters. Rebecca had a baby when she was seventeen. No one guessed; she hid it with her clothes. A lady can do that, up to a point. When the time came and she might have begun to show, she got something from an herb man that made the baby come early. This lady who wanted the dishes that you never saw in Madame's house, who never came home and never wrote a letter, gave birth all by herself when she wasn't much more than a girl. It was brave or it was stupid. There was a storm, which brings on childbirth. The air comes down low and brings down whatever is inside you. Mademoiselle hid herself in the woods, and when it was over, she left the baby under a tree outside of the graveyard. Not the Jewish graveyard. Ours. I know because I followed her.

"Maybe somebody would find him and maybe they wouldn't. Maybe he would be drowned by the rain pouring down or maybe he would swim like a fish. She didn't know and she didn't care. She ran away like a shadow or a demon, so fast you'd never know she was there. I had followed her before when her mother directed me to. I knew she had been with a sailor who came from St. Croix. He was not one of your people. He was one of mine.

"I didn't wait to find out if the baby would drown. I took that baby and brought him to Madame Halevy. Rebecca had already bought her ticket for Charleston. She was staying in the Grand Hotel, where she stained the sheets with blood—I know because my cousin worked there and I had her keep an eye on Rebecca. I thought she might do damage to herself, maybe decide to leave this world, but she wasn't that kind of girl. She was already in the future. She left the next morning. Maybe she thought good-bye, but she didn't have the decency to come around and say it to her mother. So Madame Halevy and I considered what would be best for this child and how we could ensure that he would have a good life. He was her grandson, but because I had found him he was mine in a way, too. We both knew he must go to a family where he would be loved. He had blue eyes and we decided that was a sign. We set his fate on that single fact.

Madame had a friend who had lost a baby son at birth. Her friend didn't care that this baby's father was an African man. She was in mourning and when she saw this child her mourning lifted. This baby was the man Jestine fell in love with, but couldn't have because everyone thought he was a member of your faith."

"Lydia's father?" Camille was confused. If this cousin of his and Jestine both had African blood, why couldn't they have married? Surely someone could have told this man the truth about himself. "Then why couldn't he be with Jestine?"

"The truth of who he was would have led back to Rebecca. That kind of gossip would have reached Charleston and ruined her. Madame Halevy was protecting her daughter. She made your grandmother promise to do the same." Helena put her hand on Camille's arm. "Your cousin never knew who he was. Jestine still doesn't know. Only Madame and your grandmother and me. Now you understand why I wear Madame Halevy's rings, and why they will be buried with me, and why this story will be buried as well."

"Except that I know," Camille said mournfully.

"That's why she never told you." Helena James had cut up the cake while she spoke. She set the slices onto the plates that were exactly as Camille remembered them, emerald green with a pattern of gold leaf around the edges. "I wanted you to understand why Madame wanted me to have everything. It was because I was so loyal and never said a word. I would have never told you either, but I didn't want you to think I was a thief."

"I never would have thought that. Now I'm stuck with the story."

Helena laughed. "We're together in that, Jacobo."

They went outside and had the coconut cake, which Frédéric Pizzarro declared to be delicious, though his son noticed he tossed bits of it behind him, for the rooster. Father and son walked back toward town together.

"I'm glad that's settled," Frédéric said.

"Thank you for helping, but it's never settled in this place," Camille responded. "People are treated unfairly and it's taken as due course.

Who cares what race you are or what faith or, for that matter, who you marry?"

His father clapped his son on the back. "We can't change the world, can we?"

"Of course we can," Camille said.

They were halfway to town when they noticed the path to the waterfall. They exchanged a look. They were expected home, but it was such a hot day. They turned onto the path. When they reached the pool they took off their clothes and dove in. The chill made Camille shout out as he hit the surface of the water. Tiny blue fish scattered. The bright sky shone through a tunnel of branches. Frédéric went to stand beneath the falling water, as he had when he first came to this island, when he was enchanted and knew that he would stay.

"What did the old lady tell you when she brought you into the house?" Frédéric asked when they had finished their swim and were dressing on the banks of the pool. "She took a long time to get that cake ready."

The sun was so strong their skin dried in moments. But in an hour or so twilight would drift down and all of the shadows would turn purple. Then the leaves would be damp with dew.

"She told me my father was a good man," Camille said.

Frédéric studied his son. "It took that long for her to say so?"

"She told me that she was an honest woman, and she didn't wish for us to think otherwise."

"Why would we? Rebecca abandoned her mother and came back only when she thought she had something to gain."

They set off, through the woods, then onto the road. There were a few wild donkeys that trotted away when they spied the men. They disappeared up a hill, leaving a path cut through the tall grass.

"Your mother used to have a pet donkey. She still cries over him."

Camille was puzzled. When he'd wanted a pet she'd always told him animals were dirty and a waste of time. His sisters had been lucky to have their tiny lapdog, and then only because their father pled their case. "My mother?"

Frédéric clapped his son on the back, then looped an arm over his shoulders. "Your mother."

They stopped so that Frédéric could gather some branches of the flamboyant tree, slashing them down with a knife he carried. "Your mother also likes to bring these flowers to the cemetery. She says it brings good luck. We can stop there."

Camille felt Madame Halevy's story inside of him as they went on. It had the heft of a stone, and it rattled, surprising him with its weight. He picked up some white rocks at the side of the road. While his father laid the red flowers around the family's graves, Camille went to Madame Halevy's grave and left three stones: the first for Mrs. James; the second for his grandmother, Madame Pomié; the last for himself, for he was the last one to know her story.

⤙◈⤚

NO MATTER HOW HE tried, Camille continued to fail in the store. After two years his father moved him down to the harbor to sign in goods unloaded from ships meant for the storehouse. It was a low-level position, and all he needed to do was be aware of when the ships arrived, then sign in the deliveries and have them transported. But instead of keeping an eye on things, Camille used most of his time to sketch, often forgetting appointments and having to rush to meet a ship's purser on the docks. He was meant to count and record crates that were unloaded, but he often took his paints along and neglected his duties completely. He was drawn to seascapes, though he found them difficult. To catch a moment in movement, to add time to space in a painting was a challenge. To ensure he wouldn't be seen by his parents, who had made their disapproval clear when it came to his true calling, he sometimes set up a makeshift easel on Jestine's porch. Jestine knew Rachel would not approve of his art, but when he was in her home, she felt her daughter was closer to her. Camille had seen Lyddie, spoken to her, touched her. Jestine and Lydia now wrote to each other on a regular basis, often once or twice a week. Lydia had delivered her fourth child, a boy named Leo, named after the constellation, a darling child and his father's favorite.

When I told my husband who I was it did not matter to him, but this was not true for everyone. The house with the garden where we watched stars now belongs to his brother. We no longer see his family. We live in an apartment in Paris. There is no garden, but I take my children to the Tuileries every day unless there is snow. They have a dog they love, Lapin, a little rabbit of a thing who is quite a clown. There is no maid to care for my daughters and my son, which is best. The time I spend with them is precious to me. I want to tie them to me with string so they will never get lost or wander off, as you tied me to your side when I was a tot. If I lost them, I would be beside myself. If they were stolen, I don't know how I would survive.

My husband is employed by another bank now, one run by people who are not of his faith. There are long hours, but he is excellent at his work and hopefully that will be recognized. I like to think the good in people will be seen, that it rises to the surface, like the tiny fish in the pool at the waterfall you used to take me to. I remember being there on a very hot day, and believing that the fish came to me when I opened my hand. I remember that you told me to be careful not to slip and fall. When I say the same words to my own children, it's your voice they hear.

Jestine had begun work on a dress that was unlike any she'd made before. For years she had put it off, but at last it was time to make a dress for Lyddie.

"You always said no dress was good enough for your daughter," Camille commented when he saw her bent over her work.

"This one will be."

"And how will you get it to her?"

"Let me worry about that." That was the next step; for now she was concentrating on the creation of something that would be worthy of her daughter.

"Surely you won't trust the mail." Camille then had an idea. "I know. I'll take it back to Paris." They laughed because it was clear he was desperate to go back. The time he'd recently spent in St. Thomas had been more than enough for him.

On the porch tubs of dye had been set out: heron blue and midnight, teal and a pale lilac-hued blue that was so like a hyacinth that bees rumbled nearby. Jestine had used sea urchin spines and pressed violets and stalks of indigo to tint various hues. She'd saved up for bolts of silk from Spain and had bought twelve buttons fashioned from pale abalone shell. She had three spools of thread spun in China, carried overland through the desert on the backs of camels, then sent across the ocean on a boat from Portugal. Her stitches were so small that her fingers bled and at the end of the day she needed to soak her hands in warm water and rest her eyes under slices of cucumber or bits of damp muslin. The underskirt of the dress was made of lace, dyed with inkberries and guava berries. On the bodice she had stitched the dried, preserved scales of fish that swam in the waterfall, tiny blue translucent scales soaked in vinegar and salt that shone in the dark. She had a length of ribbon she dyed haint blue. That would make certain that the dress would always protect Lyddie. No ghosts, no demons, no sorrow, no separations, no thievery, no witchery, no abductions, no spirits of any kind.

❧

CAMILLE WAS VISITING JESTINE, as he did nearly every day, when he saw the painter at the harbor, a standing easel set up before him on the sand. He stood upon Jestine's porch with a spyglass. The waves were rough that day, and the trade winds blew across the island. Palm trees rattled, and fronds that were shaken fell into the roads. The painter paid no attention to the weather and worked feverishly, glancing up now and then to watch the light on the crashing waves. Jestine came out with two cups of hot coffee.

"Everyone says he's a madman," she said of the painter on the beach.

"Do they? Why is that?"

"Just look at him! He stands out there in the wind! If he doesn't watch out a wave will carry him away. Maybe he needs to be tied to the wharf with rope."

Camille was instantly interested. A few days later, when he spied the painter in the same spot, he left his office on the dock, curious to see what this gentleman was up to. The painter was only a few years older than he, Danish, with sharp features, already balding but with a boyish appearance. He was quite approachable and not in the least disturbed at having been interrupted.

"I know no one here, so to meet a fellow artist, well, I couldn't be more grateful."

They shook hands, and the young man introduced himself as Fritz Melbye, an artist from Copenhagen, who had been born in Elsinore in 1826. He specialized in seascapes, and though he was only four years older, he had vast experience compared to Camille, and had been to art school in Denmark. He was from a family of marine painters, the youngest of three brothers, and had set off to the West Indies to make his fortune and his name. He was fearless and friendly in a way Camille would never be, willing to go anywhere and do anything for a view of a watery vision that resonated inside his soul. They went to a tavern and Camille introduced Melbye to guava berry rum, which he declared a delight. Melbye, for his part, introduced Camille to cigars, which sent him into a coughing fit. He felt embarrassed, inexperienced, a boy living with his family, doing their bidding when this fellow Melbye, at the age of twenty-four, was on his own entirely, a grown man living on his instincts and desires.

"You make your living with your art?" Camille asked, intrigued.

Melbye could hold his rum well, and the painting he was working on, a view of the harbor at St. Thomas, was impressive.

"I live as well as I can, and paint as well as God allows."

His older brothers were better known, he confided; Vilhelm had been the first to approach seascapes, and Anton was a respected teacher and painter in Paris. Fritz himself was lighthearted, a ladies' man, interested in seeing the world and experiencing all that he could.

"Death stalks us." He shrugged and called for another rum. "So why not live as we wish? I'd like to paint every ocean and every major sea before I'm thirty. If I do that, then afterward I can drop into hell for all I care, for I'll have completed my goal."

Camille laughed. He had never enjoyed another man's company so thoroughly. "So that's that? The devil can have you?"

"I'd prefer to be showing in Paris, but if I go to the devil, so be it."

They began to meet nearly every day, and took to working side by side. Camille showed his companion the Sky Tower, from which they could view nearly every bit of the shoreline. He brought him to the synagogue, made of stone and molasses and sand, then on to the inlet where vegetables were unloaded from sailboats and African laborers took carts and baskets into the marketplace. Melbye sketched at all of these places, images that he would later use in his paintings. What was familiar to Camille was exotic to the Dane, and intriguing beyond belief. Fritz wore a white suit and a white linen shirt, but he wished to leave his more refined ways behind. He'd grown a beard and he liked to go barefoot, even though Camille warned him about burrs and the local stinging bees, which nested not in trees but in the ground. Fritz spoke French and English with a clipped Danish accent. As it turned out he, too, had come from a bourgeois family; in his case, they were involved in finance. But his older brothers had fought the battle of art versus commerce with their father, and by the time Fritz was twenty his father had already accepted the fact that none of his sons would carry on the family business. "When it came to me, he gave up." Fritz grinned.

It was a pleasure to be in Fritz's company and to hear about the art world of Paris, and his brothers' experiences, and Fritz's own plans. He was wildly cheerful, so friendly local people took to calling him l'Ami Rouge, the red friend, for although his blond hair was balding, his beard was a pale red. He clearly had a desire to do as the locals did and be considered a friend among them—washing his laundry himself, learning to make maubie and drinking it with every meal. For breakfast he had sea moss, a concoction made of boiled seaweed mixed with milk and spices. He dined on plain salt fish even on Sunday, something no person with any pride would do. He meant to go to South America and back to Europe and then on to New York. While in St. Thomas he had rented a shed from a farmer in the Savan, the living area newly created for freed slaves. There were a few Jewish families there as well, but Melbye was the only Christian European to reside in the Savan, and his neighbors thought him a bit mad, for he stayed up till all hours, painting in the alleyway outside his shack, asking women and children to pose for him in exchange for a sketch of themselves or a bit of what little money he had. Once a robber broke in, thinking he was a rich man, but there was nothing to steal but paint and unwashed laundry. When Melbye protested, he was felled by a blow. The two men fought, but somehow Fritz won the thief over, and he wound up helping his victim off the floor. The robber was Maurice, son of his neighbor, Mr. Alek, and he and his neighbors soon enough had mugs of rum together, forgetting the episode entirely.

"Nobody likes that man you're friends with," Jestine told Camille when he next came to visit after stopping at the post office for her. There had been three letters on that day.

"Fritz?" he said, surprised. "He just has a big heart."

"Well, he looks like he'll bring bad luck." Jestine hated to think that Rachel's boy might be led astray. She'd heard the two friends were staying out all night, drinking at the harbor, and that there were some women involved, including a St. Thomas girl Camille used to know back when they called him Jacobo. People said this girl was married to a man who knew nothing about what was going on.

But the girl's mother, the woman who had told Jacobo Camille Pizzarro to stay away from her daughter when they were ten years old, had figured it out. In her opinion he was trouble then, and trouble once again. This lady came around to the Pizzarros' store to speak her mind, and nothing was going to stop her from doing so. Rachel was in the back room going over the ledgers. Since the time her father had first brought her to the store it had been her habit to do so once a week. It was late on Friday and Mr. Enrique had gone home to be with Rosalie. Frédéric and the boys had already set off for the synagogue, Jacobo Camille was out as he usually was, and so Rachel was alone in the shop. She looked up and there was a woman in the doorway. A local woman of her own age who looked quite upset.

"You'll need to speak with the clerk in the morning if you want to place an order," Rachel said.

"I don't need to place an order," the woman responded. She was tall, attractive, but clearly agitated.

Rachel sat back in her chair and appraised her guest. She had seen her in the market but didn't know her by name. "Did you want something?"

"Your son is the one who wants something and he's not having it," her visitor said.

Rachel rose so that she might pull over a chair. She was not surprised that her son had offended someone in some way. "Please," she said, suggesting her guest join her at her desk and continue. When the woman sat beside her, Rachel recognized her. She worked as a laundress and had sent her children to the Moravian School. "I've forgotten your name," Rachel admitted.

"Why should you remember? I'm nothing to you, as you are nothing to me."

Rachel found this woman interesting. Certainly she spoke her mind. She closed the ledger book and gave her guest her full attention.

"It's my daughter's name you should know. Marianna. Why don't you ask your son about her? And in the meantime, hope her husband doesn't find out."

Rachel remembered Marianna. She'd been one of the reasons Rachel had sent Jacobo away in the first place. She still thought of him with his old name and refused to call him Camille. She certainly wasn't about to let her hard work setting him on the right path be disrupted by this same pretty girl. She went to Jestine's the next morning and told her about her visitor. They drank coffee and sat at the old table where Adelle used to give them their lunch.

"He's not having a love affair with that girl," Jestine said. "You don't have to worry about that. But you have something else to worry about. He's painting her."

Jestine had some sketches Camille had made of Marianna carrying some laundry. He'd left them behind, and she now brought them out and set them on the table. Rachel held one up. She took note of the curve of the woman's shoulder and breast, her thin waist, the angles of her face as she looked toward the sea.

"He may not be having an affair, but clearly he's enamored," Rachel said. "How long have you known about this?"

Jestine looked stung. "Shall I not be your friend and an aunt to him? Do you feel I have stolen him?"

"Of course not," Rachel said. "You are an aunt to him and I'm grateful that you are. What I have, I gladly share with you. It's only that he tells you everything and I'm the last to know."

"Would you have told your mother anything?"

"But I'm nothing like my mother." She looked hard at Jestine. "Am I?"

"Rachel, if you were, I would not be your friend," Jestine assured her.

Still Rachel worried that she carried the seed of her mother's bitterness. The one feature that had caused her to be vain was her beautiful dark hair. But one night she dreamed of her mother, and when she awoke her hair was streaked white, as if she'd been cursed. Her mother's hair had turned white when she was a young woman, when Rachel's father began to leave in the evenings and not come home. Rachel would listen to her mother weep, but she never went to her. Perhaps there was a punishment for this, and she would always be the last to know her son.

THE PIZZARROS INVITED FRITZ Melbye to dinner, an invitation he gratefully accepted, even though Camille had warned him that it was a trap. "They've heard rumors about you. Now they want to see you for themselves."

"Fine," Melbye said agreeably.

"They'll study you as they would examine a sloth or a snake."

Melbye laughed. He had a great, strong laugh, which suited his good humor. He often had a hangover and found it difficult to leave his sleeping pallet before noon. "They'll find I'm more sloth than snake."

Camille was sure his friend had no idea of who his parents were, how fierce they could be, even his mild father when the situation called for ferocity, and how dedicated they were to keeping him tied to a fate he was more and more convinced simply wasn't his. He dreamed of Paris, often so deeply he didn't know where he was when he awoke. Until Melbye, he'd been an early riser, but not anymore. In the late morning he often lay staring at the ceiling. The crack in the shape of a lion, the mulberry-colored drapes to keep out the heat of the sun, the mahogany dresser—it all seemed so unreal. He often thought he was dreaming that he'd come back to St. Thomas, and when he truly awoke he would be in Passy, at his aunt and uncle's house, and that when he leapt from his bed and looked out the window, snow would be falling, covering the garden and the lawn, and all the birds that were singing in the trees would be doves and wrens instead of the parrots that woke him with their piercing cries.

AT THE APPOINTED DINNER, his brothers and sisters crowded around the table as Frédéric interrogated Melbye. Though Melbye was already balding, and seemed far older than their son, he was a good-looking, charming man who was used to dominating a room with his fluid conversation. Why St. Thomas, Frédéric wanted to know, and what was next? Fritz had already confided in Camille that his plan was to go to Venezuela, and he had invited Camille to go with him. Fritz had no concerns that Venezuela was politically unstable; there, the races and religions were intermixed and he could live as a local person might. Also, he'd been told the sea views were extraordinary, visions he wouldn't see elsewhere. Unfortunately, Melbye did not think to be guarded, and he slipped into his conversation his intention to head to Caracas, mentioning his hope that his friend would go with him. That was Camille's parents' greatest fear and all they needed to know about l'Ami Rouge. He was a dangerous man, at least when it came to their family. Camille saw them exchange a look and knew that the pleasant dinner, and his chances of fleeing were, at least temporarily, dashed.

Rachel stood and left the table. "This has been a long evening," she said as she excused herself, clearly dismissing their guest.

"Did I offend her?" Melbye asked when she'd left the room and closed herself into the kitchen.

"I'm afraid you have," Frédéric told the young man. The candles on the table were burning down into puddles of wax.

"I apologize," Melbye said. He hadn't known many Jews, and thought perhaps that was the problem. Perhaps the solution was merely to get to know them better. "I don't know your traditions. Perhaps I was supposed to say a prayer?"

Camille shook his head, trying to warn his friend, but Melbye blundered on.

"I haven't had a Jewish friend before, you see."

"I'm not surprised," Frédéric replied. "Jews are too busy working to engage in the nonsense you propose. I'm afraid you have no purpose and, in our opinion, no real future." He had heard the rumors after all. Everyone in their community had. The madman on the beach, the fellow who lived in the Savan when everyone else wanted to move out of that vile place.

"Is art nonsense?" Camille said, his hackles up.

"Not for other people perhaps. Just for reasonable men."

"Are we reasonable men, Father, and have you always acted so when there was something you wanted?" Camille said, a not so veiled reference to his father's past and the decisions he'd made when he first came to the island.

"I was always reasonable," Frédéric replied. "I reasoned your mother was meant to be my wife."

In the kitchen, Rachel had boxed up the molasses cake Hannah had brought for dessert. Rosalie had had her baby, Carlo, and her presence was greatly missed in the household. There was only a day woman to help with the laundry and cooking. Rachel would go see Rosalie in the morning and tell her about the foolishness that had happened at dinner and bring back what was left of the cake with her. She busied herself with chores Rosalie would have helped her with in the past. It was a bother, but tonight she was grateful to have cause to remove herself from the table. She did not wish to see that so-called painter and was waiting for him to leave when he suddenly appeared in the kitchen doorway.

Rachel eyed him, annoyed. "Excuse me," she said. "You're in the wrong place."

"That's what your son says about himself. He doesn't belong here. Although it's a beautiful island."

Melbye towered over her. With his long, uneven, red-blond hair and loping gait, he brought to mind the monsters people said lived in the hills, one of the things that turned into a werewolf at midnight and ran through the streets. Only this fellow lived right in the center of town, in the Savan, where he didn't belong.

"Did you ever wish to have another life?" Melbye said.

Rachel stiffened. She knew when she was being courted, for whatever purpose, and had no intention of discussing the intimate details of her life. "Sir, please do not address me. I have the kitchen to see to."

Melbye came to lean against the stove. He wore his white suit, which he'd had pressed by a laundress for this evening's dinner. Rachel shuddered when she realized he was not wearing shoes. This barefoot Dane had his nerve to come into her house in this manner, and he didn't even know how rude he was. She was relieved to think he'd be gone soon enough. Still he leaned back as if this kitchen was his home. As if they'd wanted him here.

"Take my advice," he suggested. "Let him go."

Rachel laughed. He really was the most preposterous man. She would have a lot to talk to Rosalie about in the morning. Rosalie would surely be jealous that she had not seen this character for herself and hadn't been there to give him a dressing-down, something she was quite good at.

"Sir," Rachel said. "I will have to ask you to leave."

"You know what it's like to want more than you have. I can see it in you." When she gave something away in her expression, Melbye nodded, pleased with himself. He theorized that an artist knew more about people in an instant than most people learned in a lifetime. "It's true. And yet you tie him here, as you were tied here when you were young."

Rachel turned to him then. He was a canny fellow, smarter than his friendly demeanor would have caused one to think. He thought he knew her, but he knew nothing. Could he imagine that she had stood on the Reverend's doorstep in the pouring rain and screamed for him to open the door until her lungs nearly burst? She removed her apron and folded it neatly.

"Let me guess," she said. "Your father pays your expenses."

"My expenses are small." He looked embarrassed all the same now that the topic had arisen, so they couldn't have been as small as all that.

"I won't do it," Rachel said. "It will ruin him."

Melbye disagreed. "It will save him."

"You were a guest in my house. Now I am asking you to leave. Go to Venezuela. I think you should. Go tonight. You'll be much better off if you do. I've heard you're called the Red Friend. Well, if you're any friend at all to my son, you'll leave him be."

Melbye's brow was furrowed as he tried to figure out Madame Pizzarro, who was a puzzle to him. She may have looked mild, the mother of a flock of grown children, her features plain, her dress modest, wearing no jewelry but her gold wedding ring, but she was hardly a simple woman.

"Meaning you'll do what if he accompanies me?" Melbye asked.

"I won't do anything," Rachel said. "It's the authorities you might need to worry about."

"SHE'S TALK AND NOTHING more," Camille told Fritz when he walked his friend back toward the harbor after dinner.

Melbye shook his head. "She's a force. Like a hurricane."

"Maybe once. Now she wants everything just so. Everyone must follow the rules, including me. But that's impossible. Wait for me and I promise, I'll go with you."

They shook hands on it, making a vow that they would both be in Caracas soon enough. That night Melbye was in bed with his robber-neighbor's sister, Jenny Alek, a woman who had been modeling for him and bringing him dinner, often pork cooked with lime juice and pepper and rosemary. There was a rooster next door and it set up a racket in the middle of the night, so Melbye rose from his pallet on the floor. He peered out the door to see the gendarmes heading to his door. He pulled on his white suit, grabbed his boots, then jumped out the window with a few belongings under his arm, leaving Jenny alone in his bed. He didn't know if Madame Pizzarro had sent them, or if Jenny's family didn't care for the nude sketches he'd made of her. Whatever the reason, his time on the island was over. He went directly to the harbor, barefoot, carrying his boots tied together over his shoulder, his easel under his arm. The next boat was to St. Croix, and he got on it. The weather had changed and rain was pouring down. Fritz's mouth was set. He'd been right about his friend's mother. She was fierce. A force he did not wish to encounter again.

Melbye wrote a letter as soon as he was settled, having left St. Croix to continue on to Venezuela, where he was set up in a makeshift shack on the beach. The letter arrived on a day when Camille stopped to get Jestine's mail. He'd been puzzled and hurt over Melbye's disappearance. When he'd gone looking for Fritz, all Jenny Alek would say was that Melbye was a coward and a werewolf. But another neighbor, a Mrs. Doogan, said he was a good man who had given her several sketches and one large painting of the harbor of St. Thomas as viewed from the Sky Tower. She hadn't a bad word to say about him.

Camille was delighted to at last receive a letter. He wasn't surprised that the gendarmes had been looking for Melbye, and suspected his parents of being the informants. Clearly the time had come to leave. He had saved enough money. He went down to a café and ordered crab and rice with shredded pork, though it was not kosher. He had come to like this dish, which Melbye always ordered and had often shared with him. He reread the letter, then burned it, to make sure his mother would never get her hands on it. He watched the smoke spiral into the air, and it was as if his past was burning up before him. That night, after he was certain everyone in the household was asleep, he packed a bag, then wrote a note for his parents that he left in the parlor. He did not mean to hurt them, but his dreams seemed realer to him than their home, and a thousand times more present than the shipping office or the streets of Charlotte Amalie. If he didn't leave now he would be trapped. He left the next morning while it was dark, on a boat set for Venezuela, where he would stay for two years. He would travel from Caracas to the harbor city of La Guaira, where the sea was like glass.

On the day that he departed, he'd already begun to feel more alive as the boat pushed off from the dock and the smells of the sea—kelp and salt and the sweat of workingmen—flooded the air. The water was a delightful blue, haint blue, the color of protection. Fritz would meet him at the dock, and everything would appear to be blue at first, but when he looked more closely at the landscape around him, the trees would be purple at dusk, the grass pale gray, the water green as new leaves on the linden trees that grew along the Seine. He would wake whenever he wished and go to sleep as dawn was blooming. He would spend hours by himself, sketching, becoming part of what arose on the pad of paper, a bird, a flower, a woman standing in a waterfall.

WHEN RACHEL READ HER son's letter of farewell, she was at her kitchen table. She knew she had no choice but to let him go, for he was gone already. She understood what it was to dream of another country and another life, the yearning that unsettled you and made your waking existence difficult to get through. She brought his note to Jestine, and they read it over together, trying to decipher its larger meaning. "Remember when he was a baby he couldn't sleep?" Jestine said. "He's still the same as he was the day he was born. Bound to cause you worry."

Instead of walking home when she left, Rachel took the road into the hills. She wasn't yet ready to tell Frédéric about their son's departure; she wanted to protect her husband until she had no choice but to share the news. Now as she went along she was thinking about her own yearning, wondering if she had transmitted her dissatisfaction to her son. Were such things in the blood? Her other children were happy enough with their lives, they dreamed of ordinary things, they married, had families, they woke to the day they were in rather than yearn for something else. She soon found herself on the overgrown path that led past the waterfall where Frédéric had bathed with fish when he first came to this island. He told her he had been enchanted. When they were alone he still told her that. Love was a spell. She thought of the day when he first came to her door. He'd sat at the table and held the baby that had been born after Isaac died. As soon as she looked at him she knew. They both dreamed of rain, and of Paris; they still slept as if they were drowning people, holding on to each other.

Rachel stopped when she saw the bones of the herbalist, the skeleton

Jacobo Camille had once lay down beside. They were so white in the grass. She had kissed the herb man once to thank him for saving her husband's life. She had trusted his medicine and his advice. Where had the knowledge that wise man possessed gone? Was it in the grass? The sky? There were some tamarind trees nearby, and birds filled the branches. A pelican sat watching her. Everything Adelle had told her had come to pass, but maybe it wasn't second sight. Maybe she could divine what was to happen because she had known Rachel so well. Better than her own mother had. You could not have all that you wanted, but if you found love, you were fortunate. *He won't be the only one,* Adelle had said when Rachel was unhappily married to Isaac.

There was a path worn into the grass. Rachel thought about her predecessor, who refused to die until her daughter was named. She thought about her dearest friend in the world, whose daughter had been gone for more than twenty years. She went through the tangles of vines. White moths rose in a cyclone when she brushed by the leaves. The red flowers were starting to bloom, red blood tears of the abandoned wives. The shack was as she remembered it, sloping to one side, the wood of the door rotting in the humidity, turning a mossy green. The garden was more overgrown, though the shells marking its outline were still there. The herb man had grown what he needed most: prickly pear, rosemary, pepper, bougainvillea, tamarind. All around were mango trees, planted long ago by the women who had disappeared and had never had their love returned.

When Rachel opened the door she expected the shack to be pitch dark, but instead she found a world of light. She had to blink. She was as still as she'd ever been. Clearly her son had been here. He'd left behind paintings of Paris, the streets he had walked on that were slick with rain, the patches of gray and white fog, the park where he'd watched Jestine's daughter for months, unnoticed, the fabled buildings of the Louvre, a miracle on earth, the white horses in the park, the garden of the Tuileries, filled with Bourbon roses. For Rachel, it was as if her dreams had been given life, for these were dream paintings, seen the way no other eyes would see, just as the herbalist had told her when he was a baby and could not leave the world long enough to close his eyes and sleep.

She spun in a circle, for every wall was covered. Some walls were of Paris, others were incandescent murals of the island, two worlds combined. There were seagulls, pelicans, stars, vines of pink flowers, women who looked like angels carrying baskets of laundry. There was a woman in a black dress, a figure much like Rachel herself if seen through a silvered mirror. He'd painted the sea the color that kept spirits away, which was why she hadn't found this glorious place until this day. It had been hidden, protected by a spell. The sheer beauty of her son's artistry made her dizzy. There were their two worlds, the place where they'd been raised and the city they dreamed of. He would go back to Paris, that much was clear. She could try to tie him here, or she could help him when he returned from Venezuela, broke and spent, but more excited about his work than ever. She would have to convince Frédéric that it would be best for all if Camille went to study in France. That's who he was to her now, no longer Jacobo. That boy who might have run their business and settled in St. Thomas with a family of his own was gone. It was a loss to give up the son she'd imagined for the one he'd come to be, but if Adelle had been nearby she might have said, *What did you expect? He is your boy, close to your heart.*

Rachel sat on the mattress that her son had filled with fresh straw. The herbalist had slept here for seventy years. If she had ever slept here, her dreams would have taken place inside her son's paintings; she would have sat in the park he had painted, wearing a gray silk dress as the colors shifted depending on the light. She found herself thinking about the donkey she'd left on the road, and the little girl who'd been told her mother would come for her but instead was taken away to sea, and the man she would have done anything for whom she saved from a fever, and the child who refused to sleep because he saw what the rest of the world did not.

CHAPTER TEN

Runaway

CHARLOTTE AMALIE, ST. THOMAS

1855

CAMILLE PIZZARRO

When Camille Pizzarro returned to St. Thomas from Venezuela, he had not slept for several nights. He'd had to scramble to get from the seaside town of La Guaira to the harbor of Caracas, where he waited for a ship that would bring him back home. He overpaid for his passage but did not care that he had nothing left. He was used to being poor, that was not the issue. He carried the news of his brother Joseph Félix's death sewn inside him like a sharp knife blade. It was guilt or grief or the two forged together. He'd been away for two years, but now it felt like he hadn't been home for a decade. His youngest brother, Aaron Gustave, had died at the age of twenty while Camille was gone, and he hadn't known for two months until a letter arrived. Now Félix, only twenty-eight, had passed on as well. Two sons gone from fever, just as Madame Halevy had lost her boys years earlier.

Once again Camille was a stranger in his own country, even more so than when he'd returned from school in Paris. Then he had hopes of escape. Now, he was not so sure. He was broke and unkempt, looking like one of the scruffy Americans who arrived on the island with nothing, desperate for a change of fate. He was no longer a boy with dreams of Paris, but a man of twenty-five who knew something of the world. He had a small bag of belongings and a trunk filled with his paintings, which he paid to have kept on the wharf while he attended to the family situation. He hadn't been close to his brother, but now he mourned that lack of closeness. In fact he barely knew his older siblings and their children, his nieces and nephews, some nearly as old as he. With this sudden death of Félix, the oldest child of his mother and father, he found himself tied with knots of regret. Who did he matter to in this world? Who mattered to him? Because of his hurry, he hadn't bathed, and his skin was covered by a blotchy rash he'd contracted from sleeping on louse-infested mattresses. Still, he was a handsome man, if perhaps too thin. Most people he passed by as he hurried from the docks didn't recognize him. Those who knew him remembered him as the Pizzarro son who hadn't a head for business, who attended the Moravian School and liked to wander off on his own, a sketchbook under his arm.

He ran all the way to the cemetery and got there as the service was ending. The service would wait for no one, especially in this weather, when dead men were packed in ice until they could be buried. Camille dropped his bag on the ground, so that he might take his turn with the shovel to offer the deceased the last favor of burying him. He wept as he helped to bury his brother. His beard and hair were long; he was too thin and emotional, consumed with bouts of melancholy over all he had failed to do. A hundred leaves fell into his hair and onto his shoulders. Was he imagining it, or were people averting their eyes? He wore no prayer shawl, no head covering. Perhaps he looked like a demon with his long hair untied, his threadbare clothes. There were well over a hundred mourners, friends, relatives, neighbors, customers of the shop, and men from the Burghers' Association. His parents were esteemed members of the congregation now, especially on this day, when they'd lost their first-born son. Camille went to his father and embraced him, then stood beside him as the last of the mourning prayers were said. His mother looked older, smaller somehow. She made him think of a blackbird in a tree. She nodded at him, her glance holding his. He noticed that she failed to cry. But of course she had never been one to show her feelings in a public place; she saw it as a sign of weakness.

Melbye would stay in Venezuela, then go back to Paris, before heading to New York, the destination he thought best for an artist. Fritz had wanted his friend to go with him, but Camille couldn't have gone even if he hadn't been called home. He'd run out of money, and everyone knew New York was a place filled with millionaires. He'd been more or less a beggar at the end of his time in Venezuela, sketching portraits with chalk for a small price. Melbye had his father's financial backing, and he'd paid for much of their expenses, but he hadn't enough to pay for Camille's passage to Paris and then to New York and, once they made it there, for a studio in Manhattan large enough for them both. When the news of Camille's brother's illness came, Fritz had said, "Perhaps it's time for you to go home and make some decisions. You may be destined to move forward on your own. Perhaps I'd hold you back."

"Unlikely," Camille had said. "It's I who have held you back."

AFTER THE FUNERAL THERE was a family gathering with too much food and too many neighbors. Had the apartment always been this small? Camille was taller than anyone else there, and long-limbed; he had to crouch when passing over the threshold. The evening was both a funeral dinner and a homecoming, a confusing combination. Let grief be grief, Camille thought. He felt shamed to have any attention paid to him. He ducked his head and said, "Please ignore me," but they did not. His sisters had arranged a dinner so lavish it covered the entire tabletop. Fish soup with tamarind, freshly baked bread flavored with molasses and cardamom, an apple tart made from the fruit of the tree in the courtyard, with apples so sharp they had to be sweetened with two cups of sugar water and molasses. His eldest sister, Hannah, the mother of nearly grown children, had gone to Helena James and commissioned a huge coconut cake. His pretty, pale sister, Delphine, however, was absent. Unknown to him, she'd been sent to France to live with relatives, accompanied by her niece, Alice, who was nearly the same age as she and already had small children of her own. When he heard this news, Camille felt a pang of jealousy. In truth Delphine was sickly and their mother wished for her to have better medical care living with the aunt and uncle outside Paris. Still, he wished he'd been the one to accompany his sister. He'd told Fritz that running away to Venezuela had saved him from the bondage of his bourgeois background, allowing him to be among real people with real concerns. Now here he was, in the thick of his family. Already he felt a noose around his throat.

Everyone greeted his return with great cheer, except for his mother, who had hardly spoken to him, and had gone to lie down in her chamber after the service. Jestine was there to embrace her old friend's son and explained that Rachel was dizzy from the heat and would soon be with them.

"How is your daughter?" Camille asked. He'd often thought of how he'd followed Lydia for all that time, how he'd sketched her before she'd known he existed, and had come to know the planes and angles of her face before they'd said a single word.

"She writes twice a week or more. She often asks for you. I informed her that you ran away to see the world."

"Not quite the world," he said ruefully.

"More than I've ever seen," Jestine informed him.

When at last Rachel came to supper, Camille went to her and kissed her three times, though her reception to him was cold. His posture straightened in the presence of his mother, and he felt a wave of embarrassment due to his patchy beard and threadbare clothes, even more so when it came to the old, ragtag shoes he had on, the same ones he'd worn when he left St. Thomas two years earlier, although now the leather was scuffed and marked up, the soles shredding. He waited to be berated for his appearance, but his mother merely greeted him in French.

In truth, after two years of speaking Spanish, it was a great relief to slip back into his first language.

"I thought you might never come back," she said. *Je ne savais pas si vous reviendriez un jour.* In French this sounded like an accusation, for she referred to him formally, as if they had only just met. If he was not mistaken there was a break in her voice. But of course this had been a terrible and trying day. All the same, his mother had a strange sort of expression, one that was surprisingly vulnerable.

"I did wish to stay away," he admitted.

Rachel pulled back inside herself. She felt this was directed not only to this island but also to her. "Jestine will have to make you a new jacket," she said after glancing at her son's clothing. "You're in dire need of it."

Camille smiled, relieved. This was his mother as he'd always known her, unable to keep her disapproval to herself. She hadn't been overtaken by another woman's spirit after all. In a way it was a comfort that some things never changed.

"I'm so sorry I wasn't here during Félix's illness," he said.

"Really?" his mother replied. "I would have thought you were quite happy to be in Venezuela. Certainly we hardly heard from you. One letter after Gus's death."

From her tone and the way she quickly moved on to greet some neighbors he could not tell whether or not she was happy to have him home. That night he slept in his own childhood room, one he used to share with his brothers. He had secretly sketched upon the wall, but during his absence his renegade artwork must have been discovered, for the wall was washed clean. He heard moths hitting against the shuttered windows and thought of Marianna, the girl he'd once thought he loved. Next time he felt such pangs, he wouldn't wait to act or give a damn about anyone's approval of the match. He longed for love, and in his too-small bed he felt more alone than he had in the alleyways of Caracas. Now that he was home he felt more lost than ever, but it was an inner loss. There was an emptiness inside him, an odd sense that the longer he stayed here, the more of a stranger he would be to himself.

THE NEXT DAY, HE went back to the wharf to retrieve his trunk, paying out a small fee to the custom man. He had very little money left, and that was an embarrassment as well. He would have to ask his parents for help, which would be humiliating. He had actually sold a few paintings and sketches, but most of what he earned had been spent on mere survival, food and supplies.

He was in such a hurry he barely noticed a dark-haired woman standing on the esplanade watching him, an umbrella over her head, for the day was brutal with white-hot sunlight. Then she called out his old name, Jacobo. He felt something go through him like a knife. He raised his eyes and recognized his mother. Her face was in the shadows and her expression was difficult to read. Jestine had always told him that he didn't know Rachel Pomié Petit Pizzarro, not as she'd been, not as she truly was, or had been once. But surely if what Jestine said about her was true, she would not condemn him for his time away, which, despite his early fears about his talents, had been glorious and instructive and wild beyond his imaginings. He had bathed in rain barrels and in river water where there were enormous green fish with teeth. He had slept on beaches where luminous fleas jumped into the black, shimmering air, and in sheds that had sheltered donkeys, and in the arms of women he knew he would never see again. Yet all the while he'd been in Venezuela, he'd dreamed of rain and of snow-covered cobbled streets and of the garden behind his aunt's house, where he would go to look at stars after Jestine's daughter had taught him about the constellations. The stars in France were pale pink, set into patterns he'd never seen before. It was Lydia who had pointed out the Lion, and the Crab, and the Hunter whose dog followed him as he chased across the sky.

"Do you not wish to come back to St. Thomas?" he'd asked Lydia once.

"That is like asking would I wish to step off the end of the earth. This is real." She nodded to the garden around them. "The other is merely a dream."

He was walking through that dream right now, sweating through it. His mother was approaching on the wharf, and there was little he could do to escape her wrath. His brother had struggled for breath on his deathbed while Camille was dozing in a hammock, staring at the stars, for in Venezuela the stars were yellow and so very far away. They would have appeared unreal to Lydia, so used to the skies of Paris, but he had painted them that way, bits of gold tossed out across the night.

"This is yours, I assume?" Rachel nodded to the trunk. This time it wasn't his father's borrowed trunk; he'd left too quickly to pack. He'd bought this one cheaply in Caracas. Already, it was falling apart, the slats of wood having become unglued. His mother pointed and said, "Open it."

"Here? Can't it wait?" It had been a long journey due to weather and tides, and the funeral had been a sorrow, and then last night he'd found himself haunted by the heat and the slapping of insects against the windows.

Still his mother insisted. "I want to see what you've been doing for two years."

Camille slid the latch over, then threw open the lid. There were twenty of his paintings, alongside countless sketches of the beaches where he'd set up house with Melbye, if a cooking pot and two cups could be considered home. There were drawings of the women he had been with, and several views of the harbor he most admired from a little fishing village where people called him le Français. He and Melbye both had aliases, which made them chuckle, most especially because Pizzarro wasn't French but Creole. They were oddities wherever they went, their hands covered with paint and charcoal, two tall, gawky men who liked to drink and laugh and meet women. But Camille took his painting more and more seriously. He could barely be drawn away from his work. He used so many shades of purple and gray when painting landscapes that Melbye had laughed and called him color-blind. "Do you need glasses, my friend?" he'd said. But in the end, Fritz had become his champion. Perhaps it was his rendering of the gold stars in a painted night so black that every tree and shrub was black as well. Melbye had come to understand that his friend saw what others did not. If the bark of a tree was gray at twilight, and the foliage purple, then so be it.

"I see you did a great deal of work," Rachel said as she examined the contents of the trunk. "If art can be said to be that." She threw a look at her son, and he shrugged, annoyed.

"It's a calling," he said. "Whether or not you wish to think of it as work is entirely up to you."

"And how do you think of it?"

She had sharp black eyes, a bird's eyes. Nothing escaped her. Or perhaps every mother could tell when her son was being forthright. Therefore he told the truth.

"I think of it as salvation."

Rachel had begun to lift a painting from the trunk. It was a study of a harbor, filled with ships. There was a cloudiness to it, as if the seascape had been viewed through a mist. On the day Camille had begun it, he'd worked so feverishly he'd fallen ill and still he could not stop. "I'll take this one." She motioned for him to close the trunk and held the painting close.

"Will you?" He laughed. "Since when do you think I can paint? You told me to put it aside. You said none of it looked right."

"I never said you *couldn't* paint. I said I didn't want you to. Now, it's clear it doesn't matter what I say."

They had begun to walk toward Dronningens Gade, up to the steps where the werewolves were said to be tricked out of catching runaway slaves when they stumbled in the place where the hundredth step should be. Camille continued to be confused. He would have expected his father to have come to help him with his luggage at the harbor, not Madame

Pizzarro. He dragged the trunk behind him. His arm was aching. He was sweating through his clothes, and he knew he looked like a man for hire found at the wharf. His mother carried her painting though it was quite cumbersome. She was clearly stronger than she looked, and she took the steps as if she were still a girl. He supposed the painting was hers if she wanted it; still, he wondered what it was that made her choose it.

WHEREAS SHE KEPT THE painting of Jestine in her bedchamber, so that few had seen it, she hung the new painting in the parlor, on the wall above the settee. People noticed. How could they not? It was so unusual, a dreamscape as much as a seascape. Something quite unique, an image you couldn't look away from. Some of Camille's older Petit brothers had laughed at how unreal it seemed, but his eldest sister, Hannah, was entranced. When she came for a visit one afternoon she studied the painting for some time, then said, "I had no idea of what true talent you had."

Camille, embarrassed by his sister's attentions, thanked her, then shook his head. "I don't know why our mother wanted it. She doesn't like art, does she? And certainly she doesn't like mine."

"You're wrong," his sister said.

Hannah believed she could remember the day Rachel became her mother, or perhaps it was only that Rosalie had told her about that meeting so many times it was fixed in her mind. She'd been a tiny baby, but young children could recall more than people suspected. She knew that Rosalie was preparing lime chicken soup, and that Rachel had held her and called her a bluebell, then had sung her to sleep. Hannah often visited Rosalie on Sundays. She liked to hear stories not only about her two older brothers, both serious men near middle age now; and her father, Isaac; but also about her first mother, the one who refused to die until she was safely named so that Lilith would not summon her. Sometimes Rachel would read to Hannah's children from her notebooks, stories which held them rapt with wonder.

"Our mother talks about you often," Hannah told Camille. "You are the one in the family with talent. She goes on and on about it. Now I understand why."

He looked at her, unsure, unable to believe that his mother spoke of him in such a light. But he saw in his sister's eyes that it was true. Hannah insisted that he come with her for a walk. She had her youngest daughters with her, and Camille felt guilty that he could not remember their names. They found themselves at the cemetery. Camille laughed when he realized where they'd wound up.

"Is this the family tradition? To go for a ramble and always end up at the worst place on earth?"

"It's lovely here," Hannah insisted. She led him to the Petit grave site. The children danced and played. He could not remember their names, but one had blue eyes, and the other had a wash of freckles across her face. They wore gingham dresses, and their stockings had been rolled down. They tossed brown leaves into the air, which then rained down to the ground.

"I come here all the time with our mother," Hannah went on. "We lay flowers on my first mother's grave."

Indeed, there were red flowers arranged in an earthen vase, so fresh it seemed as if they were still blooming on their branches. Both of Hannah's daughters had come close, perhaps because they were afraid of ghosts. He hadn't noticed that they'd slipped their hands into his, but now he did. Bees were buzzing. He was wrong and Hannah was right. This was perhaps the most beautiful place on earth. He felt tears in his eyes.

"Take this with you when you go," Hannah said, handing him a branch of flowers. "When you run out of things to paint, this place will stay with you."

"I'm not going anywhere," Camille said. "It's too late for that."

WORKING SIDE BY SIDE with his father, he had come to feel a great responsibility. His life on St. Thomas was a burden he wished he could cast off, but couldn't. Now, with his brothers gone, it was back to the store for him. There was no other option. This time he was quiet and did his work as best he could. He paid attention. He did not sleep in the storeroom or paint when he was supposed to be at the harbor, collecting shipments sent from abroad. He dreamed of Paris, though, and in his dreams he asked Lydia if it was possible to love a place yet still want to leave it. She handed him a small telescope made of steel and brass and leather with a magnifying lens. He looked and saw the constellations — the Fish, the Crab, the Lion, the Hunter—hanging above him like a canopy in the night.

In the evenings he went walking, as his father used to when he first came to this island, as he himself had when he returned from Paris and didn't know what to do with himself. He went along twisting roads into the hills. From high above the shore he watched the colors of the sea, how the water changed from green to pewter as the clouds went past. He went to the old fort that people said was the portal to hell, where so many slaves had arrived no one could count them all. The fort was empty now, and the stones were pitted from gunshots; some had fallen out altogether and were little more than dust. He went past Madame Halevy's house. Someone had carefully restored the old mansion; there was a new roof, new green shutters, and in the rear there was a proper garden, with rosebushes imported from England and South Carolina. He meandered out to the countryside, to where Mrs. James lived with her daughter and grandchildren and great-grandchildren. One young man, a grandson, came out to see who was looking for his grandmother.

"I used to talk to her when she worked in town for Madame Halevy," Camille explained. "I suppose I worked for Mrs. James as well."

As they talked Camille discovered this fellow Roland was the older brother of the boy who had run to get Camille on the day Madame Halevy's daughter had shown up. That boy, Richard, who had been so fast Camille and his father had struggled to keep up with him, had drowned just last summer. Everyone in the family still wore black cloth tied around their left arms in his memory. But there was a black band around Roland James's right arm as well.

"That one's for my grandmother," he explained. "She died six months ago." Roland was as tall as Camille, but better built and heavier, a baker himself, he said, just like his grandmother. He was employed at the Grand Hotel in town. On this day he was visiting his mother, who was old herself. He was a young man who had a great many responsibilities and burdens. He had always been looked upon as the man of the house, though he had older brothers and cousins, because of his sensible nature. "My grandmother was ninety-three when she died. On that day she was still talking about how she rescued a baby from drowning in the rain. She always wished she'd kept him. Was that you?"

Camille shook his head. He knew who that baby was but said nothing. With Mrs. James gone, he was the only one who knew the story of Madame Halevy's daughter and the son she'd given birth to, then left outside the cemetery, who grew up to be Aaron Rodrigues.

"She said Madame Halevy was certain that my grandmother was an angel," Roland went on. "That's why she gave her everything that belonged to her. But I'm going to have to sell it all now to provide for the family. I hope nobody's ghost is going to be upset by that."

"Of course you should sell it," Camille said. "It's all old-fashioned. The dishes and the furniture should bring a good price."

"My grandmother insisted she be buried with her two gold rings, so we honored that, though I'm sure they were worth quite a bit. They meant something to her and she said some things need to be buried with you when you go to the next world."

NOT LONG AFTER THAT, Camille ran into Roland again, this time in a tavern beside the Grand Hotel. After that, they began to meet occasionally for a drink. He missed Fritz and their camaraderie; he was an outsider in his own community, friendless, and his own brothers surely didn't understand him. Though he went to synagogue with his father every Friday night, he felt more comfortable with Roland. By now they realized they'd gone to the same school and had had the same teachers. They could recite the same poems in German and had memorized the same Bible stories. Their current lives were divergent however. Roland had a wife and four little children, and worked twelve-hour days at the hotel. Camille sketched Roland's wife, Shirley, and their children. He set to work on a painting of the children chasing a donkey out by the sea road. He liked to go to their family's house in the Savan for dinner on Sundays, when Shirley made the old recipes. She'd gotten them from Mrs. James before she died and written them all down in a book that she kept on a shelf. She made a perfect fish stew that Camille would have been happy to eat every day of his life. Roland James brought home cakes and tarts from the hotel. He was an amazing baker, far better than his grandmother had been, and his coconut cake had won several awards.

MORE AND MORE CAMILLE missed the old ladies of St. Thomas. The island seemed empty to him on many levels. Some days he did not wish to get out of bed, but he knew he couldn't be late to the store.

"If I were you I'd go back to Paris," Roland said to Camille one evening as he walked him partway home through the neighborhood. There were no longer any Jews living in the area; they had all moved to Synagogue Hill. People did still talk about the red-haired painter who had lived in the Savan a few years back, and how the gendarmes had come to grab him, and how he'd sprinted through the streets mostly naked in order to escape the authorities. Some people said Jenny Alek's boy was his, for he had red hair like the painter's.

"Listen to me, brother," Roland went on. "Run away. I know you're going to do it. So do it sooner rather than later. One day we won't see you around and then someone will say, Oh, he's gone and he's not coming back. Sure I'll miss you, but I'll be happy for you as well. You should do it before something happens and you wind up married with a pack of children."

Camille laughed. In truth, he hadn't the money for passage. He was still living in his childhood room, going down to the wharves to collect crates when tea and spices were delivered from ships that sailed from Spain and Portugal, waiting on customers and doing his best to be polite. "All I know is that I'll still be here tomorrow," he told Roland.

The men shook hands good night. "I know you were good to my grandmother," Roland said. "She always talked about the delivery boy who used to sit in the kitchen and pretend to eat dessert. She said you were the only child she ever met who didn't like sweets. And then you helped her when that lady came from Charleston to make trouble for her. She left something for you if you ever came back. I didn't say anything right away because I didn't know whether or not you deserved it. I had to get to know you first."

They'd kept on walking without realizing it and were already approaching Synagogue Hill. They sat on a bench outside of a shop that sold notions and buttons and clasps, along with lampshades.

Roland handed over a bit of cloth. Tied up inside was a gold ring.

"Madame Halevy's ring," Camille said, surprised. It was battered from wearing. "You said your grandmother was buried with it."

"She was buried with one, but she left the other one for you. She told me she thought you'd come back one day and I'd know you because you would look like you needed a good meal."

They both laughed at that. "True enough." Camille was still skinny, with knobby wrist bones and knees.

"She said you deserved to have the ring because the three of you shared something. I thought about selling it, I almost did, but then you came by and I thought I'd better do as my grandmother said."

Camille took the ring. His hands were huge, and the band didn't even fit halfway down his pinkie finger, so he slipped it into the small leather bag he carried, in which there was charcoal and some scraps of paper.

"My grandmother had a way to get you to do what she wanted you to do," Roland said thoughtfully. "I used to be wild and would climb out the window at night to go off looking for trouble, but she caught me and she scared me into being good. She told me that ghosts turned into birds and if I didn't act right they'd swoop down and find me."

"She didn't say anything about werewolves?"

"The old slaveholders? She didn't need to. I was afraid of them all on my own. It was those birds she told me about that changed me. I would stand outside and watch them at dusk and I knew I had better do as my grandmother said."

PERHAPS MADAME HALEVY'S RING inspired him. He had stored it in his artist's bag and often took it out to look at it. He had renounced painting upon his return to the island, for he felt he could never truly be an artist due to his situation in life, yet now his art haunted him. He returned to painting, taking what little equipment he had and venturing up to the herb man's house whenever he could sneak off. When he first arrived and pushed open the door, some mongooses ran under the floorboards. There was a film of dirt over his murals, but he was glad they were still there. The place felt like home. The sea and stars he'd set on the walls and ceiling, the women he'd seen at work he had re-created, the palm trees, worked on leaf by leaf until all he could see was green. He set up a makeshift easel and got to work. He drew out what was inside him and painted from memory. He painted everything he saw before him in the woods, but all transformed in the way he envisioned it, in a dream, in a mist, in grays and purples and blues, realer to him than the world around him.

He worked one night through in a frenzy, painting until morning. Then he hurried home in the dew and chill, and arrived with a cough. He went to bed, and when he woke his mother was there, or perhaps he was dreaming she was there, making him sip a bitter tea made of the bark of a mahogany tree, into which she'd poured salt rather than sugar. His fever lasted two days, and in that time Rosalie came to take turns with Rachel sitting beside his bed. They were all reminded of the time when

Frédéric fell ill. Rachel looked ghastly, pale and overwrought. She could not bear to lose another son, and certainly not this one. She looked through his belongings. She found a gold ring that puzzled her, for it looked like a marriage band. She wondered what she didn't know about her son. She looked through a stack of small paintings he'd brought home and hidden in the bureau. There was a very small one of the great cathedral, Notre Dame, cloaked in fog. She took it for herself, and she wept to think of his years in Paris, and to think of him now that he had returned to her, motionless in his bed.

Rosalie knew what Rachel was feeling—she thought she loved him too much, and in doing so had turned his fate against him. But it wasn't true. She brought Rachel a cup of tea, half filled with rum.

"Love him more, not less," Rosalie told Rachel.

Rachel nodded and sat beside him and did not leave. She barely slept, and when she did she dozed in the chair. When Camille came swimming up from his fevered dreams, he saw Madame Halevy's gold ring on the bedside table. His mother was there beside the bed, watching him quite carefully. Camille felt he'd been away on a far journey. His arms and legs were still weak. He had forgotten about all the fevers on the island and had sat outside painting at the hour when clouds of mosquitoes arose from the shrubbery. He struggled to raise himself on his elbows.

"Will I live?" he asked his mother.

"Do you think I would allow you to die?"

Camille laughed, or tried to, and his mother helped him settle back into his bed.

"Whose wedding band is this?" she asked, nodding to the ring on the table. For all she knew he'd been married in Venezuela; he was so secretive and kept her at arm's length.

"It's not a ring, it's a story." He was still somewhat delirious. "It belonged to Madame Halevy."

"Then it's a witch's story," his mother said.

He did laugh then. He took the ring, which felt cool in his hand.

He'd lost so much weight he could slip it on his pinkie finger. "Don't worry, Mother," he said. "I can protect myself from witches."

AN OLD CHILDHOOD INCIDENT was brought to mind after their discussion, one Rachel still wasn't certain had been real. She seemed to recall a night when Madame Halevy came to the door of her parents' house. She was wearing a black cape, for it was the rainy season and buckets were pouring down. Rachel was a small child, so perhaps she truly believed a witch had come to call. She went to her window, mesmerized. The black cape flared out around Madame so that she seemed to be floating. Rachel recited the only prayer she knew by heart. She wished her father was at home, but he was often gone in the evenings to business meetings or out with friends. It was a windy night, and the whole world shook and seemed topsy-turvy. Palm fronds swept onto the ground, fruit fell from the trees, the bats settled in the bushes, closed up like flowers that bloom only in the light. When Rachel leaned farther out her window, straining to see, she spied a bundle in their visitor's hands. The gold rings on the witch's finger shone a dull, pale light. Two rings, and one bundle. Inside the blanket, an infant slept. Rachel's mother opened the door, and light spilled out from the hall. Rain splattered in through the window. Rachel held her breath.

"*Le secret d'une autre*," the witch in the black coat said. She turned, and Rachel saw her face. It was Madame Halevy, her mother's best friend, who scared her with her questions about whether or not she was a good girl.

Rachel's mother had taken the baby in her arms. "This is a secret I'm happy to take on."

The women had kissed each other, three times, then once more for luck. Apples fell from the tree in the courtyard, the bitter ones that Rachel was not allowed to eat. Not even the lizards braved the gusts driving across the courtyard. This strong wind came across the ocean to their shores from Africa in the rainy season. There were puddles in the courtyard, and the witch, if that was what she was, held her skirts up as she strode away empty-handed. In the morning, Rachel had a cousin who would now live with them. His name was Aaron, and the servants said he'd come to them on the wind. Rachel was near the kitchen house and overheard when Adelle followed Rachel's mother into the courtyard to ask why this child was in their house. The puddles were drying up in the sun; the wind had disappeared. There were chickens in the yard, pecking at the grass.

"Don't ask me how I come to have my children and I won't ask how you come to have yours," Rachel's mother had said to Adelle.

The island was so small everyone believed they knew everyone else's business, but in a place where nothing was equal, there were always secrets, even in her household, even in this room where she sat in a caned chair and watched over her son whom she finally allowed herself to love more, since he seemed fated and determined to live.

CAMILLE WAS WELL ONCE more and back at work in a matter of weeks. He did his best, and yet he seemed unable to control his true nature. He began to commit small acts of anarchy, charging the customers he knew could barely afford their provisions less than the usual price for beans and flour and bolts of cloth. When Roland's wife, Shirley, came in, he arranged the ledgers so that it was possible to charge her nothing at all.

Mr. Enrique went to Rachel and asked if they might sit down to speak. They did so over cups chamomile tea, which was said to calm the spirit.

"Do you think this is the proper career for Jacobo?" Mr. Enrique asked, using Camille's old, familiar name. He'd known the boy all his life after all. He'd known him before he was alive if it came to that. His own son, Carlo, now was old enough to come to the store to work every day after school. He was considered a mathematics wizard and could add long columns of figures in his head, then divide and multiply them at will without pen and paper.

"I take it you think it's not his calling," Rachel replied when the question of her son's abilities were brought up.

Mr. Enrique shrugged. "We're likely to see our children as we wish to, not as they are."

"True," Rachel agreed. She had been thinking more and more about the witch in the courtyard, and how her mother always sent her out to the kitchen house when Madame Halevy came to call. When Rachel complained about being cast out, her mother called her a spoiled, silly girl.

"Do you know any reason that would have caused my mother to hate me?"

Mr. Enrique pushed his teacup away, his brow furrowed. "Madame," he said. "What a thing to ask."

She looked into his face, and there it was. He knew something.

"Was it my character? Or my birth?"

"It was not you," Mr. Enrique said formally. He could not have looked more uncomfortable. "And I could never speak ill of your father."

Rachel thought this over. "Then I will ask no more questions about my parents."

"Good. Because we are here to speak of your son, and whether commerce should continue to be his vocation. I owe the business my loyalty, as I owed it to your father."

"Has my son done something wrong?"

"In his mind it is likely right, and perhaps it is, but it is not right for the store. He believes goods should be given freely, and that charging people who cannot afford to pay is a crime. That is a good thought, but not possible if the store is to continue. I would hate to see the business handled by someone who didn't understand or care about such matters. And it would be a burden to him to do so."

.   .   .

RACHEL WENT DOWN TO the wharf. She still liked to walk the beach alone, looking for the miracles she had written down in her notebooks. There were several of them now, and she tied them together with ribbon so she would not lose or misplace them. She drank limeade and watched the boats coming in. The tepid drink was not enough to quench her thirst. She ordered a café au lait as well, for she remembered what Adelle had taught her: hot drinks in hot weather allow the skin and soul to breathe. She had left a note for her son to meet her. He likely would have it by now. It was August, white hot. The roads were chalky, scattered with shells dropped by the gulls. That morning she had watched her husband sleep, and when he woke she told him that one part of their life was over and another had begun.

"Then it will be so," he said without question.

"Tell me what you remember about Paris," she said, and he did, his arms around her, as if no time had passed since the morning when he came to breakfast and saw her in her white shift, with his eyes so wide she'd laughed and felt a shiver of pleasure after she went back into her bedchamber. She knew he was hers even then. He described the garden in the house where he'd grown up, the chestnut tree, the grass that turned silver in the dark, the streetlamps that were filled with yellow light, the women in their cloaks on the way to the opera, the men in tall hats, the horses pulling carriages, as they did in Perrault's stories, white horses whose breath came out as steam into the cold, moonlit evening.

It was the end of lunch hour, and many people were on their way home to rest during the hottest hours of the day. Soon the café would be shuttered. Rachel saw her son walking across the square. He wore a white shirt and had cut his hair. She knew he was trying to fit in and do as they wished. He walked slowly, and waved a greeting to a fellow outside the Grand Hotel whom Rachel didn't recognize, a West Indian man who clapped him on the back as they spoke a few words. Her son spied her then and ambled over, wary. He kissed her in greeting, then sat across from her, swinging one long leg over the other. On his feet were sandals

Rachel didn't approve of. She liked proper shoes to be worn. The table was small, the chair made of wood and rush. Fortunately there was a blue awning to protect them from the sun.

"I'm not quite sure why you wished me to come here," Camille said. He guessed Mr. Enrique had told her about the missing supplies and the way the ledger had failed to add up correctly. The waiter eyed them, wanting to go take his rest on a cot in the back room of the café. "Just a coffee," Camille called to him.

"The family believes you're home to take over the store," Rachel said. "But don't make yourself too comfortable. We both know you won't be here long."

"I can explain what happened," Camille began. He stopped speaking when the coffee arrived, for the waiter glared, impatient. Camille quickly paid the tab, then resumed his conversation. It was best to be honest and be done with it. "I just can't overcharge people."

"You think our store overcharges?" Her glare was worse than the waiter's.

"Not necessarily. I think any charge for certain people is too much."

She laughed. "You realize we have expenses. We have to pay for the goods we import, a rather high price, and a business is meant so that one can make a living."

He shrugged, not convinced of her argument. "It's not fair the way some people have to live."

Rachel softened then. "The world is not fair."

"Not yet," he said.

One had to be practical in this unfair world, but her son was a dreamer. Many young men were, but there was more to him than that. Perhaps it was best that he had such hope in the world. It would likely serve him well to have faith in the future. Rachel did not laugh, as he feared she would, but nodded in agreement.

"Yes, not yet." She reached for an envelope she'd brought and handed it to him. "One can always have hope."

Camille gazed at her, more puzzled than ever, then tore open the envelope he'd been handed. Inside was a ticket for passage to France and funds enough to live on for more than a year if he was careful with his money. He didn't know what to say. He was not a man of many words, least of all words of gratitude.

"Mother," he finally said, deeply moved by her generosity. "You understand that if I go back to Paris, I won't return?"

"Of course I understand. Before you go, you'll help your father in the store. Without your two brothers, he needs you now. Then, when our business affairs are more settled, you can leave."

There was a war brewing in America, and the effects rippled down to everyone. Ships were lost, ships were commandeered, with goods meant for Charleston or New York stolen. It was perhaps the bleakest time for their business, and Rachel was glad Mr. Enrique had long ago suggested to Frédéric that they no longer own the ships themselves. If they had continued in the direction Monsieur Petit had led them, they would likely be destitute by now, accepting charity from their community instead of helping those in need, something Camille seemed to have overlooked completely. Every Sunday food was brought down to the synagogue for those who were faltering in their businesses and their lives, and Rachel was more than glad to give what she could.

They had finished their coffees, and now began to walk together. The market square was nearly empty in this, the hottest hour of the day, with white cloths thrown over the fruit and vegetable stands to protect them from the sunlight. "Just do your best not to bankrupt the store before you leave," Rachel told her son.

"I promise to try," Camille said. It was the very least he could do.

That was enough for her. Rachel was ready to go home. She found herself exhausted by the heat, even though she'd known such weather all her life. The birds were so weighted down by the temperature, they didn't sing at this hour. The only birds that managed flight were the pelicans, and then only far out at sea, where there were breezes. Rachel imagined that Adelle's spirit was out where the ocean was the exact shade of gray that it was in the painting her son had given her. The idea of the wind at sea was a delicious notion on such a hot day. The clouds would be enormous, white, like a canopy. The spray would be chill, the waves as high as the roofs of the fruit stands they now passed. As for Camille, he was imagining not the sea but the street where his aunt and uncle lived, the way the dusk sifted down like black powder. He would arrive in November, the start of his favorite time of year, when the trees were red and gold and black and the grass was silver. He would write to Fritz's brother Anton immediately and ask if he might be taken on as one of his students in preparation for attending a serious art school.

Rachel paused to lean on a low stucco wall for support, cooling herself with a small fan that had been made from bone and silk in Spain. Her son offered his arm so that he might assist her as they walked on, but she waved him away.

"I don't need your help, even if you do think I'm an old lady." She began to walk on, toward home, quickening her pace. They had already begun to climb the twisting street that led to the store.

"When I used to walk with Madame Halevy, she always said the same thing."

"That old spider?" Rachel said, her mouth pursing with distaste.

Camille grinned at her response. When he did, he so resembled his father that Rachel felt her love for him rise up inside her. More, not less.

"I'll be able to return the favor to Jestine for sewing my new jacket," Camille said joyfully. Now that he knew his fate was his own, he was filled with good cheer. "I'll bring the dress she made for Lyddie to Paris."

"There's no need," his mother told him.

Soon she would be in the gardens of the Tuileries, where she would astound strangers when she told them about the turtles that arose from the sea on a single night, and the blood-red flowers that had been planted by the wives of the pirates, and the flights of stairs built to protect runaway slaves from the werewolves that chased after them. She had begun to pack that morning, making certain to leave room in the crate for Camille's paintings.

She patted her son's arm to assure him she was ready for what came next. "Jestine and I can bring the dress. We'll already be there when you arrive."

CHAPTER ELEVEN

The Season of Rain

CHARLOTTE AMALIE, ST. THOMAS / PARIS, FRANCE

1855

RACHEL POMIÉ PETIT PIZZARRO

There was trouble brewing in America, a lawlessness that sometimes portends war. Our business was failing due to the unreli-
able shipping trade, particularly along the coast of South
Carolina, where piracy was not only indulged but, it seemed, encouraged. Frédéric had made a promise to the ghost of my first husband to
watch over his holdings, and therefore would not leave until this promise
was fulfilled. I could see he was torn. He had approved my plan to finally
go to France; my daughter Delphine was seriously ill in Paris, and my
son Camille would soon be going there to study. There was no longer
any reason for me to stay. Frédéric knew my heart's desire had always
been to leave this island. He wished to accompany me, but he was too
good a man to shirk his responsibilities. Once the business was more settled, both my son and my husband would follow me to France. Mr. Enrique would then be the manager of the store, overseeing day-to-day
dealings. A third of our income would belong to him; the rest would be
directed to Isaac's family. We might have paid Mr. Enrique less, but we
owed him our lives. Had he not carried my father to the harbor in a

wicker basket I would never have come into this world and my children would never have been born. There would have been no woman to greet Frédéric when he arrived in St. Thomas and no one to pay the herb man to save him from his fever.

As the time for my departure grew near, my husband and I were both seized with nerves. In more than thirty years we had never spent one night apart. After all this time, he was still in love with me, and each time I saw him I felt the same pulse in my throat that I'd had when I gazed out the window and saw him surrounded by bees. Frédéric was fifty-three, still so handsome that women in the market nudged each other when they spied him. I knew what they were thinking when they saw us together, for I was not remarkable in any way. *What does he see in her? What spell had she used to enslave him for a lifetime?* If they wanted to think I was a witch, I didn't mind. Perhaps I was one. Perhaps I had called him to me, ensuring that he'd had no choice but to fall in love with me when he saw me in my white slip. It was the one morning I didn't pin up my dark hair. I had chosen to stand there, half unclothed, even when I saw the desire in his eyes.

ON MY LAST DAY in St. Thomas I went back to the house where I'd grown up. As I walked through the gate my skin pricked with sadness. I expected to feel the same turmoil I'd always experienced when I thought of the sort of daughter I'd been, never good enough. But there were only spirits of the past here now, jittery, fading things that sparked through the tangle of vines. If the new owners spied me, they didn't chase me away. They closed the shutters and left me in peace. Perhaps they'd heard rumors about me, or it was possible they saw me open my hands so that the last stirrings of those who had lived here could gather, drawn to the heat of my flesh before they scattered into dust.

I had imagined I would be distraught when I returned to the pathways of this garden; instead I felt a surprising tenderness for the landscape of my childhood. Despite the marriage of convenience my father had made for me, he had always loved me. He'd respected my intelligence and taught me the business. Because of this I'd always had a high opinion of myself, despite what others thought. True, I was arrogant, but perhaps that is not the worst trait for a woman to have. I knelt down to peer beneath the hedges for the lizard that had been my cousin's pet, for such creatures are said to live longer than most men. All I saw were some beetles and the neatly raked earth.

On the other side of the gate, Rosalie's son, Carlo, was cutting back hedges of oleander. He tossed me a smile when he saw me and shyly called out hello. He was at the ungainly age when he was still a boy but longed to be a man. He worked in the store on Sundays and was a good student at the Moravian School. Rosalie loved him too much, and Mr. Enrique doted upon him even more, if that was possible, but fortunately nothing bad had happened to him. Rosalie no longer believed that love brought a curse. A cruel nursemaid had been the one to suggest her own milk had drowned her first baby. "It was nonsense," she told me. "Babies die from fever, not from love."

Yet I continued to fear I would be punished for my unquenchable longing for Frédéric. I thought of the way God had let the rain fall down upon us on the day the Reverend wouldn't open the door, and how I had defied them both to get what I wanted. I felt a brand of fear I hadn't known as a younger woman, just as Madame Halevy predicted I would. We pay a price for everything, I saw that now. I walked more narrowly and thought more carefully before I acted and spoke. I knew the chaos I had brought upon my children when I refused to give up Frédéric. No one had to tell me how selfish I'd been.

I sat with Rosalie for the last time. To me, she looked nearly the same as she had on the day I met her in Monsieur Petit's kitchen.

"I was young then!" She gave me a cup of tea and a slice of coconut cake dolloped with cream. "But not as young as you were."

We had both made a promise to the same ghost, and because of that we'd been bound together by fate. That had been part of my good fortune.

"Let's not say good-bye," she said to me on my last day in St. Thomas.

I agreed it would be best not to. We both knew that I could never thank her enough. She had taught me everything about raising children when I'd become the mother of three so suddenly. Despite the fact that she'd been violated and forced into servitude, she couldn't have been kinder to a girl who knew nothing, not even what happened when a husband came into bed. "Didn't your mother tell you anything?" she had asked me each time she discovered how much I had to learn. Whatever I did know had been a lesson from Adelle and then only told to me in whispers to ensure that my mother couldn't overhear.

As I was leaving I noted that Rosalie had adopted the rose tree my mother had hated. She said it was an unnatural plant, not worth the water it needed to survive, with huge pink blooms that called wasps and bees to it, but it had been on the patio of the cottage for so long, Rosalie said, who was she to let it die?

"My mother despised it even though it was a gift from my father. Likely she wanted something more."

Rosalie shook her head, mystified by all I still had to learn. "She didn't like it because it wasn't for her. There was another woman in your house, and she was very pleased with this gift. Mr. Enrique has been taking care of the rose tree ever since your mother disposed of it."

I didn't ask any questions and she didn't offer any answers, but we understood each other all the same. We both had come to believe that Adelle was more to my father than most of us had known, except, perhaps, for my mother. As a girl I had known the world by way of my own angry heart, and hadn't paid attention to issues that didn't concern me. Children were hushed and dismissed, sent to their rooms. So much the better, I'd always thought. I was immersed in my own troubles, plotting my escape. But now my memory added all I'd failed to see: the intrigue of a closed door, three petals of a fragrant rose burning in a dish in the kitchen, a woman crying, the garden gate closing so softly I hadn't been sure whether or not I'd heard it, the redness of my father's eyes when he came to tell me I was to be wed, the way my mother would study Jestine, as if looking for features she might recognize.

I left Rosalie before either of us could cry. I had spent more time in her company than in anyone else's, and she in mine. I was fierce with other people, as harsh as my own mother on some occasions, but never with Rosalie. She had managed to see through me. She'd told me things other people would have been afraid to say to my face, but she never told me I was wrong to get into the bed of the young man from France. Now as we said our good-byes, she kissed me three times, then a fourth time for luck. She reminded me of her best piece of advice and suggested I would do well to listen to her.

Love more, not less.

IT WAS THE END of the season for the flamboyant trees, the glorious month of September. I wouldn't see flowers such as these again, not unless I traveled to Madagascar. The sailors from that country had gone to great trouble to bring the original specimens across the ocean, wrapping the roots in burlap, sharing their own precious drinking water, all for a blessing on their journey. There were only a few blooms left, but I gathered enough to leave an armful of flowers on Madame Petit's grave, and on the grave of the Reverend's first wife, for my marriage to Frédéric had been recognized and my children's names had been written down in the Book of Life and I believed I owed this to her ghost. I left white stones in remembrance of my sons, and my parents, and of Isaac. He'd known I'd never loved him, but that hadn't mattered at the time. We had an agreement and we both kept to it. When I left, leaves drifted into my hair. Usually I kept them, out of respect to the spirits, but on this occasion I shook my head, letting them scatter. They came from the bay tree and were spicy with scent. Some people folded them in with their belongings when they packed for a journey, but I left them where they'd fallen.

. . .

JESTINE AND I SET off on a windy day when the sea was green. My husband held me for as long as he could, until the captain called, insisting it was time for us to leave. There was the tide to think of, and seas that grew rougher with each day that was further from summer. Jestine and I both wore black, as if in mourning for the lives we'd once led and the people we would no longer be. We noticed a pelican swooping after our ship and left fish from our dinner on the railings. We collected feathers to keep on our bureaus. But when we were far out to sea, a chill met us and the pelican disappeared. We tossed out crusts of bread and mussels taken from their shells, but there were no birds here, so far from land, only the blue light of the open sea.

We sailed northward, and soon the ocean turned dark; there were nights a scrim of ice formed on the bow of the boat. We slipped on black gloves and woolen cloaks and drank hot tea with tiny slices of lemon. There was a bushel of lemons and two barrels of limes, and out at sea they were highly prized. We were the only passengers who braved the cold on deck as twilight spread across the horizon. Our cabins were drafty and smelled of mold, and we preferred to stay where we could gaze at the stars, as we had on the nights when the turtles rose from the sea. We'd planned to be on a ship such as this one since we were ten years old. It seemed no time had passed since then, yet we were about to turn sixty. We looked in mirrors and didn't recognize ourselves. We laughed and pointed and cried out, "Who are these old ladies?"

When the waves became so high the deck was slippery to walk upon, water sloshed below into our quarters. We needed to hold on to ropes simply to cross to the dining room. We ignored the bad weather as best we could and celebrated our birthdays together, as we always had. We ate shrimp with lime juice and drank white wine while the waves crashed against the hull of the ship. People asked if we were sisters, twins born on the same day. We were amused and said of course not, but I had always wondered about how alike we looked and now I realized other people could see it as well. I had a twinge of feeling for my mother. If Jestine had indeed been my father's daughter, surely Madame Pomié must have known. No wonder she despised the rose tree, and Adelle, and me, for my father preferred us all to her.

There was no one left to tell us the truth, so Jestine and I shrugged off such questions. We toasted each other, then cut our birthday cake in even halves and ate every crumb. It didn't matter what had happened on St. Thomas in the past. All that hurt and love was long ago. It was in the time of the turtles and that time was over. All along the harbor there were lights, and the turtles went elsewhere to lay their eggs. They would not return, just as Jestine and I both knew we were never going back. That was when we stopped wearing black.

DECADES HAD PASSED SINCE Lyddie had been abducted. I couldn't understand how time could pass so slowly when we were young, and fly so quickly now. Jestine worried that after so long apart she and Lyddie wouldn't recognize each other. She said she was now ugly and perhaps she should wear a veil so as not to frighten her daughter and grandchildren. That was nonsense and I said so. If we had been sisters, she would have been the pretty one, I would have been the one who was too smart for her own good, and too bossy. Jestine was still beautiful. Even on the ship, men had glanced at her and could not look away. She flushed, but had no interest. She might have married a dozen times during the past years—certainly there had been men who did their best to win her over, several of whom had come to me and begged me to plead their cases. Some were local men who wished to marry her; two were men of my faith who came to me secretly, certain I would favor them considering my own struggles with the congregation. One was a European businessman who insisted he would do anything to win Jestine. He was particularly ardent and had already planned her future with him: they would go back to Denmark, where no one would know her mother was a slave and she would live as a wealthy Burgher's wife. Jestine had laughed when I told her his plan. She said she would rather know who her mother was than who he was, so he gave up and went back to Denmark without her. She turned down all of her suitors without regret. Her plan was always to be on this ship, going to Paris.

ONE NIGHT, I WAS awakened by a sound I didn't recognize. Then I realized it had begun to rain. We were in the middle of the ocean, between worlds. It was a light rain that fell in endless silver streams, so different from the torrential storms we had on the island. From that time on, it didn't stop. There was so much rain that the green seed of bitterness I'd always carried inside me bloomed into a flower. It wasn't some terrible and monstrous plant, even though it had been sown from the sorrow of my mother's disdain for me. It wasn't at all what I expected. A white flower with pale green edges. I thought it was a moonflower, a parting gift from the original people on our island, who had wanted nothing more than to bring light wherever they walked.

Aboard the ship, my childhood came back to me as it had in Rosalie's cottage. What had been murky was now clear as daylight. I'd come to remember nights my mother waited for my father when he didn't come home. She would be in the parlor and I would hear her crying. I wondered where he was on those nights. At that age, I still believed in werewolves and feared he would be eaten alive. I remembered confiding in Adelle, telling her I didn't think my father cared for my mother. She whispered back that you couldn't force someone to love you. Either he did or he didn't, and no spell or trick or prayer could make it so. She ran her fingers through my hair as she spoke. I loved the way her voice sounded. I'd held on to the small hope that somehow I could exchange mothers with Jestine. But when, after a disagreement with my mother, I confided in my father that I wished I could be Adelle's daughter, he slapped me. It was the only time he did so. *Never say that again,* he told me.

As we neared France, I wondered if I would miss hearing the sea beneath me as I slept. Sometimes the waves were so big the ship rocked back and forth and I had to hold on to the bedpost or be shaken onto the floor. I knew there were turtles below us, perhaps even the woman in the story who had chosen their way of life over ours. I missed my husband most at night. We often shared our dreams as well as our waking life. Later, when we reunited, we discovered that during separation we had dreamed of each other. There he would be, standing on a cobblestone lane beside the Seine. There I was, casting off my black cape, wearing a white linen slip. We sat entwined on a green bench. *Don't wake up,* he would say. When I did I would know he'd been dreaming of me.

WE ARRIVED IN MARSEILLE, where we spent a few days at a hotel on a bluff overlooking the cold Atlantic. We laughed at our sea legs and were greedy for fresh fruit and vegetables. We slept almost till noontime. Jestine had caught a chill on the ship and now came down with a cough. We booked an extra day at our hotel so that a local doctor could visit. He assured us that if Jestine drank hot tea with honey we could continue on to Paris. We took a train to the gleaming Gare de Lyon station, which had only just opened. My heart was pounding to have finally reached the destination I'd yearned for. It was the last few days of the Exposition Universelle, a grand event attended by over five million people since its opening in May in the Jardins des Champs-Elysées. Paris was mad with joy, crowds were everywhere, and we were quite stunned when we arrived in the station. Exiting the train was much like stepping into a storm that swirled in circles. I closed my eyes and listened to the crush around us. It was like listening to the sea. At heart, we were still two girls from an island where everyone knew everyone else. This city was a gorgeous madhouse. Jestine took my hand and pulled me along. My eyes were wide. I was taking it in. The work of Haussmann, who had been commissioned by Napoleon III to reconstruct and reorder the parks and avenues, made the city a mystery, replacing my father's maps with a new and gorgeous vision. Everything I'd imagined was redesigned and brand new, the Rue de Rivoli completed, and a new square, Place Saint-Germain-l'Auxerrois, now faced the colonnade of the Louvre, as magnificent a building as there was in all the world. I was as awake as I'd ever been; I was also inside the dream I'd been dreaming my whole life long. How bright it was. How burning. I was a moth in a shabby dress, though I wore my finery. I wanted to be closer to it all, enveloped in the light.

A beautiful woman was approaching. She wore a fur-trimmed coat over a blue silk dress. When she threw up her arms to wave, I understood this was the same girl who had sat on the porch of the house built on stilts, the child who'd been lost for a lifetime.

I had given my luck to Jestine and was glad to have done so. She ran to embrace her daughter, who was soon enough joined by three lovely girls. A young boy lagged behind his mother, too shy to say hello. This was Leo, born in August and named for that month's constellation of the Lion in the sky. Lyddie's husband, a Monsieur Cohen, had arranged a carriage for us. Lydia came to embrace me and welcome me to Paris as well. "So you're Camille's mother. We would never all be together right now if it weren't for him. He has such integrity!"

We went first to the Cohens' apartment on the Île de la Cité. It had begun to rain again, and we rushed into the building to avoid the showers, making our way along a stone staircase with a mahogany banister. There was the echo of our footfalls. The three girls laughed and raced up ahead of us. We would have tea, Lyddie declared, then she would have her husband take me to the lodging Frédéric had leased, where my ailing daughter Delphine was already staying. The Cohens' apartment was small, but beautifully appointed with salmon-colored divans and crystal gas lamps, belongings, I later learned, that were the only household goods Monsieur Cohen had been allowed to take from the house his family owned. They had been disavowed by the family and the community, as Frédéric and I had once been. Beyond the issue of her African heritage, Lydia was not considered a member of our faith because her true mother had not been Jewish. The Cohens had donned black armbands and the Rabbi had read the mourning prayers just as if Henri had died, for to his family he had. Should they happen to pass him in the street he would be nothing more than a ghost to his own mother, and his daughters would be strangers though they had been cherished as babies and adored as young children.

Monsieur Cohen had been employed in another bank owned by a French company. He was not in a manager's position anymore. He did not discuss his family, nor did he see them when they suggested they meet without Lydia. I tried not to impinge on Lyddie and Jestine's conversation, although I couldn't help but overhear bits and pieces. From a window I saw Notre Dame. I heard bells and the sound of water running in the streets. At last, my dream had come to pass. It was almost too much for me, the sheer reality of this new life. I grew dizzy and leaned against the windowpane flecked with rain.

Jestine came to stand beside me. "They want me to stay here with them."

"Are you sure you'll be comfortable?"

Lyddie overheard and called out, "Of course she'll stay here. The girls are moving into one room, and Mama will have the room with the view of the river."

I went to see Jestine's room. Perhaps I hoped it would not be good enough, and I would then encourage her to stay with me.

"She has to approve," Jestine told her daughter, nodding toward me. "She's always been the bossy one."

True enough, but even I had nothing to complain about. Although quite small, the chamber was lovely, with moss-green silk wallpaper flocked with gold and creamy decorative woodwork. There was a high bed with many pillows in shades of jade and scarlet and a bureau on which there was a vase of pale pink peonies, clearly placed there to welcome Jestine. Iron grillwork covered the lower half of the window, and there were damask drapes in an apricot color. The Seine was right outside. I peered out at the still green water and the rain falling down. I knew this was where Jestine wanted to be.

"I approve," I said.

I left before Lyddie opened her present, the moon dress Jestine had sewn. She had taken my mother's necklace apart and tacked the pearls to the bodice. She'd used silk thread from China and dyes made of lavender and guava berries. That exchange was private, between mother and daughter. Jestine and I kissed each other in farewell. We had done what we'd set out to do, and we were both exhausted. Then Monsieur Cohen took me to what would now be my home. "Don't worry about your friend," he said to me. "She was loved before she came to Paris, and will be even more loved now that she is here."

I thanked him for his kind help. He and I were kindred spirits after all, willing to do anything for love.

OUR APARTMENT IN PASSY on the Rue de la Pompe was too large for us, but there was no time to look for another. Delphine was extremely ill, and I hadn't realized how serious her condition was. She was one of the twins, as we called them, for she and Emma had been born so close together they formed their own society. Delphine had been Frédéric's favorite, a flower he called her, and he gave in to her whims whenever she wanted dogs or tamed birds. "She has a kind heart," he always said to me. "Like yours." I smiled when he spoke these words, knowing full well he was likely the only person on earth who thought I had a heart at all.

I hired a nurse immediately, but Delphine did not improve. I watched her sleep in a fever, fading more each day. Perhaps I hadn't been a good enough mother to my daughters. We had company, my niece and her five children came for weekends to cheer us up, and Lydia was often a guest. But the apartment was too quiet even with visitors. I got lost in the rooms. The kitchen was vast, and my bedroom was the largest I'd ever seen, with a bed so high I was afraid I would fall off in the middle of the night without Frédéric to hold on to. I did not walk in the park or shop on the Rue de Rivoli. Haussmann's rebuilding had demolished entire neighborhoods. I did not recognize the city, for it was brand new, and when I did venture out, I often found myself lost. When Jestine came to call we had green tea and studied the leaves in our cups to see what our children's futures might be.

I had the best doctors come and still Delphine coughed up blood. I thought about the herb man in the countryside and the cures he had given me. None of the ingredients could be found in Paris, not even in the African markets in Montmartre, where I went with Lydia on Saturdays to search the stalls. We found nothing from our island, no flowers, no herbs. At night I heard birdsongs I didn't recognize. I wrapped a blanket around my shoulders and gazed out the tall leaded windows while Delphine slept uneasily. In bad weather it was not possible to get warm here in Paris. Frédéric had told me that. He'd said he'd always worn socks to bed. He was never warm until he came to St. Thomas. Now it was my turn to know the chill of this city. I could feel my blood growing colder and thinner, a pale ribbon of red. The vines outside had lost their leaves, and only twisted gray stalks were left.

Being inside of a dream was beautiful and sad. I liked to hear about Jestine's life, her mischievous grandson, Leo, who was growing taller each day. She recounted her days spent with her granddaughters, whom she brought to dance classes and then to have hot chocolate at a sweet shop across from the Tuileries. They, too, would soon be women, on to their own lives. Best of all, Jestine said, were the evenings she spent with Lydia, for after all these years apart, they simply couldn't stop talking. On Sundays, the entire family went to the Bois de Boulogne, the huge park Monsieur Haussmann, soon to be titled Baron, had constructed, where it was said there were werewolves at night, just as there had been in Charlotte Amalie, when the old corrupt families came out of their houses to drink blood for pleasure. Jestine's grandchildren begged for stories about our island as we had longed to hear about Paris. Sometimes she brought them to my house and they sat on the carpet, enthralled, while I read to them from my notebooks. They thought St. Thomas was a fairyland, and asked if I could collect magic and call spirits to me as their *grand-mère* said I could.

"That was long ago," I told them. "In a place where such things were possible."

I left Delphine while she slept in the late afternoons so I could go out walking. I tried to follow the routes of the maps in my father's library, but Monsieur Haussmann had torn up the old twisted streets from the time of Perrault's fairy tales and begun to replace them with broad, elegant avenues and plazas. I became accustomed to the new Paris and found my way. I often passed the same old lady in the nearby park, who sat with a black pug dog on her lap. The clouds were different here, so high up in the sky. I walked along the gravel paths in the park waiting for the light to turn orange as the sun began to set. I went along the river, for although some people said it wasn't safe, I was drawn to water. I imagined the wharves and docks I had known, the waterfall with the blue fish. Sometimes I cried and my tears fell into the river. I did not wish to be old or fierce. I wanted to be a woman who took a young man into her bed after she had drawn the shades and locked the door. As the dusk settled I walked back to the apartment, stopping to buy bunches of blue flowers at the shop on the corner, where the owner and I knew each other well enough to nod a greeting. Each flower had a thousand petals. They didn't grow in our country, but here they were everywhere, and as the weather grew colder they turned from blue to pink and then to scarlet.

I was a little less lonely when I employed several servants, two to clean and see to the laundry, and two to work in the kitchen, an old woman named Clara, and her assistant, Julie, a girl not more than twenty who had recently arrived from the countryside of Burgundy, near Dijon. I heard the girl, Julie, tell the other maid that she had never seen a Jew before, but I didn't hold this against her. She had spent her life on a farm, and had lived simply, and had likely not seen many things in this world. The housemaids filled up the rooms with their lively conversation and with the delicious scent of their cooking. One night Julie made a chicken stuffed with chestnuts that was perhaps the most delicious dish I'd ever tasted. I remembered reading recipes to Jestine so many years ago and how hungry we were for all the food we'd never tasted. As it turned out the assistant cook was more talented than the cook in charge. She made an exceptional apple tartine and applesauce that was extraordinary. Her family had an orchard beside their house, and she had told me that she believed apples to be a gift from God. Her God, I did not say out loud, not ours. The God that chased our people into hiding, from one country to another, in the case of my husband's family, for nearly three hundred years. I thought of the tree we had left behind in St. Thomas, the one my father had loved and Mr. Enrique now cared for, with its twisted bark and bitter fruit, our namesake. I wondered if I had cursed myself for not bringing it with us to France. Perhaps it was fate that out of all the girls I might have hired, I chose the one who could bring me apples from Dijon.

MY HUSBAND AND SON arrived in late November, in time to be with Delphine before her death. I had now lost three children. The Jewish cemetery was in Passy, where the earth was cold and hard. There were no leaves falling from the trees, no birds singing, no red flowers, only ice on the ground. We needed to hire a Rabbi and pay for mourners, for we hadn't enough family —there had been some disagreement over the fact that Frédéric had left the business in Mr. Enrique's hands— and we needed ten men to say the prayers for the dead. Afterward the only people who came to the funeral supper were Jestine and Lydia and her family. The very next day I had the maids burn my daughter's linens and make up the room for my son. Jestine returned, and we locked the door of Delphine's chamber and burned herbs in an earthenware dish, then threw open all the windows and let the spirit of my quiet, pretty daughter go. There was a horse chestnut tree just outside, leafless now, but home enough if Delphine's ghost wished to stay.

The apartment was so big there was no reason for Camille not to live with us indefinitely. Yet he looked displeased when Frédéric told him we would pay for his studies and that Delphine's room was to be his. He was now in his mid-twenties, a grown man who didn't wish to do as he was told. Perhaps he believed artists must live in an alleyway or in a canvas tent in the Bois de Boulogne. He stayed in our lodgings but kept to himself. I had dinner served every evening at seven, but he never joined us. He took his meals in cafés and came home long after we were in bed. I suppose he had contempt for us and thought of us as shopkeepers. Sometimes he was covered with paint and the parlor maid had to scrub the hallway carpets after his boots left tracks of pale vermilion and violet. He'd begun to work as Anton Melbye's assistant. This painter was the brother of the tall red demon I had chased out of St. Thomas. I'd had to pay good money to the constables in order to do so, but in the end it hadn't mattered. My son had followed the demon to Venezuela despite my wishes. He did as he pleased then and now.

ONE EVENING I CAME home from the Cohens' to hear my husband and son arguing. I'd never heard a conversation as heated and belligerent between the two. My husband was defending me in response to my son calling me a cold and heartless woman. I was in the front hall, well out of sight, still wearing my cape and gloves, unsure what to do next, when the young maid from the countryside brought some tea and cake into the parlor, where the argument was taking place. She walked right in, as if this was her home, not mine.

"So kind of you," my husband said. I could tell from his tone that he was embarrassed to have a servant observe such a private encounter.

"You needn't serve us," my son said as the maid began to pour the tea.

"Of course I must," she assured him. "And you must have large slices of cake."

I think it was an apple cake, made with fruit from her family's orchard that she'd brought back from a visit. I'd learned that her people were Catholic farmers who had a deep attachment to their land. Before coming to Passy, this girl had worked on the family farm and in their vineyards. She knew how to handle most household situations, and she clearly knew how to handle angry men. When the kitchen had flooded during a rainstorm she'd mopped up the water, then had taken it upon herself to fix the ceiling with plaster and glue. I had stumbled upon her when she was in the midst of her repairs. White dust fell as she worked away. She looked as if she were standing in a snowstorm. "It's winter!" she called out cheerfully, and indeed I had felt something along my spine at that very moment. I suppose I had a sense of what was to come even then. Julie was eight years younger than my son, but she seemed the more mature of the two. She had capable hands and a direct gaze. I could not fault her for her work. And her apple cake was excellent. As was her timing. She had ended the disagreement between father and son.

When my son looked up to thank her, I could see that he was drawn in. He had passed her by a dozen times, but now he clearly saw her in a different light. Perhaps he saw what I did at the moment I felt the chill of recognition. The snow, the peace, the purity. She wore a black dress and a white cap. Her eyes were haint blue. She was not pretty, but she was capable and serene. When I gazed at my son I was reminded of Frédéric's expression when he first saw me. He had seemed like a fish in a net, desperate for air, yet not wishing for any escape. This was the way such things happened, whether by accident or preordained, whether you wished for it or despaired over it, you could not look away.

After that first encounter, Camille began to search out my maid. It took time, but soon enough he was sitting with her while she cooked dinner, as he had long ago gone to Madame Halevy's kitchen, drawn there as if it were the only place on earth worth visiting. He still wore the old witch's ring, a single gold band. Once I spied him twisting it while he spoke to Julie. I caught sight of the glint of gold before I saw him whispering to my kitchen maid in the corridor, his hand on her waist. I did what I could to keep them apart. Julie came to me once, when I was reading.

"Did you want something?" I asked.

We looked at each other, and I knew exactly what she wanted.

"I'm sorry if I disturbed you," she said.

"Well, you have," I said.

If she had stayed at home, surely she would have married some farm-worker who could neither read nor write, but she had come here and she had seen Paris and now my son had changed the way she looked at the world. But that did not change the way the world was. I knew that from experience.

I would not let her ruin his life.

I gave Julie days off when I knew that my son would be home from the studio. But he was defiant.

"Your plans won't work," he said. "And you needn't be rude to her."

"If she wanted to see you, she'd be here," I said, wishing to plant a seed of doubt in his mind. I did not want to lose him to the world outside ours, and so perhaps I was rude, but it didn't matter. When he found Julie gone, he took the train to Burgundy and set up his easel in the snow. I came to believe that Madame Halevy had cursed me, so that I would know and understand the pain of her loss. None of the servants told me when they found Julie sitting in my son's lap in the pantry, her arms entwined around his neck. Why would they be loyal to me? I was a demanding old woman who liked my coffee hot and my husband's clothes pressed carefully. They were young and in love. I suspected that Julie smelled of apples, for I found several cores in her apron one day. The black seeds fell onto the carpet and I could not find them, even when I got onto my hands and knees to search.

That was when I knew. I should never have hired her.

1863

As Jacob waited seven years for Rachel, my son waited seven years for our kitchen maid. At first I argued with him, but my entreaties had no effect. I was honest with him, as I believe a mother should be. We sat in

my chamber, where I had hung the painting of Jestine and the tiny painting of the Cathedral. He was painting more all the time, but I adored
these two early works. That did not mean I would give in to my son,
though he was now considered a fine artist by many of his peers, not that
their respect paid his bills.

"There is nothing you can say against her that will change my mind,"
Camille said.

His hands were rough, his clothes unwashed, but he had gracious
manners, likely inherited from his father, who had never lost his French
elegance.

"She's uneducated," I said.

"As were you," he shot back at me.

"I was my father's student," I informed him.

"She'll be mine," Camille said.

He crossed his long legs. He looked out of place in our chamber. His
clothes were paint-smeared, but I dared not reprimand him for this.

"Our people have struggled in order to survive, that is why we band
together and why it is a sin to marry outside our faith."

He laughed then and shook his head. "You're not serious. Do you
dare to tell me about the rules of marriage? Was I not the one who went
to the Moravian School? Who had no bar mitzvah? Who was an outcast
from my own people? All because of you. You did as you pleased."

"But your father was of our faith. In the eyes of God we did the right
thing."

Camille stood then, sick of arguing and sick at heart.

"You loved him and that was that. So please don't tell me to do
otherwise."

There was the dull thud of recognition when I realized how pig-
headed my son was. Tell him no, and he was bound to do what was forbidden. He had never viewed the world the way others did, and that was
more true now than ever. We continued to support him, paying the rent
for a studio and then, when he moved out of our apartment, also for

lodgings on the far side of the city. I felt the old bitterness inside me, twisting through my heart, the distance between a mother and a child that I now knew from both sides. When I passed by the mirror in the corridor, I sometimes thought it was my mother's image I spied, not mine. This was her revenge. Everything I had done to her, my son now did to me.

We had made the right decision to leave St. Thomas, for the War Between the States was raging. South Carolina, where much of the trade had been, had been the first state to secede after Lincoln was elected, and no ships were safe. The Emancipation Proclamation declared that as of January 1, 1863, all slaves would be freed, but the bloody business of freedom took a toll, as it had on our islands. We read about the horrors, and were grateful to be in Paris, where the only war was in our family.

Camille came and asked for our approval to marry my maid, admitting that Julie had become pregnant. We denounced their union, for we were reminded of ourselves and we did not wish the same troubles on our son that we had experienced. Then the baby was lost. After that I couldn't sleep. I couldn't look at myself in the mirror. Who would I find there? I wondered if every girl grew up to be a stranger to herself. What would I have thought of myself if I could go back and meet face-to-face with the headstrong young woman I once was, pounding on the Reverend's door, eyes shining, convinced that love was the only thing that mattered?

Camille still wished to marry Julie, even though she was Catholic and uneducated, a farm girl who knew when an apple was ripe but had never met a Jew before her employment in our home. To marry outside our faith was unacceptable. I wondered if my mother's ghost was whispering in my son's ear, urging him to defy me just to be vindictive, or if he was still under the influence of that witch, Madame Halevy, who first turned him against me. He did not believe in our faith or our God or in any God it seemed. He had declared that his only faith was in nature: a leaf, a flower, a woman with blue eyes whose soul was as quiet as snow.

He was an anarchist and a leader of his fellow painters, all outsiders who were not wed to the old-fashioned forms of realism, all of whom looked up to him. When I saw him now, his coat flaring out behind him, his tall, awkward form lurching down the cobbled streets, he seemed like an angel who had lost his way and was plummeting into the darkness. At last I understood what my mother had told me. I would only understand her grief when my child caused me my own.

Our son was too much of a rebel to work within any academie, and soon left his position with Melbye. He studied with the master landscape painter Corot, with whom he journeyed out of Paris, declaring that the countryside was an antidote to all that poisoned our society. He grew more radical, faithful to the best interests of the workingman. He was already an outcast among the establishment and had been rejected from the exhibition by the Salon. The established painters did not care for his work, or his politics. But the Emperor Napoleon III had surprised everyone by setting up an alternative gallery, the Salon des Refusés, for new artists such as Monet and Cézanne and Manet and the American painter Whistler, and of course Pizzarro, respected and loved by this group of radical artists. I did not understand my son as a man, but I had come to understand there was a vision other than the one we had known. After living with his art in my own chamber, I saw there was more than mere mimicry, and that art was a world unto itself, with its own symbols and language. A leaf seen in a certain light might be gray or violet as well as purple, and a latticework of twigs might easily turn red as the sky paled above the city.

One afternoon I discovered a painting left in our vestibule. I saw the wet footprints of oversize shoes on the black and white tiles. The portrait was of a woman beneath a flowering fruit tree, a basket of apples beside her. This was a gift to me, an entreaty to accept his choice. Had I not wanted the very same thing, enough to stand in the rain, to defy everyone and everything, to love whom I wished to rather than whom I was told I must? I felt the sting of pride. Even I could tell it was a great work of art. Of course I recognized the model as Julie. I brought the painting inside and stored it in the wardrobe behind the winter coats.

THEIR SON WAS BORN on February 20. I did not visit the new baby, born without benefit of marriage. On my behalf, Jestine and Lydia brought presents to the countryside, where the couple was now residing. We had shopped together for blankets, quilts, baby sweaters, and britches. On the evening when these gifts were delivered, Frédéric and I went to sit in a café. We knew it was wrong not to be with our own son and grandson, and yet here we were. Though it was chilly, we found a table outside and ordered hot tea and rum. Since leaving St. Thomas I had acquired a taste not only for rum but for molasses, which I spooned onto my toast in the morning. I had begun to want the things I had thought little of when I was young. Sometimes I longed for the brilliant sunlight I had always despised. It was already dusk, and Lydia and Jestine were probably on the train home. My new kitchen maid had likely made a wonderful dinner, perhaps a savory chicken stuffed with chestnuts. The air was silver and the evening was made bright by the ice on the ground and a light falling snow. We did not hurry despite the weather. I didn't complain though my face smarted with the cold. My husband wore a felt hat and the black coat that had been his first purchase upon arriving home in France. I could hear the wood pigeons in the plane trees nearby fluttering from branch to branch, trying to keep warm. I looked up and saw three birds perched above us. I knew that sorrow came in threes and I feared that number. I told my husband we should leave for home, but he held on to my hand. When I'd first looked out the window on the day he arrived, I had expected to be confronted with an enemy. Instead I saw his heart beneath his shirt. I heard it beating.

"Perhaps we should accept the situation," he said as we walked home through the dark. "The world is changing."

"Not fast enough," I said.

"Then let us be among those who hope that the future will be less cruel than the past."

That night I tried on the earrings my mother had brought to St. Thomas in the hem of her skirt. I could barely see my reflection in the cold hallway. At that moment, I was so flooded with doubt I might have agreed with those who thought I was a witch with the power to commit the foulest of deeds. I thought Frédéric was already in bed, but he saw me peering into the silvered mirror. He came to circle his arms around me, and in the dark he told me that he knew the truth about me as no one else ever would. The woman who had saved his life with a kiss.

1865

That year Lydia's daughter Leah was to wed a doctor from Senegal, a man named Joseph Hady, whom she had met through my own doctor, Dr. Paul Gachet, for both doctors' practices included natural elements along with traditional cures. Leah and Dr. Hady were already living together in an apartment in Montmartre. I thought there might be a scandal, for although Leah was of mixed race, she was considered European by anyone who saw her because of her pale skin and gray eyes. But Montmartre was an accepting place, and no one paid attention to the actions of this couple; clearly Paris wasn't bound by the rules of St. Thomas. The Cohens had already been shunned by their family, none of whom attended the wedding. I brought the bride and groom a gift of crystal glasses along with a bottle of rum from our island. Dr. Hady had been treating Frédéric, who had fallen ill with a sort of wasting disease. For several months, my husband had difficulty eating, and the doctor often came to our apartment. He recommended no alcohol, no dairy, and no wheat. Still there had been little improvement. Dr. Hady checked in on him at the wedding reception, as Frédéric sat at the table, drinking hot tea with lemon.

"Does he complain about pain?" the doctor asked when he came to greet me.

"Never," I said.

"Well, then, that is the sort of man he is," the doctor said with clear

appreciation of my husband. I realized then he meant the pain was excru-
ciating, and that another man would not have been able to do any more
than lie in bed. Dr. Hady spoke to me about looking for a studio to rent
for Leah, for she was an accomplished watercolorist. I had two of her
paintings in my bedchamber, lovely images of the new, broad avenues in
the city. Perhaps the doctor imagined I had insights into the art world,
for my son was so well known, but the most I could offer was the suggestion that she use one of the rooms in my large apartment.

"Oh, I think she wants her very own place," the doctor said, though
he thanked me for the invitation. He then asked about St. Thomas, a
place he'd always wanted to visit, for he and Leah planned to travel after
their marriage. The doctor was a tall, handsome man, very dark, with
liquid eyes. In the St. Thomas of my childhood he and I would never
have been sitting at the same table. In the United States he would be a
soldier or a slave not a highly regarded doctor marrying my dear friend's
daughter. I recommended Malta as a possible destination, or perhaps the
south of France.

There was music playing, and Leah signaled for her new husband to
join her on the dance floor. "If you'll pardon me." He excused himself
graciously. "There is my beautiful wife."

She was indeed the most beautiful of the three sisters. Often when I
spied her it was as though I were looking back in time, seeing Jestine at
the same age. In the marriage hall, the ceiling had been strung with dozens of lanterns that floated like fireflies. At every table there were vases
of delphiniums and lilies and hyacinth and lilacs, all flowers we hadn't
known on our island. I had often gone through botanical books in my
father's library and cut out the illustrations of flowers that grew in France
so I might paste them in my journal. They were far more beautiful than
I had imagined. I took a hyacinth to carry in my cloak. I sat beside my
old friend in her place of honor, at the marriage table.

"You're not worried anymore?" I'd asked her, for we had talked at
length about the consequences of Leah marrying a man from Senegal.

"It will do me no good to worry," Jestine said. "Perhaps we should both be thankful that anyone manages to find love."

"Perhaps." I wished not to discuss this issue any further, for I knew my friend's meaning to be that I would do well to reconsider my disapproval of my son's choice. I often thought of my kitchen maid's apple cake, of her tarts that were so perfect, and how when she first came into my house I had felt a chill, as if she brought the future with her, clinging to her clothes.

There would be dancing into the early hours, and because we considered ourselves to be too old for such things, we left early. Our carriage took Jestine home first, and Frédéric waited, a blanket over his knees, while I accompanied my friend into the empty house, helping her to carry several baskets of flowers. The cold, purple air smelled of hyacinths. We went inside, then up to the parlor, where I waited while Jestine lit the lamps and saw to the fire. The rooms were chilly, and we kept our cloaks on while the flames took. It had been a glorious wedding, and we were both teary-eyed. I went to the window to check on the carriage. I do not know what made me do this—a surge of worry perhaps. I could see Frédéric in his black wool coat and black hat waiting for me, the plaid blanket warming him against the night air. I loved him too much, beyond all measure, so much that I was willing to ruin both my own life and the lives of my children. It was then, while I gazed at the scene before me, that I saw three crows in the tree outside the window. They were silent, unmoving, as the bats in our garden were so long ago, easily mistaken for dark, sinister leaves. I panicked. I let out a cry that didn't sound human. The hyacinth I'd taken from the wedding party fell from beneath my cloak. I knew from Adelle what such a sign portended. All sorrows came in threes, and black birds meant death. Jestine rushed over and threw open the window. She waved her scarf and shouted out curses and the birds took flight, screaming as they heaved themselves above the stone rooftops.

"It means nothing," she said. "Do you understand me?"

I nodded and said good night, then hurried down the cold stairs. I didn't argue with her. But I knew she was wrong.

THE NEXT MORNING THE light was dim, mauve-colored. The city had seemed darker for weeks, as if the war in America had sifted across the water to us. People dressed in black, fretted over the future, stocked their pantries in case war should come to us as well. There were no birds singing, I noticed that first. Frédéric awoke and said he was dreaming about rain, as he had when he first came to St. Thomas. When I touched his forehead, he was burning up. My husband's illness, the one I thought the herb man had cured, seemed to have returned. He appeared disoriented. When I spoke to him there was only a flicker of a response.

Doctor Hady came and, after an examination, said my husband's heart and lungs were weak and that there was a mass of some sort inside his abdomen. Frédéric was only sixty-three, but the disease of his youth had come back to haunt him and a new disease had formed in his gut because he was so run down. The raw planes of his face were shadowed blue, as if he'd been bruised. I saw faint sparks around him in the dark, the spirits of those who had passed on gathering close by, waiting. After all this time, the ghosts had come back to me, unbidden and unwanted. I wept when my husband began to mutter, his words a dark tangle of pain. And then he took a breath and said that he could see the lavender growing in his parents' garden. He laughed, delighted. There were dozens of bees, and fields of purple, and he was so young he grinned to think of all that was before him, his whole long life. He began to talk to people I didn't recognize, the dead uncles and aunts he'd seen on trips to Bordeaux when he was just a boy. "May I have some water?" he asked me in a sweet voice. He winced when he attempted to sit up, though there were three pillows beneath him. I felt him slipping away to a world beyond my grasp.

I knew that at the end of their lives many people went backward, searching for the moment when they first glimpsed the light of our world. I got into bed beside Frédéric. The doctor had been and gone. My husband was too weak to lift his head. Still, I trusted the soothing tea that Dr. Gachet and Dr. Hady recommended, to fortify his spirit and his strength.

Yet he grew weaker. One night he didn't know me. He called me Mademoiselle and said he was lost. I sent for Dr. Hady in the middle of the night, and he came right away, even though the weather was dreadful. The doctor clapped the snow from his coat in the hallway. I greeted him and took his scarf and gloves. "Terrible night," he said.

He then asked me to boil water.

"For what?" I asked, concerned. I could not imagine Frédéric would have the strength for any sort of surgery if that was what was being proposed.

"For tea," he told me. He handed me a packet that looked familiar, reddish peels of tree bark and some spices and herbs. I thought it might be the cure the herb man had given me years ago when Jestine and I saved Frédéric's life.

I had forgotten my shoes, and the kitchen floor was freezing. None of the servants were there, for it was a holiday weekend. I fixed the tea and brought it down the corridor. Everything was silent. My footsteps, the snow sifting down, the empty streets. There was a clock in the parlor, and I could hear it as if it were a beating heart. When I neared the bedchamber I heard Dr. Hady's voice. "Does your chest ache when you breathe?"

"There are birds outside the window," Frédéric said.

Dr. Hady went to pull back the curtains. Flakes of snow hit against the glass and stuck in patterns that looked like clouds. Snow was wedged to the branches of the plane trees that lined our street. "There are no birds," he said.

But from where I stood I saw the three blackbirds.

I went to the window and opened it, even though the wind came through and snow dotted the floor. I shouted at the birds and gestured with my arms, until Dr. Hady pulled me back and closed the window. I sat in a chair shivering while he drew the curtains.

I took the tea to Frédéric, but he waved it away.

"Darling," he said. He recognized me. "You see them out there, don't you?"

"Perhaps the yellow fever he had after arriving in St. Thomas damaged his liver and spleen," Dr. Hady told me when we went into the hall. The doctor said he'd given my husband quinine, made from the bark of a tree from South America, which had not been freely available when Frédéric was a young man. For this medicine to be effective, however, it needed to be given immediately after the illness became present, not years later. And then there was the growth in his abdomen, perhaps a cancer of the stomach. It was too late to remove any tissue for study, for Frédéric was too weak for anything so invasive. The doctor told me to keep my husband cool when the fever came and have him drink the tea every hour. He refused to accept a fee. "You are family to us," he said. "I am here whenever you need me."

I SOON REALIZED THAT the doctor's tea was a narcotic of some sort, not meant to cure but to ease the process of dying. My husband's lean, strong body and his fluid energy had disappeared. He faltered more every hour. Still there was a gleam of response when I got into bed beside him. We twined around each other, and I breathed into his mouth so that my soul might strengthen his, but it did no good. I wept for the young man in my kitchen, his fine features, his eyes elusive, as if he feared to look at me. But he did look, and now he opened his eyes. He still knew me. No one else had known me as he had.

It took three days. Jestine or Lyddie came to sit with me. The fevers grew worse, and the chills were so terrible nothing I did seemed to warm him. On the third day, I sent for Camille. He came immediately, smelling of snow and paint. He was thinner than before, his beard longer, his clothes fitting for a peasant. I made no mention of any of this and allowed him to kiss me three times. He had brought a handful of hyacinth, the same flower I'd had with me when I knew my husband would die. They were deep purple and smelled of both spring and snow.

"You should have called for me sooner." My son threw off his coat and went to stand at the foot of the bed. He called to his father, but Frédéric seemed very far away and he would not respond.

"Is this the end, then?" Camille asked me. I could see how shaken he was. "Is there no hope?"

"There is always hope," Adelle had told me so long ago, when I was so unhappy with my life, after I married the first time. Much to my surprise, it had turned out to be true. Now it was a lie, but I could not tell my son otherwise.

Frédéric slept in the grip of his fever, his breathing labored. The sound of him straining for air reminded me of the sound of the wind that came across the sea from Africa before the rains began. I hadn't changed my clothes in days, or washed, or had a meal, or left the room. Perhaps Camille noticed my distress, for his expression changed. He pulled over a chair and sat next to me.

"Did you know that Father and I once went to a waterfall and threw off our clothes and dove in together? He told me if I held out my hands little fish would come to me, and they did. It was near this same place I once found a skeleton, nearly hidden by the tall grass."

"I know that place." I was glad to envision it, the pool I had passed on the way to the herb man, whose death my son had foreseen when he was just an infant who refused to sleep.

"We went swimming the day we chased off Madame Halevy's daughter."

I looked at Camille, surprised to hear this. I hadn't known my husband had been a party to that. It made me love him even more.

"I've kept Madame's ring to remind me of that day. I've kept her story secret for her, but there's no real cause to do so anymore."

I nodded. "She was a great one for secrets."

"She told me that your cousin Aaron was her grandson. Her daughter abandoned him because the father was African."

"I think you're wrong," I told him, yet I remembered Madame Halevy at the door, late one night, when I thought she was a witch standing in our courtyard.

"Your mother had lost a son, and so the two made a pact. Your mother would raise the child in our faith and no one would ever know the truth about Madame Halevy's daughter. When he fell in love with Jestine, they told him he mustn't marry her; such a marriage would only bring his origins into question. These two ladies were the ones who thought it best for Lydia to be raised in France, where she would be considered a member of our faith. They were the ones who arranged for her to be taken. They thought they were doing the right thing for all concerned, but they were not."

My son tugged off Madame Halevy's ring. He'd worn it for so long it had left an indentation in his flesh. When he took my hand in his, his palm was as rough as any workingman's. He seemed older than his years because of his long beard. He painted in the fresh, cold air, and his complexion was weather-beaten. I thought of how I'd carried him through the woods when he couldn't sleep. How he was the only one of my babies I had told my stories to. I'd loved him too much even then. I saw Frédéric in him, his lanky, dignified posture, his resolve to do the right thing, his strong features.

"I had pity for Madame Halevy," he told me. "That was the world she lived in, but it isn't ours. Give the ring to Jestine. Tell her Aaron Rodrigues wanted her to have it. He just never had the chance to give it to her."

My son sat with me through the night. When morning came the bright streaks of daylight were haint blue, but in this country that color couldn't keep ghosts away. My husband died that day at noon. It might as well have been midnight, for the heavy damask drapes were drawn and the room was pitch. I did not want to look out and see Paris, the city of my beloved's death. The world was silenced by snow, but in the dark I could imagine vines of cloudy pink bougainvillea and bees rumbling through the blossoms and the young man blinking back sunlight as he stared into my window.

His last words to me were *I am no longer with you.*

I did my best to tear down the curtain between death and the living world, to ensure that light and breath would enter into my husband once more. I breathed into his mouth and pounded on his chest. I called to him, but he didn't return. He was gone from me.

There was a small service at the cemetery. Camille was there with my kitchen maid and their little boy. When it came time to move the coffin into the ground, I would not allow it. There were wood doves nesting nearby, and they all took flight when I began to scream. We had hired a Rabbi, an old man who wore a broad, black-brimmed hat and said the mourning prayers for a fee. When I could not be held away from the casket, he retreated as if I were Lilith herself, the witch who came for unnamed babies and never let them go. She had talons at the ends of her fingers and a thousand golden rings, all sacrifices from women who had tried to bribe her. But no payment would do. I held on to the coffin and banged on it. I heard an echo and thought my husband had been brought back to life by a miracle. I was not one to give up easily, no matter who my enemy might be, even death. I heard my son's voice then as his strong arms pulled me back. *He is gone and all we have is this world, here and now.*

FOR SEVERAL WEEKS AFTERWARD I did not leave my room. I took the laudanum that was prescribed to me, ten drops at a time and then twenty. When that was not enough I had the coachman bring me more, from where I did not ask. I slept all day and night for good reason. In my dreams I could go back in time. That was what I wanted. The place I'd always hated, I longed for desperately now. Every night I dreamed of sitting in the kitchen while Adelle fixed our lunch. I was out in the yard where the chickens came to me when I clucked at them. There were green moths at my window and red flowers in a vase. I was wearing a white slip made of cotton and the sunlight was blinding. I could not open my eyes because of it. There were parrots in the trees, a sign of luck, the luck I had given away. A man was walking through the door and my heart was so loud I couldn't hear anything else.

Jestine came and insisted upon opening the drapes. A dim light fell in bands across the room, but I protested even that. I did not wish to see the world, or step into it, or know it without Frédéric. We were one person, or so it had been, and now without him, I was nothing. A girl who was waiting for her life to change. An old woman who cared about nothing but what she had lost.

Camille came to see me, but I kept my back to him. He found my blue notebook in my bureau and began to read to me during his visits. He told me about a donkey with the name of a Frenchman whom I loved so well I gave him bread mixed with milk for breakfast, and of an apple tree that never grew any bigger, and a bird that flew around the world searching for love. He added stories of his own, of an old lady who rescued a baby from drowning in the rain, of people who were in love, but kept apart. He brought colored pencils and illustrated my stories, and sometimes when he left, I would study them. I cried when I saw how beautiful our world had been as seen through my son's eyes, and my tears brought me back to life.

Jestine made me fongee and insisted I eat. She then brought out my black mourning dress, the one I'd packed in St. Thomas and had worn to every funeral except my husband's. On that day I'd refused to wear anything more than a white slip under his long black coat. Jestine pressed the mourning dress with lavender water, then she combed my hair. Nothing had turned out as we thought it would. I gave Jestine the gold ring that should have been her wedding band. "From Aaron," I said. "Since you were the one he loved."

We had grown up in a world rimmed with hurt, where a lie was easier to tell than the truth. Later that day, I heard Jestine crying in the garden.

It was cold and there were no birds, only the sound of her immense sorrow. What we had lost, we could never regain. I sat in the parlor and when Jestine came inside she no longer had the ring. She had buried it under a rosebush, using her bare hands to dig deeply enough. Every day as the weather grew warmer we sat on wicker chairs and watched the leaves greening. In April the war in the states was over, and there was a great celebration in our city, but then the news came that Lincoln had been shot on April 14. Black banners and buntings were hung on houses and shops. By the end of the month, the buds that appeared on the rosebushes were white. They were Alba roses, but we called them *roses de neige*. Snow roses. We told each other that when they bloomed our hearts would be mended. But on the first of May, when the roses opened, they were red, and we still carried our pain. We then understood we would carry it forever. We had planned to cut the roses when they bloomed, and keep them in vases, but we left them. They reminded us of the gardens in St. Thomas. Just as I suspected, a thousand bees appeared one day and drank their fill.

LATER THAT MONTH I received a card from my son announcing that he and Julie had had another child, a daughter born on May 13, whom they had named Jeanne-Rachel. Jeanne for Julie's mother. Rachel after me. I had done many things that I regretted, and I had all but lost my son, just as Jestine had predicted. So I took his naming of the baby to be a message to me. I thought about the first Madame Petit, who had refused to die until her baby was named. What you are called marks you and makes you who you are. Despite my disagreements with the parents, I put aside my bitterness. This baby was mine.

When Jestine suggested we go to see my namesake, having figured out how I might avoid the mother, I quickly agreed. My friend had persuaded Lydia and Henri Cohen to invite my son and Julie to lunch, to discuss financial matters, for I had placed Henri in charge of my finances. I still supported my son's family, so he agreed to this appointment. On that same day, Jestine and I took the train from Paris to the railway crossing at Les Pâtis, near Pontoise. Then we walked, for my son and his family lived in a farmhouse outside of town. We took a beautiful old looping road bordered by purple blooms scattered through the tall grass. I realized it was lavender, which I took to be a good sign. I was wearing black boots with buttons that made for good walking shoes and my black mourning dress and also Frédéric's black woolen coat, even though the day was unseasonably warm. I did not imagine I would ever wear another color. As we approached the farmhouse I fell silent. Jestine understood that I was nervous. The sky was dull and the clouds were low. We held hands so we wouldn't stumble on the muddy road.

As we neared the house we noticed there were chickens running free in the yard.

Jestine laughed. "Don't kill anything," she warned me.

"I'm too old," I informed her.

"Don't be silly. Old women are the fiercest ones of all."

We chuckled as we traipsed along, our skirts dragging. Madame Halevy had told me I wouldn't begin to understand the world until I was her age. *Witches are made, not born.* That was what she'd whispered to me on the night my son brought us to her house for dinner. *Remember that,* she'd said before I left. *Remember me.*

We knocked on the back door as if we were expected guests, and ignored the protests of the kitchen maid, who was startled to find two old ladies calling and did her best to put us off. We said we were too tired to be turned away, and demanded tea before the poor woman could question us about our intentions. When steaming mugs of tea and small lemon tarts had been offered and accepted, the maid explained that her employers and their little boy had gone to Paris for the day. She didn't have the authority to entertain guests and might find herself in trouble if her mistress discovered she'd allowed strangers into the house. I threw Jestine a knowing look. The original kitchen maid was now an employer with a long list of dos and don'ts. We assured the maid we were well meaning, there to see the new member of the family, and that we had traveled too far to turn heel and leave.

Now that we were inside, I took the opportunity to evaluate my son's situation. The house was rough hewn, but not without charm. A good thing, since I was paying for it. My son the anarchist had no trouble letting the money from our family business pay his bills. When the maid had been convinced we were harmless, we were brought into the parlor, where lovely lace curtains had been hung over the windows There was the baby in the cradle.

"Do they call her Rachel or Jeanne?" I asked the maid. I hoped it wasn't Jeanne, the name of her other grandmother, the one who tended orchards near Dijon and likely plucked chickens each evening for a stew.

"They call her Minette."

I was pleased to hear this. It was a pet name for a little cat. They could call her whatever they wanted as long as they didn't call her Jeanne. As far as I was concerned, her name was Rachel.

I wished either Jestine or I could have remembered the words Adelle recited to protect a child from harm, but neither of us could recall her prayer. I wished Frédéric had been beside me. I still talked to him inside my head, and so I told him now how happy this visit had made me. My namesake was a beautiful child, with dark eyes. I believe she recognized me when I stood over her cradle. I told her about the butterflies who created a second moon of light, and of blue birds as tall as people, and of a woman who swam away from the cruelties of humankind. I'd brought a gift for her, my mother's diamond earrings. I left them on a tray beside my son's easel with a brief note—*de Rachel à Rachel,* From Rachel to Rachel. Most likely he would think the jewels wasteful, silly extravagant things, and would sell them in order to pay his bills. Perhaps that was what they had been meant for all along when my mother sewed them into the hem of her dress.

I'd brought a gift for the household as well, a basket of apples. But as we left the house I noticed there was an orchard just beside the house.

We picked apples to eat on the train ride home. The light was deep and gray and the fields were purple, exactly as my son painted them.

NOT LONG AFTERWARD I moved to smaller lodgings, in the Ninth Arrondissement. Our apartment had always been too large, and I had found myself going from room to room as if searching for my husband. My new lodging happened to be close to my son's studio and an apartment he rented for the nights he spent in Paris, while the mother of his children cared for their home. The children came to me on Thursdays. I marked that day of the week on my calendar with a star. Camille carried the baby and held the little boy by the hand. He reminded me so much of Frédéric, for he had the same sort of tenderness with his children.

"They're not too much for you?" Camille asked. He called the darling little boy Marmotte, sleepyhead, the same name I had used for him. "They won't tire you?"

"Do you think I'm ancient?" I said.

"I do," the little boy said. "A hundred years old. You're a very old goat."

I laughed despite myself. I liked a boy who broke the rules. "Did you teach him to be so polite?" I asked my son. "Or maybe your mother told you I was a goat," I said to my grandson, who laughed and hid behind his father, peeping out every now and then with a grin on his face.

"Be nice to your grandmother." Camille leaned down to kiss the little boy on his head. "They adore coming here," he told me.

"Why shouldn't they?" I said.

Camille laughed and kissed me three times, as we used to do on St. Thomas. "Don't let them tire you out."

My son left the children early in the morning, and returned after his day of work at his studio. I assume their mother appreciated a day to see to her bustling household without the children underfoot. She didn't mind the old goat when it came to caring for them. So much the better. I liked to sit with them in the parlor in the afternoons and tell them stories.

I took out my blue notebooks, which I had stored away for so long. My darling granddaughter was only a baby, but my grandson listened to every word I told him, eyes wide. I told him about the werewolves who couldn't count to a hundred, about fish who could become horses on dry land, about a donkey named Jean-François who could speak.

"No he couldn't," my grandson responded with certainty. "Donkeys don't talk. We have one. My mother says feed a donkey hay and he'll be happy."

I shrugged. "Maybe that's true in France. In St. Thomas, donkeys talk."

"In English?" he asked. I saw that I had won him over, despite what his mother had told him. That gave me hope for the future.

"In French," I informed him.

My grandson nodded, pleased. This made sense to him. He was a charming, practical boy. He took his nap very well, my Marmotte, and lay down on my settee so I could cover him with a green silk blanket. "I'm in the ocean," he said to me.

"Swim into your dreams," I said, as I dimmed the light.

When my pretty little namesake fussed, I lay down on the bed beside her. She was not a good sleeper, but she was a good listener, with lovely dark eyes and a mouth like a rose. I told her the story about the woman who lived with the turtles, the one who had followed me across the sea, just under the ship. All across the ocean she had slept with her long, pale arms wrapped around the anchor, she ate fish and clams, she avoided sunlight, and swam just below the surface of the waves. She came near when she heard music on board from a string quartet that was traveling to Paris. She came even closer when the captain displayed his art collection of watercolors in shades of apricot and rose and yellow, all human colors that she could never find at sea. One day a passenger's dress was missing, and that evening I spied a skirt floating in the water, a silky thing that rose and fell with the tides. The woman who lived with turtles could not make the choice between our worlds, and at night I saw a hundred of her companions floating farther out in the ocean, their green shells like stepping-stones.

The baby was often asleep on my bed when her father came for the children at the close of the day. He said it was a wonder how well his daughter slumbered when she was in my care. I told him that babies needed to sleep in order to dream. I believe my namesake dreamed of a thousand small miracles and that she dreamed of the turtle-woman from our homeland. When he arrived for the children, my son smelled of turpentine; he couldn't wash it away. He was considered to be famous now, although still a radical, and the other radicals who admired him wished to have his paintings for free. Every month I wrote him a check, just as I'd always done. Not that he was a spendthrift. Far from it. He wore old clothes that hung on his thin frame and favored boots with restitched soles. He'd rather eat an apple than have an expensive meal in a café. More than anything he was a family man. He was a good father and a good husband. He was intent on marrying my kitchen maid, but he still wanted my blessings. I understood. I'd wanted the same thing myself. Perhaps that was why he allowed me to spend so much time with the children, or perhaps it was simply because he could see my deep love for them. For now, I would let them wait for my approval, but eventually I would have to give in for the sake of these darling children. I gave them fongee porridge for dinner every Thursday. I had hired a cook from St. Thomas named Annabeth, who remembered all the old recipes; she could even make a mixture that tasted like guava berry rum by using local strawberries. It was a comfort to have her around, plus she was an excellent baker. Every now and then she made a coconut cake that I brought to share with the Cohens. "Don't you want something better than porridge for your family?" Annabeth often said to me on Thursdays, but no, I didn't want anything more. When I told Jestine about the cook's remarks, she laughed. She, too, made fongee for her grandchildren. It was good for the body and the spirit, as it had been long ago.

On warm evenings Jestine and I often walked along the river. It was nearly summer and Frédéric had been gone for several months. Still, he came to me in my dreams. He lay down beside me, entwined with me, and I could hear the sound of bees. Time was moving so quickly. Soon it would be July and the sky would be blue and heat would rise off the gravel paths in the Tuileries in radiant waves. I'd brought the roses in my garden with me to my new address and planted them in a courtyard. As the season went on they would grow pale, withering in the bright sun-light, and then, if they were carefully pruned and watered, they would have a second flowering in August. Jestine and I would sit in the wicker chairs and watch to see whether they bloomed red or white.

We liked the quiet of the river and often took the path along the Seine. Paris was never a disappointment, although often we talked about the weather back home, and how we could sit out all night long and never once be chilled, how when the rain came down I kept my window open. One evening as we were strolling the weather changed suddenly, surprising us, as it did on our island when the wind came from Africa. All at once there was a driving green rain, so cold we shivered. This was not the rain of our island. Here it fell like a curtain. We could barely see as we plunged into a tunnel and stood there laughing in the dark. We'd run so swiftly we were out of breath. I was wearing my feathered hat and Frédéric's black coat. I was never without it. I wondered what I would do once the summer was upon us. Perhaps I would wear his shirt, the one I slept in now, beneath my clothes and close to my heart.

We couldn't stay in the tunnel forever, so we darted into the rain, holding Frédéric's coat above our heads as we'd once held up leaves to be our umbrellas. Now it was the leaves from the chestnut trees that were drifting down, sticking to the pavement, a slick, coppery carpet. Eventu-ally the rain became a pale, cold drizzle. Everything was so green, the way it was when we hid in the tall grass, unnoticed by everyone but the yellow birds darting above us. We found a painted wooden bench for ourselves and swept off the rain with our hands.

The leaves on the shrubs turned silver as dusk crossed the sky, the grass was purple. We were so still none of the passersby noticed us as they hurried along the wet gravel, intent on being on their way. Jestine and I had practiced silence on the nights when we waited for the turtles. In the tall grass we could disappear if we wanted to. We could watch the hillsides turn red, one flower at a time. We had seen so much, but we had never seen the turtle-girl until now. She was there in the river, the woman who had spent a lifetime with the turtles but had arms and legs as we did and long, moss-black hair she had wound into mourning plaits. She had come across the sea from the place that was our home, alongside our ship. I'd seen her footsteps on the bow of the boat and in the hallways of our building. All over Paris lanterns were burning. It was the hour when the haint blue sky dissolved into darkness and the bats flew above us. We watched the woman between worlds climb out of the water and walk through the park. Our sister, who could not decide whether or not to be human, sat down with us at last.

Afterword

Rachel Pizzarro's life in my imagined story mirrors the known facts about her as closely as possible.

Rachel Monsanto Pomié Petit Pizzarro was born in 1795 on St. Thomas, where her father, Moses Monsanto Pomié, was a prominent merchant, having fled in the 1790s from Saint-Domingue during the revolution there. They were Danish citizens whose families had come from Spain, Portugal, and France. In 1818 Rachel married Isaac Petit, a French Jew of Marrano heritage. He had previously been married and had eight children with his first wife, Esther. Three were surviving when Rachel became their stepmother. By the time Isaac died, in 1824 at the age of fifty, he and Rachel had three more children together and one born after his death. In 1825 Frédéric Pizzarro, then twenty-two, came to St. Thomas to run the family business. He and Rachel fell instantly in love despite the community disapproval and the synagogue's refusal to marry them because of their family connection. Despite the scandal created by their relationship, which was considered highly improper, they eventually married and became the parents of four, including Jacob Abraham Camille Pizzarro (Pissarro), who was to become one of the fathers of Impressionism.

The stories of the Pizzarros' West Indian employees, neighbors, and friends are invented, although Moses Pomié was said to have been carried to safety in a basket, much like his biblical namesake, by a slave who traveled with him when he fled to St. Thomas. Rachel Pizzarro is thought to have brought a maid who was a freed slave with her when she came to Paris at the age of sixty, never again returning to St. Thomas.

Once in Paris, Pissarro (who changed to the more French spelling in 1882) studied with Corot and attended the Academie Suisse, where he met Claude Monet. He was then introduced to Pierre-Auguste Renoir, Alfred Sisley, and Frédéric Bazille and later to Paul Gauguin. He became a father figure, as well as a mentor, to Cézanne. He fell in love with Julie Vellay, a maid in his parents' home. His family disapproved because of her social class and religion and never accepted her.

In 1870 the Pissarros fled to London to avoid the Franco-Prussian War (with Rachel, now widowed, living close enough to see her grandchildren, to whom she was devoted). Camille and Julie wed there in 1871. Pissarro had asked for Rachel's permission to wed—she wrote letters giving and then retracting her consent. When Camille and Julie returned to France, they found their house had been used as a slaughterhouse and was in ruins. Fifteen hundred of Pissarro's paintings had been destroyed (several of Monet's stored there were destroyed as well). Rachel continued to help support the family throughout her lifetime. In 1874 Pissarro's beloved daughter Minette, of whom he painted several moving portraits, and who was named Jeanne-Rachel for her grandmothers, tragically died at the age of nine due to a respiratory infection. In all, Julie and Camille had eight children, two of whom died.

Rachel Monsanto Pomié Petit Pizzarro died in Paris in 1889, at the age of ninety-four. Toward the end of her life she was cared for by Julie, though she still refused to fully accept her as a daughter-in-law. It is interesting to note that when Julie's oldest son decided to become an artist, Julie was said to react much as Rachel had when her son had the same desire, with displeasure and the hope he would find a more reasonable career. She knew how her husband and family had struggled financially, forced to depend on her mother-in-law. Her son did not listen to her and became a well-known painter.

Pissarro left his Jewish heritage behind, perhaps because of the stigma and stress placed on his parents and their family when they were ostracized from their community in St. Thomas. His mother warned him against being political when he thought of fighting in the Franco-Prussian War. "You are not French," she is said to have told him. "Don't do any thing rash."* But in 1894, during the Dreyfus Affair, Pissarro could no longer avoid the issue of his background. Captain Alfred Dreyfus was convicted by a military court of treason for allegedly passing French secrets to German intelligence. Evidence pointed to Dreyfus's innocence, but France became divided into two camps—those who supported the military and those who wanted justice for the Jewish captain. Monet and Pissarro supported the search for the truth. Against Dreyfus were some of Pissarro's oldest friends, including Cézanne, Degas, and Renoir. The affair became laced with anti-Semitism. When Émile Zola wrote his famous essay "J'Accuse" in 1898, anti-Jewish riots broke out. Pissarro wrote him a letter of admiration for this act of bravery. Degas and Renoir continued to shun Pissarro and did not attend his funeral.

Camille Pissarro's childhood and school years spent with working people and the children of slaves formed his political and personal attitudes. As an outcast, he was sympathetic to those who were rejected by society. Pissarro thought of himself as an anarchist and an atheist and lived his life as an artist and a workingman, an outsider who did not let anything but his art define him. He never returned to the West Indies, but the island of St. Thomas and the people he knew there influenced his art, his philosophy, and his life. He died in Paris in November 1903, the same year the Louvre bought two of his paintings. He is considered to be one of the greatest artists of the twentieth century.

---

* Rachel Pizzarro quoted in *Private Lives of the Impressionists* (New York: Harper, 2006), p. 78.

Acknowledgments

My gratitude to Carolyn Reidy, Jonathan Karp, and Marysue Rucci for many kindnesses. This book would not exist without your faith and support.

Many thanks to Amanda Urban and Ron Bernstein for good advice, love, and patience.

Thank you

to Joyce Tenneson for your glorious photograph,

to Kate Painter for amazing assistance,

to Susan Brown for copyediting expertise,

to Elizabeth Breeden for help along the way,

to Deborah Thompson for many facts checked,

and especially to Pamela Painter, for helping me to understand my own novel and bring it to life.

And to my son, Jacob, for all you have taught me.

Bibliography

Brettell, Richard R. *Pissarro's People*. New York: Prestel, 2011.

Cohen, Judah M. *Through the Sands of Time: A History of the Jewish Community of St. Thomas, U.S. Virgin Islands*. Waltham, MA: Brandeis University Press, 2003.

Gjessing, Frederik C., and William P. Maclean. *Historic Buildings of St Thomas and St John*. London: The Macmillan Press LTD, 1987.

Lloyd, Christopher. *Pissarro*. New York: Phaidon, 1979.

Rachum, Stephanie. "Camille Pissarro's Jewish Identity." Tel Aviv University, *Assaph* 5 (2000): 3–29.

Raffaele, Herbert, et al. *Birds of the West Indies*. Princeton, NJ: Princeton University Press, 2003.

Rewald, John, ed. *Camille Pissarro: Letters to His Son Lucien*. Boston: MFA Publications, 1958.

Roe, Sue. *The Private Lives of the Impressionists*. New York: Harper-Collins, 2006.

Sherlock, Philip. *West Indian Folk-tales*. Oxford, UK: Oxford University Press, 1966.

Thorold, Anne, and Kristen Erickson. *C. Pissarro and His Family*. Oxford, UK: Ashmolean Museum, 1993.

About the Author

Alice Hoffman is the author of more than thirty works of fiction, including *Practical Magic*, *The Red Garden*, the Oprah's Book Club Selection *Here on Earth*, *The Museum of Extraordinary Things*, and *The Dovekeepers*. She lives near Boston.